THE WAY TO A WOMAN'S HEART . . .

"Oh, joy!" Ginny clasped her hands in mock ecstasy. "You're going to teach me to cook? You're going to teach me something I don't want to learn?" She frowned as Josh scrabbled through the kitchen cabinets. "What *are* you looking for?"

"Your zester. For the lemon."

"My what? It sounds like something you'd find in a triple-X-rated store in Times Square." Ginny handed him her vegetable peeler. "I don't even want to guess what you do with the lemon after you get through zesting it."

Josh laughed. Her breath caught when she saw his eyes smiling down at her. He pulled her into his arms and hugged her, then tilted her head back and kissed her once hard and then again softly and sweetly.

"Isn't the rice going to burn?" Ginny asked inanely.

Josh moved to hold her face in his hands. This time, his kiss was a promise, a preview. This, Ginny thought, is what making love with him would be like—hot and sweet enough to melt her bones. For the first time in she didn't know how long, Ginny wanted a man. Not just any man.

Josh Havilland.

NEVER TOO LATE

MARTHA SCHROEDER

ZEBRA BOOKS
KENSINGTON PUBLISHING CORP.

To
Ardath, Bobbie, and Kate
With love and gratitude for your faith
and encouragement,
And for the shared laughter and never-failing help
on all those Monday nights.
You're the best friends in the world.

One

"I'm sorry, Ginny, I know it's an imposition, but you have to meet the train."

Ginny McDougall looked at her boss with deep disfavor. "This is too much. I mean I've heard of workaholics, but this is your *father* coming to visit for heaven's sake, Denis!"

"Ginny, my dad's a lawyer. He'll understand that I have to be at this deposition. Now you better get a move on. Lunch hour traffic is murder and he's getting in at Penn Station at one-fifteen." He glanced at his watch. "With lunch, it shouldn't take more than a couple of hours. You'll be back here by three at the latest. You can draft the Ebersole deed this afternoon."

"Denis, one of the associates and I can go to the deposition, and I can still finish the deed." Ginny looked at Denis Havilland and shook her head. He was the most dedicated lawyer she knew. Except for frequent dates with some of New York's top models, he never left his work behind. "You have to meet your father. I'd die if

Lisa ever had someone else meet me. And he's coming all the way from Florida." Ginny gave him her sternest maternal stare. "You *have* to go."

It had always worked with Lisa and most of the time Denis gave in, too. Not today. He raised harassed-looking brown eyes to meet hers and sighed. It was what Lisa called Denis's "cow-eyed look," and Ginny knew she was going to meet that train.

"All right," she said, gathering up her steno pad and five thick file folders. "I'll meet him and take him out to lunch and then to your apartment."

Twenty minutes later, Ginny stood on a subway platform in Pennsylvania Station. Her train had stopped in a tunnel for what seemed like an hour and had actually been ten minutes—just long enough to make her late.

"Oh, murder," she muttered as she headed up the stairs at a steady lope. She hated to think of Denis's father, elderly and probably befuddled by his first trip to New York, looking around for his son and finding no one.

As she entered the main waiting room, she glanced around at the crowd of people, every one of them moving purposefully, intent on his or her destination. She tried to spot a bewildered gray-haired man but no one met that description.

Suddenly, Ginny felt someone standing close behind her. With instincts honed by twenty-five years in the Big Apple, Ginny stepped away and pretended to be walking toward one of the out-going Amtrak tracks.

"Excuse me," said a deep, masculine voice behind her, "but are you by any chance Ginny McDougall?"

She whirled around, to be faced by the handsomest man she had ever seen. Ginny frankly stared. Blue eyes, thick brown hair sprinkled with gray, at least six feet two and lean without being skinny—perfection in human form. From somewhere deep inside, she felt dislike and distrust coil upward and chill her spirit.

"Yes, I'm Virginia McDougall. Have we met?" Her voice was as chilly as the March weather.

His smile was every bit as devastating as the rest of him. "Only on the phone. I'm Joshua Havilland, Denis's dad."

Ginny smiled back, unable to keep from doing so. The distrust still lingered, but she smiled at him and held out her hand. "Hello. It's good to meet you in person at last." She meant it. Too handsome he might be—but she couldn't help responding to him.

Josh Havilland ignored her outstretched hand

and, still smiling, swept her into his arms. As his head lowered to hers, he murmured, "This is the way we greet old friends in Indiana, Ginny."

At last, she managed to free herself. "If you want to stay out of jail or the hospital, you'd better get used to shaking hands in New York," she said breathlessly.

Josh laughed and put his arm around her waist. "I told you, it's how we greet old friends. Are you planning on having me arrested or just disabling me with a well-placed kick? Denis said you took karate classes."

"That's not how I treat my friends." Ginny decided to drop the subject. "Where're your bags?"

"I gave them to a free-lance porter. He's going to meet me at the information booth."

"Oh, Josh," Ginny said, shaking her head. "I'm afraid that wasn't very—" She caught herself. Better not insult the man's intelligence right off the bat. "I mean, there are a lot of thieves who claim they're porters in the train stations here and then steal your luggage. I hope you weren't a victim."

Josh looked at her and Ginny could see the smile brackets around his mouth and eyes deepen, though his expression remained noncommittal. She couldn't help smiling. She'd never known anyone who could smile without really smiling.

"There he is," Josh said. "Hi, Cleavon. I found my guide."

"Hey, man, I thought you said your son meetin' you!" The young black man in bicycle shorts and a back-to-front Atlanta Braves baseball cap grinned at Josh.

"I got Ginny here instead. How much do I owe you?"

Ginny inwardly sighed. Joshua Havilland was a real babe in the woods. This time it had worked out. Cleavon was honest, but the next time Josh could wind up swindled by some three-card monte dealer in Times Square, or robbed by a gang in a subway station. New Yorkers knew how to avoid those risks, but an open and trusting tourist like Josh was trouble waiting to happen.

Clearly, Ginny decided, she had her work cut out for her.

Josh and Cleavon conferred and to Ginny's surprise, the young man hefted Josh's two bags and came with them. It only took a few minutes for Ginny to shepherd them upstairs to the taxi stand.

Once Cleavon was paid and the cab directed to Denis's apartment in the West Seventies, Ginny sat back with a sigh of relief. She smiled at her charge. "How was the trip?" she asked. "I didn't know trains still ran from Indiana."

"Well, if I'd been in Florida, I'd have flown,"

Josh said. "But I was in Elgin seeing to some business and one of my old clients wanted to go to Baltimore to visit her daughter. She's scared to fly and scared to go alone, so I took the train with her."

"That's certainly beyond a lawyer's usual duties, at least in New York."

"I don't know about that. Seems to me, people are the same no matter where they are. Everyone needs something beyond the usual sometime." Josh smiled at Ginny again, and again her heart seemed to give a little skip. "Even New Yorkers," he added.

"Maybe so." Ginny gave herself a mental shake. She was thrown off-balance by the way this man affected her. Virginia McDougall was fifty years old, a top-notch secretary and paralegal, mother of one and volunteer at several charitable groups. Her heart did not skip beats! She was way past any such giddy nonsense.

She cast about for something to say. "How did you recognize me? I never would have known who you were. You don't look much like Denis." She didn't add that her picture of him, gathered from their many telephone conversations, had been of a spry but frail octogenarian.

"No, Denis takes after his mother. She had blond hair and brown eyes, too." Ginny knew that Josh had lost his wife when Denis was in his teens. "I asked him what you look like after I'd talked to you, and he described you. I recognized the hair. And then the eyes."

"Oh." Her hair, still a gleaming cinnamon color, made Ginny stand out in a crowd. She touched her short, windblown-style hair. "Yes, I guess that made it easy." Her clear green eyes looked at him a little apprehensively.

"I like to know what my friends look like." Josh turned toward her, his eyes smiling into hers.

Ginny was uncomfortable. The cab seemed to have grown warmer and smaller. She looked down at the seat. There was still plenty of room between them. Why did she feel somehow crowded?

"There's an African proverb," Josh went on, "that there are two kinds of friends in life: friends of the road and friends of the heart. I guess you have mostly friends of the road here."

Why should that remark make her want to cry? So she had friends of the road and not of the heart—was that so terrible? *Get a grip, Ginny,* she told herself. *You haven't known this man one hour and already he's got you questioning your life.*

She took a deep breath but before she could speak, Josh changed the subject. "I thought there weren't any trees in Manhattan. This looks pretty green to me." Josh was turned away from her, looking out the window again.

"We're passing Central Park. Denis's apartment is only about a half block off the Park."

As she spoke, the cab driver pulled up in front of a small white building tucked between two larger ones. It had a curved facade garnished with limestone gargoyles.

"Here we are."

"I didn't know Denis had a house." Josh looked up at the five-story building.

"Oh, he doesn't. Just the top two floors and the roof."

"The roof?" Josh's eyebrows rose.

Ginny managed to open the triple lock on the inside front door of the house. She was about to throw her weight against it to get it to open when Josh's arm reached over her head and effortlessly pushed it. She smiled at him over her shoulder and said, "Can you get your suitcases up the stairs? We can leave it here for Hervé to take up later." Josh's eyebrows questioned her. "He's the super. He lives down in the basement. If you ever need him, just ring the bell out in the vestibule labeled—"

"Don't tell me, let me guess. It's the one marked 'super,' right?" Josh's grin robbed the words of any offense, but Ginny blushed with embarrassment. His grin widened. "I don't mind that you think I'm a hick, Ginny. I am. You'll just have to take me in hand so I don't do anything stupid while I'm here."

The smile and the idea of taking Joshua Havilland in hand made Ginny feel an unaccustomed surge of warmth and anticipation. *Cut this out!* she ordered herself.

They had reached Denis's door and Josh, who had carried his own bags up three flights, wasn't even winded. They grew them strong in the corn belt, Ginny decided. She explained to Josh how to turn the security system on and off and then punched in the code to let them in.

Denis's place was clearly the habitat of an affluent bachelor who didn't give much thought to his home. It had been decorated in an attractive but impersonal style by an interior designer, and was kept clean by an anonymous cleaning service. The living room featured an overstuffed couch covered in a muted camel, blue, and brick print. It was flanked by two sleek Barcelona chairs in butterscotch leather. There was an elegant and expensive Tabriz on the floor in the same colors, and an elaborate marble mantel over the fireplace. A huge, complicated stereo system occupied an antique walnut armoire. On the few occasions Ginny had been there, she had thought it designed for comfort and as a way station to the bedroom. It didn't appeal to her.

"Looks expensive," was Josh's only comment as he followed Ginny up the stairs and into the guest bedroom. It was small and furnished only with a queen-size sleigh bed and a heavy rosewood chest. The bedspread and curtains were white, and a small Oriental rug in glowing jewel tones lay on the dark, polished wood floor.

"Looks comfortable," Josh said, putting his bags down.

"I think I'll go downstairs and see if I can find some coffee," Ginny said, inexplicably nervous at being in Josh's bedroom.

"Tell you what, Ginny." Josh took a step toward her and, with a gleam in his eye watched her back away. "I haven't had lunch, and I'll bet you haven't either. Is there any place around here where we could eat?"

"Of course." Ginny was embarrassed. She had completely forgotten about eating. This man was doing strange things to her body as well as her mind. "There are a number of good restaurants in the neighborhood. I'll just call the office while you unpack and unwind for a few minutes." She didn't wait for a reply before hurrying down the stairs, away from the unsettling sight of Josh Havilland next to a queen-size bed.

They ate at a Greek restaurant Josh had insisted on. Ginny had tried to steer him to a hamburger and chili place she thought would be more to his taste, but Josh had voted for exotic and strange. Over lunch, they talked easily about themselves.

Ginny told Josh about her daughter, Lisa, who worked for a nonprofit foundation with offices in midtown Manhattan, and Josh told Ginny about life in a retirement community in Florida.

"She likes doing something practical about social problems, and she's very good at it," Ginny told Josh. "But I'm not sure Lisa knows how to make allowances for people who lead different kinds of lives. She looks down on people who make a lot of money, even if they give a lot to charities."

"Shellfish Cay is nice, sort of like Shangri-La," Josh said. "But I always thought I'd be bored in Shangri-La, and I must admit it's pretty dull down there."

"Is that why you were back in Indiana?" Ginny took a bite of her stuffed grape leaves.

"Yes. I thought maybe I'd move back, reopen the office, and start the practice again, but . . ." Josh shrugged and smiled at Ginny.

"But what?" Ginny leaned forward and looked at him. She found that the reason for Josh's actions mattered, more than she had imagined.

"Oh, I don't know. I guess Heraclitus was right."

"You mean that you can't step in the same

river twice?" Ginny had taken a course in Greek philosophy at Fordham.

"You know Heraclitus?" The idea seemed to please Josh. More, Ginny thought, than a long-dead Greek seemed to warrant. "I read philosophy like other people read mysteries. Keeps the world in perspective. You, too?" His smile was hopeful.

"No, I take college courses like some people take Tums. Keeps my mind from getting upset because it's empty." Her smile was a welcome.

"Working for Denis doesn't do that?" Josh stirred the tiny cup of syrupy Greek coffee the waiter had just brought him. "From the way he talks, you're busy every minute."

"That's just it. I need something to keep my mind occupied after I leave the office." Ginny shrugged. "Otherwise, I might begin to think the law is all-important."

"I'm glad you know it isn't."

"Most lawyers wouldn't agree with you." Ginny smiled slightly. "Your son, for one."

Josh shook his head. "He's young. He'll learn."

They looked at each other in unspoken accord, two people who recognized that they had learned many of the same lessons from life. Ginny glanced at her watch. Good lord, it was two-thirty already. For a moment, she could feel herself tense, ready to go back to the office and the Ebersole deed. Then, very consciously, she told her muscles to relax. She was going to take the afternoon off, no matter what Denis thought. His father deserved someone's undivided attention. Since Denis wasn't available, it would have to be Ginny's. "Would you like to take a walk in the park?" she asked. "There's a playground not too far from here. Or we can just stroll."

Josh handed the waiter a credit card. "I'm glad you don't have to get back to work right away."

"No," Ginny lied cheerfully. "I'm free as a bird."

He took her hand as they left the restaurant. "Good. I was afraid Denis was a slave driver who'd have you chained to your computer all day." He smiled. "I'm glad I was wrong."

Two

Denis inserted his key in the lock of his front door. His nose twitched. What was that smell? His hand paused in the act of turning the key. Autumn in Indiana, leaves burning, football practice. Home. Dad. Tuna fish, noodles, and mushroom soup casserole.

Oh, God, how he hated tuna fish!

It was the first thing his father had learned to cook. After his mother died, they had eaten it every night for a month, until Mrs. Cavanaugh down the street had taken pity on them and offered to come in and cook. Before she'd retired, she'd taught Josh some of her recipes, but his old standby was still tuna fish casserole.

For an instant, Denis felt a stinging behind his eyes. He blinked rapidly and opened the door.

"Dad," he called out, just as he had so many times before. "I'm home."

"Hi, son." Josh's face was beaming as he came out of the kitchen, wiping his hands on a towel he had tied around his waist as an apron. "It's good to see you. Glad you could make it home for dinner."

They gave each other a brief embrace, and stood back, grinning fatuously.

"You're looking great, Dad. Florida must agree with you." Moving to Shellfish Cay had been Denis's idea and he was happy to see how well it had worked out.

"Well. Yeah. I guess."

Denis was too good a courtroom lawyer not to notice his father's lack of enthusiasm. "What's the matter, Dad? Why were you back in Indiana?"

"Just looking up old friends, Denis. Did I mention that Coach Snyder asked about you? Said they've never had a better halfback." Denis hid a smile. So the wily old lawyer was leading his son away from a sensitive topic. "Why don't you change your clothes, Denis? Dinner's about ready."

Denis grinned. He felt as if he were in a time warp, suddenly hurtled back twenty years and a thousand miles. "Do I have to do my homework after dinner?"

His father turned at the kitchen door, a reminiscent smile on his face. "You mean you didn't get it done in study hall?"

Chuckling, Denis headed upstairs to his room.

Maybe having his father visit wasn't going to be the disaster he had feared.

That happy thought lasted through dinner. Denis managed to eat the tuna casserole, though nostalgia didn't make it taste any better than it had in high school. Over afterdinner coffee in the living room, he broached the subject of the reason for his father's visit once again.

"How come I finally got you to agree to come to New York after all this time?" Denis asked. "You always had a million reasons for not visiting."

"Right. And each one a crime statistic. I'm too old to outrun a mugger." It was Josh's standard answer.

"So? The last time I looked, Manhattan hadn't turned into the Peaceable Kingdom. What changed your mind?"

"Just got restless, I guess." Josh studied the gold-and-crimson design on his coffee cup. "And talking to Ginny McDougall whenever I called you maybe had something to do with it. She made it sound as if being here was exciting. Always something going on."

"True. Rapes, muggings, robberies—always something."

"Are you trying to get rid of me?" Josh's eyebrows rose. "You usually sound like the Chamber of Commerce and the Bar Association combined.

'Lots of parties, lots of important cases. Can't come to visit this year, Dad.' "

Denis frowned. "All true, and it still doesn't answer my question." Denis set down his coffee cup. "What brings you to New York?"

Josh considered what to say. How much should he tell Denis this early in the game? He decided on what a Nixon administration bigwig had once called a "limited total hang-out." He'd tell his son the easy half.

"Mostly to see you. As I said, you couldn't come to Indiana or Florida, so I decided to come here. And I wanted to see the Big Apple. Take in some shows, see some art galleries, window-shop—all the tourist stuff."

"Fine, Dad. Great." Josh could tell from the falsely cheerful tone of Denis's voice that he wasn't happy. "But you know, I won't have time to show you around. I've got a couple of really major cases and—"

"No problem. I have a couple of guidebooks and I've written down some of the places Ginny told me about. I'll be fine." Josh tried to look reassuring. "I've been on my own for a good while now, Denis."

"I know, Dad, it's just that I—I'm often not around much in the evening. Either I'm working or—"

"Or you have a date. I know you date a lot,

Denis, and I certainly wouldn't expect you to disappoint your young ladies. I can entertain myself. And stay out of your way." Josh stood and gathered the coffee cups. "Ginny's asked me over for dinner. Potluck, anytime at all."

"I wouldn't take Ginny too seriously on that, Dad. She's very busy. She's always taking an extension course or two and she sees a lot of her daughter."

"Lisa, right?"

"She told you about the Child from Hell?" Denis's tone was acid.

"She's hardly a child. Ginny said Lisa graduated from Barnard and works for the Barringer Foundation."

"Yes, indeed. Lisa's found her lifework— spending other people's money." Denis got up and took the cups out of his father's hands. "Got in the habit of it living off Ginny, and now spends some airhead millionaire's dough."

"Don't tell me, let me guess. You don't like her."

"Does it show?" Denis grinned. "I know, I know. I'm not being fair. But it's mutual." He moved toward the kitchen. "Just ask Lisa about me, and you'll hear about parasitic, high-powered lawyers and bloodsucking big-city law firms. She thinks I'm right out of 'L.A. Law'."

"I can't wait to meet her." Josh's voice was dry. "She doesn't sound much like her mother."

"No, Ginny's terrific. She's been like a mother—"

Denis broke off abruptly. Josh could see concern written on his son's face and he hastened to reassure him. "It's okay. I know how you feel about Ginny and I don't resent it, Denis. Your mother's been dead a long time."

"I just sometimes think you've never gotten over it." Denis's words were hesitant.

"Why? Because I never remarried?" Josh shook his head. "There just never seemed to be anyone . . ."

"I know. But I thought it was because no one could measure up to Mother."

"I've never really thought about why." Josh considered the question. "At first, it was just too painful, that's true. And later, I never had the time." He grinned ruefully at Denis. "Or I never took the time."

"Was there someone? Someone you didn't take the time to get to know?" Josh could see guilt in Denis's eyes.

"No. If there had been someone special, I would have taken the time. I didn't sacrifice myself for you. There never was anyone." *Not until now.* The thought was gone before Josh could pin it down.

Denis looked relieved. "I was sort of hoping that you'd find someone interesting at Shellfish Cay."

Josh shook his head. "I'm afraid Shellfish Cay isn't the place for me. Now, don't worry about it. I just need to get away from it for a while and think about what I want to do. I do know I have to do something. I'm not cut out for retirement."

After years of being a single parent, a lawyer, and a member of more civic boards than he could remember, let alone count, retirement was a letdown. Josh missed the sense of purpose he had always had.

"You're not thinking of relocating to New York?" Josh could hear the alarm in his son's voice. "I don't think that would be a good idea, Dad."

Josh couldn't help being disappointed. He had always thought that he and Denis were friends. But his "friend" was happier when he was a thousand miles away. *There's nothing unusual about that,* he told himself. *How many kids want their parents underfoot?*

"I don't intend to cramp your style, Denis. And I certainly hadn't planned on moving in with you." Josh couldn't help it if he sounded a little hurt. Hell, he *was* a little hurt.

"I didn't mean that, Dad. I just don't think

that you'd be happy in New York after a lifetime in Elgin, Indiana."

"Too much of a hayseed?"

"Whatever that is. No, you just won't like it here. It's big and dirty and dangerous. And no one stops to pass the time of day. I've been shopping at the same supermarket for years and I don't say anything to the checkers."

"Not even hello?"

"Not even."

"Well, I hadn't planned on staying in New York. And if I do, I'll get a place of my own."

"It costs a lot to live here." Denis was clearly embarrassed at having to mention money to his father. One of the reasons Joshua Havilland didn't have more money was that he had spent so much sending his son to Princeton and Harvard Law School.

"Yes, Denis, I know." Josh smiled a little. "Don't worry. I can afford what I'll need."

"You'd really be much better off at Shellfish Cay. It's pretty and clean. And there's golf and . . . backgammon." Denis was clearly having a hard time thinking of advantages to living in a place he himself wouldn't consider for a moment.

"And plenty of time just to sit and listen to my arteries harden." Josh shook his head. "It's not for me. But don't worry. I'll find something to do." He smothered a yawn. "It's been a long day. I think I'll go up now. 'Night, Denis." Josh patted his son's shoulder as he passed on his way up the stairs.

Funny how sad he felt, knowing Denis didn't want him around. It wasn't that he expected to live with Denis, but the idea that his son was waiting impatiently for him to leave made Josh feel his age—fifty-eight and useless.

The next evening, Josh was sitting with his feet up, reading a guidebook. He had spent the day walking around midtown Manhattan, looking in boutiques where the price tags made him put on his glasses to be sure he hadn't misplaced the decimal. Fourteen hundred dollars for a sweater? Amazing. He had peered into art galleries and read the menus of all the restaurants he passed. He thought the decimals were misplaced there, too.

He started dinner, not knowing if Denis would be in. Corned beef and cabbage. It was too hot in Florida for corned beef, but the chill March weather here was just right. Now Josh sat relaxed, sipping a scotch. He liked New York. There was a pulsing, supercharged life in its streets that he responded to. No listening to your arteries harden in this town!

On his way in with the groceries, he had encountered Hervé, the superintendent, polishing the brass mailboxes in the entryway. Stopping to chat was second nature to Josh.

In the five minutes they had talked, Josh had discovered that Hervé came from Haiti, that he was in the country legally and sent money every month to his mother, who lived on a farm outside Port-au-Prince. Hervé was working for his high school equivalency exam and was superintendent at two other brownstones on the block, but lived in this one.

Hervé was interesting and Josh wondered as he climbed the stairs why Denis had reacted so negatively to the idea of talking to anyone he hadn't been introduced to. That was the kind of idea mothers in Elgin had given up on fifty years ago! Imagine New York more old-fashioned than Indiana, he thought with an inward smile.

Josh had just finished the chapter on the Metropolitan Museum, which he had decided was a must-see on his itinerary, when the doorbell rang. Remembering Denis's lecture that morning, Josh looked through the peephole at their visitor. *Damn thing makes everyone look like a goldfish,* he thought irritably, and swung the door open.

The young woman standing in the hall was one of the most beautiful girls he had ever seen. A tall, slender blonde, with high cheekbones and enormous hazel eyes framed by incredibly long, dark lashes—she was gorgeous. Breathtaking. Josh's breath had literally caught in his throat just looking at her.

"Hello," she said in a soft, Arkansas drawl. "Are you Denis's dad? He told me I should just come ahead if the shoot finished early." She looked at Josh inquiringly.

"I'm sorry to be rude," Josh said at last. "But you're the prettiest thing I've seen since the last Miss America pageant. Come on in." Josh ushered her into the living room.

"I'm Candy Cameron," said the beauty, so softly Josh had to lean forward to hear her. "Denis and I are going out to dinner. Would you like to join us, Mr. Havilland?"

"That's nice of you, Candy," Josh said. "Come on in and sit down. Denis will probably be here any minute, with you waiting for him. Can I get you something to drink?"

Candy asked for plain water with lemon. Josh brought it to her and asked, "Tell me about your career. I've heard all about New York models but I've never met one. Is the work hard? Some of those poses look tough—draped around statues or running up the street. Are they?"

Men seldom asked Candy about the strains of her work—they were only interested in her looks and wanted to show her off. She kicked off her

shoes and, under Josh's expert questioning, told
him about shoes that pinched, dresses that had
to be pinned so tight she couldn't breathe, pho-
tographers who treated her like a piece of meat,
and advertising executives who thought going out
with her after work was part of the deal.

Candy sat back and sipped her drink. "What's
that wonderful smell, Mr. Havilland? Are you
cooking?"

"Yes. I was in the mood for some corned beef
and cabbage and they were having a sale at
D'Agostino's."

"It's been ages since I've had a home-cooked
meal," Candy sighed. "My roommates and I stick
mostly to fresh raw veggies and fruit when we're
in for dinner. I miss my mother's cooking."

There was a wistful note in the young model's
voice that touched Josh's heart. "I'd love to have
you stay, Candy. There's plenty. But I know that
Denis is looking forward to taking you out."

Candy sighed. "Yes, they always want to go
out. Sometimes I think men just want to wear
me on their arm, like a carnation in their button-
hole." Her quiet voice was still gentle, but Josh
detected an undertone of bitterness.

"Why don't you—" He was interrupted by the
telephone. It was Denis, announcing that he was
going to be late for dinner and asking to speak

to Candy. Josh went out to the kitchen to cut the celery and peel the potatoes and carrots.

He heard Candy hang up and went back into the living room. "Denis get held up?" he asked with a sympathetic smile.

"Worse than that," Candy said. "He can't come at all. There's some sort of hearing tomorrow and he's going to be at the office until late."

Josh couldn't help but wonder if Ginny McDougall stayed late on those occasions. Would she be going home alone late at night? Surely Denis would see her to her door. Wouldn't he? Josh wasn't sure. Denis didn't seem too concerned about how Candy got home.

"Well," Candy said, her shoulders drooping a little, "I guess I'd better get home. I have a runway job tomorrow."

Josh cleared his throat. The girl looked so lonesome. "Why don't you stay and have dinner with me, Candy? There's much too much corned beef for one person. I can't pretend it will be as good as your mother's, but if you'd like to stay . . ." Josh made it a question.

"Thanks, Mr. Havilland, I'd love to." Candy beamed at him.

Candy sat on a stool at the counter that set the kitchen off from the living room and chatted happily while Josh simmered the vegetables and sliced the beef. All through dinner he plied her with carrots and cabbage—in deference to her diet—and heard about life in a tiny town south of Little Rock.

After dinner, they sat in the living room and drank herbal tea and talked some more. Finally, Candy looked at her watch and jumped to her feet. "Oh, goodness, look. It's ten-thirty already, Mr. Havilland. I've taken up your whole evening and just talked and talked about myself. You must be bored to tears. You should have stopped me."

Before Josh could protest there was the sound of a key in the lock and Denis came in. His eyes widened when he saw that his date was still there.

"Checking up on me, Candy?" he said in an acid tone.

Josh could hear Candy's sharp intake of breath. "Candy agreed to stay for dinner and keep me company, Denis. I'm afraid I've kept her later than I should have, but I've always been interested in . . ."

"Beautiful girls," Denis interrupted. He flung his briefcase down on one of the couches and collapsed beside it. His shirt was wilted and his tie askew. He looked exhausted.

"You look tired, son," Josh said quietly. "Are you hungry? I could make you a corned beef sandwich."

"Thanks, Dad, but I'm fine. You made corned beef? I wondered why the whole place smelled like an Irish pub. I'll probably get complaints from the Stevensons downstairs."

"I was just about to go down and find Candy a cab." Josh was determined to ignore Denis's bad temper.

There was a pause. Denis took a deep breath and said, "I'd like to do that, Dad. I haven't seen Candy in a while." He gave the model a devastating smile and got to his feet. "Can't have you stealing my girl."

"Did Ginny stay down this evening, too?" Josh couldn't help asking while he had the chance. He had a feeling Denis was going to take a very long time seeing Candy home.

"Sure. I sent her home in a cab," Denis said carelessly.

"I should think so. You gave her dinner, too, I hope?"

"Why the third degree, Dad? Ginny can take care of herself."

His son's cavalier attitude infuriated Josh. "She shouldn't have to! A woman like Ginny should be taken care of." Denis turned his back and headed for the door. "Good-night, Candy, and thank you for your company. I trust Denis will take better care of you than he does of his assistant."

Josh turned on his heel and stomped upstairs, where he tossed restlessly until the early hours of the morning.

Three

Josh decided he had better make himself scarce the next evening. Denis had announced at breakfast that he would like it if Josh would refrain from cooking dinner unless asked to do so. "I'd also like it if you'd leave my dates alone. All I heard from Candy last night was how terrific my father was."

"Would you rather I stayed at a hotel, son? I don't mean to mess up your private life. I can see how hard you work."

"No, of course not. And I didn't really think you should have sent Candy home." Denis smiled reminiscently. "I was glad to see her. It's just . . ." His voice trailed off.

"I know. You're used to having your place to yourself."

Denis shrugged and Josh could tell he was embarrassed. "I like having you here, Dad. I guess it just takes some getting used to."

"I'll leave you a note if I'm not here when you get home. Is tonight likely to be a late one?"

"Not at work. I'm leaving at six. Janine and I have tickets for the opera."

"Janine? Not Candy?" Josh could have kicked himself when he saw the shuttered look come over Denis's face.

"Janine Ryan." Denis's voice was clipped. "Before you ask, she's a model, too, but she's studying voice and I take her to the opera. I'm meeting her for dinner at six. I don't know when I'll be home. Anything else?"

Josh smiled. "Not a thing." So Ginny wouldn't be working late this evening. Maybe he could talk her into dinner. They could go to a restaurant, Indian, if he had a choice. Tandoori chicken and lamb curry. He had tried Indian recipes, but never had the real thing. He reached for the telephone, then remembered that it wasn't yet eight o'clock and Ginny wouldn't be at the office yet.

But despite her late evening, Ginny was in the office and at work by seven-thirty. In addition to her secretarial duties, Ginny did legal research and drafted documents for Denis's review. Secretary and legal assistant was her job description and sometimes Ginny thought that didn't begin to cover it. One thing was for sure—eight-hour days were few and far between.

When her phone rang at ten o'clock she picked it up and cradled it between her shoulder and cheek. "Hello. Sanderson and Smith, Denis Havilland's office, Virginia McDougall speaking."

"Hi, it's your telephone buddy."

His voice poured over her like warm honey. "Josh?"

"Yep. I called to ask you out for dinner tonight." Ginny didn't know why her mouth was suddenly dry. Josh continued, sounding a little desperate, "I wanted to get you before I started out for the Metropolitan Museum. Sounds like there's so much to see I'll spend all day there." Ginny still didn't know what to say. "Ginny? Is something wrong?"

"No." She looked down at her blotter. For the first time she regretted her full calendar. "I'm sorry, Josh, I can't tonight. It's my volunteer night at a retirement home over in Brooklyn. I go once a week to play cards or write letters or read aloud, whatever they need done."

"Sounds great! I'll come with you. What time shall I pick you up? Why don't I meet you at Denis's office at five and we can have a quick dinner. What time did you say you had to be in Brooklyn?"

"Whew." She laughed a little. No one had taken over quite this ruthlessly in a long time. "Well, okay. That sounds terrific. They can always use another pair of hands. And five o'clock will be fine. I'm not expected until seven-thirty."

"Plenty of time for dinner. I'll see you then." There was a flattering smile in his voice. Ginny put the phone down and sat, uncharacteristically bemused, for a minute. She was looking forward to the evening. She had a feeling he would liven up the Mordecai Jackson Home.

Six o'clock found them sipping beer at a small table in a crowded Indian restaurant on Third Avenue. Josh had arrived at Denis's plush Wall Street office, with its view of the Statue of Liberty, and swept Ginny off before Denis had time to do more than remind her of five things she had to do first thing the next morning.

"Does he always give you that much to do?" Josh frowned, thinking of his son's imperious tone when he talked to his assistant. Josh found himself resenting it.

"It's a very busy office. Denis isn't the only one who gets a little short-tempered at the end of the day," Ginny said. "It's just the way things are when you practice with a big firm in the Big Apple."

"I think I'm glad I stuck with Elgin, Indiana."

"Denis said that you went to Harvard Law and then decided to go back home to practice."

"You sound puzzled. I guess to a New Yorker that's pretty hard to understand," Josh said. "I worked for a firm down here on Wall Street the summer after my second year in law school."

"Why didn't you come back after you graduated?"

"Why do you assume any big, New York firm offered me a job? Maybe I was only good enough to practice in a small town with the hicks." Josh leaned back and grinned.

"Because I know you were on the law review at Harvard, that's why. Had you always planned to practice in a small town?"

"No. It was after I spent the summer in the law library here, and only got out into court once—carrying documents for some associate who was arguing a little diddly motion. That just wasn't my idea of practicing law."

"You wanted to be in a courtroom, arguing motions yourself?"

"Partly. But I could have done that in the DA's office here. No, I wanted to have clients I knew and advised over the long haul. Real general practice, like an old-fashioned doctor." Josh leaned forward and grinned. "I didn't want to be a hired gun in a three-piece suit."

Ginny looked at him thoughtfully. "I can understand that. Sometimes I feel the same way."

"Could you get that same feeling in this city, that closeness? I thought it was impossible. That's why I left." He tasted the chicken in yogurt sauce and sighed. "I've tried to make this dish, but I can't get the sauce right. Would the chef tell me how he does it, do you think?"

"You can ask. You never know."

She saw how Josh explained what was wrong with his sauce.

"No body and it kind of falls apart into solids on one side and liquid on the other," he explained. Then he praised the smooth result of the chef's version. A little flattery, a lot of conversation about the difficulties of running a restaurant in New York, and Josh had the secret.

He explained it to Ginny as they left, leaving a family of friends behind. The best that Ginny could make of it was that the chef drained the yogurt in cheesecloth overnight. It sounded very messy to Ginny, but Josh seemed pleased with the idea. Ginny, whose cooking tended to be hurried and rudimentary, was amused to find Josh so interested in foreign cuisine.

They took a cab back downtown and across the bridge to Brooklyn, an extravagance Ginny didn't allow herself very often. She didn't ride the subway late at night, but at seven o'clock she felt quite safe and someone usually gave her a ride home when she left.

"How did you start helping out at the retirement home?" Josh asked.

"A friend, a minister I met at a course in medieval music, asked for volunteers. I went and enjoyed it and I've gone once or twice a week ever since."

"I'm looking forward to it," Josh said, and because she already had seen how interested he was in everyone he met, Ginny believed him.

Once there, it became even clearer. Josh mingled easily with the residents and the staff. Ginny went to write letters for Joe Kelly, who had children scattered all over the country and arthritis in his hands. Once a month Ginny helped him keep in touch. When she came out of the study an hour later, she found Josh deep in conversation with Sylvia Bright, who was known around the home as the ancient mariner because she fixed some hapless visitor with her beady eye and refused to let them go until she had told them the story of her life. Sylvia was seventy-seven, so it was a long story.

Ginny strolled over, ready to rescue her friend if he needed it. But Josh was winding wool for Sylvia and deeply engrossed in conversation.

"I don't know, Sylvia," he was saying as Ginny came up to them. "I don't think you should have your son-in-law draw up your will if you don't trust him."

"But he's the only lawyer I know. The only one I can afford." Sylvia's voice shook a little.

"Well, I'll look into it for you. If you make up a list before you go to see the attorney, it could take only an hour or so. It sounds like you want a very simple will." He looked up and smiled at Ginny. "In fact, Ginny and I could do it for you, couldn't we?"

"I think Sylvia should consult a New York attorney." Ginny knew she sounded ungracious, but she was annoyed with Josh. She didn't like being dragged into situations without warning. She didn't want to draft a will without instructions from an attorney. Paralegals could draft legal documents but only under the direction of a licensed attorney. Ginny wasn't about to run afoul of those rules and end up being charged with practicing law without a license. If that happened, she would be fired.

Josh's eyebrows rose. "Sorry, I didn't mean to commit you to something without asking," he said quietly. Ginny was disarmed by his innate understanding of what she felt and his readiness to apologize.

He turned to Sylvia again. "Well, I'll try to think of a solution. Maybe your son-in-law could draft it but I could take a look at it before you execute it. How would that be?"

"Josh!" Ginny tugged at his arm. "I need to talk to you."

Josh excused himself to Sylvia Bright and followed Ginny across the room. "What's wrong, Ginny?" He looked down at her, his expression soft and somehow yearning. "The lights make your hair look like cinnamon and ginger. Good enough to eat."

Ginny told her heart to settle down. What was the big deal of being compared to a spice rack? Where was the romance in that? "Josh, you've got to be careful. You're not a New York lawyer. You know how lawyers are about someone poaching on their preserve. You don't want to be accused of practicing law without a license."

"It's nice of you to be concerned, Ginny, but I don't think that just looking at Sylvia's will—"

"Her son-in-law is a weasel. I've met him. He wants her little bit of money and if you tell her how to get around that, he'll have you for breakfast."

"Fee, fi, fo, fum. I'm terrified." Josh smiled down at her. "Do you really think that a guy who picks on old ladies scares me?"

"Well, he should scare you." Ginny was ready to shake him. *Men!* she thought. *When will they get over this macho stupidity?* "His father is a past president of the Kings County Bar Association."

"Kings County?"

"That's Brooklyn."

"Oh. And is that a very important job?"

"It is in Brooklyn." Naturally, Josh wouldn't know how powerful Sylvia's son-in-law's father was.

"And I could get in trouble if I try to help Sylvia?"

"Yes, you could. A lot of trouble. With a capital T and it rhymes with B and it stands for Bar Association." Ginny lowered her voice. "You could be censured, a letter written to the Indiana Bar complaining of your conduct."

"It would be a nuisance to be reprimanded, but I don't think they'd yank my license." Josh's eyes were boring into Ginny's. "Besides, I don't practice law in Indiana anymore."

"I wish you'd back off this, Josh."

"Well, I don't like backing off and I don't do it unless I have to."

"Do you know enough about New York estate and inheritance law to advise Sylvia?" Ginny wasn't going to back off either.

"If I don't, I'll seek counsel." Josh's eyebrows drew together and Ginny could see he was becoming annoyed at her persistence.

Ginny decided she had said all she could. Her voice was cool and noncommittal as she said, "Harry Lipscomb is here visiting his father. He usually drives me back to Manhattan. I'm sure he'd be happy to take you, too. If you'll meet me back here in five minutes, we can go together."

Harry Lipscomb was a chatty fellow who seemed to know Ginny well. They talked all the way across the East River and up to Ginny's apartment on Twenty-third Street and First Avenue. She said nothing when Josh got out to open the door for her, but her mouth opened in protest when he took her arm and started to walk into the building with her. Josh's hand tightened on her arm and he growled, "Don't lecture me on how independent you are. I'm doing this for me, not for you." He turned back to Harry and waved. "Say good-night, Ginny."

"Good-night Ginny," she repeated, with a smile for Harry. "I know all the old jokes, too."

Josh kept his hand on her arm until the elevator had deposited them on the tenth floor. He waited for Ginny to open the door to Apartment 10-G, then took her, unresisting, into his arms. He kissed her slowly, gently. She had plenty of time to pull away, to say no. But she couldn't. She wanted his kiss. If she were honest, she knew she'd wanted it since one minute after he'd kissed her for the first time in the middle of Penn Station.

When he moved as if to break their kiss, she put her arms around his neck and pulled his head down to hers again. With a soft sound of satisfaction, he tightened his hold again and swept her body closer to his.

After a long moment, he stepped away from her, breathing hard. "I'd better go." His forefinger traced her cheek. "Dinner tomorrow?"

"Yes." Her voice was a sigh. "Call me."

"Yes. Yes." He took her lips in a last kiss. "Sleep well, Ginny."

His kiss had stirred back to life something long buried within her. Sleep well? Not a chance.

Four

Josh had spent the day browsing through art museums, and now stood chatting with a hot dog vendor outside the Metropolitan Museum. He ordered his hot dog with everything, discovered that "everything" included sauerkraut and chili and quickly amended his order. New Yorkers had to have cast iron stomachs, he decided. Mack, the vendor, had opinions about the upcoming election ("they're both bums,") a scandal in the Parks Department ("imagine, payoffs from tree farmers,") and the outstanding nature of all New York sports teams except the Giants ("they moved to Jersey. They're the Hackensack Pygmies now.") Just as they started to debate Mack's theory of global economic recovery, a crowd of schoolchildren gathered to place their orders and Josh moved off.

Munching his lunch, Josh sat on one of the benches lining the park side of Fifth Avenue and watched the stream of people move by. It was just after two and the street was as crowded as downtown Elgin during the Fourth of July parade. More crowded than all of Shellfish Cay at any time.

He strolled down to Fifty-eighth Street and walked across the park. Toddlers were out for an afternoon stroll with their caretakers. Josh couldn't tell which were the mothers and which the *au pairs* until he heard which women spoke with foreign accents. Satisfied he had the answer, he had to smile when one of the children addressed a dark-haired young woman as "mommy" and "mommy" answered in purest cockney. Only in New York, he told himself.

By the time he returned to Denis's triplex, Josh was pleasantly tired and surprised to find it was four-thirty. People-watching in Manhattan was clearly a full-time job. He eased his feet out of his loafers and wiggled his toes on Denis's expensive Oriental rug. Just as he stretched his legs out with a contented sigh, the phone rang. Josh debated whether to answer or let the machine pick up. Denis would probably prefer that his father not answer, but Josh could never resist a ringing telephone.

He picked it up. It was Candy.

"Oh, Mr. Havilland, I'm so glad to get a chance to talk to you instead of the answering machine. I wanted to thank you for dinner the other night." Candy sounded glad to hear his voice. Josh didn't know whether to be glad or sorry. Denis had pretty emphatically ordered his father out of his love life. Josh couldn't very well invite Candy over for dinner, or accept an invitation from her. "I had such a nice time. We'll have to do it again."

Oh boy. "Yes, I'll have to check with Denis and see when we can have you over again, Candy. I enjoyed meeting you, too."

"Oh, no, Josh. My roommates and I have a potluck supper every month or so. Just informal, you know, to pay back all our beaux."

"I haven't heard anyone call men 'beaux' since my youth, Candy. Where did you learn it?"

"My momma. We're kind of old-fashioned in Arkansas. I'll just send you an invitation, then, if you're going to be at Denis's for a while. Okay?"

"Well, sure, I'd love to come. Denis, too, of course."

"Oh, yes. Denis usually comes." Something in Candy's voice told Josh that she had no illusions about being Denis's only girl. "We'll look forward to seeing you both. Bye."

Shrugging, he dismissed Candy from his mind and called Ginny. At the sound of her voice, he smiled. "Hello, Virginia McDougall. Is it late enough in the day for you to think about dinner?"

"Much too late," she said with a sigh. "Denis

has left me with a full evening's worth of typing."

"You're a paralegal. You don't still do his typing, do you?"

"Usually. Though I suppose I could give it to the typing pool." She sounded as if the idea was a new one.

"Do they have night typists?"

"Yes. There's a whole night staff. They stay till midnight, later if they're needed."

"Good. Then you can turn your typing over to them and meet me for dinner." Josh felt like smiling. He was going to have dinner with Ginny. It had been a long time since he had felt that kind of anticipation. Since the early days with Marion. A very long time indeed.

"Where do you want to eat?" Ginny sounded apprehensive.

Josh took a chance. "How about letting me make you my famous veal piccata? I'll do everything if you'll just furnish the kitchen."

"You want to cook at my place?" Josh could hear surprise in her voice.

"Yes. Why so surprised? You do have a kitchen, don't you?"

"Of course. I just don't use it very often."

"Well, we'll dust it off then. I'll meet you there at seven-thirty. Okay?"

"Okay. Fine. Terrific!" Josh smiled at the telephone, glad that Ginny sounded enthusiastic.

He spent an unhurried half hour in the supermarket nearest Ginny's apartment. The aisles were barely wide enough for two carts to pass each other and the shelves were piled to the point of collapse with ethnic foods Josh couldn't find in Shellfish Cay. Now he could make Cuban black beans and rice and real Spanish paella with chorizo—New York was a culinary paradise.

He was surprised that Ginny's apartment was so spacious and the building so well maintained. The unadorned brick of the outside had reminded him forcibly of pictures of urban housing projects, but the hallways and elevator were polished and painted. And Ginny's apartment was warm and cozy. There was an old-fashioned camelback sofa covered in a cheerful red-and-green stripe. Two armchairs in flowered chintz, several almost-antique tables, and lots of green plants made Josh feel at home. The kitchen was small, but plenty big enough to cook in, Josh told her as he unpacked the groceries.

"I wouldn't know," Ginny confessed. "I don't cook unless I have to. And then it's salad and something broiled. Or spaghetti. I do know how to cook that. Though sometimes it's a little flabby."

"Hush. You're making my taste buds ache.

Flabby spaghetti! Woman, you need help. Fortunately, I am willing to undertake your education."

"Oh, joy!" Ginny clasped her hands in mock ecstasy. "You're going to teach me something I don't want to learn!" She frowned as Josh scrabbled through the cabinet drawers. "What *are* you looking for?"

"Your zester. For the lemon."

"My what? You mean my vegetable peeler thing?"

"That will do if you don't have a zester."

"I certainly don't have a zester. It sounds like something you'd find at an adults-only, triple-X-rated store in Times Square." Ginny handed him her vegetable peeler. "I don't even want to guess what you do with the lemon after you get through zesting it."

Josh laughed. Her breath caught when she saw his eyes smiling down at her. He pulled her into his arms and hugged her. "Ginny, you're terrific." He tilted her head back and kissed her once hard and then again softly and sweetly.

It had taken only a moment, but Ginny could feel her heart start to melt and expand, and she caught her breath in dismay. This was much too fast and too strong for her. Her hands rested on his chest, and she made herself push him away. "Enough. I'm depending on you for dinner. I can't cook all this stuff." She gestured to the artichokes, rice, and other ingredients she didn't even recognize. Veal piccata came her way only when she ate at an Italian restaurant.

"I can take time out from time to time. For a kiss, or a glass of wine." Josh grabbed a knife and began chopping parsley on Ginny's chopping board. After a few seconds, he stopped. "When was the last time you sharpened this knife?"

"I haven't the slightest idea. I'm sure Lisa did it sometime in the last decade, whether it needed it or not," Ginny said defensively. Who was Josh Havilland to invite himself into her kitchen and criticize her?

"Well, it needs it now," Josh said as he went through her cabinet drawers until he found a long, slender cylinder with a handle. He wiped the knife blade across it several times and then tested it with his thumb. As Ginny watched, he searched for and found four other knives and subjected them to the same procedure.

"That's how you sharpen knives?" she asked, fascinated. "I've always wondered what that thing was. A knife sharpener, imagine! Learn something new every day."

"Stick with me, and I'll see to it," Josh replied.

"You're going to give me a cooking lesson every night?" Ginny asked, her eyes crinkling with suppressed laughter. "I could go for that as long as I get to eat the results."

"I bet I could teach you a few things in other rooms as well." There was no suggestiveness in his voice but Ginny could feel her cheeks heat. He didn't have to suggest for her to imagine.

She rallied and tried for light banter. "I'm glad to hear you say that. I've never felt I was getting my shower head really clean. Do you think you could teach me how to scrub it?"

"Very funny. I have some ideas about your shower and scrubbing, but they don't involve the shower head." Now as he looked at her, his blue eyes were hot and slumberous.

Ginny took a half step back and bumped into the counter. The kitchen wasn't big enough for two after all. She turned and stumbled for the door. "I'll leave you alone to create. If you need anything, you'd probably better just look for it."

His hand gripped her arm. "Don't leave, Ginny. I'll behave." She looked up into his eyes. "I don't want to, but I will."

Ginny didn't want their newfound friendship ruined by false expectations. She took a deep breath and explained. "I like you, Josh. And I'd like to have you for a friend. But that's all I'm interested in. I just don't want anything more— anything *else,* I mean."

After a long moment's silence, Josh spoke. It wasn't what Ginny expected. "Is it me or is it every man?"

"Actually, not that it matters, it's me." Ginny turned away again, dismissing him.

He wouldn't let her get away that easily. His arm barred her exit and his hand held her elbow. "It matters to me. I want to know what I'm up against."

"Up against? You're not up against anything. I like you. I want us to be friends." Ginny tried to pull her arm away. "I don't sleep with a man on the second date."

"Cut it out, Ginny. That's not what I meant. It's not what you meant either." Josh's hands were gentle but implacable. "This isn't some vacation fling or one-night stand. I'm seriously interested in you."

"How can you be? You hardly know me." Ginny stopped trying to pull away. She wanted to hear his answer.

"I do know you. We've talked on the phone how many times over the years? At least a few hundred? Two? Maybe three. And how often since I moved to Florida? Every other day? I know you, Ginny. I know how you struggled to raise your daughter, how proud you are of her. I know how hard you work and all you do for my ungrateful son. I know you like Fellini movies and, God help you, Stephen King novels." He shook her gently and pulled her close to him, so he was whispering into her ear, his breath stirring her hair. "I know you and I like you. I more than like you. And I think you feel the same way about me."

"Isn't the rice going to burn?" Ginny asked inanely.

"Stop trying to change the subject," Josh growled and moved to hold her face in his hands. This time, his kiss was a promise, a preview. This, Ginny thought, is what making love with him would be like—hot and sweet enough to melt her bones. For the first time in she didn't know how long, Ginny wanted a man. Not just any man. Josh Havilland.

The thought scared her to death. How could she be stupid enough to want to make love with this supremely handsome man? Wasn't one disastrous relationship enough for a lifetime?

She shook her head, hoping to clear it. She would control her thoughts and her feelings. She would simply refuse to entertain any thoughts about Josh Havilland that were other than friendly and completely unsexual. Asexual. Whatever.

"I don't want anything other than friendship." Ginny was proud of the firm sound of her voice. Anyone could tell she meant what she said.

Anyone but Josh. "Ginny, you kissed me, too."

"I did not! You kissed me."

Josh grinned. "You kissed me back. Am I being as childish as I think I am?"

Ginny smiled ruefully. "We both are. You're right . . ." She cleared her throat. "I did kiss you, too. But that doesn't mean that I approve of doing it. Or that I want to do it again. We're just friends, Josh. That's all I want. Really."

"That's not all you want, Ginny. It's just all you'll let yourself want."

"I don't see the difference." Ginny shrugged impatiently. "If we're going to go on seeing each other, that's got to be the basis for it. Friendship. A mutual interest in ancient Greek philosophers. My kitchen, your cooking."

"All right," he said. "I can accept that, for the time being. But I want you to recognize that it isn't going to stay that way. For either of us."

There was a pause. Ginny couldn't stop staring into his eyes. She thought she could see heat and laughter and something deeper than either. Something she didn't want to see, and couldn't look away from.

"Didn't you promise me veal piccata and artichoke hearts, Mr. Havilland? My mouth is watering for the taste of that zesty lemon peel."

"You're right." Josh grinned. "Let's get to it."

"Let's? As in 'let *us*'?" Ginny said. "I thought all I had to do was supply the kitchen. Are you trying to renegotiate our deal?"

"Not at all. The deal was that you lend me your kitchen, but your true kindness of heart won't let me toil out there alone, without your friendly conversation."

"You win. I'll talk, you cook."

"That's right. We'll each do what we're good at." With a flourish, Josh pulled out the chair at her tiny kitchen table.

Dinner was the best meal ever cooked in her kitchen, and Josh the best company. Ginny relaxed now that he seemed to accept her limits on their relationship. She basked in the warmth of his company and praised his cooking until he laughingly asked her to stop.

"I know you're just trying to butter me up so I'll cook for you again."

"Have I made any headway?" Ginny asked with an eager smile. "I want to book you up before word gets out."

"You can book me for dinner any time, Ginny. Flattery is always welcome but, in your case, unnecessary." Josh's voice deepened again, and there was a light in his eyes that Ginny thought she had banished with her talk of friendship.

Apparently, Joshua Havilland didn't give up. Well, she didn't either, and there was something she wanted to discuss with him. "I hope we really are friends because there's something I want to say."

Josh looked surprised, but then his eyes narrowed. "Don't tell me, let me guess. I'm going to get the lecture again, I'll bet. No practicing law in the sacred precincts of New York for outsiders like me?" he said. "You've made your point, Ginny. I won't do anything that will embarrass Denis or get me disbarred in Indiana."

"Are you admitted to the bar in Florida?" Ginny asked as she sipped an after-dinner Cointreau.

"No. There's no reciprocity down there. I'd have to take the bar exam, and I haven't decided whether or not I want to do that. I'm not even sure I could still study hard enough to pass it." He stretched his legs out and smiled at her. "It was pretty tough the first time."

"I've heard endless horror stories about taking bar exams. I'm not surprised you don't want to do it again."

"Of course," Josh said, giving her a look she couldn't interpret, "New York would let me in if I applied. There's reciprocity with Indiana and I wouldn't have to take the exam."

"New York? You're thinking of moving here and practicing law?" Ginny was astonished. The man had been in New York three and a half days and he was thinking of moving here.

"It was just a thought. Don't panic, Ginny. I won't hang on your sleeve, no matter how short a time I'm here. I was just thinking out loud." He looked down into his coffee cup, as if he could read something there. "You know, when he was little, Denis used to say that he wanted to be a lawyer just like me and become my partner when he grew up. I've always been a little sorry that we've never worked together."

"You think that you and Denis—?" Ginny didn't know what to say. She knew Denis Havilland and the chances of his ever moving back to Indiana to practice law were nil. "I don't know, Josh—I don't think—"

Josh chuckled. "Don't look so horrified. I know Denis would never want to leave here. He's a real New Yorker—if you can be a real New Yorker when you come from Elgin, Indiana."

"Most of the people here came from someplace else."

"Did you?"

"Yes. I was born and raised in New Jersey. I made the big move across the river when Lisa was just a baby." Ginny could feel her stomach tighten. She didn't want to tell Josh Havilland about her life when Lisa was small. But she had to say something. "It was tough at first, but moving here was the best thing I could have done. There were lots of single mothers and we sort of found each other and helped each other out. And all the best-paying jobs were here. I found a job with Sanderson and Smith right away. I found a small apartment—"

Josh interrupted. "You were alone from the time Lisa was a baby? What happened, Ginny?"

He looked so genuinely concerned that Ginny couldn't refuse to answer. Maybe if she gave him the bare bones of the story, he would let it go. "Lisa's father died in a car crash two weeks before she was born."

"Ginny, honey—" The deep note of concern in his voice almost made her lose control. Then he reached out and took her hand, and Ginny found herself crying for the first time in almost twenty years.

"Damn you, Joshua Havilland!" She pulled away and stood up, hugging herself around the waist. She hurried over to stand in front of the big window that ran the width of the living room. Hunching her shoulders, she fought for control. At first, she thought she was winning, but then she felt the warmth of Josh's body right behind her and the feel of his arms as they wrapped around hers.

"I'm sorry, Ginny. God, I seem to say that to you every five minutes. I didn't mean to pry and I didn't mean to make you unhappy." He bent his head and kissed her cheek. "I admire what you've done with your life, that's all. I think you're a terrific lady—woman—person."

Ginny couldn't help but chuckle. "Don't know

the politically correct term for my gender, Havilland?"

"It seems to change daily. What do you prefer?"

"Woman is fine."

"Wouldn't 'baby' be even better?" She could hear the smile in his voice, and leaned back into the warm strength of his embrace. For just a minute, she told herself. It would be okay for just a minute.

"No, somehow baby reminds me of old gangster movies. Dick Powell and Robert Mitchum were always calling some blond bombshell like Lizabeth Scott baby. I knew then it wasn't me." She pulled away from him. She was calm again. A minute in Josh's arms and a little silly conversation and the memories that had threatened to overwhelm her were back in the deep recesses of her mind where she kept them.

He didn't let her go. Instead, he gently turned her around to face him and studied her expression. "All right, Ginny?" he asked, his voice laced with concern.

"Yes, fine. I don't like to talk about the early days. Except for Lisa, there's not much I want to remember." She smiled at him and then gently, inexorably, pulled herself out of his arms.

Josh gave her a piercing look that said the subject was closed, but not forgotten, and changed the subject. "Some girlfriend of Denis's is going to invite me to a party at her apartment. She's a model and so are her roommates and they're all about twelve years old. At least, Candy looks like she's twelve. Would you take pity on a poor Hoosier and go with me? Please?"

"Sure, if I'm free. I'm taking a course in modern French lit on Saturday mornings and there's a lot of homework. And I have my evening at the Jackson Home—and some other commitments from time to time. But if I can, I'll go with you." Her voice was friendly, nothing more, and she had left herself plenty of outs. The woman who had leaned against his chest and taken comfort in his embrace had gone.

He seemed to recognize the fact. "I know you have to get up for your French lit class, Ginny. Maybe I'd better go. But I'll call you Monday. I'll be in Connecticut for the weekend. An old law school friend invited me and it will give Denis some time away from me."

Five

On Monday morning Denis had to ask Ginny twice for a file, and that afternoon she forgot to remind him of his appointment with the dentist. Denis would have let go with some of his scathing sarcasm, except for a conversation he had had with his father that morning.

Josh had quite frankly told his son that he had a jewel of an assistant in Ginny McDougall. Furthermore, if his father ever heard that Denis had abused her in any way, there would be trouble, the kind not seen since Denis was sixteen and stayed out all night with Josh's car.

All the way to his office, Denis turned the problem over in his mind. It wasn't like Ginny to complain. No matter how hard she had to work—and Denis admitted to himself, a little guiltily, he made her work very hard—she had never complained.

And since the memorable day some five years ago when Lisa McDougall had stormed into his office and accused him of wearing her mother down and ruining her health, no one had ever thought that Ginny needed a defender. Lisa, he could understand. Even though she was a difficult, abrasive person who didn't deserve a mother like Ginny, she did have her mother's interests at heart.

Ginny had been sick with the flu and Denis had called, just to ask that she take some dictation over the phone and type it up at her leisure. All right, he thought, frowning at a toy poodle who was barking at him from the end of her leash, so maybe that wasn't very thoughtful. Still, it was pretty nervy of Lisa to tell him that he made Simon Legree look like Santa Claus!

He hadn't seen her since, but Denis scowled at the receptionist and slammed the door to his office. Lisa McDougall, he thought furiously, was an obnoxious do-gooder who looked like a bag lady and talked like a stevedore.

"Ginny!" he barked into his intercom. "I need you. Now!"

As always when he was angry for no reason, Ginny took her time answering his summons. She came in and sat in the chair across from his desk, smiling serenely. Denis looked at her. She wore a gray tweed suit and an ivory silk blouse. Slim, stylish, still pretty—

His heart sank and he began to rock back and forth in his high-backed leather desk chair. "I may have to stay late and work up the Laverman deposition. Can you stay?" His eyes bored into her.

"I'd rather not." It was Ginny's standard response when she had made other plans. She said she had adopted it from a story by Herman Melville she had read in an American lit class. She didn't confide in Denis, and Denis didn't inquire. He understood that she took college courses and saw her friends.

"Are you seeing my father this evening?" Denis gave her the gimlet-eyed look he bestowed on opposition attorneys.

Ginny raised her eyebrows at this attempt to cross the line between her business and personal life. "Why do you ask?"

Damn, he thought, but she was as good as a lawyer, answering a question with a question! "Because he's new to the city—he isn't—he doesn't—he can't—" As he sputtered to a stop, Denis realized that he couldn't think of a single thing his father couldn't do, didn't know, or wouldn't understand.

He was madder than ever now that he knew he didn't have a leg to stand on. "I don't want you to see each other," he blurted out. "It's not—appropriate." There. That sounded convincing. He leaned back, satisfied that he had made an air-tight case.

"Just what do you mean by not appropriate?" Ginny asked. "What do you think we're doing together?"

"I don't know, that's just the problem." Denis was aware that he sounded a little . . . oh, maybe "whining" was too strong a word, but he was afraid that "childish" wasn't.

"Denis, I think we'd better stop this conversation right now." Ginny got to her feet. She gave her employer an impassive stare. "Before you say something unforgivable." Turning away, she marched to the door. "I won't be available for overtime this evening. If you need someone, I'm afraid you'll have to use the steno pool."

Ginny closed the door after her with a gentle click, then found herself at her desk, shaking a little. She wasn't sure whether she was angry or frightened. Both maybe. If Denis had pushed her any farther, she knew she would have resigned on the spot.

She rested her head in her hands. What had come over her? She could handle Denis. She never had the slightest difficulty calming him down and smoothing his feathers. She could deflect his anger and keep him on course as easily as she had handled Lisa when she was a toddler. But six days after meeting Josh Havilland her calm had deserted her and she declined overtime as casually as some nineteen-year-old word processor with a new boyfriend.

She took a deep, calming breath, the kind she had learned in a yoga class. She had been working too hard, and not taking enough time off for dinner with Lisa or a movie with a friend. That was why she felt so off-balance with Josh. He had come along at a time when she was bored and needed stimulation.

Ginny brightened now that she had decided it wasn't Josh himself that had shaken her usual cool competence. It was just circumstances. She would see him tonight, just to show Denis who was boss, but then she would gently—but firmly—discourage him. There was no place in her life for a too-handsome man with silver in his hair who was invited to parties by nubile models named Candy!

By eleven that morning, Josh had finished mapping out his agenda for the day. He had lingered over a second cup of coffee, thinking about Ginny and what they could do that evening. He would be happy just cooking again and being with her. But that wouldn't do for a New York woman like Ginny. He would have to find a restaurant. Maybe in Chinatown. There were a couple of Szechuan dishes he really wanted to learn.

Perhaps he could find a chef as accommodating as Rajid had been.

He walked slowly down the stairs, thinking that as crowded as New York was, he sometimes felt very lonely. Now if Ginny had been with him, it would be different. As he pushed open the door to the vestibule, Josh heard a faint cry from inside the building. He stood for a moment, trying to identify and locate the sound. It wasn't an animal. It sounded like a man. Josh frowned and turned slowly in a full circle in the tiny hallway. It seemed to be coming from downstairs. There was a door under the stairs marked "Basement—Do Not Enter" and Josh pushed it open.

He was right, the crying was clearer now. The light in the stairwell seemed to be out and Josh felt his way down the steep flight. As he reached the bottom, a door opened and light poured onto the crumpled form lying at the foot of the stairs.

Josh could see Hervé silhouetted in the lighted doorway. At that moment the superintendent looked up and saw Josh. A look of frantic alarm crossed his face and he rushed out into the dim hallway and stood in front of the figure on the floor, as if to shield him from Josh.

"Hervé," Josh began, "who is this? And what's the matter with him?"

A torrent of what sounded to Josh like French poured from Hervé. Josh couldn't understand a word, but he could see that the man was frantic about something—presumably the man still lying on the floor.

"Hervé, calm down." Josh spoke slowly and quietly. "I came to see if I could help. Let's get your friend into your apartment and see if he's badly hurt."

Hervé began to wring his hands, and burst into another rush of French. He knelt down and shook the unconscious man's shoulder and, when he did not awaken, Hervé picked up his shoulders and began to drag him toward the lighted doorway. Josh hesitated for only a moment before he picked up the man's legs and silently helped carry him into the apartment.

Once their burden had been laid down, Josh took a good look at the unknown man. He was young, probably about twenty-five, and his face was gray. He looked malnourished and his clothes were little better than rags.

"Please, *m'sieu,*" Hervé said, twisting his hands together, "please to leave us now. I will look after François. *Merci, m'sieu. Au 'voir.*"

Josh didn't move. He thought that François looked as if he needed medical care and he wondered why Hervé was so nervous. Josh could feel the familiar mental itch begin—he wanted to know what was going on. His mother had told him many times that curiosity killed the cat, but

Josh had always insisted that he wasn't a cat and he wanted to know. He had never outgrown that itch and he prepared to scratch it now.

But first they had to look after François. Josh felt for the young man's pulse. It was rapid but strong. "Get a blanket for François," he ordered Hervé. Obediently, the superintendent went out of the room and returned with a faded but serviceable quilt. Josh draped it over the unconscious figure. "I think François will awaken hungry. He looks as if he hasn't eaten much. Do you have any soup?" Hervé nodded and jumped to his feet again.

"He'll sleep for a while. Sit down, Hervé." Josh used the tone of voice that had impressed his son and a number of juries. Denis called it the voice from Mt. Sinai. "Now," Josh continued in the same deep, solemn tone, "tell me what this is all about."

Hervé looked as if he were going to faint right alongside his friend. He looked around the room frantically, as if seeking escape. Finally, with a sigh, he sat down in a large armchair that had a colorful length of fabric thrown over it as a make-shift slipcover. He took a deep breath and began to speak. *"M'sieu* Havilland, I am here in this country since seven years. I am legal," he said proudly. "I have the green card. I work all the time, many hours. My family remain in Haiti. I write, I send money, I try what I can do. But—" He broke off sharply when François stirred. "I will bring soup." With that, he fled.

Josh looked around the cramped, dark apartment. There were bars on the windows, and all that could be seen from them were the feet of passersby on the street above. The room was low-ceilinged and crowded with furniture, including a large table and four chairs.

Hervé returned with a large bowl of steaming soup. He carefully spooned a few mouthfuls into François. He looked worried, but his face cleared as François started to look alert, and sat up. When he began to feed himself, Hervé began a low-voiced conversation in French and Josh wished, not for the first time, that he had paid more attention to his language classes.

"Hervé, let me ask you something," Josh said. "Is François here in this country illegally?"

This time it was Hervé's face that showed shock. He waited for a moment, staring hard at Josh. Then he seemed to make up his mind. "I believe you will not betray us. Yes, François came to Florida in a small boat. He managed to make his way to New York, to me.

"He is wanted by the *attachés,* the illegal civilian police force." Hervé looked up at Josh pleadingly. "Can you help us, *m'sieu?* I know that you are an advocate, like your son."

"An advocate?" Did he mean a lawyer, or just someone who shot off his mouth to officials?

"Yes. You understand, an *avocat,* a barrister." Hervé searched for a word. "A lawyer!"

"Yes, I am." Somehow, for the first time, Josh was reluctant to admit to it. Denis would have his head on a platter if he got involved in this case. Well, if he didn't want that . . . Josh grinned. An idea had just occurred to him. "And so is my son. Maybe the two of us can keep both you and François out of trouble. Let me use your telephone?"

Hervé pointed the way to the phone and Josh quickly dialed Denis's office at Sanderson and Smith. He explained François's status and asked if Denis knew of anyone who could help.

"Maybe you could go to the INS with him," Josh suggested.

There was a gusty sigh from Denis's end of the telephone. "Dad, what did I tell you about getting involved with people in New York? I've lived in that building for years and haven't had any trouble. You're there four days and you're the super's bosom pal and some undocumented alien's lawyer!"

"Now, Denis, what else could I do? I couldn't just walk away."

"Why not? Everyone else does."

"That's why not. Now, are you going to help

me?" Josh was beginning to get annoyed. He wasn't sure that big-firm, big-city practice was doing his son any good.

"Yes, Dad, I'll help. As a matter of fact, I've been doing some *pro bono* work with immigrants. I'll talk to the super and his friend this evening." Denis was clearly ready to hang up.

Josh wasn't. "I thought you were working late this evening."

"Not that late. Tell the super I'll stop down about nine or nine-thirty. Okay, Dad?"

"Yes. Thanks, son."

"Now can I get back to work?"

Josh had no objection and said so. When told what had been arranged, Hervé became almost incoherent in a mixture of Creole and English. Josh made his way out of the apartment, accompanied by Hervé's blessings. He decided to call Denis at eight-thirty, to make sure he hadn't forgotten his appointment.

Deciding that the Metropolitan Museum was worth at least one more visit, Josh took a bus across the park and walked up Fifth Avenue. This time he wanted to see the Temple of Dendur and the costume collection. He was enjoying himself, but sightseeing on his own was beginning to pall. Now, if Ginny were with him, he would really enjoy himself, he mused.

Instead, he stopped for another chat with Mack,

the hot dog vendor. But Mack was quiet. Finally, after some prodding, Mack admitted that he was having trouble with his supplier. He was vague about who was supplying him, but he did say that the supplier had told Mack that he would have to move his stand to another location. Mack shook his head. "This here's the best spot in the city. Lookin' at paintings makes everybody hungry. But if Eddie says I gotta move—"

"You can't fight Eddie?" Josh asked as he smeared mustard on his hot dog.

"Nah. He'll do somethin' tricky, see, and I won't have a license no more. I got no lawyer, see, and Eddie's got a flickin' platoon of 'em, right outta NYU. There's nothin' I can do myself. So Eddie'll see to it I either operate without a license and get busted every time the mayor needs a headline, or I go uptown and starve like he tells me to."

Josh debated with himself for about thirty seconds. Denis would just have to be angry. "I'm a lawyer and I'll take a crack at Eddie and the license bureau for you if you want."

Mack looked at him through narrowed eyes. "Thanks, but I'll take care of it." He looked again. "What's your angle, anyway? Don't have enough business?"

"So I'm pushcart-chasing? Is that what you mean?" Josh grinned.

"Something like that." Mack didn't respond to the smile. "You're from outta town. No offense, but Eddie's shysters would eat you for lunch. So thanks but I'm busy here."

"Okay. Take care, Mack." Josh sat on the wide staircase to the museum to eat his lunch. He couldn't help being a little disappointed. What was it about New Yorkers that had them convinced nobody was as smart as they were? With their city in the shape it was, they still remained steadfast in their belief in their own superiority. Josh shook his head.

Josh had just finished washing down his chili dog with the last of his root beer, when Mack called to him. "I been thinkin'," the vendor said, "and you may be okay. If you want to help, I'd be pleased. I'll bring Eddie's letter tomorrow."

Josh smiled. New Yorkers maybe weren't so different after all. "Sure, Mack. I'll be here for lunch again. See you tomorrow." He set off for Denis's, forgetting the Temple of Dendur in the pleasures of once again having a client.

Six

Ginny was uncharacteristically distracted. She transcribed Denis's dictation tape, working on automatic pilot, with no conscious thought at all. But when she went to the firm library to research the question of creditor preferences under the Bankruptcy Code, she found herself thinking instead of Josh Havilland.

This would not do. She was much too busy and self-sufficient to come unglued because a good-looking man was interested in her. All right, he was better than good-looking, he was handsome enough to turn heads on the street even in blasé New York. And he seemed more than interested. Josh Havilland was acting like a man who was . . . well, smitten.

Smitten? Ginny asked herself. Where had that word come from? She hadn't heard it in years. But a good old-fashioned term like smitten really summed it up.

But the problem, she admitted to herself as she

sat in the firm's library, was how Ginny felt about
Josh.

Scared. Once the word surfaced in her mind,
she knew it was the right one. And she knew
why. It was his looks. If only he were less handsome—

"Ginny!" Denis shook her shoulder. "What's
the matter with you? I've been having you paged
for the past ten minutes."

"Oh. Sorry, Denis. I've been lost in the Bankruptcy Code. What's the problem?"

Denis didn't answer until they were in his office with the door closed. Then he explained the
problem in one word.

"Dad."

"Your father? What's happened? Is he all right?"
If Denis looked startled at the intensity of her
questions, Ginny was too upset to notice.

"Yes, yes, he's fine. But he's going to drive
me nuts if he keeps this up." Denis ran a hand
distractedly through his neatly combed hair.

"Keeps what up? Make sense, Denis."

Ginny's concern cut through his preoccupation
with his own reactions. "He's managed to acquire
two clients in the two days he's been here. One
is an illegal Haitian immigrant on the run from
the secret police, and the other is a hot dog vendor in trouble with some supplier, who sounds
like he's got mob connections."

Ginny smiled. "You forgot the little old lady in the retirement home with the greedy son-in-law."

"Oh, God. What next? If he wants to practice law, why can't he go back to Indiana? And if he wants to get into trouble, why can't he go back to Florida? They're used to old codgers down there."

Josh Havilland an "old codger"? Ginny started to chuckle at the ludicrous idea. Denis glared at her. "That's right, laugh! He's probably got *you* under his spell, too."

So Josh kept people—women—under his spell, did he? Ginny's amusement dried up instantly. She wasn't going to be just another of his conquests. Let him go charm the Mafia.

"Look, Ginny, I need your help." Denis gave her a charming smile and Ginny's defenses went into high gear.

"What sort of help?" she said. "I don't take on dubious hot dog suppliers, Denis, even for you."

"No, I just want you to keep Dad from taking on dubious hot dog suppliers." Another disarming smile.

"Just what do you have in mind?" Ginny thought it was better to discover what Denis was contemplating before she said no.

"Well, he's getting into all this trouble because

he's trying to see the city alone. So, if you were to take a leave of absence—"

"A *what?*"

"How about a fully paid two-week leave of absence?"

"To do what?"

"Just take Dad around and show him the sights. Take a Circle Line tour, go to the Cloisters—just keep him occupied so he doesn't have time to make friends with building superintendents and hot dog vendors."

"Denis, really. If anyone should be taking Josh around, it's you. Why don't you take a day off and go to the Cloisters? It would do you a world of good."

Denis stared at her, then shook his head. "For heaven's sake, Ginny, I can't just waltz off to spend the day bonding with my father over medieval tapestries. I've had that bankruptcy case dumped on me and the Laverman trial is only weeks away. I can't even take the weekend off."

"Then how come you have tickets to the City Ballet tomorrow and the Met the night after?" Ginny glared at her boss. He was not shaping up the way he usually did.

"I have to have some recreation. And eating Dad's version of sushi just isn't the same as taking Candy to the ballet." Denis sighed, sounding, Ginny thought, like a bad actor in a melodrama.

"Besides, Candy keeps asking when Dad's going to ask her for dinner again. It's pretty annoying when she's sitting in a seventy-five-dollar seat courtesy of me. All he gave her was corned beef and cabbage. I give her Balanchine and Tommy Tune and she coos over my father." Denis was aggrieved, but Ginny had no sympathy for him.

"Fine," she said. "Let Candy show him New York."

"He doesn't want Candy. He wants you. All he talks about is you. Please, Ginny, I'm begging you. Somebody's going to put a contract out on him if he keeps this up. He's already mixed up with the Tonton Macoute and the Cosa Nostra. Please! If it were your father, I'd do it for you."

That idea made Ginny laugh. "You'd take my family on? I should take you up on it. I could sell tickets to the show."

"I would, Ginny. Truly." Denis sounded sincere.

"Good. I'll expect you for dinner on Friday. You can take Lisa home afterward. I worry when she goes back to her apartment late at night." Ginny smiled.

"Oh, well, Ginny, I meant I would if I could, but of course I can't. I mean, Friday is a really bad day and—"

"Seven o'clock. Your father's cooking. Lisa will come from work so you don't need to pick her up." Ginny gave him her maternal, obey-or-die look. "I'll take the rest of the week off—paid leave, of course. And I'll see you Friday."

"But—"

"No quid, no quo, Denis."

He sighed in defeat. He would spend an evening with the Child from Hell and in return he wouldn't have to worry about his father getting into any more trouble. Ginny drove a hard bargain, but it was worth it. "Okay. Friday night. Dinner with you and Dad—and Lisa."

Ginny was satisfied. She had always deplored the fact that her daughter and Denis didn't get along. In fact, she knew it was worse than that. They detested each other. It was wearing, never being able to mention Lisa to Denis or him to her without unleashing a tirade from Lisa or icy disapproval from Denis. With Josh there to help her, she thought détente between the warring factions was a real possibility.

In return, she'd be spending her days with Joshua Havilland. She smiled, thinking that every woman she knew would consider her lucky. But others would see only the surface and not the danger Josh posed to her peace of mind. He was intelligent, warm, funny, and he could cook. And kiss. Ginny couldn't forget his kisses. His kisses and her response to them were what made her dread the coming days.

Ginny took a deep breath. She could handle this. It was only a week or two and she could keep anyone at a distance for that length of time. Right now she would forget about Josh and bury herself in her work for the next few hours. That had been one of the ways she had kept men away over the years. Ginny picked up her pencil.

A timid knock sounded at her open door. She looked up to see the shy smile of one of the firm's young secretaries. "Anita?" Ginny said. "Come on in. What can I do for you?"

Anita DiBenedetto came in and sat down in the chair opposite Ginny's desk. Ginny had often found herself acting as a sort of mother substitute to the younger women on the staff. Anita was a quiet, pretty girl whose clothes and bearing reflected money in her background. The usual secretary at Sanderson and Smith did not come to work carrying a Vuitton bag and wearing a Donna Karan skirt. Anita was so self-effacing Ginny wasn't sure that anyone else had noticed her expensive wardrobe.

"Mrs. McDougall, I was wondering . . . I need to talk to someone. Could you . . . that is, could I buy you a drink after work and could we talk?" Anita's hands were clasped so tightly in her lap that her knuckles were white.

"Of course," said Ginny. She was relieved to have a reason not to see Josh this evening. She needed a little breather before she had to be with him all day. And all night? her traitorous brain asked before she could censor her thoughts. *Certainly not!* she answered herself sternly. "I'll look forward to it. Why don't you stop back down here at five-thirty?"

"Could we make it six? I'm a little backed up."

Ginny agreed and studied the young woman as she got up to leave. Anita's eyes were red-rimmed, as if she had been crying. She clearly needed someone to talk to. "Hang in there, Anita," Ginny said softly. "I'm sure we can work something out."

Anita smiled wanly, murmured something Ginny couldn't hear, and slipped out the door. Ginny frowned. Resolutely putting Anita out of her mind, Ginny concentrated on writing up her bankruptcy research for Denis.

Josh called in the afternoon, prepared to tell Ginny his version of the day's activities over dinner. He sounded so disappointed when she told him she couldn't see him that Ginny had a twinge of conscience. She was not planning on spending the evening with Anita DiBenedetto. It would be possible to meet Josh for a late dinner, *No,* she told herself, *it's better this way. Now he'll realize I have a rich, full life and I'm not interested in him.*

Josh might realize it, but the question was, would she?

"Do you like working at Sanderson and Smith?" Ginny asked. They were seated at a corner table in a dim bar near Battery Park City.

Anita looked across at her, her huge, brown eyes troubled, glistening with unshed tears. "I-I like it, Mrs. McDougall. Work is fine. It's not that. It's . . . personal."

Ginny took a sip of her dry sherry and prepared to listen. "If I can help, you know I will, Anita. And if I can't, our conversation will be just between us."

"Yes, I know. That's why I asked you." Anita took a deep breath and a long sip of her ginger ale. "It's Gray—Grayson Harcourt—my fiancé. My father—my family—doesn't know about him. They've met him, but they don't approve, and so I—I just didn't tell them we want to get married." Anita twisted her fingers together and took a deep breath.

"Gray's been after me, wanting to tell Papa about us, but he doesn't understand. When Papa gets angry, it's very—" She gulped and continued. "Last week I found out I'm—I'm—" Anita looked around the room as if searching for the word she couldn't say.

After a long pause, Ginny said softly, "Pregnant?"

"Yes. Now Gray insists that we tell the family and get married right away. But we have to wait until I can tell Papa. But Gray said n-n-no."

Anita lost the battle to keep her emotions under control. She bent her head and Ginny could see her slender shoulders quiver with sobs. Silently, Ginny reached in her purse and handed Anita a package of tissues. Then she waited until Anita could speak once again.

Anita said, all at once, in a sudden burst, "Last night he said he'd go to see Papa without me if I didn't agree to tell him about us."

Ginny looked over at the tearful young woman opposite her.

"Hey, everything's going to be okay, Anita. Really." Ginny reached across the table and took the girl's hand in hers.

"You don't know Papa, Mrs. McDougall," Anita's brown eyes were drowning in tears. "He hates Gray."

Maybe that was the answer. "Why, Anita? What's Gray like?"

"He's a lawyer with Hanson and Hermann on the fifth floor. We met in the elevator. He comes from Darien and he went to Yale."

This kid sounded like every parent's dream. What was wrong with Anita's father? Ginny probed a little. "Do you know why your father doesn't approve of Gray? Has he told you?"

"Yes. Gray's not from our . . . background. He's different. Papa has had someone all picked out for me to marry since I was thirteen. I've said no, I'm not going to marry Tony Carello a million times, but Papa never listens to me."

Papa sounded positively medieval, Ginny thought, but he must be a mean customer if his daughter was so terrified.

"Have you explained to your father how you and Gray feel about each other?"

"Not yet. I wanted to talk to someone first. To you. To get some ideas on what to say." Her hands twisting in her lap, Anita looked at Ginny with hope.

"Anita, you love Gray. Would it be so terrible if he went to your father and explained that you two wanted to marry?"

"Yes. And if he ever told Papa *why* we wanted to marry right away, Papa would—" Anita drew in a shuddering breath. "I don't know what he would do."

"Have you considered having an abortion, Anita? Do you want one?" Ginny thought she already knew the answer to that question. If Anita wanted an abortion, she wouldn't be sitting here crying. She and Gray would have simply gone ahead and done it.

But Anita surprised her. "Yes," she said, her mouth grim and determined. "Rather than tell my father, I would—" She couldn't finish, her tears choked her.

Ginny stared at her. What kind of a monster was Anita DiBenedetto's father? "Have you told Gray?"

"Yes. Maybe I shouldn't have. He was furious. He threatened to go to see Papa without me." Anita's eyes were dark with what looked like fear, and she caught Ginny's hand in a convulsive grip. "He can't do that. He mustn't. We can't— Oh, Mrs. McDougall, you have to talk to him. Tell him that he can't!"

"But, Anita, think for a minute. What do you want to do? Never mind your father, what do *you* want? Would you have an abortion if your father approved of your marrying Gray?"

It took a minute for Anita to answer.

"If I could, I'd marry Grayson tomorrow and have the baby." Her face seemed to soften and take on the glow of love and impending mother-hood. Ginny remembered the feeling.

"Can't you do that? And tell your father after the fact, if you have to?" Ginny reached over and took her hand. "You wouldn't have to face him alone. I'd go with you to talk to him, if you and Grayson would like."

"No, no! You must promise me not to tell my

father!" Anita's hand tightened under Ginny's and her face was paper white. "Promise me!"

"I promise I won't tell anyone you don't want me to tell."

"Thank you. Even if he asks you?"

"Yes. Even then. You must think your father is pretty persuasive." Ginny tried to lighten the atmosphere, but it didn't work. If anything, Anita looked more scared than ever.

"Yes," she whispered. "He can be very persuasive."

"Well, let me think about this. One thing I can tell you right now. I think you should see a doctor immediately. Prenatal care is very important and you don't want to wait until later—the first few months of a pregnancy are crucial."

"I know. Gray said the same thing. But I don't know any doctors—except the ones my family goes to."

"Where does your father live, Anita?" Ginny wished she could ask more direct questions, but mention of her father seemed to frighten Anita so much that she asked only what she thought she had to know.

"Out on Long Island."

"Is your mother still living?"

"No, she died when I was sixteen."

"Do you live with your father?" It seemed unlikely that she could have conducted a full-fledged affair while living under the same roof with her father.

"No," Anita said. "I have an apartment here in the city." Anita smiled wanly. "My father found it and helps pay for it. I wanted it so I could be independent and show Papa that I could take care of myself. What a lousy idea that turned out to be."

"Don't say that, Anita. You fell in love. Lots of girls do that."

"But Papa won't understand that. He wants me to marry Tony. He won't listen to anything I say."

The man really must be a mental case. "Anita, I really think you have to talk to Gray about all this. It's his baby, too, and he loves you."

"I don't know if he'll listen to me. He was so angry when I told him I was thinking of having an—I don't know if he—he—" She broke off, then took a deep breath and gave voice to what Ginny could see was her greatest fear. "I don't know if he hates me."

"Oh, Anita, honey, people don't change their feelings overnight. If he loved you last week, he loves you now. He probably regrets your quarrel as much as you do."

"Would you—could you please come with me to talk to him?"

"I would but—don't you think he might resent a stranger sitting in on such a private conversation?" Ginny looked up to see their waiter standing impatiently by her elbow.

"If you aren't going to order anything more, we could sure use this table," he said, flipping the bill down by Ginny's hand.

"Thanks. Okay." Ginny looked at her young friend. "We'd better go. I'll share a cab with you. We can talk some more. Maybe if you call Gray tonight, you'd want to have lunch tomorrow?"

As she got up, Ginny glanced around the crowded room. They really did need the table. She shrugged into her coat and waited for Anita to gather up her handbag and her mink-trimmed coat. Ginny snaked her way through the close-packed tables, heading toward the door.

Suddenly, a hand touched her arm and a familiar voice said,

"Why, Ginny McDougall, fancy meeting you here!"

Seven

"Josh! Hello." Ginny's heart gave an absurd leap at the sound of his voice. "I left a message for you on Denis's machine. Didn't you get it?"

"Telling me you had to meet someone after work? Yeah, I got it." Josh's beautifully sculpted mouth curved in a sardonic smile. "I just thought I'd come and see where the elite meet." He gave a genuine smile to Anita. "Hello, I'm Joshua Havilland, Denis's father and Ginny's friend."

"Hello," Anita responded in her soft, shy voice. "I'm Anita DiBenedetto. I'm a . . . friend of Ginny's, too."

"I can't tell you how happy I am to meet you," Josh said with a smile in Ginny's direction. "I'm just about to leave, so I can escort you ladies wherever you're going."

"We were going to share a cab home. You don't have to escort us." Ginny hadn't decided whether she was flattered or annoyed that Josh had tracked her down. "We'll be perfectly safe. Stay and finish your drink."

"Nonsense. Beautiful women are never safe in New York." Josh threw a crumpled ten-dollar bill on the bar and, taking both Anita and Ginny by the arm, managed to get all three of them out the door and into a taxi without breaking stride.

Josh told the cabbie to go directly to West Fifty-seventh Street, where Anita's studio apartment was located. He insisted that they see Anita to her door, disregarding her assurances that there was a concierge and a doorman to make sure she was safe.

"That's not how we do things in Indiana, Anita," Josh said as he pushed the button for the nineteenth floor. "A gentleman sees a lady to her door." He gave her a disarming grin and held the elevator door open. As they walked down the long corridor to her apartment, they could see someone sitting by one of the doors. From Anita's sharp intake of breath, Ginny thought she knew who it was.

"Gray!" Anita said, her voice choked.

"We have to talk, Anita. I have to make you understand—" He turned toward Josh and Ginny, clearly wishing them anywhere but where they were. He wasn't handsome, but appealing, even when his hazel eyes were troubled and his dark blond hair tousled. He stood up and Ginny could see he was of only average height. Josh towered over him. But Gray was obviously in love with

Anita. He looked at her as if, as far as he was concerned, she hung the stars in the sky.

"Thank you, Mrs. McDougall, Mr. Havilland," Anita said. She had clearly learned her manners in the old school.

Ginny leaned forward and kissed her cheek lightly. "Good-night, dear. I'll talk to you tomorrow."

"Thank you, thank you," Anita said, her expression troubled but her eyes glowing as she looked up at the man she loved.

As they waited for the elevator, Josh raised his eyebrows at Ginny and said, "Are you Sanderson and Smith's resident den mother, as well as Denis's surrogate mother and Jiminy Cricket?"

"Jiminy Cricket?" The name rang a bell but Ginny was too tired to identify anyone.

"Pinocchio's conscience." Josh smiled at her. "You need some dinner. You look beat. The young seem to have an endless capacity for melodrama, don't they?" He caressed her hair and the back of her neck, and Ginny felt herself relax and soften under his hand. She resisted the impulse to stretch and purr like a cat.

Without another word, he led her to an Italian restaurant just around the corner on Fifty-sixth Street. Josh helped her off with her coat and settled her on a red leather banquette. Then he sat back and smiled. "Are you mad at me?"

"You mean for tracking me down like a private eye?" Ginny glanced at the enormous menu. She'd just hope they had a specialty that wasn't something trendy like squid with black spaghetti.

"Yes. I know you don't like to be fenced in."

"Especially not by men I hardly know." Ginny rallied, an acerbic note in her voice. Just because she was tired, didn't mean she was going to let him get away with anything.

"I thought we straightened that out. I've known you for a long time. We're old friends. Remember?" His expression was still wary as if he feared that she would become angry once she was no longer tired and hungry.

"Do you always follow your old friends when they say they have other plans and can't see you?"

Thoughtfully, Josh picked up a bread stick. "No, I don't. As a matter of fact, I've never done it before. Felt weird."

"Then you can give it up right now. Why did you come all that way, Josh?" Ginny's anger began to simmer. She wasn't going to allow anyone—even someone she liked as much as Josh Havilland—to push her buttons and manipulate her.

"I wanted to see you, Ginny. You said you were meeting someone after work and I took that to mean that you weren't having dinner with him or her. So, I asked Denis where you were likely to go. He didn't tell me to forget about it, which he would have done if you had a heavy date with another guy." Josh spread his hands and shrugged. "I just wanted to see you."

Ginny still glared. He could have said all that over the telephone. What if she hadn't been happy to see him? What if she had been having dinner with someone else, or a drink with another man?

Josh seemed to read her mind. "If you had had a date, I would have left before you saw me. I guess I—all right, all right!" He looked at her and frowned. "I admit it. I was jealous. Okay? Happy now?"

"What are you talking about?" Ginny said, as Josh waved away the waiter who had come to take their order. "Jealous! You don't have any right to be jealous of me. I hardly know you! You can't be jealous!"

"Don't be silly, Ginny. If I tell you I *am* jealous, why do you turn around and tell me I *can't* be? Who should know better how I feel, you or I?"

"I'm just saying I think it's strange."

"That's me. Strange as a square grape." Josh looked up at the waiter, who had returned to hover around the table. He asked what the daily specialty was.

Ginny was somehow not surprised to find out it was squid with black spaghetti. Nor that Josh ordered it after a detailed and, to Ginny, disgusting discussion of how it was made. Squid ink in the spaghetti water. Ugh.

It had been that kind of a day.

Ginny ordered vegetable lasagna.

"Do you have something to tell me?" Josh inquired, as he twirled a strand of charcoal gray spaghetti expertly around his fork. Ginny averted her eyes. "Denis said you did."

"Denis would," Ginny fumed. Denis had an unsurpassed ability to avoid what he didn't want to cope with. That was the reason he had never married and hadn't ever had a really serious, committed relationship. It was also the reason he arranged it so Ginny had to tell Josh that his son had decided he needed a keeper.

"So what's the news?" Josh looked at her with a quizzical look and the crooked half smile that started her pulse racing. "Denis and I decided that you shouldn't have all the fun. We drew straws and I won, so I'm going to spend the next week or so showing you around New York." She crossed her fingers, hoping that Josh wouldn't detect her lie and take offense.

To Ginny's surprise, his smile grew, crinkling those amazing blue eyes until, against her better judgment, she found herself smiling back. His smile reached out and touched her like a warm caress.

"That's wonderful! I've been feeling a little lonesome, I don't mind telling you. I even thought—" he broke off, his smile fading a little.

"I'm delighted too. I never have a chance to see everything I want to. This will be like a vacation." To her surprise, Ginny found that she meant what she said. Despite the threat he posed to the calm routine of her life, she wanted to be with Josh Havilland. She wanted to show him the city, and to hear his reactions to its many pleasures and treasures.

Josh reached across the table and took her hand in his. "I've been thinking, wishing that you were with me. And now you've given me my wish. Thank you, Ginny."

"Don't thank me. It was really Denis's idea." Ginny tightened her fingers around his. "But I'm glad I won the toss."

"I thought it was the long straw."

"Whatever. I'm glad."

Ginny started her guide duty the next day. Denis called her early that morning, his voice uncharacteristically subdued. "Dad's not awake yet. Don't bother to come into the office. I'll get someone from the pool, or force some associates to give up their secretary. Just keep Dad out of my hair. Please. Candy wasn't bad enough. Now Janine is calling, asking me to bring my father along. One of Candy's roommates told her how wonderful my father is. I can't take it! Keep him away from me. I'll pay for dinner. I'll pay for you to take him up to Boston, so he can revisit Harvard. Or go to Philadelphia to look at the crack in the Liberty Bell. Anything!"

"This is your father we're talking about, Denis. You're behaving like a teenager when another good-looking guy comes to town. Adults don't behave this way!"

Denis was instantly penitent. "I know. I'm a slug. But do it for me anyway, Ginny. Please?" he wheedled.

"I've already agreed to it. And I've agreed with Josh to go to Candy's party with him."

"You have? Terrific, Ginny! What a godsend you are—even reading my mind. You two can sort of sit in the corner and—" Denis broke off, as if he realized he wasn't being very flattering to the woman he wanted to help him.

"Yeah, I get it," Ginny said dryly. "We'll just sit in the corner and trade memories of Grover Cleveland's Inaugural Ball."

Denis hastened to make amends. "I didn't mean it that way, Ginny. You know I don't think of you as really old. I mean, Dad's at least five years—"

She interrupted him ruthlessly. "I know exactly what you mean. If you thought about it for a minute, you'd wonder why you're jealous of your father. If he's so elderly that he needs a keeper, what are you worried about? Unless, maybe, he's just a nicer person than you are." Ginny paused for breath, and decided she had said more than enough. " 'Bye, Denis. Tell Josh I'll pick him up at ten."

Ginny returned to her coffee and found she was angrier with Denis than she had ever been before in their sometimes stormy collaboration. She liked Denis, even though his behavior could be self-centered and childish. Most of the models and girls-about-town whom he dated had no more serious interest in him than he did in them. Ginny had always taken a see-no-evil approach to his love life, though there was precious little love involved. For that, Ginny felt sorry for Denis. He seemed to skate on the surface of life.

Unlike his father, who, Ginny could sense, had both loved and lost greatly. There was a richness to his personality that Denis hadn't yet acquired. Maybe, she mused as she sipped a rare second cup of coffee, you couldn't develop the depths and heights of your character without both abiding love and aching loss.

If that was true, Ginny told herself, her personality should look like a topographical map of Kansas. Abiding love was not what she lost when she was widowed. What she had felt was relief. She pushed the thought away and headed to her bedroom to decide what to wear to go adventuring with Josh Havilland. After several false starts, she decided on camel pants and a gray blazer with a sweater that combined the two.

Josh called her from the lobby at nine-thirty, just as she was getting ready to leave to pick him up. She buzzed him up and met him at the door with a sense of pleasurable anticipation she could feel down to her toes. She couldn't remember ever being this glad to see a man.

"Hi, Ginny. I couldn't wait for you to come and pick me up, so here I am. I brought you something." Josh wore jeans and an old gray tweed jacket and looked good enough to eat. He took his hand out from behind his back and revealed a bouquet of snowdrops. Where had he found snowdrops? But there they were, a delicate harbinger of spring.

Ginny took them from his hand and was surprised to feel the sting of tears in back of her eyes. "Th-thanks," she said, annoyed that her voice shook. "These are beautiful. The first I've seen this year."

"A Korean greengrocer over on Third Avenue

had them. I stopped the cab; I thought they had your name on them and sure enough, they did." He smiled at her, wrapping her in shared warmth and Ginny found herself smiling back, helpless to turn away from the man who made her feel so special.

At last she pulled her gaze away from his. "I'd better put them in water," she said, moving to the kitchen.

Josh followed her. "They aren't the first though. I saw some at a stand near Penn Station the day I got here."

"Oh," Ginny said. She was embarrassed, though she couldn't have said why. "I didn't notice."

They strolled out of the building and decided to begin the day with a leisurely coffee and croissant at an upscale little coffee shop on Third Avenue. At ten-thirty on a weekday morning, they were the only customers.

Over huge cups of caffe latte, Ginny and Josh discussed their possible destinations, then veered off into talk of municipal politics, whether a big-city newspaper like the *New York Times* offered better insight into national news than weekly newsmagazines or the news channels on cable TV. Josh managed to involve the owner of the shop and one of her friends who had wandered in for his daily espresso.

Ginny could see that sightseeing with Josh was

going to involve more people than monuments. But she was too conscientious to permit anyone to visit the city without seeing the required sights. A quick mental rundown had decided her against Times Square, at least for the moment. She didn't feel up to what she could foresee as Josh's inter- action with the denizens of that seedy neighbor- hood. Huckleberry Finn Goes to The Sleaze Capital.

Having made plans to stroll up Madison Ave- nue window-shopping and then head back down- town for a visit to the Morgan Library, Ginny relaxed.

"You look like you've just successfully crossed a mine field," Josh said, leaning back in his chair and grinning at her. "Think you'll be able to keep me out of trouble?"

"Think you're going to get in trouble?" Ginny replied.

"I don't, but Denis does. He's worried I'll sully his reputation as the perfect corporate lawyer and all-round stuffed shirt." Josh's grin faded. "He told you to come along and look after me, didn't he? God, it makes me feel like a damned idiot!"

"Josh, please don't look at it that way." Ginny decided on the truth, even though it made her uneasy to admit even a little affection for the man who sat opposite her, the sunlight gilding his brown hair with touches of silver and gold.

"How should I look at it? That showing some-one's visiting relative around town was your idea of the perfect vacation?" Josh looked at her, disbelief apparent in every line of his body.

"Don't make it sound like that. I know you probably find it hard to believe but I looked forward to today. I wanted to spend time with you. It's people that make vacations fun, Josh, not places. To me, this really *is* a vacation." Ginny leaned across the table and took his hand. It was very important that he believe her. "Really."

"Really?" He looked absurdly pleased, as if she had given him an unexpected gift.

"Absolutely." Ginny pushed her chair away. "Now that we have that cleared up, it's time to head for some art galleries and libraries. Culture awaits."

By the end of the afternoon, Ginny was exhausted but, exhilarated. Seeing New York with Josh was like seeing an entirely different city from the one she had lived in for so long. Ginny wondered if she had ever really looked at Manhattan before.

They sat in one of the small, discreet, and superexpensive hotels in midtown, sipping tea and nibbling cucumber sandwiches. It was the New York version of British afternoon tea and to Ginny it was heaven. The only thing lacking was a way for her to take off her shoes and wiggle her toes in the sumptuous carpet.

When she mentioned that to Josh, he smiled and dared her to go ahead and do it. With the excruciating care of a cat burglar, Ginny bent and untied the laces on her unobtrusive tan oxfords. She looked around fearfully then slipped them off her feet. Just as she was about to come up from under the table, she caught a glimpse of legs in correct black trousers with a satin stripe. She unbent with as much cool savoir faire as she could, favoring the waiter with a gracious smile as she refused anything from the pastry cart.

Once the waiter had left, she dared to look over at Josh who was grinning unrepentantly. "You looked like a queen," he said. "A very cross and dyspeptic queen. You scared the poor man to death."

"That's only fair," Ginny said. "He made me feel like a hillbilly. And now we'll have to sit here while I get up my courage to put my shoes back on. But the rug does feel like heaven." She wiggled her toes blissfully.

"I'm glad you're happy." He looked as if he really was. "Can I talk you into dinner, or is that pushing a good thing too far?"

"I think I'd better spend the evening taking a therapeutic soak in the bathtub, if we're going to do the same thing tomorrow." Ginny felt a stab of alarm at the thought of spending more time with Josh Havilland. She felt threatened, as if he would undermine her carefully cultivated sense of self-sufficiency.

"Sure I can't join you in the tub?" Josh asked. It was a joke—of course it was—but there was a warmth in his blue eyes that kindled a reciprocal warmth somewhere in the vicinity of her stomach. Ginny didn't dare pinpoint it any more specifically.

"As I recall, Denis had a state-of-the-art soaking tub put in his bathroom a year or so ago. If you ask nicely, I'm sure he'll let you use it." A warm caress whispered across her instep. Josh's foot.

"It won't be the same." The warmth seemed to expand within her, as his gaze locked with hers. She had to smile back into those blue eyes, bright as candle flames.

Ginny gave herself a mental shake. What in the world was she doing, flirting and playing footsie at her age? She had no business having warm and liquid feelings. This had to stop before she made a complete fool of herself. Resolutely, she fished around under the table until she located her shoes and slipped them on. She bent to tie the laces.

"I really have to get home," she said crisply, ignoring the way the warmth in Josh's face vanished at her words. She continued ruthlessly, "I'll take a cab home. It's in the opposite direction from Denis's. Suppose whoever gets up first calls the other tomorrow. I thought we might go downtown and—"

She knew she was babbling all the way out the door. When they stepped outside, she looked around for a cab, refusing to look at Josh.

It didn't help. As a taxi rolled to a stop beside them, Josh took her face in his hands and kissed her. It was slow, sweet, undemanding, and it completed the meltdown he had started. Before she was irretrievably lost, Ginny dived into the cab and told the driver to hurry.

When she got home, it didn't help to find a message from Anita DiBenedetto on her machine. Ginny had forgotten all about her, and it was all Josh's fault!

Eight

Ginny got Anita's answering machine, both that evening and the next morning. A soak in hot water laced with Epsom salts soothed her muscles, but nothing soothed her sense of unease. Not just about Anita.

By nine o'clock the next morning, she was a little surprised Josh hadn't called. She was about to call him when he buzzed her intercom. She had counted on at least a half hour to put on her lipstick and shore up her defenses, but she buzzed him in. It seemed like ten seconds later when her doorbell chimed.

Ginny took a deep breath and opened the door, to be pulled against Josh's chest and kissed thoroughly.

"You taste even better without lipstick," he said, leaning back to take a good look at her. "You look better, too."

"Cut it out, Josh." Ginny was angry and scared. Angry at him for forcing the pace of their relationship and scared of her own responses. "We have to slow this down. I don't like playing this kind of game."

"What game?" Josh's eyes were wary. "I wasn't playing. Were you?"

"Don't give me that." Ginny poured him a cup of coffee and sat down opposite him at the tiny kitchen table. "You know damn well what I mean. This flirty stuff—kissing me all the time, and making suggestive remarks and romantic gestures. All that stuff."

"You sound disgusted. Do you dislike my kissing you? And what suggestive remarks did you have in mind?"

"About wanting to take a bath with me. And playing footsie at tea yesterday." It sounded absurd when she said it out loud. She felt like someone's maiden aunt.

Josh didn't seem amused. "And the kisses? Were they unwelcome, too?"

Ginny didn't answer for a minute. She wanted to lie and tell him yes, they were, but for some reason she couldn't. Incurable honesty? The desire, despite her best efforts to the contrary, for him to kiss her again? She didn't know.

"No, none of it was unwelcome at the time," Ginny said reluctantly. "But it can't go anywhere, so I think it would be better if we just kept it platonic and remained friends."

"Why can't it go anywhere?" Josh wore his

cross-examiner look again, and his voice was sharp. "If you weren't just trying to be nice to Denis's father, if you did like—"

To Ginny's relief, the telephone shrilled, cutting Josh off in midsentence. She hurried to answer it.

"Ginny? It's Anita. Anita DiBenedetto." The voice was small, almost a whisper. "I tried to get you yesterday."

"I know. I'm sorry. I was out of the office. I should have let you know." Ginny was remorseful. Anita sounded as if she really needed a friend, and Ginny had more or less promised to be there for her. If it hadn't been for Josh—

"Could we—that is, Mr. Havilland said you weren't going to be in the office today, but I thought maybe—" An emotion Ginny couldn't identify quivered in Anita's voice as she gulped and then added, "Maybe I could meet you for lunch, or something."

"Hang on a second, Anita, I'll be right back." Ginny pressed the mute button on her telephone and turned to Josh. "It's Anita. She sounds very upset and she wants me to meet her for lunch. Would you mind terribly? Eating lunch by yourself, I mean."

Josh shook his head. "Of course not. You go right ahead. I'll meet you somewhere afterward."

Ginny arranged to meet Anita and then turned

to Josh. "Thanks. She really sounds like she needs a friend, and I'm still not sure I understand exactly what she's afraid of."

"Well, I know just how you feel. Because I'm not sure I understand what it is *you're* afraid of, Ginny."

With a sentence, Josh had catapulted them back to their previous discussion. Ginny frowned. "Why can't you just let it go? Just let us be friends?"

"Why do you insist on it? I'm not *trying* to care about you. I just do. I feel it growing and I'll admit it scares me a little. It's been a long time, but there it is and here we are. Why won't you admit it? Deal with it?"

Ginny sank into her chair again. "I admit it. I just think it's foolish. We can deal with it my way. We can have a nice time together and then wave good-bye with good wishes on both sides. Or we can . . ." She trailed to a stop. The look on Josh's face dried up her words. He was leaning over the table, his eyebrows drawn together, his eyes flashing blue fire.

"Or we can what, Ginny? Fall in love? Would that be so terrible?" His voice was a rasp. "Am *I* so terrible?"

Ginny's throat closed. She simply knew that falling in love with Josh Havilland would be a gigantic mistake, one that could cost her all the peace she had worked so hard to find. She had never asked herself why.

"Not terrible. Of course not, Josh. But caring too much about each other would be . . . foolish." At last she had found the word. "Very foolish. At our ages." There. That said it all, and Ginny leaned back, satisfied that she had explained everything.

"Foolish? You think love is foolish?" He looked astonished. "A mistake? Why? I'm not too old to want you, and unless I've forgotten all the signals, you're not too old to want me. What's foolish about that?"

"A passionate affair at our age is foolish. I don't have the emotional resilience to survive you."

"What about a passionate relationship then? Would that be acceptable?" Ginny said nothing. "Or a passionate marriage?"

"No. Never." The words came out flat and hard as stones.

They were the truth and Josh recognized it. "Never? Was your marriage that good, Ginny? I can't compete with a twenty-year-old memory, is that it?" He took her hand and held on when she tried to pull it away.

"I don't want to talk about my marriage."

"Meaning you *won't* talk about it."

"Meaning it's none of your business."

"Okay. I can accept that. For now. But you ought to get one thing very clear, Ginny. I'm not flirting or playing some game. I care about you more than anyone in a long time. I'm more attracted to you than to anyone in an even longer time." He pulled her to her feet, and set his hands on her shoulders. "And it's not any easier for me than it is for you to leave myself open to what I feel, but I'm not going to run away from it. And I'm not going to let you run away from me."

"Please, Josh. Don't do this. I don't want this."

In reply, his arms moved to encircle her and pull her close. His lips met hers in a gentle kiss that nevertheless demanded a response. Ginny couldn't help herself. She kissed Josh, asking and taking as much as she gave.

Then, as if she had a sudden return to sanity, she broke away. "I have the Staten Island Ferry on the agenda for this morning. What do you say?"

"Why not Ellis Island or Liberty Island?" he asked.

"We can if you want. I didn't know you'd be interested in Ellis Island. Did your forebears come in that way?"

"No, actually, my great-grandfather came over when Castle Garden was still being used to process immigrants."

They had walked back to Second Avenue to

get a downtown cab. Josh hailed one and when
they had settled into the cracked leather backseat,
told the driver, whose English was marginal, that
they wanted to go downtown.

"Downtown?" the driver said.

"Yes. Downtown."

"How to go downtown?"

Josh looked slightly baffled and Ginny took
over, directing the cab to the ferry dock. She and
Josh leaned back and smiled at each other.

Once at Ellis Island, the wall of pictures and
the sheer size of the building where most immigrant processing had taken place left Ginny more
moved than she had foreseen. She stood, slowly
turning in a circle, imagining the huge room
filled with people speaking a dozen languages,
babies crying and mothers hushing them. Lonely
children, sent from Europe by themselves to seek
a better life, going through the lines alone, wearing name tags so their sponsors could find them.

She felt as if she could see the ghosts as
plainly as the Park Service guides. Josh took her
hand and smiled down at her. She blinked sudden
tears away and said, "You were right. This place
is awe-inspiring."

They lingered until it was almost time for
Ginny to meet Anita. Josh took a moment to
make a phone call and announced he was going
to have lunch with an old law school classmate

at India House, one of the private lunch clubs in the Wall Street area. Ginny told herself that she should have known that Josh was never alone unless he chose to be. Then why, some imp inside her head asked, would he choose to spend so much time with you? The obvious answer was that he meant what he said and felt more for her than for anyone else.

Why did she find that so unacceptable? Ginny asked herself as she walked over to the deli where she was meeting Anita. Ginny was incurably honest. She didn't want Josh to care about her because she was absolutely terrified of falling in love with him. If anyone asked her why loving a handsome, intelligent, charming man who seemed to be well on his way to falling in love with her was so fearsome, what could she say?

"That's exactly the problem," Ginny said aloud. Several people on the crowded sidewalk turned their heads, but New Yorkers were used to ignoring the outlandish and Ginny just smiled at them and walked on.

It was the truth. Good looks and charm worked on Ginny in reverse. Even natural good looks and effortless charm like Josh's had her closing off her feelings and running away from them.

Most people would find that bizarre. Josh clearly didn't understand it. He would if he knew her reasons, Ginny thought. If he knew about Brian. But she had decided a long time ago that no one was going to know about Brian.

"Ginny!" She heard a soft voice call her and she looked up to see Anita giving her a puzzled look. In her preoccupation, she had almost walked past the deli.

Ginny looked closely at the young secretary. Her eyes were shadowed and she looked as if she hadn't slept since Ginny had last seen her.

"Anita, how are you feeling?"

"I don't know." She sounded miserable. "I'm not sure how I feel. Right now, I don't think I'm sure about anything."

"Let's get a sandwich and take it outside. I know a bench in Battery Park that should be warm enough even today." Ginny smiled

They didn't talk until they had their sandwiches and had made their way to the park. The sun was bright and there was no wind.

"Even in March it's comfortable if the sun's out," Ginny said as she bit into her turkey-breast-on-whole-wheat-lettuce-and-tomato-hold-the-mayo.

She looked at Anita, who still held the brown bag with her sandwich in her hands. "Anita, did you and Gray talk the other night?"

"Yes." Anita stared out toward the ocean. "But we didn't decide anything. Gray still wants to marry me and have the baby." Her voice was flat.

"You make it sound as if he wanted to send you to jail. Don't you want that, too?"

"Of course I do. But I can't. I can't do that to Grayson."

"Do what to Grayson, Anita? Marry him?"

"Yes, exactly. I can't do that so I've decided what I have to do."

Something in her voice made Ginny's skin prickle. It sounded so lifeless, so final. "What is that, Anita?"

"I'm going to have the abortion and then I'm going to move back into my father's house and tell him that I've decided to marry Tony Carello." Anita looked down at her hands. "He'll have to know that I'm no longer a virgin, but I won't tell him who the man was. That way, Gray won't be involved."

Ginny opened her mouth, then closed it again without speaking. Anita was so frightened of her father that normal arguments simply didn't apply. She thought for a moment, then took a deep breath and counseled deception and lies.

"Anita, look. Why can't you and Grayson get married quietly at City Hall and tell your father afterward? Your father loves you" (*I hope!* she thought) "and surely he'll accept your marriage when he finds out that he's going to be a grandfather."

For a moment, Ginny thought she had gotten through. Then Anita shook her head. "No, Ginny, he won't. Or at least I can't be sure that he would. And I can't take the chance that he won't and that he'd try to get the marriage annulled."

"But surely he wouldn't want an illegitimate grandchild," Ginny protested.

Anita shook her head. "I don't know. I don't know what he'd do." Ginny put her arm around Anita's shoulder.

"I don't want to make it harder for you. I just want you to have a chance to be happy. I'll help you any way I can."

"Thanks, Ginny. It does help to talk to you. I will think some more about it. I'm going home for the weekend. Maybe I'll talk to my father then." Anita stood up and braced her shoulders, as if she were going to face a firing squad.

Ginny took her hand. "Please call me when you get back. I'll worry about you until I hear from you."

"Okay. I'll talk to you Sunday. Or maybe Monday." With a wavery little smile that stung Ginny's heart, Anita walked away.

Ginny's heart ached for Anita DiBenedetto, but she didn't know how to help her as long as Anita was so afraid of her father.

She and Josh had agreed to meet in front of the statue of George Washington at the Federal Reserve Building. When she caught sight of Josh, already standing beside the Father of Our Country,

Ginny caught herself smiling fondly. He was so solid, and wise and . . . and sexy. Resolutely, Ginny straightened her expression. She must not have looked fond, for when Josh looked down into her face, he said, "What's wrong, Ginny? Is Anita in more trouble?"

"No, no—the same old trouble," Ginny said. "A man, I suppose."

"What makes you say that? Women do have other problems, you know. Not all of us are obsessed with the opposite—" Ginny sputtered to a halt.

"Sex." Josh smiled at her and Ginny's heartbeat sped up. "I know they have, Ginny. But when that young man met her at her apartment and they both looked like the most star-crossed lovers since Romeo and Juliet, I naturally concluded that her problem had something to do with the man in question. What was his name? Gray?"

"Yes. And yes, it does have to do with Gray. And her father."

"Really? That has a real old-fashioned sound. Does Daddy not approve?" Josh took her hand and started walking up Wall Street to Trinity Church.

"I can't talk about Anita's problem with you, Josh. It's personal."

"Of course, I'm sorry. I didn't mean to pry. Or to make light of what's troubling her." Josh squeezed her hand. "But you will tell me if there's ever anything I can do, won't you?"

"Thank you. Of course I will."

For the rest of the afternoon, she and Josh walked around the financial district, the oldest part of the City. Wall Street had once actually been walled, Josh informed her, having read his guidebook. It had been the northern boundary of the city. Now it was scarcely past the southern-most tip of Manhattan.

Ginny spent that evening on household chores that had piled up since she had been spending her days with Josh. He and Denis were going out for dinner. Maybe it would give them a chance to get to know each other better. The next night was the dinner she had insisted on with Denis and Josh and Lisa.

Josh was full of information, and laughter, she thought as she scrubbed the bathrooms. Ginny admitted to herself that she hadn't had so much fun in years. He made her laugh and notice things she wouldn't have seen without him. He made her feel that she'd been existing rather than living. And, though she hated to admit it, he also made her aware of just how long it had been since she had been in love. Not, of course, that she was in love with Joshua Havilland.

Of course not. The idea was absurd.

Nine

Ginny had to scramble to hold her dinner party. The Mordecai Jackson Home had asked that Ginny change her visit from Thursday to Friday, necessitating a switch in the dinner from Friday to Thursday. It just made a dinner party, always nerve-racking for Ginny, more difficult than usual.

She was pleased that the evening started perfectly. In fact, as Ginny told Josh later, it was great until the last guest arrived. As long as only Josh and Denis were there, things went perfectly. Just when Ginny began to relax, Lisa arrived, and the temperature in the room went down twenty degrees in as many seconds.

Lisa looked beautiful in her mother's eyes because she was Lisa, and in Josh's because she looked so much like Ginny. Lisa was a little taller and little slimmer but her hair was bright as a new penny and her eyes were the same green as Ginny's. She was dressed in a style that owed a little bit to boutiques and a lot to thrift shops. A purple silk tank top fought to a draw with a bubble gum pink sweater and both gave off sparks next to her coppery hair. A paisley wool skirt flared above steel-toed work boots.

Denis cringed when this technicolor vision drifted into the living room. Lisa embraced her mother warmly, shook hands with Josh after subjecting him to a long, sober appraisal. As an afterthought, she nodded to Denis.

After a few minutes of conversation, to which both Lisa and Denis contributed only monosyllables and nods, Ginny decided dinner had better come sooner rather than later. She hurried to the kitchen.

She hadn't lied when she said that she didn't cook often. When she did, she bought the best ingredients and cooked them the simplest way. This evening, she offered an out-of-season Thanksgiving dinner, with roast turkey, sweet potatoes, green beans, and pecan pie for dessert.

Of course, she bought the pie and the sweet potato casserole from a gourmet shop. When Josh came out to her kitchen to offer his help, he noticed the telltale boxes.

With a grin, he whispered, "What will you give me for not telling your guests where you got dinner?"

"Not a dime, you extortionist," she replied. "Lisa knows and Denis doesn't care." She had to smile back at him. "But if you don't trust me, you can see to the green beans. Unless you like them gray and limp."

"I'll take care of them," Josh said hastily. "I'll even make the gravy."

"Gravy? We never have gravy."

"What do you put on top of the stuffing?"

"What stuffing?"

"Ginny, I may have to marry you, just to ensure that Lisa has a decent Thanksgiving dinner sometime in her life."

Ginny froze and stared at him for a moment. With relief she saw the twinkle in his eye. "You don't have to make the ultimate sacrifice. Just invite Lisa to Florida, or wherever you are next year. For stuffing and gravy, she'd probably walk from here to Key West."

"That won't be necessary." Josh gave a crooked half smile. He hadn't missed her reaction to the "M word." He knew that Ginny didn't believe they knew each other well enough to use it, but, dammit, he was fifty-eight years old. It frustrated him that she didn't see their relationship as clearly as he did. In fact, she didn't seem to see any possibilities beyond casual friendship.

The silence from the couple in the living room was broken by the low murmur of conversation. Ginny smiled. She had been right. Both Denis and Lisa were grown-up enough so they could get along like civilized adults. She opened the oven to check on the turkey. It looked brown.

"Do you think this is done?" she asked Josh.

"How long has it been in?"

Ginny furrowed her brow. "An hour, I think. More or less."

"How much does it weigh?"

"I don't know. I don't ask my turkeys personal questions. We're not that close."

"It says on the price tag, Ginny."

"Oh. Right." She fished it out of the trash. "Ten pounds."

"That should take about . . ." Josh looked around. "Do you have a pencil and paper?"

"What for?"

"Never mind. Do you have a meat thermometer?"

"I might." Ginny rummaged in a drawer. "Is this one?" She held up a metal object.

"Yes. Thank you, Ginny." Deftly, he inserted the thermometer. After a minute, he took it out, looked at the oven temperature gauge and said, "It will be about another forty-five minutes, Ginny."

"Oh, lord, what will I do with them?"

"Who? Denis and Lisa?" Ginny nodded. "Nothing. They're behaving. They aren't calling each other names or hitting each other over the head with their toys."

As the words left his mouth, the decibel level in the living room escalated suddenly. Words could be distinguished.

"You're a leech fastening on society," Lisa said.

"Nonsense, child. I perform a necessary service." Denis's voice was precise and pedantic. "If more people used the law, and lawyers were put in charge of society, the world would be a better place."

"God forbid!" Lisa's voice rose. "Lawyers *are* in charge! That's why the world is in the shape it's in! Lawyers! Do you know what fifty thousand lawyers on the bottom of the ocean would be?"

"Yes, Lisa. 'A good start.' I've heard that joke. And all the other lawyer jokes you're dying to repeat." Denis sounded both annoyed and bored. "Now tell me all about the good deeds you're doing at your little foundation, applying Band-Aids to society's wounds. What's your new project? Setting up prison basket-weaving courses for multiple murderers? Or do you have something *really* useless this time?"

"Cute, Havilland, very cute," Lisa said.

Ginny picked up a crystal decanter of sherry and handed it to Josh. "There are glasses on the chest by the couch. Give them each a glass of

sherry—and be generous. I'm willing to try anything to make this evening work."

Josh shrugged. "I'm not sure even pecan pie
can stop the carnage. What do those two have
against each other?"

"It's a long story. Basically, it's a feud and,
like most feuds, the reasons for it have been lost
in the mists of time."

"I'd bring out some cheese and crackers, if you
have any. They'll need a snack to keep from kill-
ing each other."

Ginny nodded. She was ready to shake her
boss and her daughter until their teeth rattled.
She had hoped that by this time the two of them
could at least act civilized.

Damn! She was out of crackers. She knew she
had forgotten something at the store. Well, they'd
just have to eat cheese on toothpicks. Ginny hurriedly arranged a tray and headed for the living
room, hoping to head off any clash.

She needn't have hurried. Josh was talking to
Lisa and Denis was staring morosely into his
sherry. Ginny shot Josh a grateful smile and
turned to Denis, missing her daughter's frown.

But Josh saw, and wondered if Lisa McDougall disliked him or his friendship with her
mother. He wondered why. Most grown children
he knew were eager to have their parents remarry.
Lisa didn't live with Ginny and, as far as he

knew, didn't depend on her mother for monetary help.

Ginny soon had Denis smiling. It was only when she tried to introduce general conversation, that the knives came out again.

"Did you know that Denis's firm represented the newspaper that won the big libel case last week?" Ginny asked Lisa brightly.

Silence. Then Lisa looked up and gave her mother a smile as shiny as it was phony. "Yes, Momma, I knew. And I must say I wasn't surprised to find that Sanderson and Smith were on the side of the big bucks."

"What case was this, son?" Josh asked, rushing to fill in the silence after Lisa's remark.

"A newspaper accused of libel by a public official in a small town in Tennessee. We got involved because we do a lot of First Amendment work."

"Don't forget to tell them that the newspaper Denis's firm defended was the *New York Journal*," Lisa added sweetly. "One of the biggest in the country. As I said, big bucks."

"It was the principle that was being litigated, Lisa," Denis said with great patience.

"Oh, right. And I'll bet all of you voted to give your fee to feed the homeless, right? Because all you care about is principles and not money." Lisa turned her shoulder on Denis, dismissing him from the conversation.

Ginny was about to ask her daughter to come with her for a quick lesson in manners, when Josh's quiet voice intervened. "Well, now, Lisa. Didn't you tell me that you worked for a non-profit foundation?"

"Yes. The Barringer Foundation."

"That's Barringer of Barringer Aviation, world's foremost manufacturer of military aircraft. Sells to everybody and anybody, regardless of whom they're shooting." Denis grinned at his adversary. "Right, Lisa?"

"Mr. Barringer is trying to use his part of the profits—"

"To pay your salary," Denis finished. "Just don't pretend to be so pure and idealistic. Defending the First Amendment is every bit as disinterested and idealistic as some of the far-out schemes you come up with. Practical, too."

"The Barringer Foundation's pilot project on nutrition for teenage mothers has been used as a model by ten cities." Lisa's voice was proud. "Tell me when that has happened to your money-grubbing, overpriced, justice-for-the-rich law firm?"

There was a moment of silence. Ginny looked down at her hands. When Lisa got on her high horse about Sanderson and Smith, she forgot that her mother had worked there for years. Ginny's salary had kept them clothed and housed and had paid for college degrees for both of them.

Ginny wouldn't remind Lisa of that in company, but Denis had no such scruples. Just as he opened his mouth for what was sure to be a blast at Lisa, Josh smiled and said, "Tell me about this nutrition project, Lisa. Back in Elgin, we considered trying something along those lines, but we couldn't get it off the ground. Do you have any reports or literature you could send to Indiana?"

Before Denis could interrupt, Ginny grabbed his arm in an iron grip and said through her teeth, "I have some work for you in the kitchen, Denis."

Once safely out of her daughter's hearing, Ginny handed him a paring knife and set the pan of green beans in front of him. "Cut them. Neatly. Here's a piece of newspaper. Put the discards on it."

Denis looked at her, horrified. "Me? You've got the wrong Havilland. It's Dad who cooks."

"Then it's about time you learned. After your mother died, why didn't you learn to make dinner? School got out before your father got home."

Denis just stared at her. "What gives, Ginny? Dad and I lived the way we wanted to. It's none of your business—"

"Exactly!" Ginny glared at him. "And what Lisa thinks of my job is none of yours."

Denis looked guilty. "How did you know what I was going to say?"

Ginny shook her head. "How long have I known you, Denis? And in those years, how many times have you told me what you thought of Lisa's attitude toward the firm that paid her way? A hundred?"

Denis grinned at her and took her hand. "Closer to a thousand. I will be on my very best behavior for the rest of the evening." He held up his hand. "I promise."

As he turned back to the green beans, Ginny said, "I don't understand why you two can't get along. You're both adults. You both are good at what you do and admire competence in others. I like you both. What's the problem?"

"Natural antipathy. Think dogs and cats. Snakes and mongeese. Mongooses. Whatever." Denis smiled. "Some things are fated never to mix, except explosively. Phosphorus and water. Denis and Lisa."

"Well, I wish you'd both grow up and learn to get along."

"Yes, teacher."

"Thanks for doing the beans."

"You're very welcome, ma'am." Denis bowed and left the kitchen.

If she could keep Josh in the living room with the combatants, Ginny was sure she'd have no further trouble with them. She was going to have trouble with her dinner, however. After a few frantic moments, Ginny called for Josh.

He took one look at Ginny and her kitchen and sat her down at the table, out of harm's way. "I'll take it from here, Ginny. I don't think there's room enough for two cooks."

She was happy to agree. Probably, she thought, she should get up and go into the living room to referee, but it was too pleasant to sit and watch Josh. He moved with grace and economy. In minutes, beans were cooking, the turkey taken out of the oven and covered with foil, and Josh was leaning against the sink for a moment, smiling at Ginny.

"Don't frown, Ginny. Denis is treating Lisa like a particularly difficult client."

"And Lisa?"

"She seems confused. That's slowed her down too."

"I never thought they'd bore each other, but that's what it sounds like."

"It's good for them. I don't want to spend dinner refereeing a childish quarrel." Josh turned back to the stove, took the beans off the burner, and deftly drained them.

Ginny was impressed. "You make cooking look easy. No wasted motion at all. Like a ballet."

"That's me. The Baryshnikov of beans." He grinned down at her.

Dinner was on the table in record time. Josh carved and Ginny passed the beans and sweet potatoes.

Lisa was impressed. "Gosh, Momma, you really can cook now that you have the time, and I'm not underfoot."

Ginny blushed. She was about to tell Lisa she hadn't done anything but put the turkey in the oven, when Josh intervened. "It is terrific, isn't it? Only Ginny would think of a turkey dinner in March." His smile was so warm and promised so much more than warmth that Ginny had to smile back.

This time both Denis and Lisa were looking, and they both wore identical frowns. Their parents were too involved with each other to notice.

"When are you going back to Florida, Mr. Havilland?" Lisa asked.

"I'm not sure. I'm having such a fine time here in New York, I'm in no hurry to leave."

Lisa frowned.

"I think I'm going to have to cut short your leave, Ginny," said Denis. "We have a lot of work on our plate and the subs from the steno pool just aren't working out. No one can take your place."

"But, Denis, you told me just yesterday that the blonde with the long legs was doing just fine."

"I lied," Denis said, his jaw set in a stubborn line.

"Typical employer," Lisa fumed. "First it's take time off. Then it's no, you can't. It's maddening. We're people, too!"

"Oh, right. I can see that you're a member of the downtrodden herd, Lisa." Denis's eyes swept down her outfit. "You clearly have plenty of time to shop. No single store could put that outlandish outfit together. You must have to go everywhere to get things that clash so perfectly."

"Stick to the subject, Havilland. The fact that you don't like anything that doesn't come from Brooks Brothers and make you look like an undertaker, has nothing to do with the way you jerk my mother's chain!"

"I am not jerking anyone's chain!"

"Yes, you are. Your attitude is sexist and stupid," Lisa said.

Before Denis could load and fire, Ginny said, "Children, children, what am I going to do with you? You're going to have to learn to play nicely together."

Lisa flushed and Denis laughed apologetically. "Sorry, Ginny," he said. "I forgot myself."

"Well, both of you have to try a little harder."

Ginny decided to play her trump card. Guilt. "It makes my life difficult when I can't mention one of you to the other. I wish you'd *try.*"

They were both instantly contrite. Ginny waved away their apologies and began to clear the table. Lisa got up to help.

"I'm sorry, Momma," she said once they were in the kitchen. "I don't know why Denis Havilland makes me so mad. He just does." She neatly arranged plates in the dishwasher. "What a pompous—"

"Enough, Lisa!"

"Well, he is!" Lisa turned the pie knife around in her fingers. "Do you like his father?" she asked at last, looking at her mother out of the corner of her eye.

"Yes," Ginny replied, looking at her daughter's averted head. "Why? Don't you?"

"I guess he's all right."

"Such enthusiasm." Ginny's disappointment was sharper than she would have imagined.

"Well, he's taking up a lot of your time. When are you going back to work?"

"Next week, probably."

"Good," Lisa said under her breath.

"What? Why 'good'?"

"I think it's an imposition for Denis to expect you to entertain his father. Why isn't Denis doing it?"

Forgetting that she had once told Denis the same thing, Ginny said, "Don't blame Denis. It's not an imposition, I'm enjoying myself. Josh and I have more fun than I've had for years."

Ginny began to cut the pie and slip the pieces onto her best flowered dessert plates. "There's whipped cream in the little paper carton on the top shelf of the fridge. Would you get it?"

"Sure." Lisa handed it to her mother and said, "I don't want to spoil your fun, and I'm glad you're enjoying yourself, but I don't want you to be hurt."

"What are you talking about?" Ginny looked up into Lisa's troubled eyes. "Why would I be hurt? Who's going to hurt me? Josh?"

"Yes, Momma. Say what you like, he's still Denis's father and you've told me yourself what a Romeo Denis is. You know what they say, like father . . ."

"Like son. Yes, I've thought of that." Ginny found herself wondering how a man as handsome as Josh Havilland had remained widowed all these years. One answer was that he was as dedicated as his son was to sampling all the women he could.

"Well, then, just be careful. Don't spend too much time with him. Remember, he's leaving New York in a little while." Lisa smiled, clearly happy at the thought.

"I know. Come on, let's get this pie out to our guests," Ginny said with an unnaturally bright smile.

Meanwhile, in the living room, Josh and Denis had been making desultory conversation. "You don't see any reason to alter your life in any way?" Josh asked, having brought the conversation around to the point where he wanted it.

"Like how?" Denis asked without much interest. He was sure his father was going to start lecturing him about marriage and his biological clock.

"I don't know. Maybe going with a smaller firm. One where you aren't on call twenty-four hours a day."

"Like yours in Elgin?" Denis asked with a smile. "That's a little sleepy for me, Dad."

"No, I didn't really mean back to Elgin," Josh said, a little uncomfortable now that Denis had reminded him of his long-forgotten dream of practicing law together. A new idea was germinating in the back of Josh's mind. A way to make old dreams—and new ones—come true. Meantime, he wanted to go on seeing Ginny.

"Do you really need Ginny back next week?" he said casually.

"I guess not." Denis's tone was grumpy. "But

I meant it when I told her that no one could take her place. She's the best."

"Yes," Josh said, smiling a little. "She is. The very best."

Denis didn't even try for subtlety. "You're interested in her, aren't you, Dad?"

"I'm not sure what you mean," Josh responded, playing for time.

"You know exactly what I mean. You're interested in her. You like her. You feel just precisely the opposite of the way I feel about her daughter. Does that make it clearer?"

Josh wasn't quite sure what he wanted to tell Denis about his feelings for Ginny, but whatever it was, he wasn't going to discuss them here.

To his relief, Ginny and Lisa came in with the dessert. "That looks wonderful," he said, winking at Ginny.

"Au Bon Gout's finest," Lisa said.

"You mean you didn't make this yourself?" Josh said in pretended horror. "And here I've thought you were the best cook in New York."

Ginny laughed. "You know perfectly well what kind of cook I am."

Lisa's smug smile turned to a frown. Josh looked at her. "I don't admire your mother for her cooking, Lisa. She's a lot more valuable for what she is than what she does. You should know that better than anyone."

"I do." Lisa snapped out the words. Her fork hovered over her piece of pie. *"Much* better than anyone."

"Josh, what do you think of the cinnamon whipped cream?" Ginny asked at random. She didn't like the undercurrents she sensed between Lisa and Josh.

"It's fine, Ginny." Josh's tone was soothing, as if to say *nothing's wrong.*

For a moment, Ginny looked at him without saying a word. He was, without doubt, the handsomest man she had ever seen and the fact still scared her. Josh seemed so unaware of his looks that Ginny's fears had been lulled, but Lisa's words had brought them back.

Maybe Josh was the same kind of womanizer his son was. How could she know? Was there some fatal flaw in her character that made her fall in love with—

Wait a minute! She replayed her words in her mind. She wasn't in love with anyone. She was way past that kind of thing.

Ginny was so unnerved by the very thought of being in love with anyone that she scarcely heard the rest of the conversation. She didn't come to until the evening came to an end. Lisa didn't stay for a chat after the others had gone, as she usually did. Instead, to her mother's surprise, she put on her orange pea jacket and murmured to Denis, "I'd like to talk to you."

Josh lingered, telling Denis he'd meet him downstairs. When the door had closed behind the two young people, he turned and smiled at Ginny. "It was a lovely evening, and unless I'm mistaken, Denis and Lisa have reached some sort of détente."

"That puzzles me a little." Ginny's brow was furrowed. Josh took a forefinger and gently smoothed out the wrinkles.

"Don't worry so, Ginny." He took her in his arms. "Kiss me good-night."

In the lobby, Lisa turned to Denis. "Did you see what was going on up there?"

"You mean my father and your mother? Yes, of course, I saw. I'm not any stupider than you are, Lisa."

"Well, then, what do you think of it? Considering the fact that it will mean either you'll lose the best assistant you've ever had, to quote you, or you'll have your father in New York permanently."

Denis stared at her. "You've certainly got this all figured out, Lisa. Why are you so down on my father?" Perversely, although neither alternative she had mentioned appealed to him at all,

Denis resented her slur on his father. Denis Havilland's father was good enough for anyone!

Lisa shrugged. "I have nothing against your father." *Except you,* she added silently.

"Well, I love Ginny. But I'm not happy about this either." The elevator door slid open and Josh stepped out. "Call me tomorrow and let's talk about it," Denis said in a hurried undertone.

Ten

The next day, Josh asked if they were going to make another trip to the Mordecai Jackson Home. Ginny hadn't thought he'd want to go visit the retirees again. But Josh Havilland was full of surprises. He refused to be pigeonholed as a graduate of a top school, a retired small-town lawyer, or a devastatingly handsome man. Instead, he was just Josh—funny, kind, intelligent, interested in everything and particularly, everybody. All the things most women wanted.

On their way across Brooklyn Bridge in a cab, Josh put his arm across Ginny's shoulders and leaned closer to look out the window at the intricate fretwork of the bridge's cables.

"What a fabulous piece of work this is," he said. "Even though there are newer and longer bridges, this one is still the first, the queen."

"The bridge 'whose leap commits the agile precinct of the lark's return,' " Ginny quoted.

"Hart Crane," Josh identified. " 'Brooklyn

Bridge.' I took American Poetry too, during my early retirement."

They smiled at each other and Ginny could feel herself being drawn deeper and deeper into the pool of warmth and happiness that seemed to surround her when they were together.

The mood lasted until they arrived at the home. When they walked through the door they were confronted with what looked like a scene from a bad play.

Sylvia Bright was seated in a large wing chair in the lounge. In front of her stood a plump, red-faced man in a well-cut navy blue suit. He was gesturing to Sylvia and his voice was loud. He sounded very annoyed.

"Mother Bright, you can't be serious. I am hurt! I am wounded! You refuse to sign the will your own son-in-law has drawn up for you? How do you think that makes me feel?" He towered over Sylvia. "Bad, that's how. And it makes Cecilia, your own daughter, feel bad, too."

"I never said I wouldn't sign it, Simon." Sylvia's voice had a quaver, and she had to tilt her head back to see him, but her eyes met her son-in-law's bravely. "I just said I want to read it first."

"But we've discussed the provisions a thousand times, Mother Bright." Simon shook his head. "I'm here tonight so we can get this all done, before Ceil and I go to Florida. Otherwise, Ceil will worry."

"Tell Cecilia not to fret. I have no intention of dying while you're on Sanibel Island. I can promise you that." A slight smile hovered on her lips for a moment.

Then she caught sight of Ginny and Josh. "Ginny! And Mr. Havill! How wonderful you've come." Sylvia's smile grew warm and genuine. "Come, Mr. Havill, I want you to meet my son-in-law, Simon Miller. Mr. Havill's a lawyer too, Simon, like you."

Simon eyed Josh coldly. Ginny could see that in Simon Miller's eyes, Josh was just a tall man, casually dressed in khakis and a sport jacket.

"How do you do, Mr. Havill. I've heard a lot about you from Mother Bright. You seem to have given her quite a bit of free legal advice last week." Simon's tone was not friendly. "Was she correct when she told me that you practice in . . . Illinois, was it?"

"Indiana. No, she's not completely correct. I have retired from the active practice of law in that state." Josh's expression was pleasant and his tone casual.

"Well, here in New York we take a dim view of outsiders coming in and giving legal advice about New York matters." Simon stared hard at Josh for a moment, then turned away.

"I'm sure you do. We feel the same way in Indiana. But as a matter of fact, I wasn't giving Sylvia advice about New York law."

"You weren't?" Simon was clearly skeptical.

"No, Simon," Sylvia interjected. "That's what I've been telling you. Mr. Havill just said I was entitled to get the will I want. And I should see another lawyer if I wasn't happy with the one you wrote me." She set her jaw firmly. "And I'm not. How can I be? I haven't even seen it."

"Mother Bright, you can't let this guy from who knows where come in here and give you some dumb, far-out—"

"He's not from who knows where. He just told you, he's from Indiana. And he's a friend of Ginny's. That's good enough for me."

Sylvia looked around at the people who were gathered around, frankly listening to her conversation with Simon. "All these people know Ginny. They know what a fine and caring person she is. And Ginny knows Mr. Havill. And she likes him. You can see that, can't you?"

The people near her nodded in agreement.

"Likes him a lot, I'd say," said an elderly gentleman in a bright red sweater.

"Sweet on him," added a tall woman, peering over her glasses and giving a decided nod.

Ginny didn't know whether to blush or laugh.

"We're just friends. Nobody's sweet on anybody," she said in a firm, no-nonsense voice.

"Mr. Miller," Ginny said in a soothing voice, "maybe you'd better leave the will here with Sylvia and she can read it and then ask any questions she may have on your next visit."

Simon Miller's round face got red and his mouth turned down. He looked like a thwarted baby. When he looked down at his mother-in-law, he tried unsuccessfully to smile. "Very well. I can see we're not going to get anything done tonight. Ceil and I will come to see you before we leave, Mother Bright. We can straighten this out then." He turned to Josh and his expression hardened. "Don't try anything cute, Havill. I happen to be an officer in the bar association, and I will be watching you very carefully. Keep that in mind." He turned on his heel and marched out the door.

Sylvia looked after him and shook her head. "My Cecilia could have done so much better for herself. But no, she had to have Simon. 'Ma,' she said, 'he's going to Brooklyn Law School.' I told her, lots of people go to Brooklyn Law School. Should you marry them all? Is that all it takes?" She shook her head again. "Children. They never listen, do they, Mr. Havill?"

"It's Havilland, Sylvia, Josh Havilland. But I wish you'd call me Josh."

"Is that Josh for Joshua?" she asked. When he nodded, she said, "I'd be proud to, Joshua. Now," Sylvia had perked up remarkably since Simon Miller had left, "you two sit right down here, and let's talk about my will."

There was a long pause, while Ginny telegraphed her disapproval to Josh, which he ignored. He gave her a warm smile. It didn't reassure her, but it did make her feel soft and yielding.

"I really can't give you advice about New York law, Sylvia," Josh said. "Your son-in-law is right about that."

"Can't you at least tell me what it means? I can't understand a word that Simon says. I don't even know who I'm leaving my engagement ring to! All those bequeaths and devises and issue. What's an issue? A magazine? What? Why can't I just give a few special things to my nieces and then everything else to Cecilia?" Sylvia clasped her hands in her lap and her mouth tightened. She swallowed and looked down at her hands.

Compassion overrode caution and Ginny said, "Of course, we can. But we'll have to look it over first. Can we take it? Just for a few minutes, to make a copy?"

"Take it away!" Sylvia said. "I certainly don't want it!"

Josh put a hand over hers on the arm of her chair. "This will may do exactly what you want it to do, Sylvia. Don't be too quick to judge Simon."

"Quick? The man's been married to Cecilia for thirty years. I know him and I know it's not the will I want. I want to leave my garnet earrings to my sister Anna's daughter, Carla. Carla's name was not in that paper. That much I'm sure of, Joshua." Sylvia nodded for emphasis.

Ginny picked up the will and headed for the office. It was still open and she came back in a few minutes with several copies.

"We'll both read the will and talk to you about what it says." Ginny gave the original back to Sylvia.

"Good. Wonderful. I won't sign anything until you tell me what this means." Sylvia slid off the chair cushion and offered her hands to Ginny and Josh. "Thank you both. I feel much better now. I can tell Simon I'm thinking it over."

"If you need to talk to me, here's my number." Josh scribbled on a scrap of paper he found in a pocket. "If I'm out, just leave a message on the machine. I'm staying with my son, Denis, so he's the one answering. Just leave the message. Okay?"

"Okeydokey," said Sylvia.

Ginny and Josh stayed for another half hour and then headed back to Manhattan. Josh didn't put his arm around her in the cab. Ginny was annoyed to find that she missed it. Wrapped up in her thoughts, she paid no attention to the conversation Josh had started with the cab driver. It wasn't until the cab pulled up outside her building on East Twenty-third Street that she tuned in. Just in time to hear Josh say, "Hey, I agree that you guys need protection. But if you're going to carry a gun, you should learn how to use it."

"A gun? You have a gun in this cab?" Ginny said. "Don't you know you could get yourself killed?"

"Lady, if I *don't* have a gun, I'm liable to get myself killed. Don't you read the papers?"

"Yes, I read the papers." Ginny had completely forgotten that they had arrived at her building. "And the papers tell me that unlicensed guns in this city cause most of the trouble. You're not solving the problem, you're adding to it!"

"Now, lady, you just listen to your husband. He knows what's what. Women!" the cabbie said in disgust as he slapped change in Josh's hand.

Josh maintained a careful silence as they made their way to the elevator in Ginny's building. "We were talking about safety in the streets," he said, his eyes fixed on the lights indicating floors. "As you would know if you paid the slightest attention to anything I say or do."

Ginny jerked her head around to stare at him. "What do you mean? I've spent four days paying attention to you! I listen. I respond. I respond too damn much." Ginny was horrified. Why couldn't she keep her mouth shut?

"Not that I've noticed. I see someone who pulls away from me at every opportunity, and denies that she feels anything beyond some kind of tepid . . . liking." He stared down at her, tight-lipped. "Has it been such a sacrifice, spending time with me?" Josh's tone was still sharp.

"No, of course not. I've loved it! You know that." Again, Ginny told him the simple truth, without thinking about it first.

"How the hell would I know that? You don't act like it." Josh waited, his face set in a formidable frown Ginny had never seen. "You tell people there's nothing between us, as if I had some social disease!"

Opening the door, Ginny motioned him inside. Josh stayed where he was. "Aren't you coming in?" She wanted him to.

They had to talk. But she didn't know what to say.

"No. Not tonight. I'll call you or . . . Look. Why don't you call me tomorrow? If you feel like it, that is." He turned to go.

"Wait! Josh, don't go."

He turned and without a word, walked back to her. Standing only inches from her, he gazed down into her face. What might have been a smile twisted his lips for a moment. He swept her into his arms and Ginny put her arms around his waist and held him tight. She lifted her face for his kiss.

It wasn't what she expected. Instead of warmth there was heat. The comfortable sense of having known this man for years, of being at home in his arms gave way to the passion and demand of a man who wants a woman.

Ginny's world reeled. She opened her mouth while Josh's hot, voracious kiss plundered it. She held him tighter, wanting to melt, to merge with him. She knew nothing and wanted nothing but this man who held her senses in thrall. But soon, all too soon, Josh broke the kiss. Breathing hard, he stepped away from her. His dark blue eyes blazed down into hers and Ginny waited, breathless.

"That's what we have together, Ginny. Something I've never felt before. And I'm not feeling it all alone. Stop trying to deny it. You want me the same way I want you." His fingers bit into her shoulders, even through the thick wool of her coat. "And, whether you know it or not, you need me. But you keep turning me away as if you didn't. I'm tired of being the only honest one around here." For another heartbeat, he continued to fix her with his stormy blue gaze. Then, with-

out another word, he turned and strode off to the elevator.

"Josh . . . wait . . . maybe you're . . . right." Ginny's voice was a tremulous whisper. She could feel her hand, cold and shaking, grip the doorknob.

Josh didn't answer. Standing, watching until the elevator arrived and he disappeared, Ginny felt tears begin to burn behind her eyes.

"Good-night," she said. "Good-bye."

Eleven

Josh needed to walk. He started up First Avenue at a quick pace, his long legs eating up the sidewalk. No matter how fast he walked, he couldn't leave his thoughts behind.

What had made him blow up at Ginny like that? He never lost his temper without warning. Shoving his hands in the pockets of his raincoat, Josh frowned. He knew damn well what was the matter with him. He wanted Ginny. Wanted her more than he could ever remember wanting a woman.

Even Marian. He slowed his pace as thoughts of his late wife surfaced. Marian had been his high school sweetheart and they had stayed in love all through college, although her parents had sent her away to a small women's college in California, hoping to separate them. They had married after Josh's first year at law school. And throughout their married life, neither had looked at another. Their love, Josh thought, had always remained the sweet, tender affection of youth. He had loved Marian deeply, had taken care of her always, as if she were a flower that would wither if not carefully tended. Yes, he had loved Marian.

But not the way he was coming to love Virginia McDougall. And not the way he had wanted Ginny from the moment he saw her. A lopsided smile curved his lips momentarily as he thought of that first kiss in Penn Station.

He took a deep breath of cold city air. Whew! You could smell the air in New York. And taste it, sometimes. But despite all the things that were wrong about the city, Josh liked it. He felt more alive here than he had since—he rummaged through his mind and couldn't think of anywhere he had felt so vital and full of spit and vinegar. Maybe Harvard. There too he had felt anxiety that had kept him trying to do more and better, just to stay in the running.

He had never considered working in New York after law school, and he realized now that it was because Marian would have been overwhelmed. But now, at fifty-eight, he felt ready to try. Could he make a life here?

He walked on, turning west on Thirty-fourth Street, still walking, as if his legs could outpace his thoughts. He saw an open coffee shop and decided to stop.

The room was steamy and fragrant with the smell of hamburgers and french fries. Josh sat at the counter and ordered coffee. When it came, it was as thick and black as tar. Idly, he stirred it and looked into the swirling liquid as if he could find answers there.

He wanted Ginny and he wanted to stay and answer the challenge both she and the city posed. He had never known a woman like Ginny—one with opinions and ideas, whose whole life was of her own making. He thought with a pang of the young Ginny, alone and pregnant after the death of her husband. She was an incredibly strong woman to have survived that and brought up her daughter to be as independent and strong-minded as she was.

He sipped his coffee, without tasting it. Ginny was so strong, why did she deny her feelings for him, shrink from his touch? There was no false modesty in Josh, and he knew that Ginny cared for him. She cared for him, she wanted him, but something kept her from admitting it, yielding to it, enjoying it.

Was it the memory of her long-dead husband? Had their love been so perfect that she was unwilling to risk disappointment? That didn't seem like Ginny. She faced life head-on. Except for this.

Josh shook his head. It was Ginny's refusal to face her feelings for him in the same fearless, honest way she faced the rest of her life that had triggered his anger. It wasn't just that he wanted to make love with Ginny—though God knew he did! It was her stubborn insistence that she didn't feel desire or love for him that had made him erupt.

He slipped a dollar on the counter and headed for the door. He wasn't going to accomplish anything by getting angry and stomping out like an adolescent. Or asking himself questions only Ginny could answer. Tomorrow he would have it out with Virginia McDougall. Win or lose, he was going to find out where he stood. All his other ideas depended on the answers he got from Ginny.

He hailed a cab, ready to go home now that he knew what he was going to do.

On his way home, Josh rode by the café on Columbus Avenue where Denis and Lisa had met earlier in the evening.

Before Denis had reached the subway stop three blocks from the café, he asked himself for the fortieth time why he had asked Lisa McDougall to meet him anywhere. At any time. To discuss anything.

The chance that the two of them could ever agree on any given topic was minuscule. Lisa would look out the window to check if Denis told her the sun was out. If Lisa announced that Christmas was on December twenty-fifth, he would call the *New York Times* to confirm.

Shaking his head over his stupidity, Denis entered the tiny coffeehouse. He spotted Lisa immediately. Who could fail to notice the only woman in the room wearing a school bus yellow minidress and thigh-high plastic boots in stop sign red, topped by a floppy rain hat in iridescent flag blue?

"All the primary colors this evening, I see," Denis murmured as he took the seat opposite her.

"Are you going to start with a fashion critique?" Lisa replied, flipping her mane of red hair over her shoulders. "Because if you are, I have a few thoughts on dull gray, boring maroon, and sleepy-time khaki." She gave his suit, tie, and raincoat a disapproving stare. "Or are you required to dress like a fifties undergrad interviewing for a job?"

"Very amusing, Lisa. Perhaps we could take our disagreement on the fundamentals of dress as a given and move on."

"I didn't start it," Lisa replied.

Denis noticed her lower lip stuck out in a sulky pout. Childish, yet somehow provocative, too. "Stop looking like an overage Lolita, would you?" he demanded, his palms suddenly damp. "We have serious business here."

Instantly, Lisa's expression changed to a worried frown. "I know. What's going on with them? How could you ask Momma to look after your father? Don't you realize what he looks like?"

"What?" Denis was amazed. What was wrong with the way his father looked? He looked just like a father, didn't he? "What do you mean, 'how could I'? My father is a very nice person. And he looks like a very nice person."

"I'm sure." Lisa was clearly not sure at all. "But he looks at my mother as if he'd like to have her for dessert."

"I beg your pardon!" Did she have to insult his father? The honor of the Havilland males was at stake here. "My father has never looked at anyone as if he wanted to stick a fork in them!"

"Well, he looked at my mother that way!" Lisa slapped her menu down on the marble-topped table and glared at her escort. She was ready to order. "A chocolate éclair and a cup of hot chocolate." Lisa seldom ate anything but fruits and vegetables, but tonight she needed chocolate and sugar.

"What happened to the veggies and tofu?" Denis taunted. He ordered a martini. Very dry. He seldom drank anything but wine, but tonight he needed gin.

"What happened to the wine connoisseur?"

Denis didn't answer and they sat in silence until the waiter returned with their orders.

"Here's to success in our joint venture," Denis said, lifting his glass in a toast.

"Just what is our joint venture?"

"To make sure our parents don't make fools of themselves."

Lisa took a big swallow of her hot cocoa. "My mother wouldn't be in danger of making a fool of herself if it weren't for your father."

"Stop acting as if he's trying to seduce her." Denis could feel his temper slipping. "He's Joshua Havilland of Elgin, Indiana, and he's never seduced anyone. And certainly not Ginny. He likes her. He's told me that. They go sight-seeing. He's asked her to a party a friend of mine is giving. It's all perfectly innocuous." He swallowed a long sip of martini and shivered a little as the gin slid down. "At least, I thought it was."

"What do you mean? Do you think he has designs on her?" Lisa paused, a forkful of éclair halfway to her mouth.

"Designs on her? Where do you get language like that? *Little Women?*"

"Never mind my language." Lisa put her fork down, the éclair untasted. "Is he trying to get it on with her? Is that a better way to put it?"

Denis laughed. Slang should have sounded natural coming from the glossy, red lips of Lisa

McDougall. Instead, it sounded like a foreign language, one she didn't understand very well. Could it be that inside the exotic disguise there was an old-fashioned girl? He took another sip of his drink. What did he care what made her tick?

"I don't know what's happening," he said, suddenly serious. "I can't figure it out. I know he likes her—a lot. But I don't know how Ginny feels. Has she said anything to you?" Denis didn't know much about the relationship between Ginny and her daughter. He loved his father, but there were things he wouldn't dream of telling him.

"Just that she likes him, and that they have fun. The same stuff your father tells you." Lisa's green eyes, carefully made up to accentuate their size and color, stared into his. For a moment Denis lost his place in their conversation.

"What?" he murmured.

"They have fun." Lisa's voice was patient. "But somehow I thought there was more to it than she was saying. You don't think there's any more to it than that?"

Denis frowned into his empty glass. "I don't know. For a while during dinner I thought I did. I hadn't seen them together and somehow—maybe I just imagined it."

Lisa nodded. "I felt the same way. There was something. A feeling."

"Electricity."

"Chemistry."

They stared at each other for a long, frozen moment. Denis felt his mouth go dry as he watched Lisa's pupils dilate and swallow the green irises of her eyes.

Electricity. Chemistry.

He cleared his throat. "Maybe we should each have a serious talk. Sound them out. Find out what's going on. Then we can meet again."

"Okay. You have my number?" Lisa didn't meet his eyes. "Of course you do. You called me." If he didn't know better, Denis would have sworn she sounded positively flustered.

Impossible. Lisa McDougall, world champion know-it-all, flustered? It must be the martini. He was seeing things.

Before they stepped out into the street, Denis turned to her. She stood so close to him, he lost the thread of his thought again and simply stared at her.

"You'll call?" she murmured.

Denis just nodded.

When Josh arrived at the house on West Seventieth Street, he was ready to go to bed and wait for the morning to determine what to do about Ginny. But on his way home in the cab, he began to feel uncomfortable about the way they had left things. He regretted having pushed her. Maybe she wasn't ready for anything beyond friendship. Maybe she didn't feel what he felt.

He would call her tonight and tell her that he didn't want to pressure her. If friendship was all she was willing to give, he wanted her as a friend.

New York was making him rush things. Better do things on Indiana time where Ginny was concerned.

Josh opened both front doors to the building and started to take the stairs, when he heard what sounded like an argument going on downstairs. He paused and, seeing that the basement light was on and the door open, went over and started down. As the voices grew more distinct, he recognized them.

Hervé and Denis were arguing—that much Josh could tell. But they were doing it in French, and he understood nothing except "oui" and "non." Denis was the one saying "yes" while Hervé repeatedly insisted "no." Josh reached the foot of the stairs and stood, astonished by the sight of his usually immaculate son with his suit jacket off, the sleeves of his wrinkled shirt rolled up to the elbow, and his expensive silk tie shoved into the pocket of his raincoat. He was standing toe to toe with Hervé, and the Haitian was gesturing broadly, and interrupting Denis in mid-tirade.

Josh couldn't understand a word, but he could tell that Denis was losing his grip on his temper. Yet while he watched, Josh saw him take a deep breath and clap Hervé on the shoulder, smiling and talking a mile a minute.

All this was very unlike his son. Josh decided to question him later. "Hi, Denis, Hervé. What's wrong? Something happen to the water or something?" It was the only reason he could think of for Denis to be in the basement.

"Non. M'sieu," said Hervé. "It is not the building which we discuss."

Denis sighed. "It's Hervé's friend, François, the illegal immigrant. You asked me to see about it. Remember?"

"And you have? Already?" Josh couldn't help being surprised. He had thought that, if Denis remembered at all, he would assign some lowly first-year associate to work on François's visa application.

"Of course I have, Dad. But Hervé won't let me meet with François. Won't even tell me where he is. And without that, I can't do anything."

Hervé turned to Josh, his eyes pleading. *"M'sieu,* you will understand. I cannot risk hav-

ing François sent back to Haiti. *Les attachés,*
they will kill him, as they have others. I have
talked with my family and we are agreed.
François will stay here, hidden. He will not risk
going to the law. The law will not help him."

"You see what I'm up against, Dad," said
Denis, shoving a hand through his disheveled
blond hair. "If they catch François, they'll send
him back. And he isn't getting the medical care
he needs. Hervé, please tell me where he is. I
promise we'll get him a full hearing before the
authorities decide his case."

Hervé listened, but in the end, he shook his
head. *"Non.* I cannot do this. But I will speak
again to my family. I will tell them what you
say."

"Could I go with you to see them?" Denis
asked, earning Josh's admiration. Devotion to
your client, above and beyond the call of duty,
had always been Josh's creed.

Hervé shrugged. "I will ask. I will see what
they say."

Denis's shoulders sagged a little. "Okay, I guess
that's all we can do for tonight." He reached out
and took Hervé's hand. "Good-night, Hervé. Tell
François what I said."

"Oui, m'sieu."

As they trudged upstairs, Josh said, "You look
like it's been a long, tough day, son."

"Dad," Denis responded, thinking more of Lisa than Hervé, "you don't know the half of it."

Twelve

"Hello." Her voice was slow, a little sleepy, incredibly sexy.

"Ginny." Josh wasn't sure she'd want to talk to him.

"Josh?" Was she pleased or shocked that he'd called after midnight? He couldn't tell. "What do you want?"

He grasped the phone receiver tighter. "Ginny—I just wanted to say—" But he didn't seem to be able to say it. Not to a telephone.

"Josh, we don't have to talk tonight." Ginny sounded uncertain. Maybe she didn't want to hear what he wanted to say.

"I'll see you tomorrow, Josh."

"Good. I'm glad you still want to see me."

"What do you mean?" Ginny's voice was low-pitched and tentative. "The way you stormed out, I wasn't sure you were still speaking to me."

"That's why I called. I've been behaving like a prize jerk. I lost my temper and I want you to know that I'm sorry."

"Thank you." Ginny cleared her throat. "I guess I must seem a little strange—"

"No, you're not. Not a bit." Josh wished he could see her, be with her. "I was trying to rush you and I knew you didn't—"

"Oh, Josh, I know that most women would want—and I am flattered. It's just that I . . ." Ginny trailed to a halt. "I don't seem to be able to make much sense."

"You don't have to. I was being pushy. You know what they say about Midwesterners. They get to New York and start pushing the natives around. Listen, forget about all the stuff I said. I take it all back. We'll just go on having a good time. No strings and no pressure. Okay?"

"Yes. Okay." Relief sang in her voice. She sounded buoyant again. The way Ginny McDougall ought to sound.

Josh sighed with relief. She wasn't angry. "Then you'll still go with me to Candy's party tomorrow night?"

"Who's Candy? What party?"

"Denis's friend. You know, the model from Arkansas I told you about. She and her roommates are giving a party tomorrow and you have to come with me."

"I don't think I'd better." Ginny gripped the telephone hard. "The last people young single women want at their parties are old single women."

"You're not old. Besides, Candy said she'd love to meet you. I thought we'd go up to Columbia tomorrow afternoon, if you'd like. They're having a seminar on legal services for the middle class. Is that too much like work or would you like to come along?"

"No. I'd love to go to the seminar. But not to the party. I really don't think—" Ginny tried not to sound as rattled as she felt. She was glad Josh couldn't see her, clutching the telephone with a sweaty hand because he wanted to go to a party full of beautiful young women. With her.

She couldn't. She just couldn't.

"We'll talk about it tomorrow, Ginny. If you don't want to go, we don't have to. There's a new off-off-Broadway play that got good reviews. John Lahr loved it. It's about Irish terrorists. It's in blank verse and all the actors wear Mickey Mouse masks. We can see that instead." Mickey Mouse as an Irish terrorist? Even Candy sounded preferable. He must have taken her silence for assent, for he said softly, "Good-night, Ginny. Sleep well."

"Good-night, Josh." She hung the phone up gently and smiled a little. Josh Havilland was a good friend. He understood. Well, no, he was a good friend because he was willing to do things her way even though he *didn't* understand.

And she couldn't explain. To do so would take

her all the way back to her disastrous marriage, and she couldn't talk about that, even after all this time. She had told Lisa the sugar-coated lie about the death of her father—that he had loved them both and died the blameless victim of a drunk driver. After that, she didn't feel safe telling anyone else the truth, so she had never spoken of it.

And she wasn't about to break her silence by telling Josh Havilland what a failure she was as a woman and a wife.

Ginny reached to turn off the light at her bedside, but at that moment the telephone rang. Everyone seemed to have insomnia tonight.

It was Lisa. "Hi, Momma. I just wanted to let you know I got home all right the other night."

"Did Denis take you?"

"No." Lisa sounded surprised. "Did you think he was going to?"

"Yes. I asked him to."

"Momma, for heaven's sake. I'm not a child. I can get from East Twenty-third Street to East Ninety-fourth Street without help from Denis Havilland." Lisa sounded annoyed, but only slightly.

"I never doubted that for a moment. I did it for me, not you. I don't like to think of you walking around in the dark alone."

"Mother! Please." Lisa was half laughing.

"I can't help it. Worrying about children when they're out in the dark is an occupational hazard of mothers."

"Well, try to get over it. Maybe by the time I'm forty you'll believe I can cross the street alone."

"Maybe. Don't count on it."

Lisa laughed. Then Ginny could hear her take a deep breath and her next words were sober. "I liked Denis's father. He seemed like a nice guy."

"Yes, he is, very nice."

Ginny thought she sounded calm and not terribly interested, but Lisa must have heard something else. "Momma, are you serious about him?"

"Why, no, Lisa, of course not. Whatever gave you that idea?" Ginny hoped she sounded as if she were telling the truth. Because she was. Mostly, anyway.

"Well, I just wouldn't want you to get involved with a man who's going back to Indiana in just a few weeks."

"He lives in Florida now," Ginny said. Then, before she could censor herself, she added, "And he's thinking of moving here."

Dead silence. Then, "Here? You mean New York?"

"Yes, New York. Where else is 'here'?"

"Oh. Well. That's really a surprise." It didn't sound as if Lisa found it a pleasant one.

"Of course, he's still thinking about it. It was just an idea. Probably, he won't do it. I mean, Florida weather must be hard to leave." Ginny knew she sounded much too eager to convince Lisa that Josh would go back. She wondered if she was trying to convince herself or her daughter.

If he stayed . . . The thought frightened her.

"So, Momma, are we on for tomorrow night?"

"Tomorrow? What were we—"

"The new Wim Wenders movie."

"Wim Wenders? Isn't he the director who did the movie about angels sitting on rooftops in Berlin? The one where I didn't even know they *were* angels until it was over and you told me?" Ginny couldn't believe she had agreed to see another incomprehensible German movie with Lisa, who adored them. When had she said yes?

"Yes, Momma, that was *Wings of Desire,* but this one is much more accessible. I'm sure you'll understand it."

Ginny decided that Candy's party was a delightful prospect compared to an evening with Wim Wenders. She explained to Lisa that Josh had asked her to a party given by a friend of Denis's. "A model," she added unwisely.

"You see? He's just like Denis." Lisa's tone

brooked no dissent. "Aren't those the only women Denis dates? Bimbos with teeth like Chiclets and silicone injected God knows where. Ugh. Like father, like son."

Lisa sounded downright angry. But why did she care whom Denis Havilland dated? Ginny decided to ask.

The question seemed to make Lisa even angrier. "I *don't* care. Why should I care? But any woman who calls herself a feminist would have to condemn such frivolous—"

"Oh, come on, Lisa! A feminist shouldn't prejudge a woman based on her occupation. Or a man based on whom he dates."

There was silence from Lisa's end of the phone. Then, she said—surprising Ginny no end, "You're right, Momma. I shouldn't judge those women by the company they keep or what they do."

"You might bear that in mind when you're passing judgment on Josh—and on Denis, too, for that matter. And you might remember that both Josh and Denis are friends of mine, so there's at least one woman they don't judge on the basis of looks."

"Sorry, Momma. But you look terrific. And if he has any sense, Josh Havilland *does* like you for your looks as well as all your other wonderful qualities."

"Thank you, dear, but that's prejudice speaking."

"No, it's not." Lisa paused for a minute. "If you're going to this party tomorrow, I'd better let you get some sleep. I just wanted to check in and say hi. 'Night, Momma."

"Good-night, Lisa, darling. Sleep tight." Ginny hung up the phone and smiled. Lisa was prone to leap to her mother's defense when Ginny didn't need any. She had done it for years, just as Ginny had worried over how Lisa was getting home. Ginny slid down under the covers and went to sleep with a slight smile on her lips.

The next morning, Ginny slept later than usual and enjoyed the sight of the sun shining through the yellow kitchen curtains as she sat drinking a leisurely cup of coffee. It was Saturday and she was prepared to coast along until time to go uptown to the seminar Josh had mentioned.

She was still in her robe when the telephone rang. Ginny answered it and was greeted by an unfamiliar, feminine voice, one drenched in a Southern accent. "Is this Miz Virginia McDougall?" the voice asked.

"Yes, it is."

"I'm so glad to get you. I'm Candy, Denis Havilland's friend. Joshua told me that you'd be comin' with him this evenin' and I just wanted to invite you myself." Candy sounded as friendly and unaffected as Josh had described her.

"Thank you, Candy, that's very kind of you, but I don't know—" There had to be a graceful way of declining the invitation to spend an evening with a bunch of nubile glamour girls. Lisa would never know if her mother spent the evening alone with a book instead of partying with the beautiful people.

"Oh, don't say you can't come. No, really, please come. We have an *awful* time getting enough girls—I mean, women, we're not very PC down in the country—to come to our parties. I don't know if it's because we're models and everyone thinks they won't look good, or if it's just that they think we can't cook. But whatever it is, they don't come. So when Joshua said that you were comin' I was just so *glad.*"

"Thank you, again. It's very nice of you to call. I'm looking forward to meeting you." Ginny didn't know if this call was Josh's idea or Candy's, but she was now committed to going.

Candy told her to dress informally and be there by eight or there wouldn't be any food left. The evening ahead looked interesting, but Ginny wasn't sure she was up to it.

Josh called and they agreed to meet for lunch

at a Japanese restaurant on the Upper West Side, close to the Columbia campus.

The law school was a single building on Amsterdam Avenue and 116th Street. "It looks like a toaster," Ginny said as they approached the street level entrance. "With two slices just popped up."

"But it's a toaster we love," said a bearded student wearing a camouflage jacket and toting a tattered backpack. "Are you here for the seminar?"

When told that they were he directed them back across the street and up to the higher level. "These doors tend to be locked. The upper level entrance is the one you want. It's much more impressive." He pointed them back across Amsterdam Avenue and told them how to get to the upper level.

The main part of the campus was bracketed by two enormous libraries and a set of steps with a large statue in the middle. The law school entrance was reached via a footbridge across the avenue.

"This is definitely more impressive," Ginny said. "But I'm not sure it's worth climbing all these stairs."

"It's good for us, Ginny. I'll bet Columbia law students have great cardiovascular systems."

The seminar was chaired by a Columbia professor and the speakers included a woman who particularly interested Ginny. Her name was Sheila Margolies and she was speaking on behalf of a divorced women's support group and advocated that paralegals be provided free so that people who were caught up in the legal system in the most wrenching way, in battles over custody and visitation rights with children, who couldn't afford a lawyer, would be better able to defend themselves.

"These people have to appear for themselves. They aren't poor enough to get publicly paid attorneys and they can't afford to pay over a hundred dollars an hour for a lawyer who knows the ropes." Sheila Margolies was not a lawyer and she was passionate about her cause. "As things stand, ordinary people have to navigate the system by themselves or risk bankruptcy because of legal fees—*if,* and it's a big if, they can find a lawyer willing to represent them. A half hour's consultation with a paralegal, at public expense, or at a nominal fee, could help these people enormously."

Ginny thought the idea had a lot of merit. A well-trained paralegal could help get court papers together and show a litigant how to fill them out and where to file them. With a computer programmed with court forms, it shouldn't take more than an hour for most people. Ginny turned to ask Josh what he thought, and found him frowning.

He wasn't the only one. Most of the audience was made up of practicing attorneys and they criticized the proposal on a number of grounds. It wouldn't work, it would allow paralegals to give legal advice without the direction of a lawyer, it might cause some litigants to lose cases they could have won with the help of a lawyer.

Nobody seemed to want to speak for the people—or the paralegals. Finally, Ginny decided that if no one else would do it, she would. She raised her hand.

When the moderator recognized her, she rose and cleared her throat. Looking around the large room, Ginny wanted only to sit back down and become invisible. All those disapproving lawyers. She took a deep breath and charged ahead.

"I have heard a great many lawyers speak on this issue today, but you haven't heard anything from the professional people who would be most directly involved—the paralegals."

She stood a little straighter. "I'm a paralegal, and I'm proud of my profession. But you people can stop worrying. I don't think I'm a lawyer. I don't know any paralegal who does. We don't do the work of lawyers. What we do, and do wonderfully well, is fill out forms and do the work that is meticulous, difficult, technical, completely necessary—and still not worth a lawyer's time.

"That may not sound like much, but with thousands of cases in court, and hundreds of hearings before a million state, federal, and local agencies, and all the forms to be filled out in triplicate, paperwork rules us all. We paralegals understand the paper blizzard and know how to find our way around in the maze. I think this program could save time and money. Maybe even a forest or two. Why not give it a try?"

Breathless, she sat down. For a long minute there was nothing but silence. Ginny turned her head to see Josh's reaction and found him frowning down at the legal pad he was writing on.

Oh, God. She had hoped that Josh would be the one to break the silence and stand up and vote with her, but he was still making notes. And frowning.

His silence and refusal to look at her hurt more than she would have believed. She wanted Josh to be on her side and to announce it publicly. Just as she was giving up hope, Josh rose and began to speak in a slow, quiet voice that could nevertheless be heard throughout the room.

"I've heard a lot in the past hour about how we, as a profession, can't help the middle class find reasonably priced legal services. I think we can, and I think we must." Ginny turned to stare at him in admiration and surprise. She wanted to applaud.

"In my mind, the idea should be carried beyond family disputes," he continued. "There are people in this city who need help and aren't getting it. That's where a lot of the distrust of lawyers comes from. People think we're not trying to help them, just trying to feather our own nests.

"For now, as a pilot project, why not provide paralegal help with the forms needed for custody and child support and visitation cases? The program can be monitored, and in a year or so you'll know whether all of you are right or whether Ms. McDougall and Ms. Margolies and I are.

"I'm sure you can find a lawyer willing to volunteer to monitor the project, and to provide supervision and guidance to the legal assistants if you find that any is required. As Ms. McDougall has so eloquently said, why not give it a try?"

A dismissive murmur ran through the crowd, but Ginny could see it didn't bother Josh.

He leaned over and whispered in her ear, "We sure shook them up. They'll never let us into another seminar around here."

"Tell you what. We'll go in disguise next time."

"What kind of disguise did you have in mind?" Josh's lips twitched, but he sounded suspicious.

"Something simple. How about angels dressed as Mickey Mouse?"

Josh turned to look at her, his eyebrows raised and his mouth quirked in a smile. "Good idea, Ginny. Dignified and unobtrusive."

"I was thinking of wearing a Mickey Mouse mask tonight, as a matter of fact."

"Coward."

Ginny didn't bother to deny it. "You bet."

"I'll pick you up at seven-thirty. No mask, no wings. Just Ginny, please." They had walked out to the street. Josh hailed a taxi and kissed Ginny's nose before helping her into the cab and waving her off. He was going to walk.

Ginny leaned back against the tattered upholstery and closed her eyes.

Coward she told herself.

You bet, she answered.

Thirteen

Clothes lay heaped on Ginny's bed. She had searched through every item in her closet and found nothing to wear. Candy had said informal, but what did informal mean to a top New York model? Jeans? Sequins? Sequined jeans? Ginny had no idea.

Her clothes veered sharply between conservative and businesslike and casual verging on sloppy. "Your wardrobe looks as if you didn't do anything but go to the office and watch TV in sweats," she said aloud in disgust.

It wasn't true, of course, but most of her social activities took place after work, so she wore her workday suits and tailored dresses. She didn't have much need for dressy clothes, formal or informal. Ginny McDougall didn't go to opening nights or, for that matter, to parties given by a gaggle of supermodels.

Oh, lord. She sat down on the edge of the bed and tried to think. But nothing came to mind. She thought for another minute and then, with a sigh and a shrug, reached for a pink silk blouse and a pair of jeans. Maybe it wasn't the best choice for a woman on the shady side of fifty but it was her idea of informal and if it wasn't Candy's—too bad!

She had cinched a turquoise-and-silver belt around her waist and slipped into woven leather moccasins, when the buzzer rang. She threw on a navy-wool blazer and headed for the door. Stopping short, she rushed back into the bedroom and sprayed herself with Chanel. *Come on, Coco, I need all the help I can get.*

She heard the elevator door clang and sensed that it was Josh. She opened the door at his knock. He stood in the doorway for a moment looking at her. He smiled.

"Ginny, you look beautiful."

"Thank you." He looked wonderful in gray flannel trousers and a blue broadcloth shirt and tweed jacket. The same thing he would wear in Elgin, Indiana, or even Shellfish Cay if the weather was cool. Men's clothes didn't vary as much as women's. Ginny was sure Josh hadn't left a pile of discards on his bed this evening.

"Well," he said, still smiling, "aren't you going to tell me I look terrific?"

"Of course. But you always look terrific. I thought by this time you'd take it as read into the record."

"Nope. I still need to hear it. Same as everybody else. Why would you think I didn't?"

"I don't know." Ginny was uncomfortable talking about Josh's good looks. "I guess I thought handsome men knew they were handsome."

"I'm sure Elizabeth Taylor knows she's gorgeous, but I'm also sure she doesn't mind being told now and then. When she's made a particular effort, maybe. Worn the good diamond tiara instead of the everyday one."

"Is this your good blue shirt?" Ginny said, reaching out to touch his arm. "It looks wonderful on you."

"That's my girl. Now where's your coat? It's time to go play with the kiddies in the sandbox."

Ginny looked over her shoulder at him as he helped her on with her coat. "Is that your idea of an evening with Candy and Friends? Children in a sandbox?"

"Isn't it yours? She's a very sweet girl, but barely out of pigtails." Josh tucked her hand in the crook of his elbow and escorted her to the elevator. "Are you dreading tonight? Candy said she was going to call you and convince you to come. Did she?"

"Yes. I wondered if you knew." So Candy had been calling him, trying to get him to bring a date. Peculiar behavior for a reigning beauty queen.

But it took Ginny only a minute after they arrived to decide that Candy was indeed a very different kind of beauty. She was gorgeous all right, with legs that went on forever, a waist that hardly existed at all, and a smile that could melt a polar ice cap. Candy greeted her at the door of the crowded apartment, where music and conversation filled the air.

Ginny glanced around and saw mostly quite ordinary-looking young people, with a smattering of tall, awesomely slim girls with big eyes and manes of hair. They had to be models, Ginny decided, but none of them looked as real or as happy as Candy.

Ginny smiled back at her. "Thank you for the special invitation this morning. I appreciated it."

"Thank you." Candy beamed at her. "That's real nice of you." She put her arm through Ginny's and led her through the crowd to the bar. "I have the most awful crush on your date."

"On Josh?"

"Yes, ma'am. What would you like to drink?"

"White wine spritzer, please."

"Claudio?" Candy gestured to the bartender.

When Claudio put her drink in her hand, Ginny turned again to Candy. "He's an easy guy to like."

"Yes. So much nicer than his son. Oh, I'm sorry," Candy grimaced. "I forgot you work for Den."

"Yes, I do," Ginny said, a little stiffly.

"You're very loyal. I admire that. And I like Den, really I do. But I don't take him seriously. His father, though, there's a man you can count on."

"How do you know so much about men, Candy?" Ginny had to smile at Candy's air of age-old wisdom.

"My mama taught me all I needed to know before I was out of pigtails. And I can tell that Den will get serious, but not about me."

"Hmm." Ginny thought it over. "You may be right, but tell me why you think so."

"He's happy as a pig in slop right now. Somebody's goin' to have to come along and just throw him off his stride. Somebody different. Somebody who'll shake him up."

"You don't think you're that someone?" Ginny and Candy had crossed the living room to a bow window looking out over the East River. They stood looking out over the lights of Roosevelt Island.

"No, ma'am. I'm the same old thing as far as Den is concerned. And he is for me."

"I'm sorry you feel that way. I think it's Denis's loss." Ginny didn't like to hear that Josh's son was so shallow and predictable.

Candy excused herself to look after the rest of her guests and Ginny looked around the room, sipping her drink and wondering who everyone was.

There were a number of men who did look like lawyers or maybe stockbrokers, as Candy had indicated. One of them even wore a vest. Some of the women looked like lawyers and stockbrokers, too. They didn't sport vests but there were some very conservative pants, shirts, and blazers being worn by some very conservative-looking ladies. The women who looked like models were dressed casually in jeans and silk shirts very like Ginny's, a thought that made her smile.

She looked around for Denis but either the crowd was too dense or he hadn't arrived yet. Josh had disappeared, too. Ginny wasn't worried. Standing by herself at a party had led to some very interesting encounters over the years and Ginny wasn't in a hurry to become part of a group. People-watching was a fine art anywhere in New York.

Josh seemed to surface from the crowd like a swimmer coming out of the water. He came over to Ginny and took her hand.

"I didn't want to interrupt your tête-à-tête with Candy. But this crowd is pretty intimidating when you're not used to it. In Elgin, a combination Fourth of July picnic and Christmas bazaar at the Methodist church wouldn't draw this many people."

Ginny laughed. "Come on, Elgin isn't that

small." She looked at Josh as he shook his head.
"Is it?"

Josh smiled. "Ask Denis if you don't believe
me. By the way, where is Denis? Have you seen
him?"

"Not yet, but I'm sure he'll be here. He wouldn't
miss it."

"Maybe. Maybe not."

"What does that mean? Did he say something?"

"No, but he's been acting out of character
lately," Josh said. "He seems to be developing a
conscience."

"Denis has always had a conscience," Ginny
said sharply. "I don't think he's as cold and
greedy as everyone says Wall Street lawyers are."

Josh put his arm around her shoulders. "Loyal
Ginny, always sticking up for her friends. But
you don't need to defend Denis to me. I didn't
mean to imply that he was cold and greedy. Just
that he seems ready to admit his life isn't completely satisfying the way it is. Maybe Lisa has
something to do with it."

"Lisa!"

"What's so astounding about that?"

"But they hate each other!"

"Well, now," Josh said with a smile, "that may
be, but you know what they say is next door to
hate."

"Do you mean love?"

"Is that so hard to believe?"

"Hard?" Ginny gulped the last of her drink. "Lisa and Denis? It's impossible!"

At that moment, they both caught sight of Denis, coming in the front door. He looked as if his mind was miles away and he wasn't paying much attention to what was going on around him. Ginny and Josh looked at him and then at each other. The unspoken question vibrated between them: What had happened to Denis?

Denis wasn't quite sure what had happened to him. But he knew that something was changing. He didn't know what had begun it but, like an avalanche, the feeling kept getting stronger and stronger. His life began to chafe him. He felt constrained by his law practice and his social life.

For some reason, it was now unsatisfying to regard the law as a high-powered, high-stakes poker game where the most skillful player won. Working with Hervé on his cousin's visa had brought him more satisfaction than all his last year's corporate litigation work.

Now he looked around the party and felt none of the pleasure he usually felt when surrounded by young, beautiful, and successful people. Instead, he had an uncomfortable sense of irritation mixed with boredom. The people all looked the same, the snatches of conversation he overheard all sounded the same. Nothing but pretty faces and petty gossip.

He wondered what Lisa would say about them. No, on the contrary, he knew damn well what she would say. Lisa believed that he fitted in perfectly with this crowd.

She had telephoned Denis soon after Josh had left for Columbia that morning, insisting that the attraction between their parents was more pressing than they had thought.

"He calls her at night, just so they can talk. After they've spent the whole day together! What can they have to talk about?" Lisa had sounded excited, but then she seemed to be excited by life in general. Denis had thought Lisa was exaggerating, but when he told her that they were going to the Columbia seminar together and then to a party given by a model, Lisa had gotten even more upset. Too upset to watch her words.

"Denis, don't you understand? I don't want my mother going to your friends' parties! She won't fit in at all. She doesn't make an obscene amount of money, and she doesn't have a fit over a broken fingernail. How can you stand back and let her get involved with those people?" Then she had stuck the knife in. "They're all right for you and your father, but Momma's too good for them."

For a moment, Denis was so angry he couldn't

answer. "I see. Do you already have one of your fellow do-gooding drones picked out for Ginny? I'm sure they must be much more worthwhile than anybody earning a six-figure salary by actually doing some productive work."

"Is that what you call posing for pictures to sell people a lot of stuff they don't need? Productive work?"

"I don't have to justify Candy's salary to you." Denis could still feel the fury course through him. "And I don't have to justify mine, or my father's—" He stopped and caught his breath, then came back angrier than before. "My friends are my business. Your only concern is my father. And let me tell you, you little bigot, that my father has never earned big money, and he has helped more people in real, concrete ways than you and your entire cockamamy foundation ever has or ever will! Joshua Havilland is good enough for anyone in this world. Even your mother, Ms. McDougall."

The conversation had ended at that point, as both phones slammed down simultaneously. Denis found he was still angry after all the intervening hours. And still defensive, he realized, and that made him even angrier.

"Evening, son." His father's voice awoke Denis to the present. "We thought you'd be here earlier."

"Sorry, Dad. Got held up." Denis looked at Josh as if he hadn't seen him in weeks instead of hours. What he had told Lisa was right. Josh Havilland was a father to be proud of, a man to admire, to love.

"You look all riled up, as if your mind is still back where you were. Maybe you'd better get a drink. Candy was looking for you."

"Okay. Where's Ginny?"

"Over there, talking to some guy who was in her Italian class a couple of years ago."

Denis finally spotted her, deep in conversation with a young man who couldn't be more than twenty-two. He was dressed all in black, a flowing poet-sleeved shirt and skintight jeans. "Hey, Dad, this guy looks like he's trying out for a part in *Interview with the Vampire.* Do you think Ginny would appreciate a rescue mission?"

"No, she can take care of herself," Josh said, looking fondly over at Ginny. "If she needs it, she'll rescue herself."

"Okay. I'm going to get a glass of what passes for scotch around here and hunt up Candy. See you later." Denis drifted off and was soon swallowed by the small, but dense crowd.

"There's a man here who wants to meet you," Candy said, a secretive smile curving her lips. "I think you might be interested." Without waiting for a reply, she took Josh's arm and led him over to a short, balding man with a mournful face that reminded Josh of a basset hound. "Luther," said

Candy, "this is the man I wanted you to meet, Josh Havilland. Josh this is Luther March." She said it as if he were somehow supposed to respond to the name. But Josh had never heard of Luther March.

Josh watched as Luther looked him up and down as if he were a side of aged, prime beef. Without saying a word, Luther and Candy smiled at each other.

"Didn't I tell you?" Candy said.

"You do have an eye, sugar," Luther responded in a Southern accent much heavier than Candy's.

"It's very nice to meet you, Luther," said Josh, not meaning it. "But I see someone over there that I really should talk to."

Josh started to move away when Luther March held up a hand like a traffic cop.

"Wait. I want to talk to you. I think that you are about to become a very lucky man."

"I'm already very lucky," Josh said with a thin smile. Who was this odd little man?

Luther continued as if Josh hadn't spoken. "You are about to become the Indigo Man!" Clearly, Luther thought he had made a monumental announcement and was waiting for the trumpets and drumrolls.

None were forthcoming. Josh was beginning to think that Luther was more than a little crazed, possibly from ingesting some controlled substance. His opinion must have been clear from his expression because Luther began to explain. "Indigo. The new line of men's fragrance products for baby boomers. Youthful but not young, mature but not old. Indigo—for the man who knows."

Luther waited but Josh simply looked at him. When was he going to get to the point? Candy took up the explanation. "Luther's agency, March, Hare and Hatter, has been searching for the perfect man to become the Indigo Man."

"And you, I think, are he," said Luther, his arms folded across his chest as he eyed Josh.

"I must be sure to try it when it comes out," Josh said politely.

"No, Josh, I want you to be the Indigo Man. Your face will be known all over the country. You'll be famous, the symbol of a vigorous, exciting life after fifty."

Josh stared at him, trying to keep from laughing. "I'm afraid I'm not really interested in being famous. But thanks, it's very flattering to be considered as a symbol of aging."

"But, Josh, you don't understand." Candy was earnest. "There's a lot of money involved. Luther's going to build a whole campaign around you."

"Candy, I know you like modeling, but I'm not—"

"We know you're not a professional, but that's

just what we're looking for. Reality. Naturalism. Almost a cinema verité quality. You're from the Midwest, aren't you? That will be perfect. Perfect." Luther's basset hound jowls quivered with emotion.

"Look, I don't know how to make you understand, but I don't want to be famous. I don't want to be recognized on the street. It's just not something—"

"Don't make a decision yet, Josh," said Candy. "Talk it over with Ginny, why don't you? She seemed very savvy. I'll bet she'll think it's a great idea."

Josh turned, looking around for Ginny, when he heard her voice behind him. "You look like you're having a serious discussion of some earth-shaking topic. Candy, one of your roommates told me to tell you that you were running out of salsa."

"Luther has just told Josh he wants him to be the Indigo Man."

Unlike Josh, Ginny knew what Candy was talking about. "The sexy older man's fragrance?"

"Please, not older. Mature." Luther looked pained. "Don't you think he'd make the perfect Indigo Man?"

Ginny felt tears start behind her eyes. She had known, known absolutely, that somehow Josh would become what handsome men always became—shallow, trading on their looks, trying to stay young, obsessed with their looks—everything Ginny dreaded.

"Yes," she whispered, "yes, you're right, he'd be perfect. Absolutely perfect." She could feel her lips begin to tremble and the tears begin to form. She had to get out. She had to get away from Josh Havilland and all he represented, all she wanted to forget.

"Good-bye, Josh," she murmured. Then she turned and all but ran for the door.

Fourteen

Josh stood for a moment, gazing after Ginny as if she were an apparition. What the hell had happened? He hadn't a clue. Suddenly, a funny incident had turned into melodrama complete with tears and sudden farewells.

Well, not this time. Josh Havilland was not a melodramatic man, and he wasn't going to put up with it—not even from Ginny. Curtly, he excused himself to Candy and Luther and hurried after her.

By the time he retrieved his coat from the pile on Candy's bed and made it to the elevator, he was in time to catch a glimpse of a cinnamon-colored head as the door closed with an inexorable whoosh.

"Damn!" He looked around for the fire stairs, then remembered Candy's apartment was on the twenty-eighth floor. He jabbed the elevator button and stood in barely restrained fury until it came.

Of course, he thought angrily as he sprinted

out of the building to see a cab just pulling away, she just got the last cab! He was sure Ginny was in it. It was the way his luck was running.

He started the long walk down to Ginny's apartment, then stopped abruptly after he had gone half a block. Why was he chasing after her? Why should she run away from him as if he all of a sudden sported fangs and hairy palms? What had he done, after all? Nothing. Not a single, solitary damn thing! Whatever was eating Ginny was her problem, damn it. Why should he go after her, begging to be let into her apartment, her life? He had some pride, damn it. She could explain her crazy behavior to him and beg his pardon for running away like that.

He looked around, wondering what to do with himself when he saw a familiar figure walking some distance in front of him. It looked like Mack, the hot dog vendor in front of the Met. Josh hurried to catch up, when he saw the man go into a bar. In profile, Josh was sure it was Mack.

The bar was nondescript, one of the neighborhood saloons that hadn't yet been crowded out by trendy singles' spots or tapas bars in Manhattan. Josh seemed to recall that Mack had said he lived in Brooklyn. Curious as always, Josh pulled open the door and stepped into the enclosed vestibule of the bar. The inner door was frosted, and as Josh pushed it open, he was conscious of a mild shiver of apprehension. Absurd. What could possibly happen to him if he stopped for a beer at a perfectly respectable bar?

If the man he had seen was Mack, he could take the opportunity to talk to him about the letter Mack had received from Eddie Tyrone, his supplier. It was a very strange letter, and as he read it, Josh had the feeling that it had been written in code. Eddie and possibly Mack could understand it, but Josh couldn't.

The bar was dark, with dim yellow lights and dark wood chairs and tables. The bar itself was polished to a sheen, and glasses glittered in shelves along the mirrored wall behind it, but the customers in the booths were indistinct. Josh made his way toward the bar, taking a look around as he went. There was no sign of the man he thought was Mack.

Josh mentally shrugged and ordered a beer from the bored-looking bartender. Glancing into the mirror behind the bar, he saw the image of a dark-haired man in a leather raincoat hunched over a table, talking to someone whose back was to the bar. Without seeming to do so, Josh tried to overhear their conversation and get a look at the dark man's companion. Their voices were too low to hear until the dark man got up and threw a bill down on the table.

"Eddie is not going to be happy, Mack," the man said, his voice menacing. "The letter means just what it says. Be a good boy—" He broke off as Josh came up behind him.

"Hello, Mack, I wondered whether it was you," Josh said in what he hoped was a jovial tone. He extended his hand. "Good to see you again."

The dark man looked Josh over, taking in his tweed topcoat and chinos. *A tourist. A jerk. No problem.* His opinion couldn't have been clearer if he'd spoken aloud. "So, Mack," he said with a smile like a knife, "introduce me to your friend. How did you two happen to meet? Over hot dogs at the museum?" A chuckle escaped.

"Sure," Mack said. "This here's Josh Havilland from Florida, Mikey. Josh, this is Mike Scanlon."

"Hello, Mike." Josh hoped he sounded like a dumb tourist. Antennae, sharpened by years examining witnesses, were shouting "red alert" in his head. Even so, his insatiable curiosity about people and their lives got the better of him. "Are you a friend of Eddie's, too?"

The silence was deafening. Mike Scanlon stared at him out of red-rimmed eyes the color of dirty ice. "You know Eddie?" he said.

"No, we've never met." Josh was hoping for a break, some indication of what Mike Scanlon was doing with Mack. Whatever it was, Josh was sure it wasn't having a friendly beer.

"Then how—" Mike broke off and turned to Mack. "Did you tell this guy about Eddie?" The menace in his voice was clear.

"No, no Mikey, I didn't. Of course, I didn't." Sweat was beginning to bead Mack's brow.

"Then how come he knows about him?"

Josh intervened. "I think his name came up when I was buying a hot dog from Mack one day. Someone came up and said something about him to Mack. I wasn't really paying attention, but I guess the name stuck with me."

Mike stared at him for a moment. Then he turned and, without another word, walked away from the table and vanished out the door.

"Thanks a lot, shyster," said Mack, his face white with fury or fear. "That'll get back to Eddie in about twenty seconds. And then I'm probably a dead man. Or at least a retired man. And I didn't want to retire."

"So why do you have to?"

"Are all you guys this dumb in Indiana? Or is it just you and Dan Quayle?"

"It's the water. Gets the smartest of us in the end. Even Marilyn Quayle succumbs now and then." Josh tried out a smile and got back a scowl.

"Well, now Eddie's gonna think that I'm meetin'

with you after I hear from him and that you're
some kind of cop or, worse, some kind of a lawyer."

"So Eddie will think I'm working for you?"

"Yeah. And that's the last thing I need anyone
to know." Mack glanced around furtively. "I'd
better get out of here."

"Wait a minute. The damage has been done.
You might as well tell me what's going on. Why
do you think Eddie's going to be mad enough to
kill you just because you've been talking to a
lawyer?"

Mack spread his hands in a gesture Josh had
come to recognize as a New Yorker's unspoken
version of "if-you-have-to-ask-you're-too-dumb-
to-understand-the-answer."

"Just explain. You're good at what you do.
Why does Eddie want you to move?"

Mack sighed. He had clearly decided to humor
the idiot from out of town. "Because Eddie's
cousin needs a job, and naturally it has to be a
good job, which means that he gets the best location Eddie can find for him. Which is my location. And I get to retire, willingly or otherwise."

"Do you have any agreement with Eddie, other
than the verbal one he talks about in his letter?"
Josh asked.

"Nah. You don't ask Eddie to put it in writing."

"Demonstrates a lack of trust?"

"You got it."

"Well, can we negotiate with Eddie? Offer to take on a helper?" Josh tapped the table with the edge of his coaster. "There must be some way for you to keep your location."

"Why must there be a way?" Mack asked, his round, potato face screwed up in a cynical smile. "Just because it would be nicer? No fairy-tale endings here, pal. Sorry."

Josh shook his head. "We don't need fairy tales. It's a simple business problem, with no hard feelings on either side. That kind of thing is solvable. There's no reason why it can't be negotiated."

"Sure there is. The reason is because Eddie doesn't want to negotiate. If he negotiates with me, what's to prevent everybody he does business with from wantin' to change his deal? Eddie's a businessman. He can't afford that."

"You're missing the point. You don't negotiate so you win and the other guy loses. You negotiate so you *both* win."

"You're crazy, and I can't sit around here anymore listenin' to you yak. I gotta get home and tell Marie that the gravy train just stopped to let us off." Mack stood up. "You get the check, It's the least you can do." He strode out of the bar without a backward glance.

Josh sat for a few minutes without moving, frowning in concentration. There had to be an answer, a way for Mack to keep his business. All it took was a little imaginative lawyering. Slowly, he rose and paid the check. All the way home in the cab he had hailed outside the bar, Josh thought about Mack's problems. He could think of at least a couple of possible solutions. Maybe, he thought before he could censor himself, he could talk to Ginny about them. No, not Ginny, not anymore. Denis.

As he turned out the light in his bedroom half an hour later, with Denis still not home, Josh smiled a little wryly. A good, tough legal problem seemed to be the only thing that could keep Ginny out of his thoughts for more than two minutes at a stretch.

He must have gone at least five minutes.

Denis had seen his father and Ginny leave the party separately. His first thought was that he needed to talk over this new wrinkle with Lisa.

Why Lisa? he asked himself. She didn't know any more about the dynamics of Josh and Ginny's relationship than he did. Talking it over with her hadn't led to any big revelations.

And she was so annoying. The way she looked with that riot of red hair, the way she dressed in those outlandish clothes, her attitude toward the law, and lawyers—all of this was so irritating that Denis couldn't understand why he even considered talking to her.

Because she's twice as smart and five times as savvy as any other woman you know. And she doesn't give a damn how she looks.

But he was wrong. Lisa cared. She tried very hard to annoy him. She spent much more time than she wanted to admit planning her outfits when she was to meet Denis. The more outrageous the better. Yet, despite her need to annoy him, Lisa never wore anything unbecoming. She would irritate him, but she didn't want him to avoid her.

Why not? she asked herself.

Herself didn't answer.

In order to avoid thinking about Denis and the party everyone but Lisa had gone to the night before, Lisa called her mother on Sunday morning.

Ginny sounded more subdued than usual. Yes, the party had been fun. Denis's model friend was delightful. Ginny had met several interesting people, including an agent who wanted to represent Josh in his new career.

"What new career?" Lisa wanted to know.

"He's going to be a model," Ginny said. She didn't sound as amused as Lisa was by the idea.

"Great!" Lisa said. She couldn't help laughing. "Old Denis will be horrified! His father, a lawyer, on the cover of *Playgirl*. I love it."

"Don't be silly, Lisa. It's nothing like that. They want him to be the Indigo Man."

Even Lisa had heard of that forthcoming ad campaign. The company had already begun running teaser ads. "Good Lord, Momma, do you realize what that means? The man is going to be the newest media darling. He may even get a half hour of fame instead of the usual fifteen minutes!"

"Right." Ginny sounded tired, almost dispirited. Except that she never sounded dispirited. "That's what everybody at the party was saying."

"Where did he take you afterward to celebrate?"

"Nowhere."

"Oh, a cozy evening just the two of you." Lisa thought she could picture the scene.

"No. I went home alone. I didn't feel well."

Lisa was instantly concerned. "Momma, are you all right? I tell you what. I'll pick up some oranges and be right over and squeeze you a nice big glass. You can lounge around and do the *Times* crossword and sip Vitamin C. How does that sound?"

"Don't fuss, Lisa." Ginny's voice was sharp. "I'm fine. A good night's sleep was all I needed."

"Well, if you're sure . . ."

"I am. I have to run now. I'll call you later."

"Okay, Momma, be sure to call me."

Lisa hung up the phone and gnawed at a fingernail while she considered the advisability of calling Denis. While she detested the man, she had to admit that she enjoyed crossing swords with him. When he wasn't being totally obnoxious, that was.

Would Denis really have any idea what was eating her mother? Probably. He had been at the party last night with all the gorgeous models. The one Lisa hadn't gone to. Not that she'd wanted to go, of course. All those beautiful, shallow creatures, and Denis drooling all over them. It was a recipe for indigestion.

She wouldn't call him, Lisa decided at last. She would wait until he called her. Something must have happened last night, and Denis would want her slant on it. Of course he would.

She would wait.

Fifteen

Ginny sipped a second cup of coffee and found her mind still circling around the same unacceptable truth: she had behaved like an eighteen-carat idiot last night.

Running away from problems was not Ginny McDougall's way of dealing with them. Starting out life on her own at nineteen with a baby in her arms had been a recipe for reality. There is nothing in the world more real than an infant. Lisa had been so tiny, with a scrunched-up face like a wise old monkey. Beautiful and awesome as she had seemed to her mother, Lisa didn't know how hard things were for them. She knew what she needed, though, and she had put her trust in Ginny to provide those things for her.

Lisa had been Ginny's life for years. Between her job and Lisa, Ginny sometimes went to bed as soon as Lisa fell sleep, so exhausted she couldn't eat dinner. Taking care of Lisa, making sure Lisa had the best that Ginny could possibly give her, had been Ginny's goal and she had been single-minded in pursuing it.

For years, there hadn't been much more to her life. Ginny hadn't regretted it for a moment. As she sat now, thinking of those early years, she smiled. She hadn't been interested in a relationship with a man. She hadn't even been interested in dating. Friendships with colleagues at work and with other mothers at the playground and the park bench had been enough.

But what about now? she asked herself. What was her reason *now* for refusing to get involved?

What are you running away from? She could almost hear Josh's voice asking her the question. And what could she say in response?

I'm running away from you. The answer slid fully formed into her mind and Ginny knew it was true. She was running away from Josh Havilland, and she had been from the first moment she saw him. The moment he had kissed her.

Her thoughts still in a jumble, Ginny curled her feet up under her. She had never been afraid to face things before. So what was the matter with her now? Nothing, she told herself firmly. She would simply deal with her feelings for Josh the same way she had every other obstacle in her life.

Obstacle?

Did she really think Josh was an obstacle? To

what? Her peaceful, quiet, totally predictable life? Was that the kind of life she had?

Yes. Until Josh came along. Was that the life she wanted to go back to? Ginny had never faced these thoughts before, yet they felt curiously familiar, as if they had swum just below the level of her consciousness. She had been unwilling to allow them to surface.

Right now she wanted someone to talk to. Maybe someone else could make sense of what seemed hopelessly tangled and contradictory to her. But she didn't have a close friend to whom she could unburden herself. Ginny's friends turned to her when they were in trouble, and she was glad to help them. She was the rock, the one everyone else leaned on. But Ginny herself never asked for help.

The phone rang. Never in her life had Ginny had a premonition, but she knew who was at the other end of the telephone line.

"Hello, Josh."

"Ginny, don't move. Don't you dare run away again. I'll be over in fifteen minutes and this time, lady, we're going to talk." Josh's voice. Josh's anger.

Could that be her answer?

"All right."

"All right? You'll be there?" Suspicion laced his voice.

"Yes." There was a pause which Josh didn't fill. "I'll be waiting," she said softly and hung up.

He was there in ten minutes. "You must have flown," Ginny said when he entered.

Josh was clearly not in the mood for small talk. His hands were jammed into the pockets of his jeans and his shoulders were hunched. "Just what the hell were you doing last night?" he demanded, his voice harsh. "Was there a reason you ran out of that party like the hounds of hell were after you? Or did you just suddenly decide you couldn't stand to be near me another minute?" He stood, frowning like a hanging judge, waiting for her answer.

Ginny took a deep breath. "I don't know. I think it was the modeling job."

Whatever he had expected, it clearly wasn't that. "For God's sake, Ginny, there is no modeling job!"

"But I heard—"

"You heard a half-assed kind of offer! But you didn't hear me accept, did you? I have no intention of spending my sunset years as some kind of geriatric pinup. Instead of running away like a frightened virgin, you could have asked me whether I was going to accept that so-called job offer."

Josh's anger added to Ginny's confusion. "I—I'm sorry."

"I don't want an apology. I want an answer."

"Well, I don't have one."

"Then who the hell does?"

"Look, I'm sorry. Strike that," she added when his already thunderous look grew even blacker. "I'm not sorry. I—I have a problem, and I have trouble talking about it . . ."

"Ginny, this is me you're talking to. Josh. I know you. I care for you. So just take a deep breath and tell me what the hell's wrong." His frown lightened a little. Ginny knew that her distress was probably visible. She could feel tears clog the back of her throat and sting behind her eyes. Josh sat down in one of the club chairs and waited silently for her to speak. Ginny sank into the corner of the couch.

"I spent last night thinking about it," she said after a long pause. "I don't know what's wrong, but it probably is my husband. He—he was a model." She had trouble getting the words out. Ginny wasn't looking at Josh. Her eyes were fixed on her hands.

Josh didn't speak. Ginny waited, hoping he'd say something, but he left her to tell him what she wanted him to know. She took a deep breath and plunged into her past. "I think that I fell in love with Brian because he had such wonderful, black Irish looks. Tall, dark, and handsome, just like the cliché. And he had that proverbial Irish charm, too. Every woman from ten to ninety fell for Brian. And I was no exception."

Josh sat expressionless, but inwardly he cursed himself. It was absurd to be jealous of a man who'd been dead for a quarter of a century, but he was.

Ginny continued. "I was amazed when he told me he loved me and I was in heaven when he asked me to marry him. I felt as if I was the chosen one. Out of all the girls who adored him, I was the one he wanted to spend his life with. Of course, I said yes, and we were married as soon as I graduated from high school. I was just a few weeks past my eighteenth birthday."

He really didn't want to hear this. "Can we skip the honeymoon?"

Ginny flinched at his sarcastic tone. "There wasn't one. Brian didn't have a job, so we didn't have enough money for a honeymoon. My secretarial job in Newark was the only money we had. We were married for a year and in that whole time, Brian never held a job for longer than a few weeks."

She looked up at Josh at last and he could see the pain in her eyes. "I got pregnant almost immediately. It was a difficult pregnancy. I was sick all the time and Brian was . . ."

She searched for a word to describe her husband, but Josh knew what he'd call Brian McDougall: a selfish bastard who didn't deserve a woman like Ginny. He didn't want to hear any more about her handsome, charming idiot of a husband.

"It's all right, Ginny, you don't need to say any more." The hurt he felt for her closed his throat and his voice sounded rusty.

"There's only a little more," she said drearily. "You might as well hear it all. When I was six months pregnant, I developed edema in my legs and had to go into the hospital for a few days. Brian didn't come for me that evening to take me to the hospital, so I told the woman in the next apartment where I was going and she said she'd tell Brian. He didn't come to see me until the next afternoon, and then he had a hangover."

"I hope you told him where he could go if he treated you that way," Josh said. How could anyone treat Ginny that way? She deserved the best a man could give her. He remembered Marian when she was expecting Denis. Josh had cooked, cleaned, carried her up and down stairs, and her pregnancy hadn't been difficult. He had wanted to treat her that way. She was his wife, carrying his child. She deserved all the consideration and care he could give her.

"No," Ginny said, "I didn't. I couldn't give him an ultimatum. It seemed to me as if it must be my fault. Something I had done. Maybe he didn't want to be around me because I looked so unattractive. Anyway, where would I go? My mother had told me that once I was married I was a grown-up and I shouldn't come running home to momma when things went wrong."

Damn her mother, too, Josh thought. Didn't Ginny have anyone she could turn to? Anyone who would help her, talk to her husband for her?

"Besides, I thought that once the baby came things would be different. Brian would want to take care of us, and he'd get a job and not stay out nights drinking with the boys. At least, I thought he was drinking with the boys."

"Is that what he told you?" Josh didn't want to hear any of this. It made him angrier than he could remember being in a very long time. Angry at a dead man, furious that a man he'd never met had treated his wife so badly all those years ago. It would be crazy if Ginny weren't still living with the fear and sense of inadequacy that dead man had given her.

"Yes. And I believed him, because I wanted to. Then, when I was eight and a half months along, Brian came to me and told me he was leaving. He didn't want a baby. He wanted to be young and have a good time. Marriage had been a mistake. Particularly marriage to me, because I'd changed. I wasn't any fun, and never wanted to do anything anymore. And with the baby he could tell things were just going to get worse."

Ginny took a ragged breath. She looked at Josh. He couldn't take any more. He got up and went over to her. He sat down on the couch next to her. He wanted to hold her, but something in her face held him back. "Ginny, don't go on with all this."

She shook her head. "No. 'All this' is the reason I don't want to—" Tears clogged her voice. She cleared her throat and went on. "I've never talked about this. I told Lisa that her father died in a car crash just before she was born. I never told her he'd already left us and was driving drunk with another woman in the car when he was killed. And after it happened, and Brian was buried, it was as if he'd never existed. Lisa doesn't look anything like him; I burned all the pictures I had of him. And for all this time I never really thought about him. I just shoved him out of my mind."

"Until now?"

"Yes. Until now. Un—until you." Ginny's voice was so low he leaned toward her to hear it.

"Why me? There must have been lots of men in the years since Brian died."

"No, not many. Lisa and working were all I had time for at first. When she got older I did date some, of course, but never seriously. I was never interested in a serious relationship."

"Because of Lisa?"

"Up to now, I always thought I never met anyone because I only had time for Lisa," Ginny said. "But Lisa's been grown a long time now. And maybe she would have wanted me to find someone and remarry when she was young, so she could have a father. But I never even considered it."

She was silent for a minute. Josh wanted to tell her that it didn't matter, he didn't need to hear all this. But he knew that she needed to say it, so he would listen, no matter how painful it was for both of them.

Ginny continued. "Now I know it wasn't because of Lisa, and how much she needed me. It's because I couldn't love anyone but Lisa enough. I didn't love Brian enough. I thought I did. I thought that my love would be strong enough to make him change. That once he knew how much I cared, he'd give up drinking and get a job and—"

"Ginny, for God's sake, you're not blaming yourself for not being able to save him, are you?"

"Of course not," she said quickly. She paused, frowning in thought, then said, "Yes, I guess I am. I should have been able to save him from his bad habits and bad friends. I should have made a home and a marriage he wanted to come home to. But I didn't." Tears sounded in her voice.

"You couldn't," Josh said. "Ginny, listen to me. You couldn't save the man's soul. You couldn't help him if he didn't want to be helped!"

Ginny was silent. Then she said, "I might as well finish it. One of the jobs Brian had toward the end was as a model for television ads. Nothing big. Just local stuff. But he thought it was his big chance to get out of Newark and go to New York and be somebody. The girl he was with when he died," she said calmly, though her voice shook a little, "was a model.

"That's why I came unglued last night. It's always bothered me that you're so handsome and that everyone likes you. But I never stopped to wonder why until that man told me last night that you were going to be the Indigo Man. Then somehow it all seemed to blur together—you and Brian and modeling and looks, and I had to get out of there. I'm sorry if I embarrassed you."

Ginny's face was empty of expression. Now that she had explained, she clearly expected him to thank her kindly and leave, never to return. Well, she would just have to learn that Josh Havilland didn't handle relationships that way. Nothing was too much trouble for him when he cared for someone as much as he did for Ginny.

"You didn't embarrass me, you worried me. And you made me very angry because you wouldn't talk to me."

"Yes, I know. I didn't know how to tell you, I didn't even know *what* to tell you until I'd had a chance to think about it. But you can see now that I'm just not the one for you." She shook her head and the sun lit her cinnamon-colored hair with dancing gold-and-bronze lights. "I've just got too much baggage."

"No," Josh said. "I don't see that at all. You're not the same scared girl you were when Brian left you. You're strong, Ginny, and loving. And lovable."

The ghost of a smile played on her lips for a moment. "It's nice of you to say so. But I haven't grown up all that much if I still run like a scared gazelle when a handsome man comes along."

Josh smiled down at her. "You didn't start to run until that guy offered me the job as the Ink Man."

"The Indigo Man." Ginny corrected him absently.

"Whatever. Before that, you seemed to be able to bear to have me around. Up to a point."

"Yes, that's it exactly." Ginny looked at Josh earnestly, as if pleading with him to understand. "I just can't ever go beyond . . . a certain point." Ginny blushed. Josh felt his heart expand at least one size. He wouldn't have thought there was a female in Manhattan over the age of two who blushed. But Ginny did.

"Ginny, do you honestly think there's something wrong with you because you don't want to go to bed with me? There's nothing wrong with you. It could be that I just don't appeal to you, period. But I don't think that's it. You respond to me, I've felt it. You know it. You just aren't ready yet, that's all."

"You don't understand. I've never been ready. I've never—" She stopped abruptly and closed her lips firmly.

"What have you never, Ginny?" Josh asked, his voice soft. "Never wanted to make love? Never enjoyed it?"

"Yes." The single word told Josh everything he needed to know.

"There's nothing wrong with you. It's not so unusual, Ginny. And it's not your fault, either. Did Brian tell you it was?"

"Yes." There it was again. That soft, defeated sound as Ginny admitted to what she thought was abject failure. Josh found his fists clenching. That selfish bastard had left his wife with a baby and an enduring sense of inadequacy. Brian McDougall was—

Josh stopped himself. Right now, Ginny was the only one who mattered. "Well, he was wrong.

And so was anybody else who made you feel that way." Josh felt sweat trickle down his spine. Being understanding was hard work when it involved thinking of Ginny making love to another man. "If you don't mind, I'd rather talk about us. Brian's dead. I'm not."

"I know." There was a faint smile in Ginny's voice for the first time. It gave Josh hope.

"What I can't understand is why you think I'm like Brian." That was what stuck in his craw. He understood that Ginny felt so vulnerable that she wanted to avoid sex entirely rather than risk humiliation and failure. But that didn't explain why she thought he was cut from the same cloth as her husband.

"I don't think you're like Brian."

"Then why the dramatic exit last night? Why would you think I'd turn into Mr. Hyde if I ever got in front of a camera?"

Ginny looked at him, her hazel eyes huge with pain. "I didn't think that. I didn't think anything. It's not a question of thinking. I just reacted." She reached out for him, but drew her hand back before she touched him.

"I don't think you're being honest, Ginny. If you didn't think I was like Brian, why did you wait to do your disappearing act until the exact moment when you found out I could model?" Josh was determined to get to the bottom of

Ginny's feelings. "As long as I was a lawyer, you let me stick around, even though you were pretty discouraging, when it came to anything but friendship." Josh smiled for a moment. "Except when we kissed. But the minute you thought I might fall prey to the lure of fame and my face on the side of a bus, you ran out."

"I guess I've always thought that all handsome men are narcissists to some degree," Ginny said flatly. "For some reason the only men I've ever been attracted to have been really good-looking. And sooner or later they all turned out to love themselves much more than they loved me or anyone else."

Josh could feel his anger heating up. "I see. It's not enough that I remind you of your rotten husband, now I fall into a category called 'handsome men' and we're *all* self-absorbed jerks."

"I didn't say *you* were a self-absorbed jerk."

"Not in so many words, but that's what you meant. Admit it, you've already judged me and found me guilty on the basis of some stupid idea of what I look like." Josh spit the words out. "Talk about shallow! Who cares what I look like? It doesn't govern my behavior. I don't tell you that all redheads are hot-tempered so I don't like you, even though you've never lost your temper! What's wrong with you?"

"Nothing's wrong with me! And I do lose my

temper." Ginny got to her feet. Her fists were clenched and her eyes had gone from dark with pain to bright with anger. "I just know what I know. Beautiful people are inherently selfish and narcissistic."

"God in heaven, Ginny, first I'm handsome and now you think I'm beautiful? Beautiful!" Josh ran his hand through his hair.

Ginny had to smile. Josh looked revolted, as if he'd never been so insulted in his life. "All right," she said in a soothing voice, "I didn't mean it. I take it back. You're not beautiful."

"Well, thank you for that," he responded. "Now you can tell me why you think anybody who reminds you of your husband is automatically someone you can't love."

"Who's talking about love?"

"We are."

"I'm not," Ginny said flatly. "But even if I were, it's not that simple or that stupid. Brian wasn't the only one. Before him there was my father."

Ginny looked at Josh. She didn't want to spend the day talking about her past. Especially with Josh. "Let's go to the top of the Empire State Building today. It's clear. We should be able to see for miles."

"Your father." Josh was relentless.

Ginny shrugged, assuming an air of unconcern.

"He was a handsome man, a real charmer. He was also an alcoholic. A falling-down drunk. The talk of the town. When he was sober, he was the nicest person in the world. The kind of man who never met a stranger. Warm, charming, funny. Like you."

Josh was silent for what seemed like an hour. "Did he run out on you and your mother?"

"Not exactly. He left the neighborhood bar one night. It was payday and he was drunk, as usual. Only this time the street was icy and he slipped and cracked his head on the curb. He died the next day. The doctor told my mother that he would have gone soon anyway. His liver was shot."

"I'm sorry, Ginny." His voice was soft, but with an undertone of steel. "And I can see why you might possibly feel that I had a certain amount to prove to you when we first met. But you know me now. Do you really think that I'd turn into an alcoholic or run out on you? Is that what you think of me?"

"No, of course not."

"Then why are you punishing me for what Brian and your father did?"

Ginny tried to think. It had been so clear last night, but now, with Josh here and his eyes smiling at her, she couldn't think. "You make it sound crazy," she complained.

"*I* make it sound crazy? I don't think I'm the one who sounds crazy around here, Ginny. I wouldn't judge anyone on the basis of what they look like. But you lump me in with your husband and your father, who each seemed to have a problem with alcohol and responsibility. And all because you think we were all handsome. I think I'm fairer than that."

"Well, bully for you, Mr. Fair and Impartial."

Josh's mouth tightened. "I like to think I am. Patient, too. But I can run out of patience, Ginny, with something as crazy as this."

Ginny ran her hand through her hair. "I don't want it to end like this, with you angry at me, thinking I'm stupid."

Josh smiled and held out his hand. "Who said anything about ending anything? Not me. Nothing's over between us, Ginny. Not by a long shot."

Sixteen

Ginny looked at Josh's hand and slowly reached over to clasp it. "You're not leaving?"

"Not until you kick me out."

Ginny smiled. "Good. So. What shall we do today? How about the Empire State Building? You haven't been there yet, have you?"

Josh exerted a little pressure and pulled her over so she sat next to him on the couch. "I don't think so, Ginny."

"Why not? It's a marvelous example of Art Deco. You should see the lobby. It's—"

"I don't want to see the sights today, Ginny." He grinned at her. "Do you always turn into a tour guide when things get too intense for you?"

She smiled, but didn't meet his eyes. "Yes. A trip to the movies or the zoo usually worked when Lisa was small and started asking about her father. You're a little harder to convince."

"Right now, I'm impossible to convince. Come here, Ginny and relax. We're about to have lesson one."

"Lesson one?" She sounded doubtful.

"Yes, lesson one of the Havilland-McDougall courtship ritual."

"Courtship?" Ginny's eyes were startled. "You did say courtship?"

"That's right. I'm going to court you, and you're going to respond, and court me right back. Then I respond to you, and it keeps going like that. Like a bird's mating dance."

"Oh. I don't think I know how to do that."

"Neither do I. We're going to make it up as we go along. Just think of all those specials on the Discovery Channel."

"But I thought I explained that I didn't have much"—she searched for a word—"experience."

"This may come as a surprise to you, but I don't either." Josh saw the disbelief in her face and smiled ruefully. "Look, for a minute, try to just see *me,* not some aging stud, okay? Go with your instincts."

"I always see you," Ginny objected. "And you *are* a stud," she added with a grin. "And my instincts are to run like a rabbit."

Josh sighed and shook his head. "Then, that's lesson one. Beauty is in the eye of the beholder. Not everybody sees what you see, Ginny. The rest of us just see an ordinary guy. That's what all the women in Elgin seemed to see, just good old Josh Havilland. First baseman of the high school team, Marian's husband and widower, the lawyer with the office next door to the First National Bank on Main Street. Nothing exotic or strange. Or sexy. And certainly not threatening."

"I don't think you're threatening, Josh." Ginny said, trying to be as honest as she could. "You're much too nice to be a threat."

"Then why do you run, or change the subject, or pull away when I do this?" Josh's long fingers cupped her chin and Ginny felt the same frisson through her body that Josh's touch always evoked.

Gently, he framed her face in both his hands and smiled down into her eyes. Ginny met his gaze. "I'm not running now, Josh," she whispered.

With excruciating slowness, he lowered his head and took her lips with his. It was a gentle kiss. Josh's lips explored hers and Ginny responded with unforced tenderness and welcome. She put her hands on his shoulders and felt their width and solidity as if for the first time.

In many ways it was a first kiss, for Ginny knew now that her past had colored her view of Josh. Now she was seeing him for the first time without the distorting prism of her relationship with Brian.

Or at least she was trying. For all its tenderness, Josh's kiss was exciting. Ginny could feel the thrill of his touch like a gentle stroke along her nerves and skin. Josh had power but it was leashed, held in check. With a tiny movement, she pressed closer to him. His arms swept around her and held her close, yet she didn't feel constrained. She could slip out of his arms at any time, but she didn't want to. Being held by Josh felt wonderful, and Ginny gave into it, leaning into his hard frame and opening her mouth under his.

"Oh, Ginny, Ginny." His husky whisper sent the blood coursing through her veins as fast as lightning. "Come closer, love." His hand swept down her back and curved around her hips. With a slight tug, he pulled her into his lap and held her cradled there. "Come closer."

"Yes," she sighed.

It was all he needed to hear. His hand began the same sort of gentle caress across her breasts and down to the curve of her waist that he had given to the long line of her back. Ginny could feel herself ignite inside. She was melting at the core of her being, and it was Josh who was making it happen. His hands cupped her breasts and Ginny could feel them tighten and grow heavy at his touch.

He turned her in his arms and once again his lips met hers. This time his tongue swept over the seam of her lips and as she opened to him, he growled softly, deep in his throat. His hand moved under the soft wool of her sweater to touch her skin.

For a moment, Ginny remained still, frozen in his arms. This was too much. When this happened, an alarm went off in her head. This was what Brian would do, fast and hard, before he told her to get undressed and then dived into her. This touch brought pain in its wake. Afterward, Brian would roll over onto his back, light a cigarette, and tell her how inadequate she was, how much better all the other girls did it.

Josh felt her freeze and looked down into her wide, frightened eyes. So this was it, the point at which Brian McDougall had made his wife afraid and ashamed. Slowly, Josh let her go, though his body was screaming for more. The fleeting touch he had of her warm satin skin had aroused him more than he could ever remember.

He hadn't felt this way since he was sixteen years old. Not even then, in fact. Marian had never aroused him as Ginny had done from their first meeting, their first kiss. Josh took a deep, shuddering breath.

"What's wrong, sweetheart?" He thought he knew, but he needed her to tell him. "What didn't you like?"

"Nothing. It's not that. It's me." Josh had never heard that note in her voice before. She sounded like a small, weak creature. That wasn't the

Ginny he knew, the feisty lady who spoke up before a group of high-powered Columbia lawyers. It wasn't Lisa's mother, Denis's supercompetent assistant, or the warm shoulder Anita DiBenedetto cried on. He thought that probably this Ginny was one only Brian McDougall would recognize.

"What do you mean, it's you, Ginny? Are you afraid of me?"

"No, no. I mean . . . I just . . ." *Stop babbling,* she told herself sternly. *You're behaving like a Victorian heroine! Say what you have to say.* "It has always hurt." She decided she should clarify that idea. "Sex, that is. Always." She waited for the sky to fall.

"Well," Josh spoke slowly as if feeling his way, "I think that's something that we can fix. If you want to."

Ginny tried to collect her thoughts. She had never had this kind of conversation with a man before. "I would like to. Because I've never understood what all the fuss was about. For me the earth never moved, and it never rained stars and planets. Sex always seemed very—" She searched for a word in her limited vocabulary on the subject.

"Painful?" Josh asked gently.

"Yes, but also embarrassing." Ginny decided that total honesty was the only way she would get out of this conversation with her dignity and her self-esteem intact. Josh wanted to know how she felt. If she stammered and blushed and said nothing, she would deserve to be left high and dry, like the Victorian heroines she had compared herself to. Literally. Permanently.

"You know, love," Josh's voice was still gentle and slightly hesitant, "there is a school of thought that says that there are no bad violins, only clumsy violinists?"

Ginny had to smile. "I've never really thought of myself as a stringed instrument."

Josh smiled back, and she felt that they shared a moment of delight in the human comedy. "I never thought of you that way either. And I don't think I'm Itzhak Perlman."

Josh put his arm casually around her. She welcomed the touch. "I just meant that the person who knows more has more responsibility to see that their partner is—" He searched unsuccessfully for a word.

"Comfortable?"

"I'd aim a little higher than that."

"Pleased?"

"Happy," he said, "at least. Preferably, delighted. Hopefully, with you, ecstatic."

"That's a heavy responsibility."

"Well," he said, then stopped. He tried to think of a way to say that any man, at any age, who left his lover feeling as Ginny did was the next thing to a gorilla. On second thought, that really was a slur on our close animal relatives, he thought.

"Look, love, the best pleasure is shared. With someone you know and trust it happens naturally. When it doesn't, there's something wrong with someone. And, in this case, it wasn't you."

"How do you know?" she said. "You weren't there. I was awful. Cold and—"

"The hell with talk." He pulled her into his arms and kissed her. Her lips opened and welcomed his invasion. She felt warm and melting again, as she had before. Only this time, when his hands began to explore and fondle she didn't hear the alarm bell. This time she heard Josh growl deep in his throat and felt the delicious shivers start deep within her, as if her blood were bubbling like champagne.

He broke the kiss at last, but only so he could kiss her eyelids and the corners of her mouth. His lips found the sensitive spot behind her ear and he kissed her there, while his warm breath played along her neck. Ginny sighed and drifted along with the tide of her feeling.

"You can kiss back, if you want to." Josh's seductive voice seemed to drift in her ear. "I don't object."

With a soft sound of pleasure, Ginny turned her head and kissed his nose. "You have a beautiful nose. Very classic. Greek. Fifth century B.C."

He groaned. "Will you stop that?"

"Kissing you? I thought you said—"

"Not the kissing. The classic fifth century nose stuff. It makes me feel like a jerk."

"But it's true." Ginny pulled his head down and worried his ear lobe with tiny nips. "Your ear looks wonderful. Tastes good, too."

"Just promise you won't make any comparisons about other body parts, when we get to them." His laughter was warm against her skin.

Josh's hands again reached under her sweater, touching the sensitive skin of her midriff. Ginny stiffened for a moment, then, with a shuddering sigh, relaxed against him.

"You okay?" he asked.

"Umm."

"Is that an umm-yes or an umm-no?"

"Shut up." Ginny turned in his arms and put her hands on his shoulders. Her mouth met his in a series of light, teasing, butterfly kisses.

"Thanks for explaining it to me," he murmured between kisses. " 'Shut up' is really helpful."

"Good. Glad I could clarify it." Ginny's arms went up around his neck. "So do it. Otherwise, I can't kiss you."

Ginny wondered how much farther she could

go before she heard the alarm bell in her head
and froze once again. Then she thought she really did hear another bell. What was he doing
to her?

"Umm," she said again. "You're making bells
ring."

"I wish I could take credit," he murmured into
her hair, "but it's your phone."

Slowly, as if coming up for air, Ginny pulled
away from Josh. The warmth and laughter didn't
fade. She looked into his eyes and saw a light
she wasn't sure she recognized. She ran her
hands through her hair, then shook her head as
if to clear it and reached for the phone. "He—
hello." Her voice was husky.

"Momma, hi. Sorry to bother you again. You
weren't busy, were you?"

Earlier that morning, Denis had watched with
a worried frown as his father left for Ginny's.
The old man was really steaming. Denis couldn't
remember the last time his father had been so
upset. Usually, Josh Havilland was totally unflap-
pable. Around Elgin, his calm demeanor had
been a byword. Once he had talked a suicidal
client down off a silo she'd threatened to jump
from. Now, look at him. Denis took another sip
of double espresso and tried to reassure himself.

Sure, Dad liked Ginny. Who didn't like Ginny? Ginny was wonderful, a combination secretary, associate lawyer, and mother hen all rolled into one. But to go chasing after Ginny McDougall as if she were some glamorous model was ridiculous. Wasn't it?

Denis told himself that he was only thinking of Ginny as he looked up Lisa McDougall's number in his well-thumbed address book. He didn't want Ginny to be hurt when Dad went back to Florida, as he was going to do all too soon. Well, he amended his thought, not really *too* soon. At least not for Denis.

Josh had been the hit of the party last night, and Denis admitted to a little bit of surprise. He just never thought of his father as attractive to women, and he certainly never thought of him as a sex symbol. Good lord, what was the world coming to when a man of almost sixty was considered for a huge modeling contract?

Sighing, Denis decided he needed to speak to Lisa. Maybe she'd have some ideas. It would be worth putting up with her obnoxious behavior if she did.

Lisa answered on the first ring. "Oh," she said when Denis identified himself, "it's you. What do you want?"

"Gracious as always, Lisa. A graduate of the

Sean Penn School of Charm and Tact, I see. I'm terribly happy to be talking to you, too."

"Sorry." She sounded completely unrepentant. "I was expecting another call."

"Oh." For some reason he didn't want to identify, Denis was annoyed. Why should Lisa be waiting for some man to call her? And he was sure it was a man. Denis didn't have a date for this afternoon. Or this evening. He was doing Lisa a favor by calling her. One she clearly didn't appreciate. "Well," he said, "I think things are heating up between our parents."

"Damn! Why can't that man leave my poor mother alone?"

" 'That man' just happens to be my father!"

"I know. That's exactly why I worry."

"Thanks a lot. Everyone else looks at my father and sees Jimmy Stewart. You see Bela Lugosi with oily hair and fangs. I'll have you know that Andiamo Cosmetics wants my dad to be the Indigo Man."

"The what?" Lisa was grinning. Denis was so easy to dupe. He decided Lisa was unaware of the biggest news in advertising.

"The Indigo Man. You must live under a rock. Everyone knows about the search for the spokesman for the new men's cologne!"

"Your father is going to pose for some cologne advertisements?" Lisa's tone made it sound as if

Josh were going to pose nude in Rockefeller Center at high noon.

"No, he's decided—"

But Lisa wasn't listening. "I knew it, I knew it! Now we really have to get her away from him! He's just as shallow and obsessed with petty and meaningless good looks as you are. Why can't Momma see it?"

"I beg your pardon?" Denis's tone was freezing. "What are you babbling about? What's wrong with appreciating beauty wherever one finds it?"

"Not a thing, except you seem to find it exclusively in pneumatic blondes with body measurements bigger than their IQs."

Denis took a deep breath. Why did this woman make him so angry? He didn't give a damn what she thought of him, or his father. Did he?

"This isn't getting us anywhere. We need to come up with something that will keep them apart. I'll order Ginny back to work and you—"

"You'll *what?* Order my mother back to work? Just who do you think you are? *I'll* convince *my* mother to quit that miserable job with you and work for someone who'll appreciate her." Lisa's voice was choked with fury.

"Hey, back off! I appreciate Ginny. She's like a mother to me!" The instant the words were out of his mouth, Denis knew he'd made a mistake. He could swear he felt the telephone line vibrate with the force of Lisa's passionate anger. Then she surprised him. After a long pause, she spoke in a calm and considered tone.

"That is the most revolting thing you have ever said. The idea of you as my brother—" Denis could almost hear her shudder.

"You make it sound like I'm Charles Manson," he complained, his feelings inexplicably hurt by her total rejection. "Your mother likes me," he added defensively.

"Charles Manson *might* be worse. It is just barely possible. And I'm aware that Momma likes you. Probably someone liked Charles Manson. Everyone has a blind spot. You're Momma's."

"I keep trying to keep this conversation on track but you just want to dwell on my flaws. Alleged flaws. Look, my father's over at your mother's. While you're busy insulting me—"

"I think it was Charles Manson I insulted."

"—insulting me, they are doing—whatever older people do when they're together." Denis didn't want to think about what his father and his assistant might be doing together. Playing chess, perhaps. Or gin rummy. Discussing Tolstoy's theory of history.

"Okay," said Lisa, "we'll go into a temporary crisis mode. I'll call Momma and get her to come over. Maybe she can stay for dinner. My stove's newer than hers, so she won't mind cooking."

"Wow, Lisa, that sounds like an offer no sane person could refuse. 'Come over and cook for me!' What devotion! You're a daughter in a million."

"Shut up. Call me tomorrow at work and we can share intelligence." Lisa hung up without saying good-bye.

She took a deep breath. That annoying, superior, stuffy—*lawyer!* Why did she let him get under her skin? Why did she bother teasing him, by pretending she didn't know about his father's job offer. Denis wasn't worth the energy she spent hating him. Thinking about how hateful he was. Seeing his hateful face in her dreams. Once she got her mother out of the clutches of Josh Havilland, Lisa assured herself that she would be happy if she never saw his hateful son again in her entire life!

She picked up the phone, punched her mother's number, and waited for Ginny to pick up. Her mother's voice sounded a little strange. As if she'd been interrupted in the middle of something.

"Momma, hi. Sorry to bother you again. You weren't busy, were you?"

"Well, yes, honey, as a matter of fact I am a little . . . busy right now." Was there a hint of laughter in Ginny's voice?

"Oh. I was hoping we could go to a movie or a museum or something this afternoon." Lisa tried to make her offer sound exciting. "Then this evening, I thought maybe you'd come over here for dinner and I'd cook for you."

Ginny didn't answer for a minute. Then she said, "Lisa, is something wrong? Are you sure you're feeling well?"

"Of course. I'm feeling wonderful. Why? What made you ask?"

"I don't know. It's just that you've never cooked a meal in your life that I'm aware of. I wondered what the occasion was."

"Don't be silly, Momma. Of course, I can cook. I've cooked for you before. Haven't I?"

Ginny smiled into the telephone. "No, darling, you haven't. Hang on just a minute and I'll see—" She felt Josh move closer.

He whispered in her ear. "Lisa wants you for dinner?" When Ginny nodded, he added, "Can I come, too?"

"Lisa? I have a . . . kind of a date this evening. With Josh. But, if you'd like, we can both come." Josh whispered something else and Ginny added, "Josh says Denis isn't doing anything tonight. Maybe you could ask him, too."

"Oh, no, Momma," Lisa said hurriedly. "I wanted it to be just the two of us. Like the old days."

"That sounds wonderful, darling, but in that case we'll have to make it some other time."

"Oh, all right, bring him along. It's better than having you two alone togeth—I mean I wouldn't want Josh to be alone."

"Are you going to call Denis?" Ginny was still trying to get Lisa and Denis to stand each other's company. It was like trying to mix oil and water. She hoped that if they saw each other often enough, their mutual antipathy would wear off.

"If you want." Lisa sounded glum all of a sudden, all her sparkle gone. "I'll see you around seven. Okay, Momma?"

"Fine. Are you sure you don't want me to come early and help you cook?" Ginny wasn't sure what Lisa, who as far as Ginny knew was no more of a cook than she was, would come up with. Left to her own devices, Lisa would probably spoil an ambitious feast and send out for Chinese.

"No, really. I can cook. And if I ruin it, we can always send out for Chinese. Bye."

Ginny put down the phone and turned to Josh with a smile. "I don't know what I'm letting you in for. As far as I know, Lisa's culinary talents begin and end with pouring cereal."

"Let's not worry about dinner now." Josh

pulled her into his arms. "Let's get back to the subject at hand."

He leaned back, pulling Ginny closer, and began to kiss her again.

Seventeen

"How does the Empire State Building sound now?" Ginny asked as she drew back to look at Josh's face. "Good preparation for a jolly evening with our warring children?"

"What is it about the Empire State Building that entrances you, sweet? I'm beginning to think you have an edifice complex."

"Bad joke, Joshua." Ginny swatted at him playfully. "I just meant I thought that we'd have trouble behaving like ordinary, everyday friends tonight if we spend the rest of the afternoon . . . you know."

"Making love?" Josh smiled down at her. "That's a very ordinary, everyday activity, Ginny." Ginny remained silent. "Well, we could just keep going until we get to a natural stopping place and then think about going somewhere and doing something else."

Ginny felt his hands begin to press her body closer to his. Then they reached under her sweater and began to caress her back. It seemed less dangerous than when he had done the same thing to her breasts. Somehow she could relax. Well, not exactly relax, she thought as her heart started to pound. Josh's hands had reached the clasp of her bra.

He paused. "I'm having a little trouble here, sweetheart. I hate to sort of pause and ask permission every time I do something new. But I'd hate it worse to have you kick me out because I do something you don't like or aren't ready for." His hands had stopped their gentle but exciting movement. "Can we talk about this?"

Ginny opened her eyes. Whatever happened to unspoken signals, she wondered.

Welcome to the nineties, Virginia.

"I guess we can talk." She looked at Josh. "I never have talked to a man about love or sex or . . . anything like that." To her disgust, she could feel the telltale heat of a blush steal up her cheeks. "Oh, God," she blurted out, "I'm blushing!"

"I know. I think it's kind of cute."

"Cute? At my age?" Ginny shook her head. "Well, I think maybe we'd better try to engage in a dialogue, like college kids are supposed to do nowadays." She paused. "The problem is that I don't know what to say."

Josh cleared his throat. "I don't either. I guess we're both doing things now that we haven't before. I feel, a little foolish myself. Falling in love at fifty-eight makes me feel that way. But I like it."

Ginny sat absolutely still. Surely she had misunderstood. "Falling in love?" she asked carefully. She was afraid even to say the words. Afraid he meant them. Afraid he didn't.

"I probably shouldn't tell you all this so soon. But things seem to move pretty fast in this town." He sounded worried.

"No, I think we should be honest with each other. I'd tell you how I feel but I don't seem to know. I know I've never felt this way before."

"Oh. I guess that means you aren't mad about me and happy that I've chosen you over all the other women who adore me."

"What?" Had he gone crazy? Josh had never said anything as conceited as that before. "Where does that come from?"

"It's how you said you felt when Brian asked you to marry him. As if you'd been chosen from all the other girls," Josh explained. "I guess you don't feel that way about me."

"Josh, I'm not eighteen. Do you feel as if you've just crowned me Queen of the May with your love?"

"No. But I didn't feel that way when I was eighteen and the star of our baseball team."

"That's because you're not conceited. But I'll

bet Marian felt you had." Ginny grinned at him. "And I am pleased that the Indigo Man says he cares for me and not Ivana Trump."

"Was Brian conceited?" Josh asked.

Ginny looked hard at him. "I thought we were going to talk about us. About how we feel. What we want to do. How did Brian get mixed up in this?"

Josh looked down at his hand as it mechanically smoothed the crease in his jeans. "I'm jealous," he said after a long pause.

"You have no reason to be." Ginny put her hand over his where it rested on his thigh. "Absolutely none. Brian was childish and unloving and sometimes mean. Once he even hit me. And I was childish, too. I should never have married as young as I did. I would say it was all a mistake except that out of it I got Lisa."

Josh gave her a wry smile. "Thank you for pandering to my adolescent fears. It's dumb, but they're very real."

"I know. I told you, I'm afraid of how you look."

"Don't explain. I know it's these long, curved canine teeth that drip blood at midnight."

"That, too, but mostly the Greek nose," Ginny said, her smile turning to laughter as he pretended to loom over her, vampire style.

"Enough, woman. Let's get serious here. How

far can I go with you before you freeze up on me? Can we discuss this seriously?"

Ginny tried to smile and shook her head. "I won't know until we get there. But I'm feeling better about it. How will I know when we've gone so far you can't stop?"

Josh looked at her. "I can always stop. I will always stop if you ask me to."

"I don't want you to give up in disgust if it takes too long."

"I don't want you to give in because you think you're taking too long."

Ginny sighed. The man was too good to be true. She told him so.

"Don't be silly. You deserve the best anyone can give you, Ginny. You should never settle for less." He took her hands in both of his. "I have a feeling we may have talked ourselves out of the mood. I hadn't figured on that. Do you still want to go to the top of the Empire State Building?"

Ginny thought. She wanted to be sure of her answer, but she had never been asked the question before. Brian had given her no choice. She was supposed to meet his demands, not make her own. In the few other sexual encounters she had had over the years since, any discussion had been hurried and embarrassed. Now here was the most attractive man she had ever met asking her to decide what she wanted to do. Did she want to explore the sexual possibilities of their relationship? Would she rather remove herself temporarily from the risks of physical intimacy?

She could feel Josh looking at her. When she dared to look back at him, he was smiling. "Don't agonize, Ginny. Let's go sight-seeing." When she frowned, he added, "Pleasure postponed is doubled. We'll come back here after dinner, and meantime we can think about what we'll do."

"Yes," Ginny said. "I think you'll need something to think about besides Lisa's cooking. We can keep our minds on higher things."

"I was thinking more of lower things."

"Get your coat."

Lisa's apartment looked just the way Denis would have imagined it. He looked around in disapproval he didn't bother to hide. It was small, just an all-purpose living-room-dining-room-library-office and a tiny bedroom, where he left his coat.

The entire place vibrated with color. There were chairs and a couch slipcovered in prints reminiscent of Matisse paintings, pillows in a rainbow of colors and patterns, curtains and walls in clear bright shades.

"I think I need sunglasses in here," he said crossly. But Lisa could see he was smiling.

"Good. I like to have sunshine around me."

"I thought so. I noticed the posters of Cancún and Cozumel in your bedroom. Have you been often?"

"Never," Lisa said. She untied her apron and threw it over the back of a slat-backed chair that had a bright calico cushion on the seat. "That's why I have the posters. They remind me of sunshine. In the summer I put up Telluride and Gstaad."

"To keep you cool," Denis guessed.

"Exactly." Lisa leaned forward and Denis got a whiff of some light, sophisticated scent that made him think of dimly lit cafés and seduction. He jerked his mind back to what Lisa was saying. "I told Momma and your father to come a half hour later than you, so we could have some time to talk."

"I'm not sure what we can do. I'm afraid things have gotten really serious. Dad went racing out of the apartment this morning looking like thunder. Then, when he got back around six he said they'd gone to the Empire State Building. But he had this big, shi—happy grin on his face. I'm not sure what they were doing, but I don't think they went sight-seeing."

"Oh, lord." Lisa closed her eyes for a moment.

When she opened them, Denis could see that they were bright with what looked like tears. "I really don't want Momma to get hurt. My father was a bum. One of Momma's friends from Jersey told me about him when I was in high school. She said she wanted me not to make the same mistakes Momma did. Anyway, Momma doesn't know I know, so don't you dare ever say a word, Denis. If you do, I'll slit your tongue."

"Ah, the real Lisa surfaces again. For a minute there I thought you might really have turned into a conventional daughter worried about her mother."

"I *am* worried about my mother. And you are one of the reasons why. Working for a yuppie jerk like you has taken its toll. Otherwise, I'm sure she would never get involved with your father. Excuse me, I have to see about the white peppercorn sauce." With a haughty look at her guest, she stalked out to the kitchen.

The sauce was fine. She looked around the kitchen. The rest of dinner was ready to cook. Swordfish on the broiler pan, asparagus washed and peeled. New potatoes scrubbed and ready for steaming. Dessert in the refrigerator. She had taken a cooking video out of the library and was carefully following the directions for what the video chef assured her would be a simple but delicious dinner for four.

Planning and organization were second nature

to Lisa, but something perverse made her hide the fact from Denis Havilland behind brilliant colors and outrageous remarks. If she were more ordinary, he might approve of her.

When she went back to the living room, Denis was sitting lost in thought. "Everything's under control. Would you like something to drink? I have celery and carrot juice, apple and prune juice, and natural spring water." She also had Chardonnay and Pinot Noir, but she couldn't resist bringing that horrified look to Denis's face.

Denis closed his eyes, clearly wishing he were anywhere else in the world. Should she take pity on him? She shouldn't, but she would. "How about a nice glass of domestic Chardonnay?"

He opened his eyes and looked at her suspiciously. "Why the prune and carrot juice come-on? You know I'm not a health nut."

"I just thought you might be changing to more healthful habits now that you're not young anymore," Lisa said sweetly.

Denis glared at her. "The Chardonnay, Lisa, please. I'll need it if we're going to play these childish games of yours."

"Yes, Grandpa." Lisa got the wine from the cooler. She poured two glasses and handed him one.

"I'm worried, Lisa." Denis sounded serious. "I don't want either Ginny or Dad hurt. But he lives in Florida and she has been a New Yorker for over twenty years. He's a small-town lawyer and she's— Anyway, you get the idea. I think they're just infatuated, but I'm not sure. Can we wait until they come to their senses?"

"I don't think so. You know older people. They get swept away. Taken in by insurance salesmen and stock manipulators. They just don't think straight anymore. I worry that they'll up and decide someday to get married."

"Married?" Denis sounded as if they might decide to go over Niagara Falls in a barrel.

"Yes, married. What's wrong with you? People get married every day. It's not some dreadful pagan ritual, you know. Nobody sacrifices virgins, or even goats. Just a nice little ceremony."

"Women always say that." Denis swallowed his whole glassful of wine at a gulp.

"Do all men like you think like you?" Lisa asked scornfully.

"What do you mean? Who are 'all men like me'?" He eyed her suspiciously.

Lisa took his glass and poured him more wine. She wasn't sure of her answer. *Good-looking, successful, self-absorbed.* "All middle-aged professional—"

"Middle-aged! For God's sake, Lisa, I'm only thirty-three!"

Lisa hid a smile. She had certainly hit a nerve.

"I'm sorry, Denis. I guess it's all the late hours that makes you look a little older."

"*Older!* You—I—" Lisa couldn't hide the smile any longer. Denis saw it and scowled.

So the little brat was giving him a hard time, was she? She dared to tease Denis Havilland, the youngest partner at Sanderson and Smith? She presumed to make the fair-haired boy of Wall Street the butt of her childish humor?

Two can play that game, Lisa. He managed to give her a patronizing smile. "I keep forgetting how juvenile—I mean, how *young* you are. Even this dreary little apartment. You use those bright, Crayola colors. Just like a playroom. So right for you, Lisa, at your stage of development."

Lisa sprang to her feet as if on springs. She put her hands on her hips and glared down at him through slitted eyes. She opened her mouth to reply.

The doorbell rang.

For a moment, Lisa continued to stare at him. The doorbell rang again. Lisa closed her mouth and turned on her heel. She stalked to the door and flung it open.

"Momma!" She threw her arms around her mother. "I'm so glad to see you!"

"I'm glad to see you, too, dear. But it's only been a few days, and I'm not leaving for the Antarctic." Lisa continued to hold Ginny in a death grip. "Do you think you could let me go and say 'hello' to Josh? Lisa?"

With a deep sigh, Lisa let go of Ginny and looked, unsmiling, at Josh. "Hi," she said, and turned her back on him. "Come on in, Momma. You, too," she added as a curt afterthought.

Josh grinned at Ginny and Denis noticed that she grinned right back at him. Denis frowned and Lisa fussed over her mother. Josh ambled into the living room and sat down beside Denis.

"Hi, son. What did you do this afternoon? You look kind of tired."

"Tired? I'm not tired. I can keep going till four in the morning if I have to, and get up at seven and do it again the next day." Denis's voice rose and he pounded his fist on the arm of the couch.

"Okay, son, I'm sorry. I know you're tireless in the pursuit of justice for the rich and famous. Didn't mean to insult you." Josh held up his hand. "Tell me where I can get some of that wine. And let me get you some more. You seem a little tense."

"Dad, if you had to spend a half hour alone with Lisa McDougall, you'd be a little tense. And annoyed. And frustrated. And—" Denis stopped suddenly, as if he realized that he sounded more than just a little tense, annoyed, and frustrated. He sounded furious.

"It's nice to see you looking so well, Denis." Ginny's tone was formal but her eyes sparkled. She had overheard the exchange with Josh. Denis didn't admit to negative emotions very often. Lisa had annoyed and frustrated him in only a half hour and he admitted it. Lisa had her mother's admiration.

"Dinner will be ready in a while. I have to check on some things. Talk among yourselves; I won't give you a topic," Lisa said as she disappeared into the kitchen.

"I'll see if I can help," Ginny said.

"Sit down here and talk to us." Josh held out his hand. "I don't think you can help." He smiled into her eyes and Ginny felt her heart turn over. She couldn't help thinking about what might happen afterward. It lent a certain spice and sense of adventure to the evening.

Denis looked at the two of them. "Ginny," he said, "I want you to come back to work on Monday."

"The temps aren't working out?"

"The last one was so dumb I had to write her a memo on how to answer the telephone. And she still couldn't get it right. 'Hi, there. This is Denis's office. Like whatcha want, huh?' " Denis was a clever mimic. Ginny could recognize the hapless temp from the steno pool.

"I hope you haven't been too impossible to

work with, Denis," Ginny said. "It takes a long time to train women for the pool. We don't like to lose them because lawyers can't behave like gentlemen."

Lisa came back into the room and sat down cross-legged on one of the floor cushions. "Gentlemen lawyers. Isn't that an oxymoron, Momma?"

"Lisa, behave yourself."

Denis ignored her. "Ginny, you wound me." He pressed his hand to his heart. "I am the nicest little gentleman you could hope to meet. I can't help it if I am surrounded by fools and idiots when you're not there. So, please consider your vacation over and come back to the office."

Josh twirled the wine in his glass, and spoke without looking at Denis. "I understood that looking after me was an assignment for Ginny, not her vacation. I wouldn't like to think that she's losing her time off just to show me the sights."

"Of course not. I wouldn't dream of charging Ginny with vacation. I just meant that going to the Empire State Building with you isn't exactly like going to a deposition with me. Not as much fun, I mean."

"I'll be there, Denis. Don't worry." Ginny was surprised at how little she wanted to go back to work. Ordinarily, she spent the second week of her vacation wishing she were back at the office.

She had tried trips to national parks, cruises to Caribbean islands, flights to Florida resorts, but nothing had held her interest compared to the fascinating world of the law. Now she found that she was going to miss Josh and their excursions, meeting people with Josh, talking with Josh.

Josh. She was going to miss Josh.

"Will you be going back to Florida soon, Dad?"

"Are you trying to get rid of me, son?"

"No, no, of course not. It just sort of came to mind. With Ginny going back to work, that is."

"Maybe I'll go to work, too."

"What!" said Denis

"Where?" said Ginny. Then she thought she knew. He couldn't resist the pull of money and fame. He was going to agree to be the Indigo Man. The depth of her sense of betrayal overwhelmed her. He had told her, insisted that he wasn't going to—

"I've been thinking about applying for admission to the New York bar," Josh said calmly. "Nothing to get so excited about, you two."

"But Dad, you don't want to stay with me while you apply. Do you?" Denis looked horrified. "Not that I'd mind, of course, but I just think—I mean, you're retired. Living in Florida. Happy."

"I'm retired, living in Florida, miserable," Josh replied.

"But, Dad, I thought . . ." Denis trailed off. "Miserable?"

"Okay, maybe not miserable. Bored. Terminally bored."

"So, what you're telling me is that you are going to leave Florida and move here, to New York City to work. And to live. Right here in Manhattan." Denis sounded more depressed with every word. "Close to me."

"Well, you could look at it like that," Josh said with a grin. "I'm glad you're so enthusiastic about it. But my real reason, aside from working where I think I might be needed, is not to be near you, son, though I know that has to disappoint you. I really want to spend more time seeing the city. I have such a wonderful guide, I think it would be foolish to leave before I've seen everything."

Denis and Lisa exchanged a look. "I'd better see about dinner," Lisa said. "I could use some help, Denis."

Ginny started to get up. *"Denis,* I said I could use some help," Lisa repeated with heavy emphasis.

Denis still looked blank, but when Lisa came over and gripped his arm he rose and went with her. Josh went over to Ginny, where she sat in one of Lisa's brightly covered chairs, and perched on the arm of her chair.

"I hope you realize that our helpful children are out in the kitchen plotting how to break us up." Ginny didn't answer. She looked up at Josh and he could see the worried look in her eyes. "Ginny? What's the matter?"

"You just made up your mind? You didn't say anything—I mean, no input from anyone. You just decided you'd like to spend more time with me—"

"I don't understand why you're upset. It's not just you. It's Sylvia and Mack the hot dog vendor and Hervé—all of them could use some legal help and they can't seem to get it. They're either too rich for Legal Aid or too poor for big-time help, or they're stuck with a system they don't understand and don't trust." He reached over and put his arm around her. "I think maybe what New York needs is a small-town lawyer."

Ginny shook her head. "You have a perfect right to do whatever you want wherever you want, Josh." Her voice was tight, as if she were forcing the words out. "I just thought if I was supposed to be a part of your plans, you might want to mention them to me."

"You're being sarcastic," Josh said. "You're mad at me." He bent over and kissed her. She smelled so wonderful. Powder and lipstick and just a maddening hint of that elusive perfume of hers. "I'm sorry. I haven't decided anything yet. And I planned to talk to you about it."

"Oh, really? When?" Ginny looked into his eyes and he could read the hurt in her clear, green gaze.

"Tomorrow morning." He smiled at her. "Now, what do you suppose those two are cooking up in there—besides dinner?"

Ginny gave him a small smile. "I shudder to think. I imagine you're going to be asked to go home with Denis so you can fix a faucet or discuss Hervé's case. And Lisa will think of a reason why she has to come home with me."

Josh ran his hand over the smooth expanse of her shoulder. "And if that fails, Denis will tell you he has an early morning meeting tomorrow at six-thirty in Queens."

Ginny's soft laughter wrapped itself around his heart. She wasn't going to pull away. She would allow herself to be close, to care. She could laugh at her daughter's fears. Maybe someday soon she could laugh at her own.

In the kitchen, a furious dialogue was going on in angry whispers.

"What else can I do, Lisa? I'll call the damn meeting. I'll call it for six if you think that will help. But, damn it, she's going to know something funny's going on when no one else shows up for it!"

"Well, okay! All right, just tell me what that great legal brain of yours can think of that's better." Lisa stuck her chin out and waved a wooden spoon at him.

"Tell Ginny you're afraid to be alone in this high crime area and want to sleep at her place."

Lisa rolled her eyes in disbelief. "You must think my mother's an idiot. I'm twenty-four years old. I don't need my mommy to get a night's sleep on Ninety-fourth and Second."

"Well, excuse me, Miss Independence." Denis's voice escalated to a low rumble. "I didn't realize that big, grown-up girls didn't need their mothers anymore. I thought you loved Ginny." Denis watched as a hurt look flashed in Lisa's eyes for a moment before they flashed with angry sparks again.

"Don't you talk to me about loving your parents, Denis Havilland." Lisa, too, had forgotten to whisper. "The way you practically asked your father to leave town! Like you couldn't stand to have him around." She felt a shiver when Denis fixed her with his blue eyes, so much like his father's. He looked sad and hurt. Of course, it was just a trick. Lawyers could fake that sort of thing so easily.

"I do love my father, but I think we would both prefer to live on our own," Denis said.

Lisa turned to the stove and slid the pan of

fish under the broiler. She set the timer and turned on the burner under the asparagus. With a deft movement, she started the microwave.

"In other words, you want him back in Florida so he doesn't cramp your style." She turned her back on him and bent over the broiler.

She was as obnoxious as she had been when he first met her, but Denis had to admit to himself that she had a cute bottom. In fact, if you didn't mind the poisonous tongue, she was good-looking. Almost pretty. "You know, Lisa, you're not bad-looking."

She stood up slowly and faced him. "Gosh, Den, I'd return the compliment. If you'd paid me one, that is." She gave him an acid smile.

"Look, Ms. McDougall, I was trying to be nice."

"Yeah? Well, you might as well give up the attempt. You couldn't be nice if you worked at it day and night for the rest of your life!"

"Wait a minute! You've done nothing but give me grief all evening. I didn't ask to come here this evening. There are people who would love to have me for dinner."

"Really?" Lisa advanced on him, her hands on her hips and her chin stuck out at an aggressive angle. "Right now, *I'd* like to have you for dinner. Stuffed and roasted."

Her eyes were spitting green fire, and her

cheeks were flushed. Denis couldn't help but notice her chest was rising and falling rapidly with the force of her anger. It was a beautiful chest. "Stuffed?" He took a step toward her.

"Stuffed! With an apple in your mouth!"

It was the last straw. Denis had had all he could take. "Damn you!" he said through clenched teeth. Then he reached out and dragged her into his arms. "You—" He captured her mouth with his, and the world exploded. Never before had Denis felt anything like the earthquake that rocked him when his lips met Lisa McDougall's. He was vaguely aware that he was being kissed very thoroughly in return, and that two strong, feminine arms were twined around his neck. He tightened his hold on her waist and opened his mouth over hers.

The sudden cessation of hostilities in the kitchen, made Ginny and Josh uneasy. The silence was deafening.

"Do you think they've killed each other?" Ginny whispered. "There are knives in there."

Josh grinned at her. "Let's go see."

Hand in hand they tiptoed to the kitchen door. Ginny let out a gasp, but before the couple locked in each other's arms could react, Josh pulled her away to the tiny bedroom where their coats were. "I think we should leave and let those two work it out on their own. Don't you?" said Josh as he helped Ginny on with her coat.

"Where are we going?" Ginny's mind was still on the scene in the kitchen. She'd heard of love-hate relationships but this looked more like lust-loathing.

"We're going to your apartment and see what we can cook up." Josh opened the door. "Come on. Voyeurism is not a nice trait in parents."

Ginny took his hand. "I hope you know what we're doing."

"I do, Ginny, I promise." He bent toward her and gave her nose a feather-light kiss. "Come with me and I'll show you."

Eighteen

They took a cab to Ginny's apartment. They rode in silence. Ginny might have preferred to talk, but Josh preferred to spend the time kissing her. After a few moments, Ginny relaxed and enjoyed it. She'd never done it before, but by the time the cab arrived at Twenty-third Street, she was looking forward to doing it again soon.

Tucking his arm around her waist, Josh walked toward the door. "That was the nicest cab ride I've ever had," he said.

"Me, too."

"I thought I detected some enthusiasm on your part." He held the outside door for Ginny to enter. A dark figure rose from the corner of the vestibule. Instinctively, Josh pushed Ginny behind him.

"Ms. McDougall? Ginny?" Under the light, Ginny could see that it was a young man. He looked familiar, but his face was drawn and he huddled inside his duffel coat.

Suddenly, it came to her. "Gray. Grayson Harcourt. It's Anita's fiancé, Josh."

"Hello," Josh managed. He was not feeling as welcoming as Ginny sounded. There seemed to be a cosmic plot to prevent them from ever making love. He took a closer look at Gray and saw the desperation in his eyes. "Why don't you come up with us to Ginny's and tell us what's wrong."

Ginny smiled at him, pleased that he wanted to help Gray, too. They rode the elevator in silence. When they entered the apartment, Ginny snapped on some lights and took a good look at Gray. He looked even more drawn and desperate than he had seemed under the dim hall lights.

"Sit down," she said, and went to the cherry table that served as a bar. "Let me get you a brandy, Gray. You look as if you could use it."

Gray sat in the first chair he came to and sank down into it as if exhausted. He took the brandy and looked at it but made no move to drink. "I don't know why I've come to you. I couldn't think of anyone——" He held his hands out helplessly. "Anita's gone."

"Gone?" Ginny took one of his hands in hers. It was icy. "Where? What happened?"

"I left her at her apartment Friday night at about eleven. We'd gone to a movie. Decided

NEVER TOO LATE 267

to just forget our problems for a couple of hours. She said she'd rather I didn't stay. She didn't say why. I thought something was wrong, but I left." Gray swallowed convulsively. "I should never have left her! When I called Saturday morning, I got the answering machine. That went on all Saturday. Then this morning, there was a new message on her machine. She had gone home for the weekend and didn't want to talk to me."

"She just went home for the weekend?"

"That's what she said on the machine. But when I tried to call her father's place I was told that she wasn't there." Gray ran his hands through his hair. "I'm worried. More than worried. Scared. Afraid that her father is putting some kind of pressure on her to break off with me."

"I'll be back in my office tomorrow, Gray. If Anita isn't there, I'll check into it." Ginny patted his hand gently. "I'm sure her father won't refuse to speak to me."

"I don't know why he hates me. I've only met him once, and that was for five minutes out in front of Anita's apartment."

Josh looked at the two figures locked together in some kind of parent-child bonding. Ginny reached out to everyone. What had she said about her father? That he never met a stranger? She seemed to have inherited the trait.

"I'm going to go check your kitchen, Ginny," he said softly, smiling at her. "I think all three of us could use something to eat."

She looked up at him and smiled. He could feel the warmth of it from across the room. "Thanks. I think so, too. When did you eat last, Gray?"

"I don't know. Anyway, I'm not hungry." He shook off the distraction. "I can't eat. I have to find out about Anita. don't know what her father will do if he finds out about—"

"About the baby?" Ginny said softly.

"Yeah. Anita said she told you. I don't even know how I feel about the baby anymore. At first I wanted it so much. I thought we could get married right away, down at City Hall and then again for our families, if her father didn't disown her."

"What about your family? How do they feel about Anita?"

Gray took a long sip of his brandy. "They like her." He seemed to want to leave it at that. Ginny said nothing. "Well, they don't know about the baby. I don't know how they'll feel then. They're pretty 1950s about stuff like that."

"But they like Anita?"

"Of course. How could anyone not like her?" He sounded as if Ginny had criticized his love.

"I agree with you, Gray. I think she's a lovely girl. I just wanted to know what the situation was. I'm glad your family isn't being difficult."

"No, it's just Anita's father. And I don't know what's wrong. I can't believe he really intends for her to marry some guy he picked out years ago. It just doesn't make sense."

"Not to us, maybe, but the DiBenedettos have different values." Ginny patted his hand, then rose to her feet. "I'll go see what's holding up our dinner."

Josh came out of the kitchen. "Dinner will be ready in fifteen minutes."

"What have you managed to scrounge up out of my refrigerator?" Ginny said. She was a little embarrassed that Josh knew the meager contents of her kitchen. But then, he didn't seem to mind.

"A cheese soufflé, and toast. Sorry there isn't a vegetable or salad. You're going to get beriberi if you don't get some greens in your diet, Ginny."

"Fuss, fuss, fuss." Ginny shook her head. "Come and sit down while the soufflé puffs or breathes or whatever it does. I promise I'll eat a salad for lunch tomorrow."

Josh sat on the couch and looked over at Gray. "I wish you could tell us a little more about what happened on Friday. I take it you two usually spend the weekend together. Is that right?"

"Yes." Gray looked a little embarrassed. "Usually at my place. But Anita said she had an upset stomach and wanted to be by herself."

"Do you think she was telling you the truth?" Josh was cross-examining the witness.

"I thought so then. She looked a little pale. But now I don't know. She might have wanted to go out to her father's on Saturday, but I don't know why she wouldn't tell me about it."

"Would you have insisted on going with her?"

"I would have tried, but she can be very stubborn where her family's concerned. She really tries to keep me from meeting any of them." Gray shook his head. "I just don't know what to think anymore."

Josh glanced at his watch and thought for a minute. "Why don't you try calling her again, Gray? She may be back in the city by now. It's almost nine o'clock."

Ginny and Josh waited in silence while Gray dialed. "Anita?" he said at last. "Are you okay? You're sure? I'd like to come by for a few—"

Gray waited impatiently for Anita to finish speaking. "I won't stay long. I just want to be sure you're— Okay, I understand. I'll call you tomorrow. Good-night, darling."

When he hung up, Gray turned away from Ginny and Josh and walked stiffly to the window. Ginny thought he moved as if he were in pain. He stood for a long, silent moment, looking out at the city lights below. At last he turned around and tried to smile. It was a dismal failure. Ginny reached out toward him, but he backed away. "I've imposed on you enough, Ms. McDougall. I'll just go home now and get a good night's sleep. Thanks for taking me in." He extended his hand.

Ginny took it and said, "I'd really like you to stay for dinner, Gray."

"I can't. Thanks anyway, Ms. McDougall. Please, look after Anita at work, would you? Her father's at her place now and she says she's fine, but she doesn't sound like it."

"Of course, and I'll call you if there's any reason for concern." Ginny smiled, trying to reassure him.

"Thanks. Anita and I owe you a lot."

"Don't be silly. Anita's my friend. Try not to worry too much, Gray."

He reached a hand to Josh who clasped it warmly. "Good luck, son. Keep us up to date on your plans. We want to be at your wedding."

Gray's smile looked forced. He hurriedly grabbed his coat and headed out the door.

After the door closed behind Gray, they sat in a silence neither wanted to break. When the oven timer went off, Josh rose and dropped a quick kiss on Ginny's hair. "Dinner's about ready. If madam wishes to aid the program, she may set the table."

Dinner looked delicious. The soufflé was tall and puffy. Ginny had seen such wonders in restaurants, but she had never known anyone who made them. "It's gorgeous," she breathed. "How can you bear to cut into it?"

"Because I'm starving. And if I don't, it will start to fall when it begins to cool."

"I wish you hadn't told me that. I like to think it was all magic."

"Nope. Just hot air. Sit down, Ginny, and let's see if it tastes magical."

Ginny took a bite. "Ambrosia. You must teach me how to make it before you leave."

"Before I leave?" Josh raised an eyebrow and gave her a hard look. "Am I leaving? I thought I was staying for a while. Though neither you nor Denis seems particularly happy about it."

Ginny could see the hurt underneath the dry tone. "I didn't mean it the way it sounded."

"How many ways could you mean it? It seems pretty clear to me."

"You weren't planning to stay in New York just to be near me, were you?" Ginny was sure the answer was "no."

"You're certainly one of the big reasons I'd like to stay," Josh said, confounding her. "Do you want me to leave?"

"No." Ginny hadn't meant to say it so quickly and baldly. But she meant it. "No, I don't want you to leave. I'd like you to stay in New York. But I don't want you to stay because of me."

Josh looked at her and shook his head slowly. "Explain, please."

"I don't want to feel responsible for your happiness. I mean, if things don't work out for us, I don't want to feel that I've ruined your life."

"You can't ruin it, Ginny. You can only enhance it. Don't you know that?"

"But if you stay here and then we stop seeing each other—"

"Why would we do that?" Josh sounded genuinely curious.

"Well, because you might not want to see me anymore." Why was he asking these questions? Didn't he know that people broke up, divorced, moved away, got bored? "A million things might happen."

"Nothing's going to happen, Ginny. I'm not going to be disappointed in you."

A hint of mischief lurked in her smile. "And are you so sure that I'll never get tired of you?"

"Absolutely." He grinned at her. "You just haven't let me demonstrate my many exciting moods and moves. Once I do, you'll never let me go."

"Oh, yeah? What makes you so sure of your manly charms? I might get very tired of a good-looking lawyer who can cook."

"It's my noncooking skills I want to demonstrate." He grinned at her again. "Finish your soufflé, sweetheart. I beat a lot of egg whites a long time for this masterpiece."

Ginny wasn't sure what she wanted to say, so she took refuge in her dinner. The soufflé was delicious, but she found she couldn't really taste it. She was anticipating, with a jumpy stomach and a beating heart, what would come after dinner. Those sexy, nerve-tingling smiles Josh was sending her way were just the appetizer, she knew. She wondered what the main course would be. Her? And if she were, would she be enough for him? After all, Josh was the Indigo Man, or he could be.

". . . don't you think so?" Josh's voice suddenly broke in on her chattering thoughts.

"What? I'm sorry, I guess my mind was wandering." Ginny gave him a weak smile.

Josh got up and came around to Ginny's chair. "Come on, stop worrying." Gently, he lifted her to her feet. "Your dinner's cold and you're not eating anyway. If I were the sensitive type, I'd be wounded."

"But you are sensitive," Ginny said softly, as she put her hands on his shoulders. "And I loved dinner. It's just—"

"Ginny, relax. Nothing's going to happen that you don't want to happen." His hands ran up and down her back, tracing random patterns that soothed and excited at the same time.

"I know. But that's the problem. I don't know what I want. I've never really wanted something like this before."

Josh buried his nose in her hair, hiding a smile. She did want him, whether she knew it yet or not. "Your hair smells wonderful. You always smell wonderful. Is it a special perfume?"

"Chanel. I guess that's special."

"Umm. It's great." He drew back slightly, and stood, looking down into her face. "Ginny, sweetheart, don't worry. You're supposed to be slightly apprehensive and a lot excited. Remember high school?"

"Dimly."

"Well, return with me now to those thrilling days of yesteryear," he said.

"Heigh-ho, Silver." She closed her eyes. "Okay. I'm there. Where are you?"

"Right in front of you. Asking you for a dance. Remember? I told you I'd meet you at the sock hop after the pep rally."

"Good lord, Joshua, you really do go back to the fifties." She smiled and laid her cheek on his shoulder. "What are they playing?"

"Tony Bennett, I think. Yes, it's 'Rags to Riches.' My favorite." He began to hum softly and swung Ginny tightly against him. "Close your eyes, and just enjoy the feeling."

He must have hypnotized her, Ginny thought later. She was back in some fantasy of high school, where she and Josh met and found each other, went steady, and danced at the prom, at homecoming, at parties. All the things she had done with Brian somehow became new again and she was doing them with Josh. Those years, which had become tarnished in her memory, now emerged bright and shining, the way they should have been. The way they would have been with Josh.

Sizzles of awareness slid up and down her nerves like sparklers in the Fourth of July sky. She smiled and at the same time felt her body tighten. This was something new, this feeling of delight, the lack of fear. Ginny sighed and looked up at Josh.

"I'm having a lovely time."

"I'm glad. But now it's time to leave. We're going to go and neck in my car."

"Josh, come on. Enough is enough." Ginny laughed.

He wrapped his arm around her shoulder and walked with her to the couch. He sat down and pulled her onto his lap in one smooth motion.

"You clearly had a lot of practice with this maneuver," Ginny said.

"Hush. Kiss me." Josh's long fingers turned her chin up and his lips found hers. He skimmed over her mouth, tasting and teasing. His lips found her eyelids and the sensitive skin behind her ear. Never giving her enough to satisfy, he left her heart pounding and her senses at a peak.

"No high school boy ever knew how to do that," Ginny gasped when he at last pulled back. "But you're right. It isn't enough. I want more."

Josh's arms tightened around her. "Gladly." This time his mouth demanded, compelled a response and Ginny answered it. She parted her lips instinctively for him and his tongue entered her mouth and aroused feelings in her she couldn't remember. Arching toward him, wanting to be closer to him, wanting to be part of him, Ginny moaned softly. She didn't think, she didn't fear. She loved, felt, wanted, and all those swirling emotions left her gasping, clinging to Josh when they finally broke their kiss.

"Josh." It was the merest hint of sound. Ginny lay across his lap, her body open now and trusting. Gently, Josh ran his hand over her curving softness.

"Ginny, sweetheart." His voice was gravelly and harsh. "You're so sweet, so lovable. I want to stay but—"

Ginny sat bolt upright. It had happened again. She had failed. What was it about her that men—

some men, she amended, two men—found so un-
appealing?

"I want to stay but it's already midnight. And
you have to get up in the morning. And I want
to take all the time in the world with you. I want
it to be right for you."

"Oh, Josh." Maybe he meant it. Maybe he did
want her.

He looked down at her. "It should be perfect.
Romantic." He grinned. "I'll work on it."

"You don't need to." Ginny's voice cracked.
"You're perfect. Romantic."

"Oh, God, Virginia McDougall, you are hell
on a man's good intentions, you know that?"
He gripped her waist in both hands and lifted
her from his lap. He stood up without letting
her go.

"I don't want you to leave." Ginny put her
arms around his neck.

He tried for a light touch. "But you have to
remember high school. All anticipation, no satisfaction."

"I'd like both. Next time let's try for college."
Ginny stepped back. "I commuted by subway
and had a baby, but it seemed as if there was a
lot of hanky-panky going on."

Josh considered. "As I recall there was a lot
of hanky but not much panky." He put his arm
around her and walked to the door.

A thought struck Ginny. "I forgot all about Denis and Lisa." A tendril of guilt tried to invade her mind, but she ruthlessly squashed it. "I wonder if they've killed each other yet."

Josh shook his head. "I keep telling you, murder wasn't on the menu at Lisa's."

Josh was right. The kiss in the kitchen ended abruptly when Lisa and Denis heard the door close. That mundane sound catapulted them back to reality. They broke apart instantly and backed to opposite corners of the kitchen. The room was so small that opposite corners didn't take them more than three feet apart. That was much too close for comfort.

Lisa's lips were swollen and Denis could see her run her tongue over them. She was still breathing hard, as if she'd just finished a 10K run. Denis tried to keep his gaze from her heaving breasts, but he found it all but impossible. He felt more unsure of himself with a member of the opposite sex than he had since junior high school. His hands and feet felt larger than life, like a cartoon character's.

Lisa took a deep breath. She was clearly trying to calm herself, but the effect on Denis was the opposite. He had kissed women before, for heaven's sake. Lots of them. Why should Lisa

McDougall affect him this way? It was ludicrous. She was an obnoxious brat. With incredible lips and a breathtaking—he censored himself, chest.

"I'd better go." Denis felt as if he were being strangled. He wanted to stay.

"You can't go. I'm cooking all this swordfish. It cost a million dollars. Somebody has to eat it. It looks like our parents have run out on us, so that leaves you."

"Dad!" Denis called. "Ginny?" Silence responded. "I think they've left."

"Yes, Denis, they have," Lisa answered, in a tone usually reserved for extremely slow two-year-olds. "That's why we heard the door close."

"Why would they leave?" Denis was bewildered. He couldn't forget about the effect Lisa was having on him.

Lisa tried again. "Because they knew we were trying to keep them from being alone together."

"They knew?"

"Yes, Denis, they knew."

"Oh. Do you really want me to stay?"

"Just for dinner. Don't get any ideas." Lisa crossed her arms across her chest and gave him a threatening look.

"No, no. God, no." He was horrified. What did she think he was thinking? "I wouldn't want you to misunderstand. I mean, it was just a moment of madness. It will never, ever happen again. I can't imagine what came over me."

"Probably the cheap Chardonnay. You don't have to make it sound as if I'm some ugly troll who bewitched you into kissing me against your will. Who do you think I am? The Frog Princess?" Lisa took the fish from under the broiler. "Allow me to assure you, Prince, that under no circumstances will I permit you to kiss me again. Ever. No matter how crazy you get."

Denis stiffened. "I do not get crazy. Wall Street lawyers, simply do not permit themselves that kind of behavior." Even to his own ears he sounded pompous.

"What would you call it? Kissing me in my kitchen?" Lisa stuck her chin out belligerently.

Denis thought about it for a moment, then gave up. "Madness. Pure madness." He brightened. He had a co-conspirator. "But you kissed me, too."

"I did not!"

"You most certainly did."

"Did not."

"Lisa, your arms were around my neck. You were strangling me."

"There. You see. I was trying to strangle you. You just misunderstood in your typically male, egotistical, self-absorbed way." Lisa smirked at him.

"You plastered yourself against me like wall-paper."

"You . . . used your tongue." Her voice was deeper, softer.

"You dug your nails into my shoulders." He took a step nearer.

"You growled."

"You moaned."

They stopped, inches away from each other.

The kitchen timer buzzed and they jumped away as if they had been given an electric shock, glaring at each other wildly.

"I can't stay." Denis ran for the bedroom to retrieve his coat, then sprinted to the door.

"Get out!" he heard Lisa say. A breakable object crashed against the inside of the front door as he closed it behind him.

Nineteen

Josh looked across the breakfast table at his son and tried to suppress his curiosity. Denis looked as if he hadn't slept in days. There were dark circles under his eyes and he hunched his shoulders as if he were cold. What on earth could have happened at Lisa's after Josh and Ginny left?

The mind boggled, or at least Josh's did. Still, he couldn't help joking. Denis took this much too seriously. In fact, Denis took life much too seriously.

"You didn't kill her, did you?" Josh asked. He couldn't hide a smile, but Denis was not amused.

"What? What are you talking about, Dad? Kill who?"

"Whom. Lisa. You look as if you have something catastrophic on your mind. That was all I could think of." Josh helped himself to a large spoonful of Denis's imported Scottish marmalade.

"Thanks a lot. No, I didn't kill her. Not that I wasn't tempted. That child—girl—"

Josh helped him out. "Woman."

Denis rejected it. "Person. That person is the most annoying person I have ever met. She could turn St. Francis of Assisi into an ax murderer in an hour." Denis's eyes brightened as he contemplated Lisa's flaws.

"I'm happy to hear she's still alive and irritating you. The world would be a less colorful place without her."

"Yeah, well, I could live with that."

"So ignore her. You told me you hadn't seen her for years. Now all of a sudden you're having dinner together as if you're related."

"God forbid."

"I don't agree." Josh crunched his toast and took a long sip of Denis's imported Kenyan coffee. "I'm hoping that maybe someday you two will be related."

"God above, Dad, you don't think I'm going to *marry* her, do you?" Denis leaped out of his chair.

Josh tried to hide his surprise. The thought had never entered his mind. He picked up his coffee cup again and looked at his son thoughtfully. Something had given Denis the wrong idea about which Havilland male was going to marry which McDougall female.

What, indeed, had gone on last night at Lisa's? Something earth-shattering, that seemed certain. "No, actually, I was thinking that I'd marry Ginny," he said calmly.

"What?" Denis shouted. He put his head in his hands. "Oh, please, no, Dad, not that."

"What's the matter with you? You sound as if I were thinking of becoming a drug dealer. It can't just be that dog and cat relationship you have with Lisa. You wouldn't have that much difficulty just being polite to her at dinner every month or so would you?"

"No, it's not that. But you hardly know Ginny. And she has a whole life here. She belongs here."

"With you and Lisa." Josh's sarcastic tone was lost on Denis.

"With me. And also with Lisa. Not with me *and* Lisa," Denis said, apparently thinking he made sense.

"Don't you think Ginny might want more out of life than mothering you and Lisa? Why can't you just let Ginny and me decide whether we can make a life together, okay? It may be she won't have me."

Denis stared at Josh. His father was really thinking of marrying Ginny McDougall. A shocking thought occurred to him. "Dad, you and Ginny haven't—I mean you aren't—" He broke off suddenly. "Are you? I mean, have you?"

"None of your business," Josh replied, guessing what Denis was driving at from his red face and unfinished sentences. "I don't ask you what you and your models do, and why you want me out of your apartment. Some things grown-ups don't need to talk about."

"Oh." Denis had never heard his father talk in quite that tone before. He had never thought Josh understood his life. Clearly, he had been wrong. Josh understood very well indeed.

"What I'm trying to say, son, is that I'd appreciate it if you and Lisa would stop this heavy-handed attempt to separate Ginny and me. We're big kids now, and we can make our own decisions. Just the way you can."

"Dad, Lisa and I are only trying to help. We care about you—both of you. We want you to be happy. We just don't think you've given this enough thought. You're behaving very—" he searched for a word.

"Childishly?" Josh smiled.

"No, of course not. Just . . . impulsively."

"Well, maybe you're right. But I can tell you, if you're lucky enough to meet a woman you can love when you're fifty-eight, you're not going to want to waste time either."

"I guess you're right." Denis frowned into his

coffee. "You really think you're in love? At your age?"

Josh held on to his temper. "I'm still alive, Denis. I'll make fog on a mirror for you if you have any doubts."

"Dad, please. That's not what I meant. It's just that you're—" Denis floundered.

"Come right out and say it. Old. You think I'm too old to fall in love."

"Of course not. I've read the articles. I know that with diet and exercise, people can remain active well into their sunset years. It's just that you're my father and I can't think of you . . . you know, in love."

"Denis, do you know that when I was eighteen I thought that men of thirty-five were too old to really know what love was all about." Josh smiled for a moment. He could remember vividly seeing his chemistry teacher kissing the school nurse one evening when he had stayed late to work on the yearbook. He had been shocked. Why, they both were at least thirty-five—and Mr. Schneider even had gray in his hair!

"Very funny, Dad." Denis sat up a little straighter, as if his thirty-three years suddenly weighed heavily on him.

"It's not funny. It's sad that young people think they have a monopoly on passion."

"Dad, I don't think that for a moment." Denis

got up and headed for the door. "I'll be back late this evening."

"If I'm not going to be here I'll leave a note." Josh turned back to the *New York Times*.

"Ginny, for God's sake, it's two o'clock. Where's my coffee? Where's the Cummings brief?"

Ginny stood in the doorway of Denis's office, trying not to lose her temper. She spoke in a calm, pleasant voice. "The brief is on top of your 'In' box. Just where I told you it was twenty minutes ago. The coffee is still in the pot because you haven't asked for any until now. Is there some reason why you're behaving like a consummate jerk today?"

Denis looked up at her, an arrested expression on his face. He sat in silence for a minute. Then, "No, I don't think so. It's probably some conflict in the stars. Or the result of dinner with your daughter."

Ginny zeroed in on the important statement. "Why should dinner with Lisa upset you?" Knowing Denis as well as she did, Ginny wanted to find out his intentions toward her daughter. Murder or mayhem came to mind.

"You know she and I have never gotten along, Ginny. That isn't going to change just because she's older and prettier."

Briefly, Ginny debated telling him that she and Josh had seen the steamy kiss in the kitchen. Realizing that Lisa would be horrified if she found out, she decided to refrain. "I'm sorry you still feel that way," she said.

"It's not your fault. It's not even Lisa's fault. It's just one of those unfortunate things. We can't stand each other. I don't know what we'll do when you and Dad get married." Denis took one look at Ginny's shocked face and realized he had blown it. Big time. His father hadn't yet broached the subject with Ginny. When Josh found out, Denis would be cat food.

"M-married? *Married!*" Ginny's voice rose. One hand went to the pulse beating at the neck of her silk blouse. The other hugged her waist. "Where in the world did you get that idea? That's ridiculous. It's as silly as asking if you and Lisa—" Ginny looked at Denis's furious red face and turned on her heel. She headed for the ladies' room. Once there, she stared at herself in the mirror. Who was this white-faced woman with huge, frightened green eyes? She no longer knew.

Married! The very word turned her stomach to acid and her brain to aspic. Marry Josh. But the thought had never even occurred to him, she was sure. They hadn't even—he hadn't even—

"Ms. McDougall? Ginny?" A soft voice brought her back to reality.

"Anita," she said. "I'm so glad to see you. I was getting a little worried about you. I hadn't heard from you in so long and then last night Gray stopped by and called you."

"Oh, was he calling from your apartment?" Anita smiled nervously. "I couldn't really talk because my father was there."

"Are you all right, Anita?" Ginny noticed the young woman's nervous gestures. "Have you talked to your father?"

"No. No, I couldn't. I just couldn't." Anita looked at her pleadingly. "You have to understand."

Ginny thought of the kiss she had observed last night. Denis hadn't told her about it, and Lisa wouldn't either. She understood. "I know, Anita, it's hard to talk to parents about some things."

"Yes. Yes. Ginny, could I talk to you? Could we meet?" Anita looked at her as if willing her to say yes.

"Of course. Tonight? After work?" Ginny had a sense that it was important that Anita talk to her right away.

"Yes, please."

"At the bar where we met before?" Ginny suggested.

"Could you come to my apartment instead? It will be more private. Would that be all right, do you think?"

"Of course, Anita. I'll be there as soon as I can get away."

Josh decided that morning it was time to see whether New York wanted him before he asked the same question of Ginny. Today, he would inquire about bar admission and then go see his "clients." Sylvia could wait until he and Ginny went to the Jackson Home later in the week. But he worried about Mack and he wanted to check in with Hervé.

It felt good to be thinking about the law and clients again. He had missed it more than he'd ever expected to. Sure, he knew he'd liked the life he led in Elgin. But he'd expected to slip into retirement like a comfortable pair of slippers and settle back to enjoy the easy life. Instead, he learned that life without a goal just wasn't fun for him.

Since he'd come to New York he'd realized that he still wanted to practice law. He liked it and he was good at it. He'd never have expected to find both a job he wanted and a woman he needed here in the heart of New York City. You didn't grow old, Josh decided, until life stopped surprising you.

Whistling tunelessly, he headed down the stairs. As he came around the last turn, he saw Hervé polishing the brass fronts of the tenants' mail boxes.

"Hi, Hervé, how goes it?"

"Goes it?" Hervé seemed puzzled. Then his face cleared. "Oh, I get. *Comment ça va,* you mean. Fine, *m'sieu,* fine. And you?"

"Just grand. How's François?"

Hervé looked around. "He is better. My, *tante,* my aunt that is, looks after him. She is very good healer. Not voodoo, witchcraft, you understand. *Les herbes.* You comprehend?"

"Yes. Herbal medicine. Natural remedies. And François is better? The wound is healing?"

"Yes. Is healing."

"And Denis is going to go with him to get a visa?"

Hervé's face was wiped free of all expression in a moment, as if a sponge has been wiped over a blackboard. "We will do what is needful for him. Do not worry yourself, *m'sieu.*"

"But I am worried, Hervé. The immigration people aren't going to be lenient if they find François has been here illegally."

"Many people are never found," Hervé said, rubbing the brass and not looking at Josh.

"Yes, I know, but they have to live by taking jobs no one else wants, with no medical insurance, no social security. Is that what you want for François?"

Hervé turned to look at Josh. His brow was furrowed and he twisted the polishing cloth in his hands. "No, I would wish for him that he become a citizen here. But it is better to live poorly here than to go back. François will be killed if he returns to the island. You must understand. And you must make your son understand, *M'sieu* 'Avilland."

Josh put his hand on Hervé's shoulder for a minute. "There's got to be a way to keep François here legally. Give Denis and me a chance to find it, Hervé. Okay?"

Hervé said nothing. His answer was a fatalistic, Gallic shrug.

Josh walked across the park to the Metropolitan Museum. He looked up at the long flight of stairs and wondered why it was so quiet.

"It's Monday," said a familiar voice behind him. "Museum's closed."

"Mack, hello. I was looking for you. I'm a tourist, but you must have known the place is closed. What are you doing here?" Josh grinned and held out a hand, but Mack stepped back and glowered at him.

"Enough of the happy talk, shyster. What the hell did you think you were doing Saturday? Signing my death warrant?"

"Mack, come on. That guy was a low-level errand boy. Whatever he says isn't going to get you in trouble. Eddie will check before he does anything. You know that."

Mack's eyebrows rose. "Maybe Indiana isn't full of hicks after all. Yeah, you're right. I've done good for Eddie. But he's gonna come lookin' for me." He nodded at Josh. "And for you, too, counselor. Bet you didn't think of that."

"I was counting on it. Look, Mack, Eddie knows you don't want to give up the location. The fact that you told me is going to make him wonder. You're not doing the expected thing."

"Whaddaya mean?"

"He expects you to give in or try to get some money out of him. He won't expect me."

"An ambulance chaser."

"A negotiator, with no strings attached and no agenda except you."

"And that's going to make Eddie scared? I don't think so, counselor."

"Not scared. Just bothered enough to meet with us. And then we discuss what you might take to give his nephew a job."

"And what would that be? I'm fascinated." Sarcasm was Mack's preferred tone of voice.

"There are a lot of possibilities."

"Like a one-way ticket to the Pine Barrens?"

"Like a partnership between you and Eddie for several locations, one of which his nephew could operate." Josh noticed that Mack looked interested now. "Or, another location for said nephew. Or another job for you. One in Eddie's office—"

"No, thanks. Eddie's got nobody but relatives working there and they're all jerks. I'd end up doing all the work."

"You might still consider it. Become indispensable and you can be a partner."

"You just don't get it, Hoosier. When you're indispensable to Eddie Tyrone you stay where he puts you, or you may stay permanently unemployed because you are permanently dead."

"Do you really know people Eddie had killed? Personally? People who disappeared and the police couldn't find? People on the 'Six O'clock News'?"

Mack thought for a moment. Then he pursed his lips and pulled his cap down over his eyes. "Actually, put it that way and—no, I don't personally know nobody Eddie had killed. But I've heard stories—"

"Hell, Mack, I could make up stories about doing away with my enemies in unspecified ways and have some people believing I was king of the underworld."

Mack looked at him. "In those khaki pants and tweed jackets from Brooks Brothers? I don't think so, counselor."

"Okay, I won't argue with you. Look, when Eddie calls for a meeting, you tell him that you'll come only if I come, too. Then you call me and we'll talk strategy. Be thinking about where you'd like to end up."

"I already know. Here. Selling hot dogs. Alive."

"You're thinking too small, Mack. Here's my number. Call me when you hear from Eddie." Josh waved, and set off down Fifth Avenue, whistling tunelessly again.

Anita wandered aimlessly around her small apartment. She had everything ready. If only she knew how to talk to Ginny. How to make her understand about her father. To people like Ginny and Gray, Anthony DiBenedetto would seem an anachronism, a throwback to old movies and newsreels of Congressional hearings in the days of Senator Kefauver.

The doorbell rang. Anita took a deep breath before answering it.

"It's a lovely room," Ginny said as she looked around at Anita's studio apartment. Everything was light and airy, with sun-washed colors of turquoise and coral and sand, and light wood finishes.

"Thank you. I did it myself." Anita was clearly proud of her efforts. "Please sit down. May I get you some wine?"

In a few moments, Anita put a silver tray of

crackers and cheese and Waterford wineglasses on the coffee table and sat down across from Ginny. She clasped her hands and rested them on her knees. Leaning forward, she swallowed hard and asked Ginny, "Ms.—Ginny, I have a great favor to ask of you."

When she didn't continue, Ginny said, "Yes, Anita? What is it?"

There was another long silence. "I would like to ask that you not tell Gray what we discuss tonight."

Ginny hesitated. "All right, Anita. But I may ask that you tell him about it."

"Please, Ginny. Would you just promise not to say anything? You don't need to agree or disagree with what I tell you. I just want you to listen, and to know my plans. As a sort of . . . foster mother." She gave Ginny a wan smile.

"Of course. I want to help, Anita. If it would make things easier, I'd be glad to go with you to talk to your father." Ginny had a perverse desire to meet Anita's father, who sounded like some sort of Renaissance prince—a Borgia who poisoned his enemies.

"No, that won't be necessary. I've decided that neither Gray nor my father need ever know what I'm going to do."

Ginny was beginning to get an idea of just what Anita's plans were and she was not happy about it. She opened her mouth to ask Anita point-blank what she intended when she turned to Ginny and said, with passionate intensity, "I can't stand being torn apart like this anymore. My father wants me to promise not to see Gray and Gray wants me to marry him. I feel like a bone between two dogs."

Ginny took her hand. "I know. You probably need to get away from the pressure you're under. Maybe a short trip—"

"My father would have detectives after me. That's why he sent a car and driver. To keep watch over me and report to him." Anita's mouth twisted bitterly. "That's why I didn't ask you to leave with me. I don't want my father pestering you afterward."

"Afterward?" Ginny began to feel a chill around her heart. It seemed more and more as if Anita had decided on an abortion as a way out of her difficulties.

"I am going to disappear, Ginny. I am going away where no one can find me, and I am going to have my baby and take care of him all by myself." Anita stood with her chin high as if daring Ginny to say she couldn't do it.

"Oh, Anita, I'm so glad!"

That was clearly the last reaction Anita expected. "Why? What do you mean?"

"I—I thought you were going to terminate—"

"Abortion?" Anita's hands went protectively around her still-slender waist. "No. Even when I talked about it, I knew I could never do that. No, no, I want this baby more than anything. It's all I can have of Gray. And it will be a reminder of my father, too, in a way."

"Anita, what are you planning? Can you tell me? Don't you think—"

"I have a list of homes for unwed mothers that I can go to. One is in South Carolina, and I think that may be far enough away. I've arranged a change of name."

"How? If you petition a court for a name change—"

"Oh, no, Ginny. My father would find out. No, I found the name of a baby who died shortly after I was born. I've requested a birth certificate and I'll get a social security number in that name. I'm not going to tell you what name I've chosen."

Ginny stared at her. Gentle, shy Anita Di-Benedetto had planned a campaign worthy of General Patton and was already putting her plans into operation.

"I can't stay here and let my father try to wear me down. He will make me ill. It's happened before."

Ginny reached out a hand. "Honey, I know I don't understand about your father, but Gray loves you, you can tell him. He'll surely want to go with you to bring you and the baby back."

"I'm never coming back." The statement was as simple and final as a key turning in a lock.

"Maybe Gray would be willing to leave New York just because he loves you and the baby." Ginny took both Anita's chilled hands in hers and chafed them, as she had Lisa's when she was a child.

"I can't ask it of him." Again, Anita's tone was final.

Ginny tried to think of a way to ask Anita the question she had needed answered from the beginning. "Anita, please don't misunderstand. I know that you've made your decision and your plans, but, honey, *why?* I just can't believe that you have to go to these lengths in order to escape your father. What can he do to you?"

Anita withdrew her hands from Ginny's and rose. She went to stand in front of the large window that looked down on the busy lights of Fifty-seventh Street. "My father is what used to be called a gangster. A mob boss. Occasionally, they write an article about him. Not often. He keeps a very low profile. But you may have heard of someone called 'Tony D.' That's my father."

Ginny simply stared. Tony D. Anita was the daughter of the shadowy kingpin of organized crime. Hidden behind a hundred dummy corporations, covered by lawyers, accountants, and stand-ins, Tony D was reputed to run gambling on the East Coast. His operation had never been infiltrated by the FBI or any other law enforcement agency. He had never been arrested, much less indicted or tried. What was known of him was vague and often contradictory. Yet here was a young woman who had an ordinary job and an ordinary life, telling Ginny calmly that her father was that legendary figure.

Ginny said nothing for a long while. "And you have to run away because—"

"Because my father loves me and will do anything to protect me. Because he can't bear the idea that I will marry a young man from Darien and Yale who will scorn me and leave me when he finds out whose daughter I am. To avoid that he may very well decide to kill Gray. In his eyes, Gray will have dishonored me." Anita turned back to Ginny and looked warily at her. "Can you understand?" she said.

"Oh, yes, Anita, of course. And I can see how difficult all this is for you. But I still think there's a way we can solve this without—"

Anita's doorbell chimed, and the two women exchanged startled glances. "It must be Gray," Anita said, moving toward the door.

Ginny sat back and closed her eyes for a moment. Now that Anita had explained it, she could begin to understand the young woman's fear.

It was Gray. Anita murmured something and Gray answered her in a whisper. They were in love, it shimmered around them like an aura. There must be a way to help them.

"Hello, Gray," Ginny said, holding out her hand.

"Ms. McDougall, I didn't expect to see you here." And he didn't look very pleased about it, either, Ginny thought.

"I asked Ginny to come this evening. I wanted to talk to her."

Gray sat down, his eyes watchful. He looked at Ginny and she could see the dawning fear on his face.

"You want to have an abortion," he said in a whisper. "Oh, Nita, no. Please."

Anita bowed her head. "I'm sorry, Gray. My decision is my business. My baby is my business."

Gray got up and went to kneel in front of Anita's chair. When he tried to take her in his arms, she pulled away.

"Anita," he said in a low, urgent voice. "Please. Marry me now. Then we'll go to your father. Together. You can tell him then. That you're married and we're going to have a baby."

"I can't. I can't." Anita's voice was less than

a whisper. "I don't know what he'd do if we did that."

"What can he do? For God's sake, this is America. It's damn near the twenty-first century. We're not living in some old-fashioned melodrama. What the hell can he do to us?"

"Not to us," she whispered. "To you."

Gray was silent for a long time. "I don't believe he can do anything to either of us, but I can see that you do," he said at last.

"I don't want to discuss this anymore. Whatever I decide to do, it's none of your business." Anita's voice was as soft and cold as snow.

"What the hell are you afraid of? Exactly what? That your father will kill me? Is that it?" Again Gray tried to take her in his arms, but Anita pulled away from him. "The guy's going to take a gun and shoot?" Gray gave an angry laugh. "For God's sake, Anita, that's ridiculous!"

Anita shook her bent head. "You don't understand," she whispered. "He has a terrible temper. He's very proud. He would never accept an illegitimate grandchild and he will never accept you."

Ginny could see from the resolute look on Anita's face that no arguments Gray could make were going to make the slightest impression on Tony D's daughter.

"Nita, please," Gray said, unwilling to admit

defeat. "Let's talk about this. I'm willing to do whatever you want, but don't have an abortion. Please, baby." Gray put his arms around Anita and held her as her shoulders began to shake. "Don't cry, honey. We'll work it out. Just let's do it together, please."

"Gray, you don't understand!" Anita's voice teetered on the brink of hysteria. "Just let me alone! That's all you can do for me. Just leave me in peace."

Ginny rose and went over to Anita. "Anita, I'll respect your privacy. But if you want to talk to me, you can call anytime. And I'll come to you if you want me to."

"No!" Gray cried, and got up to take Ginny's arm in a bruising grip. "You can't let her do this! Ms. McDougall, you can't."

Ginny took Anita's paper white face between her hands. "Anita, I understand. But I wish you would talk to Gray. Listen to him. Think about your decision." Ginny took hold of Anita's hand and squeezed it. "I'll come to you when you need me, and I'll be with you wherever you are. Okay?"

"Thank you, Ginny." Anita's tear-drenched eyes looked up to her with such gratitude that Ginny felt her own eyes begin to sting. "But I'm not going to change my mind."

"I'll see you tomorrow, dear. Gray, good-night." Ginny gripped his hand with hers and then made her way out of the apartment, closing the door softly.

Twenty

It was still early when Ginny arrived home, but her steps were lagging and she longed to see Josh. She checked her machine for messages. He had called. She had left one telling him about her meeting with Anita.

To Ginny, hearing Josh's voice was like grabbing hold of a lifeline. Surely Josh could think of something. If she could just talk to him, tell him about Tony D, and Anita's fears. There had to be a way, without risking Anita's fragile composure, of helping her and Gray.

Ginny changed into a soft blue sweater and a pair of jeans, made herself a cup of tea, and stared at the contents of her refrigerator without interest. Instead, she sat in the living room with her feet up and sipped. It felt good, but not as good as talking to Josh.

She called him, and he picked up on the first ring. "I've been waiting for you to call. What happened, Ginny?"

"Anita saw her father this weekend all right but she didn't tell him about the baby."

"That's what Gray was afraid of. Has her father talked her into anything?"

"No. Anita's talked herself into what she thinks she has to do."

There was a pause at Josh's end of the line. Then he said quietly, "Abortion?"

"No. Look, there are some factors that she didn't tell me before."

"Something that changes the way you think about it." It was a statement not a question. He understood, Ginny thought. "Can you tell me, or is it a secret?"

Ginny thought for a moment. "I can tell you some of it, but Anita has asked me to keep part of it confidential. I promised I would."

"Okay. What can you tell me? First off, is Gray going to be part of her plan?"

"No. She's determined to do this alone, though I think she may let me help. After seeing her father, she's at the end of her rope. There's no telling what she'll do if anyone tries to stop her, or tells her father. She's terrified of him, Josh. Anita honestly thinks her father will kill Gray if he finds out about the baby."

"Well, I hate to say it, but it is just possible that she's right. Not all parents are well-meaning or even rational when it comes to their children."

Again, he understood the basics without Ginny's explaining Anita's fear of her father. Ginny didn't want to betray Anita's confidence, but she did need Josh's advice. She leaned forward, as if that would bring her closer to him.

He spoke after a long silence. He sounded reluctant, as if he didn't like what he was proposing. "I hate to go behind Anita's back, Ginny. She already feels that her father doesn't listen to her. But if he wants to, I'll go out to Long Island with Gray to talk to Mr. DiBenedetto."

"Oh, no, absolutely not. You mustn't go near her father." Ginny felt a cold prickle of fear up her spine at the thought of Josh trying to see Anthony DiBenedetto.

"What's wrong, Ginny? Is he dangerous? There's more to this than you're telling me. Are you in any trouble?" Anxiety sharpened his tone.

Ginny thought carefully before she spoke. "Anita is very concerned about what her father might do. I don't think she's afraid for herself so much as for Gray. If you and Gray tell him about the baby, he may do something drastic. I think she may be right about that. And at that point, Anita might run away and never be found."

Josh said, "I'm going to the library tomorrow. Where do you think I could look?"

"For what?"

"For anything in print on DiBenedetto."

Ginny stared straight ahead. There was plenty in print about Tony D, some of it somewhere probably naming Anthony DiBenedetto. She bit her thumb in concentration. If Josh found information independently, what would he do with it? Should she tell him and risk Anita's trust? She decided to compromise.

"Why don't I check Mr. DiBenedetto out? I'll see if there's anything on him in any newspaper or magazine. I'll run him on Nexis tomorrow."

"Ah, the research queen at work. Good thinking."

Ginny leaned back in her chair and smiled a little. Now that she had talked to Josh she felt better. As if Anita's problem were in good hands. She and Josh made a good team. "Will I see you tomorrow?" she asked.

"You can see me anytime you want, sweetheart, you know that. As much of me and as often as you'd like." His voice had lowered to a soft growl.

"Mmm." She wiggled her toes and relaxed. She would let Anita go until tomorrow. "I miss you now that I'm back at work. I had a whole list of things we were going to go see."

"I'd rather see you."

"I was included in the tour. Services of a first-class guide, isn't that what the brochures say?"

She smiled and twisted the phone cord around her finger.

"Have you had anything to eat?"

Ginny sat bolt upright. "What a way to spoil the mood, I was having a lovely, flirtatious conversation and you want to talk about salads and green beans."

"Is that what you're eating?"

"What do you think?"

"I think I'll bring you something nice and nourishing. I'll be there in twenty minutes."

"Now, Josh, I don't need a nanny. You just stay where you are. I've been feeding myself for years."

"You need a nanny, a cook, and a nutritionist. Not to mention a friend, a lover, and—"

"Are you applying?"

"I thought I'd been hired. On a trial basis, of course." Josh laughed softly and a shiver ran up Ginny's spine. "Twenty minutes."

She didn't argue. It was symptomatic of how far she'd fallen for the man that she didn't think to protect her independence. Worse yet, she didn't even feel it was threatened.

Virginia, she thought, *you're a goner.*

A half hour later, Ginny was eating a chicken and vegetable sandwich on pita bread and spooning up lentil soup. "This is so healthy, my stomach is wondering what happened to the tea I was feeding it before you arrived."

"Explain to your stomach that it's going to have to get used to me, just like the rest of you." Josh grinned and reached over to snag a carrot stick from her plate. "Now, let me tell you about my day." He pulled a sheaf of papers from his jacket pocket.

"Looks official," Ginny commented, through a mouthful of sprouts.

"It is. Application for Admission to the Bar, New York Appellate Division, First Department." He put them on the table. "I went down to the courthouse and got them this afternoon. I fill out the forms, get a couple of colleagues from Indiana to agree to tell New York what a great lawyer I am and what an asset I'll be to the New York bar, and I'll be in."

Ginny put down her sandwich. "Josh, are you sure you want to do this?"

He looked at her, the expression on his face serious. "It's not just because of you, Ginny. I really want to practice law here. I think that I can be useful. I practiced in Elgin for over twenty-five years and I needed something different, new. But I found out I don't want to retire. It's fine for lots of people, but not for me. Even if we . . ." He spread his hands in a gesture of dismissal. "I'll still want to stay."

"Are you planning on hanging out your shingle in some storefront or what?"

"I haven't decided yet." His voice hadn't changed, but there was a glint in his eye that said he had some interesting ideas.

"I'll do anything I can to help."

"You do that for all your friends, don't you?" Josh smiled at her and Ginny felt her heart speed up.

Josh came around the table and put his hands on her shoulders. "You never let anyone go away unhappy if you can help it."

"Come on, Josh, you make me sound like Mother Teresa." Ginny laughed to hide the shivers that went through her at his touch. *Keep it light,* she thought. But it was getting harder and harder to do.

"Somehow 'saintly' is not the first word that comes to my mind when I think about you." His lips touched her neck and moved with exquisite slowness to her ear. She could feel the click of his teeth on the tiny gold stud she wore as he worried her lobe. Her throat arched back and a low sound of pleasure and need came from somewhere deep inside her.

Slowly, Josh pulled her chair back and lifted her to her feet. His arms wrapped around her and Ginny felt her body give and mold itself to his.

With a murmur of need, she flung her arms around Josh's neck and pulled his head down to meet hers. Their mouths opened to each other, their tongues dueled and explored. Ginny was as eager as he was. When Josh pulled back, breathing hard, Ginny pursued him.

"Ginny, Ginny," he groaned as her hands swept down to stroke his chest. "Don't start something you don't want to finish. Talk to me. Tell me what you want,"

"Enough talking. Kiss me."

"Ginny—"

"How do I know what I want if you don't show me what I can have?"

"Ginny, are you sure—"

"No! I haven't been sure of anything since I met you. All my arrangements and decisions about my life that I've been happy with for twenty years have just gone up in smoke." She grabbed handfuls of his hair and shook him. "Damn you anyway! You tell me you're falling in love with me, shake up my whole life, and then ask me to tell you what I want! I'm damned if I know anymore. Except that now I want to try everything. With you!" Her voice lowered, the anger drained away. "I just want you, Josh."

She backed away then, but Josh wouldn't let her go far. "Lady, you've already got me. Don't you know that by now?" He pulled her back into his arms and held her.

Their lips met and clung. Ginny felt herself melting, turning hot and liquid deep within her, electricity sparking wherever Josh touched her. She was excited, curious, eager to find out where love would take her. For the first time, making love seemed an adventure, a glorious voyage, where the outcome was less important than the trip itself.

Josh's hands slipped under her sweater, and the touch of his hands made her tremble. Josh felt it and stilled his hands. He wanted Ginny McDougall, needed her the way he needed air and water, but only if she wanted him with the same urgency.

"Please," she whispered, her voice husky, "don't stop. I want to try everything. I want to make love with you, Josh."

"Oh, God, Ginny." He buried his face in her hair, inhaling deeply. Ginny could feel him drop a kiss on the top of her head. "I want you, too. So much."

He twirled her around as if they were dancing, then fell with her onto the couch. She landed on top, breaking her fall with her hands, and looked down at him, laughing. "At last, I have you where I want you!" Ginny cried, and ran her tongue over her lips and then bent to nibble at Josh's lower lip. "Delicious!" she murmured.

Josh's hands reached up under her sweater to cup her breasts and Ginny arched back, throwing her head back and closing her eyes. He circled his palms on her nipples, pressing them through the lace of her bra. Ginny could feel heat arc through her, leaving her nerve ends awakened, sensitized, wanting.

She arched and pressed closer, wanting to feel his touch on her naked breasts. "Take it off, Josh. Please."

With a groan, he unfastened the front clasp of her bra, catching her breasts in his hands as they tumbled free. It was almost too much. For a moment, Ginny thought she would lose consciousness from the emotions that coursed through her. "Yes. Yes." It was all she could say.

Josh looked at her rapt face and felt his love run hot and sweet within him. This was an experience different from any he had ever had. His feelings for Ginny were so much stronger than any he had felt before.

"Touch me." It was a whispered command.

He obeyed. His fingers played with her breasts, swirling around her nipples and moving to caress their round fullness. Ginny moaned softly. He pulled her sweater over her head and down her arms. Impatiently, she freed her hands, and Josh's mouth fastened on first one nipple and then the other.

"Oh, Josh. Oh, yes." She moved, straddling his hips, conscious only of her need to be closer to him, close enough for him to still the ache, satisfy the hunger within her. Still kissing her breasts,

Josh's hands found the snap of her jeans and pulled the zipper open.

Ginny gave a half laugh, half groan as his fingers found her, warm and moist and waiting. "I can't stand this," she whispered. "I'm going to fly apart. Josh, what are you doing to me?"

He didn't answer. The feel of her, slick and soft, warm and willing, was everything he had known it would be. She was responsive, eager—in every way the lover he had dreamed of. His lips suckled her and his hands found the secret places within her. He felt her tighten and clench around his fingers for a moment. Then the tremors began and she sank down against him, shivering

She lay against his chest for a timeless moment, as Josh stroked her back and kissed her hair. At last, she raised herself enough to look into his eyes. "That was it, wasn't it? For the very first time." She was smiling, and her cheeks were rosy. Blushing again. Josh loved it.

"Sure seemed like it from where I sat." He couldn't help it, he was grinning like a self-satisfied idiot. "Was it . . ." No. He was not going to sound like a seventeen-year-old.

"Oh, Josh, it was—it was indescribable. Thank you."

"Please don't say thank you. It makes me feel

like you're going to stick ten dollars in my Calvin Klein briefs."

"Do you really wear Calvin Klein underwear? Let me see!" Ginny was feeling giddy, as if she had successfully scaled a mountain. She was happier than she could remember being in—she didn't know how long. Maybe ever. Champagne ran in her veins. She looked down at Josh's face, his eyes half-closed and burning with desire and the same desire began to trickle through her again. Without a word, she began to unbutton Josh's shirt, and spread the two halves apart. She bent and kissed both his nipples. Then she lifted herself up and swung off the couch. With a shimmy of her hips, she sent her jeans and panties to pool on the floor. Then she held out her hand to Josh.

"Come," she said. He looked at her and his breath stopped. She was so lovely, so exactly what she should be that he could scarcely believe his luck. How had he found her? He kicked off his shoes, but Ginny gave him a mock scowl.

"Let me undress you," she said, and kissed his nipples again.

"Lord, yes. Anything you want." He felt helpless with need everywhere she touched him, hot and hard where her hands caressed him as she shoved his jeans down to the floor.

"No Calvins," she said, and moved her hands

inside them to caress his tight buttocks as his briefs went to join his jeans.

"I'm afraid I'm strictly a Fruit of the Loom kind of guy," he said breathlessly as he pulled off his socks. Naked, he stood in front of her and reached out to her again. The proof of his need was hard against her. Ginny moved, smoothing her body over his.

"I have to have you. Now," he said, and swept her up into his arms. He made his way down the hall to her bedroom and fell on the bed with her still in his arms.

Laughing, they untangled themselves. Their mouths met in a voracious kiss and slowly, easily, he slid inside her. For a moment, they held their breaths. This was what they both wanted, needed. They were together and that was enough.

Then need began to snake through Josh, as he felt himself sheathed tightly in the welcoming channel of the woman he loved. Slowly, he began to move, holding himself in tight control. He wanted Ginny to come again, with their bodies joined. His satisfaction, their loving, wouldn't be complete without it. He could feel Ginny begin to echo his movements, her breasts moving against his chest, her hips rising to meet his.

He moved deeper within her and he could hear her gasp. "Are you all right?" His concern for her overrode his own body's needs.

"Oh, God, so much better than all right. Don't stop, Josh, don't ever stop." She reached up and pulled his head down so she could kiss him. His tongue mated with hers, their bodies moved in the same rhythm, and sooner than he wanted, later than he needed, they exploded, shattering into a million iridescent pieces, at the same moment.

Neither spoke for long minutes, until their heartbeats had returned to near normal. Then Josh caressed her cheeks with his thumbs and Ginny tunneled her fingers through his hair.

"What are you thinking, Ginny?" he said at last.

"I was wondering what you'd say if I told you that—" She was going to say she loved him, but something held her back. "—that that was one of the most wonderful things that has ever happened to me."

He rolled off her, and lying on his back he grinned up at the ceiling. "It didn't just happen to you, Ginny. It was us. We made it happen. For both of us."

"Did we really?" Ginny looked at him anxiously. For the past hour she had felt invincible, as if she could do no wrong. Now reality was beginning to seep back into her consciousness and she was afraid.

"Oh, yes, lady. Believe me. I've been fantasizing about this since the moment I met you. And you definitely exceeded anything I could have imagined." He reached out and stroked her arm gently.

Hearing that made her euphoria complete. She didn't know what to say, so she leaned over him and kissed him, letting her soft lips speak to him silently, telling him what she couldn't say. Then, afraid of the emotions roiling within her, she backed away a little, and teased him. "Darn! I just find out how I really want to spend my vacation, and I have to go back to work!"

"People do manage to fit love in, you know, Ginny. Even when their schedules are jammed." Josh rolled over to his side and propped his head on his hand. He gave her a slow smile that speeded up her heart beat.

"I hope we can, Josh. I don't want to lose you." This time she wasn't afraid. She would ask for what she wanted. "Can you stay the night?" Ginny couldn't think of anything more pleasurable than sleeping next to Josh.

"Are you sure you want your boss to know you've been sleeping with me?"

"Denis? Why should he care? He loves you. He wants you to be happy."

"He'll make sure Lisa knows. And then we'll be in for a family discussion. Are you ready to go public?"

She sank back on the pillows. "I guess we'd better wait. But this is worse than being a teenager in love. Sneaking around behind our children's backs is really bizarre, Josh."

He grinned at her. "There's a certain thrill in sneaking around, don't you think?"

"I think I'll get enough thrills just from making love with you." She leaned over and kissed him. "But you're probably right. We'll keep it a secret for a while. So, go on, leave before I change my mind and hog-tie you."

"I love you, Ginny."

"Oh, lord, Josh." She almost quailed at the enormity of what she was about to say. "I'm afraid I love you, too."

Twenty-one

It was raining the next morning, the kind of steady downpour that filled New York's gutters to overflowing in minutes and caused every empty cab in the city to disappear.

Ginny had never seen a more beautiful day.

She woke early and for a few seconds she couldn't identify the source of the faint soreness in long-unused muscles. Her heart felt like a hot air balloon that had lost its ballast and was floating free, bouncing against her ribs. She felt free. And happy.

She was in love. And she felt freer than she had ever felt in her life.

The thought filled her with surprise. How could falling in love free her? Her happiness was now tied irrevocably to another person. She needed Josh Havilland and yet somehow that emotion itself gave her a sense of unfettered joy.

Last night had rid her of her crippling fears and doubts about herself. Until that moment, Brian's opinion of her femininity, her basic worth as a woman had somehow been hers as well. Their relationship had colored her life and her view of herself. Then Josh had appeared and in a matter of days he had changed all that. Changed her.

Irrevocably.

Now, she knew that even were she to lose Josh—and her heart quailed at the very thought—his gift to her would always be with her. She wouldn't go back. Without thinking, she rolled over and picked up the phone. It had rung four times before she looked at her clock and realized the time.

Oh, dear. She had a cowardly urge to hang up when she heard a familiar voice, still husky with sleep. "H'lo."

"Josh." It was enough to hear his voice, say his name.

"Morning, sweetheart, what are you doing up at six-fifteen?"

"Thinking about you."

"Me, too. I love you, Virginia McDougall."

Ginny snuggled down under the covers and smiled from ear to ear. "Say it again."

"I love you." Ginny savored the words, running them through her mind. "Hey, I could stand to hear from you, too," Josh said into her continued silence.

"I love you." Ginny was struck by a sudden attack of self-consciousness. "I think. I sound like a love-struck teenager."

"I like it." Josh's low growl sent shivers down her spine. "I'd better go. I hear Denis moving around upstairs. Did he stick you with a seven o'clock meeting?"

"No, but if he's going to be in early, I'd better prepare for gale force winds. Will I see you this evening?"

"Yes, love, I'll call you at the office. Good-bye."

"Good-bye, Josh. Darling." The receiver fell back onto the handset and Ginny gave herself another thirty seconds of wallowing in happiness before she got up and readied herself to face the day, and Denis.

Later that morning, she saw that Denis looked puzzled, a worried frown on his brow. When Ginny went into his office to see which of the dozen things she had to do should take precedence, he looked up without answering.

Denis was never absentminded. He dived into work with single-minded zeal.

"Are you all right?" Ginny asked. "You look a little preoccupied this morning."

"Uh—no, of course, I'm not preoccupied. I just need some coffee." He lifted his fast-food paper cup and took a long sip. "See, better already."

He didn't look better. The travesty of a smile didn't reassure Ginny. "Well, if you say so. I'm going to do a little research. Is there anything you need right away?"

Denis looked at her. "Did you know your daughter has changed?" Ginny looked puzzled. Changed? Lisa?

"What do you mean?"

"She's not so childish anymore." Denis looked vaguely out his window.

"She's twenty-four years old now. She was fourteen when you saw her."

"Yes. You brought her to the office. It was when I first arrived here. She was drawing pictures of long-haired rock stars all over the brief I had to file the next day." He spoke reminiscently, as if it were a cherished memory. As Ginny recalled it, he had screamed like a soul in torment and threatened to have her fired and Lisa shot at sunrise.

"I remember," she said. She had reprinted the brief. It had taken most of the afternoon. Lisa had not been popular that day.

"She's changed, Ginny. A lot."

"Well, she's given up the idea of marrying Peter Frampton, it's true."

"But her apartment is like a child's painting. So bright and cheerful."

Ginny frankly stared at him. Denis might say that nothing was wrong with him, but this conversation was exceedingly odd. Denis hadn't sounded this dreamy and strange since he came back from lunch two years ago after having sat next to Christie Brinkley in the restaurant. Much as she loved her daughter, Ginny knew Lisa was no Christie Brinkley. So what was going on?

Could Josh be right? He seemed to think the two of them were drawn together and were fighting it. Maybe, Ginny thought doubtfully. Stranger things had probably happened—but what could they be?

"So why don't you go ahead with your research," Denis said, with a smile.

Ginny hurried out of the room, before the real Denis came in and denounced this impostor.

An hour later, she had notes on a number of articles that mentioned either Tony D or Anthony DiBenedetto. They described a shadowy figure, reputed to have great power and to wield it ruthlessly when necessary. Most of the time, it seemed, just the mention of his name sufficed. There was one grainy picture of a burly man getting out of a limousine that was reprinted with every article. Ginny thought the photograph only added to the aura of mystery that surrounded the man. It was indistinct yet menacing.

She leaned back in her chair and wondered again what to do about Anita. If she had to, Ginny would be there when she gave birth. But the idea of trying to keep his daughter's whereabouts a secret from a man like the one Anthony DiBenedetto was supposed to be—well, Ginny would rather face Denis, an angry federal judge, and a pond full of alligators!

Her phone rang. When Josh responded to her businesslike greeting with, "Hi, darling," her day brightened to sunshine despite the rain that still drummed against the windows of Sanderson and Smith.

"Josh, hi." She sat looking, she knew, every bit as fatuous as Denis. "How are you?"

"I missed you this morning. I woke up very lonely."

His deep voice started strange vibrations in her heart. "I know. I missed you, too."

"I have a solution for our mutual problem," he murmured. "I'll tell you about it this evening."

"Mmm," was all Ginny's short-circuited brain could come up with. "I can't think."

"Good. That's a very good sign. How about I pick up some dinner stuff and meet you at your apartment about six?"

"How about five-thirty?" She was shameless and she didn't care.

"I'll be there. Right now I'm off to the library. Have you had a chance to check out Anita's father?"

Ginny tried to think. Should she tell Josh, or

would that be a betrayal of Anita's trust? No, she could speak. It was Anita's plans that had to be kept a secret.

"I found him," she said.

"I wondered. For a minute I thought maybe you weren't going to tell me what you knew." His understanding of her thoughts was sometimes a little scary to a woman who had kept her own counsel for so many years.

"I was debating. But I think it's okay. Anita's father is also known as Tony D." Ginny gave Josh all the information she had gotten from the computer database file.

"No wonder she's scared of him, if she thinks he's an organized crime figure."

"She's not the only one who thinks so, Josh. The *Times* and the U.S. Attorney's Office think so, too."

"Well, as a lawyer I'm a born skeptic. And I've known some U.S. Attorneys who didn't know what they were talking about a good part of the time."

Ginny shook her head. Surely a daughter couldn't be that far wrong in her assessment of her father and the danger he posed to her and anyone who cared for her. "I don't know, Josh. If you'd heard her last night. I don't think she's just an overimaginative girl who's mad at her father."

"Okay. Let me do some checking. I have a

source who might know something. We'll talk over dinner." Josh's voice sank to a low murmur as he said, "And later maybe we won't talk at all. 'Bye, Ginny."

" 'Bye, Josh," she whispered, her eyes dreamy, her voice low.

After talking to Ginny, Josh decided that before he set out for the main branch of the New York Public Library on Fifth Avenue and Forty-second Street, he would detour around to Fifth and Eightieth Street and talk to Mack. Maybe he'd know something about the mysterious Tony D.

Mack probably knew more than the *National Enquirer*, and since his lunchtime crowd wasn't coming for some time, he was willing to talk to Josh.

"I haven't heard nothing from him, and I know Mikey talked to him. So maybe you weren't so dumb after all, Hoosier."

"Thanks, Mack. Can I quote you, in case I need a testimonial to get into the bar here."

"Whaddaya mean get into the bar? You were in the bar Saturday night."

Josh wasn't sure whether he was kidding, so to be on the safe side, he explained. "Not that kind of bar, Mack. The kind lawyers belong to. You know, attorneys are members of the bar."

"Oh, yeah. Hey, I thought you were already a

lawyer." Mack's brow grew more furrowed than ever.

"I am, but not in New York."

"How can you be a lawyer in Indiana and not a lawyer here? Lawyers are lawyers, right?"

"You could get some argument on that from clients who win and those who lose." Josh smiled. "Laws differ from state to state, and only lawyers in that state are expert enough to understand and explain them."

Mack thought for a moment, then glared at him through slitted lids. "So how come you're telling me what Eddie can and cannot do in New York? You ain't a lawyer here, are you, shyster?"

Josh responded to the challenge in Mack's voice. "I've been a lawyer for over twenty-five years. And I've met a lot of guys who wanted to play Wizard of Oz. I think your Eddie is one of them."

"Whaddaya mean, Wizard of Oz? Whaddaya talkin' about?"

"Remember the scene in *The Wizard of Oz* where the little dog pulls the curtain aside and you see the old magician making the smoke and lightning that scare everybody?"

A smile broke on Mack's face. "Yeah, yeah and he says 'pay no attention to that man behind the curtain.' Sure I remember."

"Well, that's what I think Eddie is trying to

do. He's scaring a lot of people so they don't look behind the rumors and the tough talk and small-time punks like Mikey Scanlon. And do you know why, Mack?"

"Because he ain't as scary as we think?"

"Exactly. That's what I think. There are guys like that all over, and I think Eddie's one." Josh let that sink in for a minute before he asked, "So, tell me, as far as you know, is Anthony DiBenedetto a Wizard of Oz, or is he the real thing?"

Mack thought for a moment. He seemed a little shaken by Josh's comments about Eddie Tyrone. But finally he said, "I've heard a lot about Tony D, most of it smoke, like you say Eddie is. I don't know, though. Most people I know, they won't talk about Tony D. I think they're scared."

"Have you ever read anything about Tony D?"

"Nah, I don't read much. Every once in a while you hear he's been called in for questioning in a murder at a social club in Brooklyn or something. Or tax evasion, or bribery or something. But nothing ever comes of it."

Josh thanked him and told Mack to be sure to call him when Eddie made his next move. "Don't agree to anything, don't even talk to him by yourself." Mack agreed, though Josh thought he still seemed a little doubtful, and Josh set off for the library.

At a little after five-thirty that afternoon, he left

the market near Ginny's apartment and headed for her building.

When Ginny answered her door, looking good enough to eat in a soft sea green outfit that made her eyes seem greener than ever, Josh deposited the grocery bags on the floor and swung her into his arms. "Hi, gorgeous," he said with a big smile. And then he kissed her.

She felt so soft, so warm and responsive that he quickly revised his plans for the evening. "Let's eat later," he said as he walked Ginny backward to the couch.

"Aren't you hungry?" she asked, breathless from his kisses.

"Starving. I'll just nibble on you." His mouth opened over her neck and as Ginny arched back, Josh took tiny nips of her skin. "You taste so sweet." He turned them both around and sat down on the couch with Ginny in his lap. With his fingers, he traced the contours of her face, while his other hand moved gently across the swell of her breast. "And you feel so soft."

Ginny finally got her breath back. "How are you?"

"Tired, happy," he caught her lower lip between his teeth for minute, then he kissed her, long and lingeringly. "In love."

She looked up at him, searching his face. There was a tiny frown between her eyes. "What's the matter, sweetheart?" he murmured. "Don't you believe me?"

Ginny looked embarrassed. "I guess I still find it hard to believe."

"What is it you can't believe? That a sophisticated New Yorker like you could love a Hoosier hick like me?" He gave her a crooked half smile. "You are in love with me, aren't you? You said so." His smile might be teasing but there was a note of concern in his voice. "Ginny?"

"I don't understand how it could happen. I mean, I hardly know you. I've never been to Indiana. You can't really mean that within two weeks you're sure that you love me and want to move to a place you've never lived before."

"Why can't I mean it, Ginny?" His voice was soft, but there was an implacable look in his eye. "Is there some time limit on falling in love? Some law that says it should take not less than two nor more than thirty-six months. Is that it?"

"No, of course not. It's just that it seems so—fast."

"It's really not me you doubt, is it, Ginny?"

"No," she murmured. "It's not me either. It's us."

He grinned at her. "I know. I've never felt this close to anyone else either. I'm a little scared."

"You are?" Somehow it made Ginny feel better to know that.

"It's frightening to meet someone I care for so much and understand so well. And it was all so easy." He bent and kissed her lightly. "Like something out of a movie."

That was what was so incredible. No one, least of all Ginny herself, had ever thought of her as a fairy-tale princess, too good to be true. Now, Josh on the other hand was typecast as the handsome prince, senior division. The thought made her smile.

"Maybe we should talk about Anit—" She never got a chance to finish the thought.

"Maybe we should not talk at all." Josh pulled her into his arms and caught her mouth with his. Ginny sighed and grasped his shoulders. As the kiss lengthened and deepened, she could feel herself soften and mold her body to his. It was as if her very bones had begun to melt.

At last, when they moved reluctantly apart enough to catch their breath, Josh said, "I could keep this up all night, but your groceries are still sitting on the floor by the door."

Ginny sighed and ran her hand through his thick, brown hair before she pulled herself away from him and got to her feet. "I'd better get them into the kitchen. What are you planning to cook for me?"

"Burgundian chicken." His hands closed around her waist and she could feel his warm breath on her neck. It made her shiver, and Josh tightened his hold.

"What have I done to deserve you?" she said.

"You mean what have you done to deserve my cooking."

Josh bent to kiss her again when the telephone rang. Reluctantly, Ginny went to get it. She was tempted to let the machine answer it, but it might be important.

A voice with a pronounced Brooklyn accent asked if a Joshua Havilland was there. "Who may I say is calling?" Ginny responded in her best Sanderson and Smith voice.

"Just tell him it's Mack from the Met."

"Of course, how are you? I'm sorry we've never met. I'll get Josh." Ginny's cordial voice raised Josh's eyebrows. Who could Ginny want to meet?

"It's Mack from the Met." She held out the receiver.

"Hello, Mack. Have you heard from Eddie?"

"Yeah, yeah, that's why I'm calling. Who's that lady? You tell her about me?"

"Yes. That's Virginia. My . . . fiancée." Josh felt himself smiling, feeling warm and satisfied. Virginia was his fiancée. Or would be as soon as he could ask her—convince her— For a moment his happiness slipped away. What if she didn't want to marry him? What if she didn't want to be with him, love him? He shook his head and turned his mind back to his client.

"What did Eddie say?"

"Not much. He wants me to know that if I don't give up the location, he'll see to it that I don't sell hot dogs. Anyplace. Ever." Mack's voice was apprehensive. He clearly believed Eddie's warning was a threat.

"Are you going to meet with him?"

"Nah. Eddie said that wasn't necessary. He's going to send any message by Mikey Scanlon." Mack's voice began to shake a little. Eddie's messages were rumored to be very painful.

"Is the address on the letter you showed me Eddie's office? What was it, some street in Brooklyn?"

"Yeah. Clinton Street. But the place I know you can find him is a bar near there. The Shamrock. Most every night, Eddie's there."

"Would he be there now?" Josh looked at his watch.

"Likely."

"Is it near you?"

"Yeah." Josh could hear anxiety tighten Mack's voice.

"Why don't I come to your house and we can go to this bar together and talk to Eddie."

"No." There was a click as Mack hung up.

For a moment Josh stood frowning, looking

out the window but seeing nothing. He was going to help Mack whether Mack wanted him to or not. Quickly, he picked up the phone again and asked for information and then tried a ploy that had worked for him in Indiana. "I have the name, but I'm not sure this is the right place. Is this the Shamrock Bar on Clinton Street?"

"No," the operator replied, "there isn't a Shamrock Bar on Clinton, but there is one on Fulton. Could that be the one?"

Josh assured the voice that it was and then hung up. He turned to find Ginny looking at him with cool detachment.

"So much for Chicken à la Jersey City, I guess. Are you off to beard the mysterious Eddie in his lair?"

Josh smiled a little sheepishly. "Yeah. I really want to meet the guy. Mack's terrified of him but I think—"

"You think you should go over to Brooklyn, where you have been twice in your life, at night, to a place you know nothing about to meet a man who terrifies his associates." She glared at him. "That's the dumbest stunt I've ever heard of. A child of ten would know better than to do that."

"Don't be silly. A lot of work gets done at bars. It's a guy thing," he added.

"I can see that. It's too stupid for a woman to

try it. Only the sex that produced Rambo and the Terminator would think it was a good idea." Ginny walked over to stand in front of him, and Josh could see the glint of fear, and something else he couldn't identify, in her green eyes.

Josh grinned at her. "You're only saying that because you can't come."

"That's where you're wrong, bucko," Ginny said, sliding her feet into a pair of flats. "If you're going, I'm going too." She smiled at him. "I'll take notes."

Twenty-two

There was absolutely no way to stop Ginny when she had made up her mind. She reminded Josh that while he knew nothing about Brooklyn, she at least knew where it was.

"A cab driver could have you in the Bronx before you even knew you were going the wrong way. Besides, you need some credibility. I'm a New Yorker, plus I'll make you look official. You'd have to be somebody important to have a secretary along at this hour."

She had sounded so confident that they were in the cab heading downtown before Josh realized that she had never said she knew her way around Brooklyn. When he reminded her of that she waved a map in his face. "Always prepared. Every true New Yorker has maps and a guidebook. Even we can't know everything."

"Is that how you sounded like you knew everything about everything in this town?" Josh smiled at her. "I'm learning more about you every day.

As well as smelling terrific and looking good, you're devious."

"You should have suspected. I've spent twenty years working with lawyers. How could I not have picked up some of their traits?" Ginny smiled back. She had changed her clothes and now looked almost mousy. Her hair was held by a neat headband and she wore a gray skirt with a blue blouse and a gray jacket.

"I must say you look every inch the dedicated secretary. Right out of a fifties movie. If you had glasses, you could take them off and turn into Susan Hayward or Rhonda Fleming."

"Well, it's not the fifties, and I'm not Rhonda Fleming. Just let's not have this turn into the Two Stooges Meet Eddie the Killer Hot Dog King."

Josh laughed. What a woman! He hugged her tight against him. "When we get back, remind me to ask you to marry me."

That did what the prospect of meeting Eddie the Hot Dog King couldn't. Ginny pulled away from him and stared at him, her mouth slightly agape. Disbelief personified.

Josh couldn't resist. He held her face up to his and met her open mouth with his own in a kiss that ignited a brushfire along all the pathways of his body. God, he wanted Ginny! The hell with their children and her job and his ragtag group of clients. "Let's run away to Cancún or Acapulco," he said. "We'll drink margaritas and make love to the rhythm of the waves."

"You're crazy," said Ginny.

"You're right," said Josh.

"You're here," said the cabbie, a young, bearded black man wearing a Mets jacket. "The Shamrock Bar." He looked at his fares as if they were Hansel and Gretel. "You two have any idea how you're going to get back to Manhattan?"

Josh shrugged. Ginny shook her head. "Okay, look," said the cabbie. "I can't leave you here. My conscience would bother me." He lifted a tattered paperback from the seat next to him. "Thomas Wolfe was right."

"You mean *You Can't Go Home Again?*"

"Very good," the cabbie said. "But no. I was thinking of his short story, 'Only the Dead Know Brooklyn.' Great story. Great title."

Josh shook his head. Were Ginny and the cab driver going to sit here discussing great American novelists or were he and Ginny going to go into the Shamrock and make fools of themselves? A hard choice.

"I know," Ginny said.

"So how about I come back and pick you up in about . . ." he consulted his watch, "half an hour?"

"Thank you, Theodore," Ginny said.

They stood on the sidewalk, staring at the bar.

It looked mysterious, almost threatening with its windows covered in black paint.

"How did you know his name was Theodore?" Josh asked, as he took her hand.

"His name's on the hack license that's posted in the cab right next to the meter," Ginny said. She took a deep breath. "How will we know Eddie?"

"We won't. But I'll know Mikey Scanlon, if he's here. And if not, we'll just ask the bartender."

They entered the Shamrock, which looked to be one of the Irish political bars that dotted New York. On the wall were pictures of Republican heroes, from Parnell to Bobby Sands. The bar was crowded and the lilt of the voices said the customers were Irish. The tables weren't full, most of the activity was at the bar. Ginny could see that Josh found whom he was looking for right away. He turned and stared at a table in the middle of the room. There was a tall man in a black raincoat standing behind one of the chairs.

Josh walked over, an easy smile on his face. "Hello, Mikey, you remember me, don't you? Joshua Havilland. I'm a friend of Mack Dermott's." He held out his hand. Mikey ignored it. Josh looked down at the man sitting in the chair Mikey guarded. "You must be Eddie Tyrone," Josh said easily.

Ginny tried not to stare at the man she had heard so much about, but it was difficult not to. He was tiny, no more than five feet tall, and old. How old, Ginny couldn't guess, but his face was seamed like a walnut and his child-sized hands were white with large purple veins. He certainly didn't look like Don Corleone, Ginny thought irreverently.

Eddie Tyrone nodded once and gestured toward the chair opposite his. He looked at Ginny and frowned.

"My partner, Ms. McDougall," Josh said smoothly. "I thought she should be here. In case anything happens to me."

The old man nodded again and a grimace that might have been a smile passed across his face. He bowed his head to Ginny in a polite acknowledgement of the introduction. Then he jerked his head at Mike Scanlon. Apparently, Scanlon understood.

"You want something to drink?" he asked as rudely as he could.

Josh looked at Ginny. She smiled. "Half and half, please." Scanlon looked surprised for a moment. Apparently, not many women ordered that.

"Whiskey," Josh said and nodded to the halffilled glass in front of Tyrone.

Scanlon left and Tyrone picked up his glass and took a tiny sip. He set the glass down, precisely in the middle of the coaster advertising Guinness Stout. "What do you want?" he asked, and Ginny understood instantly why he preferred gestures to speech. His voice was a high-pitched, shaky whisper. It wouldn't have scared a toddler.

"I want to talk to you about Mack's stand at the Metropolitan." Tyrone gestured for him to continue. "I understand that you have asked him to give up that location." Josh waited for a moment, and Tyrone nodded once. "It is because you wish to give that location to a relative of yours." Again, Tyrone gave a single nod. "I wonder if we couldn't reach some mutually satisfactory agreement." Tyrone shrugged. Josh took that as an invitation to continue.

"Look, Mack has done well for you at that location." A pause, and again, Tyrone nodded. "He can continue to do well. But there is no guarantee that somebody else at that same location would make it as profitable." This time, Tyrone sat, as impassive as a Buddha, his small, black eyes narrowed to slits. He waited.

Josh went on. "It's a prime location, because it gets so much traffic. Someone less quick than Mack, someone who couldn't make change and take orders and hand out frankfurters all at the same time, might not do so well. Isn't that so, Mr. Tyrone?"

Mikey Scanlon, who had waited nearby with

Ginny's and Josh's drinks in his hand, came to the table in response to a glance from Tyrone. He set the glasses down without a word and went to stand behind his boss's chair.

Josh took a sip and smiled. "Wonderful stuff. I've never understood why anyone who could get whiskey like this at home would leave Ireland and come all the way to America, where it has to be imported."

Tyrone made a small gesture with his hand, which Josh interpreted as an invitation to continue. "Now, when I talked to Mack, he indicated that he might want to retire in a few years' time, if he could afford to. In the meantime, Mack indicated that he might be willing to train someone to follow in his footsteps. So maybe that someone could learn to take orders and make change and fix frankfurters all at the same time." Josh took another sip of whiskey. "That way, everyone would be happy." He sat back and waited for a reaction.

Tyrone looked at him without expression. Finally, the old man leaned forward and spoke, his harsh croak so whispery that Josh had to lean forward to catch the words. "I don't make deals. I want the location. Now. It doesn't matter what kind of deal you offer, how good it is. I don't make deals."

Ginny had sat quietly during the entire conversation, taking down every word in a shorthand notebook in her lap. Now she watched the two men lean together like conspirators. What next, she wondered.

"Did you get all that, Ginny?" Josh asked without looking at her.

"Every word," she said, feeling like Sam Spade's secretary, Essie or Effie? Whatever her name was, she had sat meekly taking notes and worshiping Sam from across the desk. It was not a comparison Ginny liked.

"You think about it, Mr. Tyrone. There are other locations for a top drawer vendor like Mack. But you're going to lose a lot of money if you give it to someone who can't do the job." He stood up and took Ginny's arm, almost lifting her to her feet.

"I'll be in touch. Come on, Ginny."

"Don't bother. You got Mr. Tyrone's answer." Mikey Scanlon's raucous voice almost made Ginny jump after the guiet tones of the other two men.

Josh said nothing. He and Ginny walked out, followed by the strains of "A Nation Once Again," someone had started to play on the accordion.

"Now what?" Ginny said in a tense voice. If Theodore the cab driver hadn't come back, how were they going to get home? Stand under a streetlight and study a map? She looked around for a cab.

Around the corner came Theodore in his wonderfully reassuring yellow cab. When they arrived back at Ginny's apartment, Josh whirled her around and put his hands on her shoulders. "Eddie Tyrone doesn't look very scary to me. I see the old magician cranking up the smoke machine. Mikey seems to be his only worker bee. I think we can get him to see reason."

"Josh, you're crazy. Maybe everybody in Elgin, Indiana, acts from rational motives, but here in Sin City people do things out of spite and jealousy and pride. All that messy, emotional stuff. So, I'm not so sure Mr. Tyrone is going to give in."

"We'll see. I have a few other ideas, if reason and self-interest don't work." Josh took her into his arms, holding her close for a moment. Then he spoke, very softly. "Do you think you could ever see your way clear to marrying me, Ginny? Given enough time, and assuming I don't have some horrible habit or a wife in the attic or something? What do you think?"

Ginny didn't pull away. She wanted to be in his arms, where she had felt at home from the very first. But she didn't want to think about marriage. ''I don't know,'' she murmured, her face half-hidden against his chest. "I don't much like to think about marriage."

Josh lifted her chin with his long, strong fingers and looked into her eyes. They were troubled and uncertain. He felt a sudden surge of fear. "Damn it, Ginny! Are you really going to let the past rule you?"

He waited, looking down and seeing the struggle in her face. Smiling a little, he smoothed her hair back from her face. "Don't live in the past like Eddie and his one henchman. Am I going to be standing behind your chair in twenty years like Mikey, while you think about someone else? Will you ever be able to marry me?"

Ginny knew she felt as deeply as he did, cared about him as much. But marriage? "I don't know, Josh. It's not something I've ever considered."

"Well, I'm glad of that. I like being the first. But do you think you could consider it now? I get impatient when I think you don't see me because you're so busy looking back over your shoulder at the past."

"I think I understand how you feel, but I can't help being afraid. This is all so new to me." Ginny could see disappointment wash over his face. She hated to think that she had caused it.

Slowly, Josh released her. "If you ever decide to give me a chance, let me know." He turned and started toward the door. "In the meantime, maybe I'd better just go home. I'll call you."

"Josh!" She couldn't lose him. He couldn't just leave.

"What?" His hand was on the doorknob. She couldn't see his face but his voice sounded defeated.

"Don't go."

He turned around. His expression was unreadable, but he walked back to her and took her into his embrace. "I'm sorry. You're right. I'm pushing you because I'm so sure, but I can see that you aren't. And I understand." He swung her easily up into his arms and carried her to the couch. He sank down into the cushions and held her on his lap, his lips buried in her hair.

"Thank God." He heard the tremor in her voice and felt the slight shiver that ran through her body. "I don't want you to go."

"I know. And I didn't mean to push you. I know your life has belonged only to you for a long time, and it's hard to think of changing that." He ran his hand over the sweet line of her shoulder and arm. She was so lovely, so precious. "I just lose it sometimes. I need you and I'm afraid you've been independent for so long that you'll decide you don't need me. Or at least, that you don't need me the way I need you."

Ginny closed her eyes. She was happy to be with him, at ease with him no matter where they were or what they did. It was enough. For now, for her, it was enough.

She struggled to find the words. "Josh, I don't want to lose you. But I can't decide the rest of my life in a week. I'm not sure why you think you can. You know, you could be wrong about me. Maybe we won't get along, or you'll get tired of the fact that I can't cook. Or I'll get tired of the fact that you can. How can you be so sure?"

Josh said nothing at first, just silently sat stroking her cheek and ear. "I don't know. Maybe I see things clearly because I left my rut. I lost my wife and sold my law practice and moved away from home. If you'd pulled up stakes and moved to Elgin after Marian died, while I stayed there, maybe I'd be the one clinging to the past. Maybe."

Ginny sat silent, listening to the beat of Josh's heart under her ear. "I guess I am being a coward. I won't be anymore." She sat up and looked him straight in the eye. "I love you, Joshua Havilland." She took a deep breath. "And I'd like you to stay the night. Please."

For a second, Josh debated whether he should push for an acceptance of his proposal. Then he remembered the old adage about half a loaf. He kissed Ginny hard and said only, "Yes."

When she rose and held out her hand, Josh took it and let her lead him into her bedroom.

Twenty-three

They hadn't been thinking very clearly when they went to bed, Josh decided as he approached Denis's building the next morning at eight o'clock. He could have stayed undercover in Ginny's apartment until he was sure Denis had left, but somehow he felt that would be cowardly. And useless.

He felt wonderful after a night in Ginny's arms. He was still smiling a little when he let himself in to Denis's apartment.

He stopped smiling abruptly. Denis and Lisa were sitting side by side on the overstuffed love seat. There was a smell of coffee in the air, and Josh thought irrelevantly that he would have to buy Ginny some of those special Kenyan beans. And a coffeepot. Ginny believed coffee grew powdered in jars.

Two pairs of eyes glared at him accusingly. "Where have you been?" the outraged children said in unison.

"None of your business." Josh was not about to be bullied by his child, or Ginny's. "What is

Lisa doing here at this unseemly hour? How long has she been here?"

"Lisa called Ginny several times last night and got the answering machine." Denis frowned. He wore that expression much too often, Josh thought. "You didn't come home at all last night."

"I know. But I'm a big kid, son. I've been allowed out on my own for about forty years now. As for your mother," he said to Lisa, "she also comes and goes as she pleases. As it happens, we were together last night." He went over to pour himself some coffee. "We had an interview with a gentleman in Brooklyn."

"All night?" Lisa demanded.

"That is none of your business. You may ask your mother any questions you want, and she can humor you if she wants to. I don't care to be cross-examined at this hour of the morning." Josh gave Lisa a long, unsmiling look and started out of the room.

"Just a minute, Dad," Denis said. "You can't talk to Lisa like that. She has a right to be concerned about her mother."

"I agree, Denis. But I am not her mother."

"No, but you've been spending a lot of time with her," Lisa interjected. "You act as if you care about her. And I think you just spent the night with her." Lisa's voice was accusing. "I want to know what's going on. My mother doesn't date much. She's a little naive about men. I don't want her hurt."

"Believe me, Lisa, I don't want Ginny to be hurt either. But I have to tell you, she's a lot smarter and a lot more sophisticated than you give her credit for." Josh came back into the room and sat down on one of Denis's butterscotch leather Barcelona chairs.

"You'd like to believe that, wouldn't you?" Lisa said, real hostility showing now for the first time. "It would ease your conscience when you take off for Florida and leave her here."

"What makes you think that's what I'm going to do?"

"I know about men like you." Lisa's glance slid over to rest for a revealing moment on Denis. "Love 'em and leave 'em, that's you."

Josh looked at Lisa to see if by any chance she was smiling. She couldn't possibly think he lived the way Denis did. Lisa wasn't smiling. It appeared she was serious. "I thought Denis must have explained that there isn't a lot of scope for a Don Juan in Elgin, Indiana. And Shellfish Cay is not a Club Med location, no matter what you may have heard."

Lisa was not amused. Her green eyes, so like her mother's, were glacial, and her mouth was pinched and disapproving. "I don't think joking about breaking susceptible women's hearts is very funny, Mr. Havilland."

"Denis, explain to your friend that I am not trying to take advantage of Ginny." Josh gestured helplessly to his son. Denis just shrugged.

"I can't convince Lisa of anything. And we're not exactly friends," he added after a moment's consideration. "We're allies." Lisa nodded.

"And what is your complaint, son? Am I behaving badly to your assistant? Is that what you're so disapproving about?" Josh could feel his happiness draining away. He and Ginny were just a couple of overage delinquents as far as these two were concerned. He couldn't wait to hear what Denis's complaint was. He didn't have to wait long.

"You can't just come to New York and act as if you know all about living here, Dad. You're really very unsophisticated, if you don't mind my saying so."

"Well, you know, son, I do mind. Quite a lot as a matter of fact." He smiled because it was amusing in a way. But it was also damned annoying. "I think both Ginny and I have earned the right to live our lives as we see fit. If we want to give all our money to a home for aging belly dancers and take off to study with a guru in Nepal, I don't think you should try to stop us."

"Would you try to stop me?" Denis stood up

and stared down at his father. "As I recall, you had a few words to say when I wanted to drop out of Princeton and become a rock drummer."

"You did?" said Lisa, with an admiring glance at Denis. "A rock drummer?"

"That's because you were a lousy drummer." Josh stood up and faced his son, grateful for his one inch advantage in height. "And at the time I was paying your way so I thought I should have some say about the manner in which my money was being spent."

"It was also because you thought you knew the world better than I did." Denis looked at his father and gave the sort of hopeless gesture that parents did when their children wanted to leave school and join rock bands. "Well, now I know it better than you do. You can't just hang out your shingle in New York City and expect to find clients and make a living. I don't know what you and Ginny are up to and, frankly, unlike Lisa, I don't want to know. I want you to be happy, that's all. And I don't think jumping headfirst into life in Manhattan is going to make you happy. This is a tough town, Dad, and I don't want to see you become an unhappy failure instead of a successful small-town lawyer."

"I'm grateful that you're concerned about me, son. And I'll certainly bear what you've said in mind. But, again, I think you'll just have to have some faith in me and what I can do."

Lisa had listened to the two lawyers discuss things with growing annoyance. "Listen, you two. If you've quite finished being very masculine and lawyerlike, could we get back to what's important around here?" She stood up and put her hands on her hips.

"And what is that?" Josh asked politely.

"What do you mean, what's important?" Denis said irately.

"My mother, that's what I mean. I don't give a flying fig whether your father makes money practicing law. But I care very much if he breaks my mother's heart." She walked over to stand directly in front of Josh. "So, if you aren't going to treat her right, just leave her alone. She's not some man-hunting little widow like you've been playing with at Catfish Hollow."

"Lisa, I'm trying very hard not to lose my temper." If he had not been so completely in love and so afraid that Ginny wasn't as certain as he was, he might have found this whole scene funny. "You have got the wrong guy if you think I'm some practiced charmer and your mother is Little Nell from the country."

"Don't give me that stuff. I know all I need to know about you." She was practically sneering.

"And what is that?" Maybe it was the coffee

but he was beginning to get his sense of humor back.

"You're the Indigo Man. Just another aging pretty face. The poor man's Robert Redford."

This really was funny. "The *very* poor man's Robert Redford," Josh said with a grin. "It's none of your business, but I have no intention of being the Indigo Man or the pink, blue, or heliotrope man."

Lisa looked at him in disbelief. "I don't care what ad you pose for. Just don't go around playing games with my mother."

"Lisa," he said, "has it ever occurred to you that it is your mother who may be playing games with me?"

"Mother?" said Lisa, in complete disbelief.

"Ginny?" said Denis, at the same time and in the same tone.

"Why can't you two see her as a grown-up in charge of her own life? She's been looking after both of you for years, but neither one of you thinks for a moment that she can look after herself. Not to mention me." Josh looked at both of them in time to see a glimmer of doubt in both pairs of eyes. He thought he had knocked a hole in their belief and decided it was a good time to quit.

"I'll drink my coffee upstairs, if you two think I can manage that task. You can stay here and wring your hands about your foolish parents."

In the living room, Lisa said, "Denis, is he right? Are we being stupid? Are we," she could barely bring herself to speak the last thought aloud, "are we acting like—like *parents?*"

Denis looked into her troubled green eyes and found it hard to think about either of their parents. "No, of course not. We're naturally concerned, that's all. It's just typical of my father that he'd think that."

"He doesn't seem like a bad person," Lisa said.

"Oh, no, he's not. I didn't mean that. It's just that he's always so calm and judicious. Always manages to make me feel like a kid."

Lisa smiled. "Momma does the same thing to me. Will we ever grow up?"

"Will they?" Denis responded. "I'd better get to the office and see how Ginny is." He stood up and looked down at Lisa. "Dad's right about one thing. Ginny's really very strong and smart. She won't do anything foolish."

She already has, Lisa thought. *She's seeing your father. And if we're right, she's sleeping with him, too!*

Twenty-four

He needed an office, Josh decided as he spread papers around Denis's antique walnut hunt table and tried to separate the notes he had taken on Anthony DiBenedetto from those on Sylvia Bright's will. If only Ginny and he worked together and lived together . . .

He leaned back in the uncomfortable Jacobean chair Denis used at the table. It ground into Josh's back and spoiled his daydream. Damn. Back to work.

The telephone rang and Josh immediately thought it might be Ginny. He snatched the receiver up but the female voice was unfamiliar.

"This is Sheila Margolies, Mr. Havilland. You may not remember, but I was one of the speakers at the Columbia Symposium you attended."

He did remember now. She was the woman who wanted help for people in family disputes who couldn't afford lawyers. "Yes, I remember, Ms. Margolies."

"I've been in touch with the Mayor's Commission on Judicial Reform and with a couple of private charities, including the Barringer Foundation. They've agreed to help fund a pilot project, if we can find the right people."

"That sounds like a good start," Josh said.

"I wondered if you and Ms. McDougall could meet with me and a member of the Mayor's Commission and several other interested parties. I'm sure you could help us." She paused a moment. "You were there together, weren't you?"

"Yes, and I'm sure she'd be interested in meeting with you, too." Josh smiled as a thought began to take shape. Maybe New York wasn't as chancy and difficult for a seasoned lawyer as some young people thought!

"Then why don't we arrange to meet for lunch? Would Thursday be good for you?" Josh thought of his and Ginny's visit to the Mordecai Jackson Home on Thursday evening. He suggested Friday and they agreed, subject to everyone else's approval.

Josh hung up the phone and whistled a chorus of "Happy Days Are Here Again." Maybe Ginny's life would get a little shaking up. Besides whatever vibrations he had managed to bring her.

Once more, he went to see his favorite hot dog vendor, ready to report on his meeting with Eddie Tyrone. As Josh approached, he thought that Mack looked worried. Instead of cheerful commentary on the world at large, Mack seemed morose. He looked up and saw Josh and seemed to do a double take.

"Shyster!" he called out, waving a frankfurter. "Good to see you! Have a dog, on the house."

Josh came up to him and took the hot dog. "Thanks, Mack, I appreciate it. But do you think you might possibly call me 'Hoosier' when other people are around? I'm trying to impress people around here with what an ace attorney I am. Calling me 'shyster' at the top of your voice isn't helping me."

Mack looked abashed. "It's a term of endearment, shys—I mean, Hoosier," he said.

"Well, call me sweetheart or darling if you need a term of endearment," Josh replied, talking through a mouthful of hot dog, chili, and cheese. "These are damn fine hot dogs, Mack. Damn fine."

"Yeah, they are. So, tell me the truth. You didn't go to see Eddie, did you?"

"Who told you that?"

"Nobody. Nobody had to. I mean, here you are."

"Right. Here I am. So?"

"So, if you had bothered Eddie with my troubles, you wouldn't be here." Mack opened a bottle of orange soda and took a deep swig.

"Listen, Mack, I did meet Eddie and I have to ask. Who's gone missing because of him?"

Mack smiled triumphantly. "I knew you didn't believe me. I knew you thought that I was running scared over nothing. So, here. I brought you these. My Uncle Liam cut these out. He had the stand before me. See. Eddie is a mean dude." He handed Josh a manila envelope. When Josh opened it and looked inside, it was full of newspaper clippings.

"Mind if I take these over to the steps and look them over?" Josh said.

"Okay. Only be careful, my Uncle Liam treasures these."

Josh finished his hot dog, and decided it made a delicious breakfast. He bought a Coke and took it over to his favorite spot on the steps and opened the envelope.

Uncle Liam's clippings detailed Edward James Tyrone's rise from petty crime to head of a gang in Hell's Kitchen, made up of Irish toughs who ran the rackets in that part of town. Eddie had been arrested several times but had never even been indicted. He kept himself out of the line of fire both from rival gangs and from the police. It was a colorful account of a colorful life.

It was also about forty years out of date. Josh looked at the mastheads of some of the clippings. The *New York Journal American,* the *World-Telegram & Sun*—papers that closed a quarter century ago.

The clippings were yellowed with age. Eddie

Tyrone's last arrest had been in 1954. That didn't mean that his reign had ended then, of course. But the age of the clippings and the age of Eddie made it seem likely that his power was limited, if not gone. If Mikey Scanlon was his only muscle, he couldn't have much business.

Josh carefully folded the clippings and put them back in the envelope. He leaned back against the balustrade and closed his eyes. The early-spring sun warmed his face, and made him think of sleep. He hadn't gotten much last night.

Last night. Ginny. He sighed. "Hey, Hoosier, whatcha doing with my Uncle Liam's clippings?" Mack's voice opened Josh's eyes and sent him back to reality. Hard stone and old newspapers.

He handed the envelope back to Mack, who tucked it away tenderly in his jacket pocket. "Well," said Mack, "you see? Uncle Liam had his problems with Eddie, believe me. He tried to argue with him once. Just once. Eddie sent a couple of his strong-arm boys to talk to Uncle Liam. Told him what would happen if he caused any trouble again. Scared Uncle Liam, man."

"That was a long time ago, wasn't it, Mack?"

"Yeah, musta been thirty—no, more like forty years ago." Mack smiled reminiscently. "I was just a kid, but I can remember Aunt Fiona crying and carrying on and telling Uncle Liam not to make Mr. Tyrone angry again or she might lose her husband and her children their father. She was calling on the Blessed Virgin. The whole family had a big meeting about it. Uncle Liam never gave Eddie Tyrone any trouble after that."

Josh could understand why Uncle Liam had believed the two strong-arm boys. "But why do you think Eddie has the same kind of power now?" he asked Mack. "Do you personally know anybody he's had beaten up or killed?"

Mack looked horrified. "Do you think I'd've let you even talk to Eddie about his nephew if I did? I'd feel as if I'd set you up. Not to mention making my wife a widow and my children orphans."

"Well, after meeting Eddie I'd still say he's a Wizard of Oz."

"You may be convinced, but is Eddie?" Mack turned to take someone's order. "Oh, hello, Mikey."

Josh looked up to see Mikey Scanlon, still wearing his black raincoat, giving Mack a very cold stare.

"You send this guy to talk to Eddie, Mack?"

"He's a friend."

"Mr. Tyrone's your friend, Mack. But he ain't gonna be if you keep making new friends like Mr. Havilland here." He looked at Josh, his eyes still without expression. "You oughta stay out of other people's business. You oughta leave Mack here alone. Mr. Tyrone don't like it."

Josh ignored the threat. "Tell me, Mike, who is this nephew Mr. Tyrone wants to take over this location? Do you know him?"

Mike Scanlon didn't like questions. He frowned at Josh, his face like a stone. Josh said, "Who is he? Mack ought to know. Tell me."

He might not like questions, but Mike was used to obeying orders. "It's me."

"You're Eddie Tyrone's nephew?" Mack said. "I never knew that. Gee, Mikey, no wonder Eddie looks after you."

Mike scowled. "I don't need looking after. I look after Uncle Eddie." He looked even angrier after he spoke.

Josh thought Mike was probably right. The frail old man he had met in the Shamrock needed looking after. On the other hand, Mike wasn't the brightest guy in the world. Slow but thorough, Josh thought. Mike would have problems with a busy hot dog stand. New Yorkers didn't wait happily, especially not for food at an outdoor stand.

Maybe, just maybe there might be room for a little competition.

"Tell Mr. Tyrone that I'll be back to see him later this week," Josh said.

"Mr. Tyrone told you that he didn't have

nothin' more to say to you." Mikey clenched his
fists and glared at Josh.

"Okay, Mikey," said Mack. "It's okay. We
won't bother him." Mack offered Mikey a hot
dog. It seemed to be his universal panacea. Whatever bothered you, one of Mack's hot dogs would
cheer you up, calm you down, or clear your head.

"Just tell him what I said." Josh gave Mike
Scanlon his best icy stare, honed by years at the
bar. Mikey frowned. He nodded his head at
Mack, the same way Eddie Tyrone did, and left
without another word.

Mack spent the next ten minutes trying to persuade Josh that Eddie would have him beaten,
shot, drawn and quartered, or otherwise disposed
of if he dared to bother him again. Josh nodded
absent-mindedly. "Don't worry, Mack. Eddie will
come around."

"You just never see reality, shyster. I don't
know how you've survived to get gray in your
hair." Mack turned away in disgust.

Josh had some thinking to do. He walked down
Fifth Avenue without seeing much of it. As he
passed Rockefeller Center, he noticed a travel
agency with posters of colorful resorts. He paused
and stood staring for a few moments.

It was possible that he could solve several of
his problems right here. He went inside and spent
half an hour discussing where to find the bright-

est sun and the clearest water at the best price. When he left, travel brochures to Caribbean islands bulged in his pockets. Once they got all their clients, families, friends, and the Mayor's Commission straightened out, he and Ginny could take off for paradise.

That evening, he arrived at Ginny's ready to cook. Rubbing his hands, he headed for the kitchen after a long and very satisfying kiss.

"I never even started dinner last night," he said as he washed the chicken and set out the other ingredients. "No wonder I ate one of Mack's hot dogs for breakfast. I hadn't had any dinner. What made me forget to eat, do you suppose?" He gave her a wicked grin.

Ginny smiled back. She sat at her tiny breakfast table while he cooked. She loved to watch him, particularly when he wasn't looking at her. The way he moved with such economy, his long legs encased in worn denim, his hands chopping and blending and frying, always purposeful, graceful.

Dreamily she concentrated on Josh, not on the chicken or the comments he was making as he went along.

"You're not paying attention," he complained. "Here I am doing my best Julia Child imitation and you're completely zoned out."

Ginny smiled. "But if I listen, I might learn something."

Josh waited, but she said nothing further. "That's the general idea," he said.

"If I start learning, sooner or later I'd probably know enough to cook on my own."

He waited again for her to say why this was a bad idea. "By George, I think you've got it," he said at last.

"Well, you see how foolish that would be," Ginny said. "Then I'd be cooking and you'd be sitting here looking at me cook."

Josh had to smile. "I see I have been bested by a superior strategist."

Ginny tried to look modest. "Of course," she said, "if you were to talk about something other than how to sauté chicken, I might listen."

"Then let me tell you about an invitation we have received for lunch this Friday." Josh balanced a knife on a cutting board at both ends and cut carrots faster than Ginny could blink.

"I can't go to lunch during the week. I have too much work."

"Ah, but this is a business lunch." Whish, whish, and minced onions joined the carrots. "It was Sheila Margolies from that seminar we went to."

"What does she want with us?"

"Well," said Josh, turning to look at her, his

face serious, "I think she wants to pick our brains about how to set up a pilot program of help to laymen—"

"And women," said Ginny.

"And women," said Josh, bowing slightly to her. He turned and briskly added the chopped vegetables to the sauté pan. "Anyway, to help members of the lay public represent themselves in court. Any ideas?"

Ginny smiled. "Hey, that's great. A legal assistant on a committee for a change instead of being given all the work by the lawyers when they get back from lunch."

"Yeah, I thought so, too." Josh smiled. "Plus, I think if we play our cards right, we may be asked to head the project."

"What makes you think that?" Ginny grabbed a carrot and bit into it.

"Just a hunch. We're probably the only people they know who are interested and have the combination of qualities that they need. Plus, we just may be suckers enough to take it on."

Ginny thought for a moment. "I don't see how I can, Josh. I'd have to take a leave of absence from Sanderson and Smith, and they're not very eager to give those unless there's some kind of medical reason, like pregnancy."

"We'll just have to talk to them. I think it would be a real coup for the firm to have you take on a job like this. Think of the good public relations when you get your name in the papers. Not only does Sanderson and Smith have the best lawyers, their legal assistants are the best, too."

"I think it sounds wonderful, but I don't think the managing committee has ever given it a thought. Every now and then, associates get leaves of absence to go to work for some congressional committee or a special prosecutor, but the staff doesn't ever get them."

"There's always a first time. Besides, if they don't give you time off, you can quit."

"Quit!" Ginny was horrified. "I couldn't do that. I've been there for years. What would Denis do?"

"He's a big boy now. He can hire himself another couple of assistants. It would take at least two to replace you." Josh combined the chicken, some other ingredients that Ginny hadn't paid much attention to, and a large splash of red wine in a casserole and set it in the oven. "There, now we can go sit down and have a glass of wine while we talk."

They sat next to each other on the couch and for a few minutes neither said anything. The idea of being with each other at the end of the day held them both silent.

At last, Ginny said, "I guess we should talk

about what you're going to do about Eddie Tyrone and what I'm going to do about Anita."

"And what we're both going to do about our meddlesome children." Josh picked up his wineglass. "But I don't feel like talking about that now."

Ginny reached over and took his hand. "I know. This is so nice."

"The two of us, just sitting here while dinner cooks and problems wait outside the door." Josh picked up their joined hands and kissed Ginny's fingers.

They sat in contented silence for a few more minutes, exchanging a smile of understanding and love. Josh had just turned to Ginny when the doorbell rang. "Damn," he said.

The telephone rang. "Damn," she said.

The stove timer buzzed, and the two of them turned to each other and burst out laughing.

"You get the telephone, I'll answer the door and check dinner," said Josh as he headed for the door. Whoever it was had stabbed his finger on the bell. "I'm coming, I'm coming." He jerked open the door to find Gray, his face pale and tense.

"I'm glad you're here," the young man said. "I need to talk to both of you."

"Come on in," said Josh, as dreams of a leisurely dinner and a long, romantic evening disappeared like smoke. "Ginny's on the telephone and I have to check dinner. Come on in the kitchen with me."

Ginny smiled at Gray and turned back to the telephone. "I'll let you talk to him, Mr. Scanlon. If you'll hold on, please." She went into the kitchen and told Josh that Mikey Scanlon wanted to talk to him. She took one look at Gray and sat him down at the small round table and poured him a glass of wine. She was sorry she had left hers in the living room.

"What's the matter, Gray?"

"Anita won't talk to me, but her superintendent told me that she has asked him to try to sublet her apartment. Her lease has a year to run." He looked at her and she could see the pain in his eyes. "What is she doing, Ginny? Do you know where she's going?"

Ginny took a deep breath. "No, Gray, I don't. Anita didn't tell me where she was going or when. I'm sorry, but even if I knew, I couldn't tell you. She asked me not to talk about her plans with you or her father."

Gray put his head in his hands. "I don't understand why she's so damn frightened of him. I could protect her, if she's afraid he'll do something drastic."

"I don't think she's afraid he'll hurt her."

"It's me, isn't it? She has some idea that he'll come after me with a shotgun." He gave a brief bark of laughter. "I thought that's what happened when the guy didn't want to marry the girl."

"I'm not sure Anita's thinking too clearly, Gray. But after she's had awhile to think when she isn't under pressure, maybe she'll agree with you." It was all Ginny could say.

"She has confidence in you. She talks to you. What can I do, Ginny? Don't tell me just to wait until she decides whether our child is going to live or die. I don't think I can do that." Gray finished off his wine in one gulp. "I'm going crazy. Tell me what to do."

"I know it's hard, Gray, but I think all you can do is wait and let Anita know you love her and will stand by her." Ginny hated to let Gray go on thinking that Anita was considering an abortion, but she felt deeply that Anita was counting on Ginny's loyalty to her. Two people telling Anita that they knew what was best for her was enough. Ginny might think that some of Anita's decisions were unwise, but she had to respect her right to make them.

"You staying for dinner, Gray?" Josh asked as he came back into the kitchen. "It's a masterful chicken in red wine sauce tonight, and if you'll both give the chef room to chop and dice, we'll also have a fantastic risotto and a matchless mushroom and spinach salad with balsamic vinaigrette."

Gray smiled slightly and looked at Ginny. "Would you mind very much if I stayed?"

"Of course not. I was about to ask you but I wanted to check with the chef to see if there was enough for three." Ginny smiled. "What did Mikey want, Josh?"

"He's going to meet me at Mack's stand tomorrow at eleven. The three of us are going to talk." Josh shrugged. "I don't know if this is good or bad. I hope that Mikey doesn't deliver some threat from Tyrone that terrifies Mack."

"It doesn't sound that way, does it?" said Ginny after some thought. "I mean, if they wanted to scare him, wouldn't they have Mr. Tyrone talk to him? Two words from Eddie and Mack would turn to quivering jelly. At least that's the impression he gave you."

"We shall see. Now, if you two would leave the artist to work his magic, we'll eat in twenty minutes or so."

Ginny and Gray sat in silence in the living room for a few minutes. Only one light was on, and the early-spring evening sky, purple and gray above the buildings to the west of Ginny's apartment building, cast a shadowy light in the room. Ginny couldn't see Gray's expression, but from his hunched shoulders and bowed head she knew he was tense and unhappy.

"Gray," she said softly, searching for a way to

tell him enough to calm him, but not enough to betray Anita, "what kind of a person do you think Anita is?"

His head jerked up and he stared at Ginny. "What kind of a question is that? She's wonderful. Gentle and strong and beautiful."

Ginny let the words hang in the air for a minute. "What do you think a gentle, strong, beautiful woman would do in a situation like Anita's?"

Gray said nothing, but his body remained alert and poised, like a dog on a scent. He was thinking about her words and, though Ginny could not see his face, she could tell he was testing his fears against the kind of woman Anita was.

"She's brave, too, Ginny," he said at last. "Is that what you're trying to help me see?"

"I want you to see who Anita is, Gray. This hasn't changed her. She'll deal with this crisis the same way she's dealt with the rest of her life." In other words, Ginny thought but couldn't say, she'll take the courageous course but she'll insist on running away and doing it all by herself. Just the way she left her father's home and the way she's refused to tell you about her family.

Gray thought for a moment, then leaned forward into the pool of light cast by the one lamp. He was smiling a little. "You've made me feel better, Ginny. Anita was born and raised a Catholic, and she's brave and determined to do the best she can for the people she loves. I know she loves me." He took a deep breath. "And being Anita, she loves our baby. I don't think she'll have an abortion." He leaned back in the chair and took a sip of wine. "Thank you, Ginny."

Ginny breathed a sigh. She had gone as far as she could. Surely a Yale-trained lawyer could figure out the rest. Or had he gone to Yale undergraduate and Harvard Law School? Without further thought, she asked him.

Gray stared at her, with the same bemused look she had seen on Josh's face more than once. "Sorry," she said. "I guess it's not important."

For the first time, Ginny saw a genuine smile on his face. "Yale College, Harvard Law. Is that okay?"

"I think so. If you can't go to CUNY and learn about life while you're studying literature and history the way I did, I guess doing your studying in Gothic buildings in New Haven is the next best thing."

"Dinner's ready," Josh called from the kitchen. "Come and serve yourselves."

Josh had left everything in the cooking pots. Ginny shook her head. Her meals might be uninspired at best, but she did serve them nicely. A silver serving dish did a lot for tuna-noodle casserole.

"What's wrong?" asked Josh.

"Nothing. Not a thing." Ginny lied without a blush. To keep him happy in the kitchen, she would praise anything. "It all looks heavenly and smells better."

"You don't like not having serving dishes." Josh nodded his head as he spoke. "I don't know why women insist on using twice as many dishes and utensils as they need to."

"On that theory, everyone should grab a fork and we could just stand around the stove and dig in," said Ginny, her voice tart. Damn, she thought, he'll never peel another onion in this kitchen. Why did she have to open her mouth and ruin everything?

Josh laughed and gave her a hug. "Don't look so stricken, sweetheart. I'll still cook, only after this you can serve it. Chef and maid, okay?"

Ginny grinned. Josh didn't need to be coddled. She served herself some chicken and creamy-looking risotto and took her plate in to the dining room table. Josh brought out the salad. He and Gray set heaping plates down on the table. For a minute everyone was absorbed in the delicious meal. Then both Ginny and Gray complimented Josh on the food. Conversation was strained. No one wanted to bring up Anita or her father, and both Josh and Ginny had to be sure they didn't mention Tony D. Fortunately, dinner was so good that there didn't seem to be any need for conversation beyond food.

Ginny made the afterdinner coffee—instant decaf. Josh reminded himself to get her a coffee-maker and some really good beans. As they sat around the table, all three tried to relax, but the subject they weren't talking about, Anita and her baby, loomed over the table like a ghostly presence.

At last, Josh cleared his throat. "Gray, you look a little better. Have you decided what you're going to do?"

"Yes. I've been thinking about what Ginny said before dinner, and I think my greatest fear is groundless. Now that I don't believe Anita wants an abortion, I'm not as afraid to give her some space, and let her think about things." He looked down at his coffee cup. "As long as she doesn't just disappear."

Josh was looking at Ginny as Gray spoke and her expression told him as clearly as words that Anita was planning to do exactly that. She must have told Ginny about it and sworn her to secrecy.

Josh looked at Gray's face and saw that he had remembered that Anita had asked to sublet her apartment. She was going somewhere. The worry was back in his eyes. Gray was once again thinking that he might lose both the woman he loved and their child.

Ginny said nothing. She stared down into her coffee cup. "Ginny, are you all right?" Gray asked.

"Yes, I'm fine." The words were a dispirited whisper.

"Well, you don't look it. It's okay. I know that you owe your first loyalty to Anita. As long as she's talking to you, I can just manage not to panic. Somebody knows what she's up to. I try to think of that when I can't sleep."

Ginny looked over at him. She was trying to think of something she could say, when the downstairs buzzer sounded. She sighed and started to get up when the doorbell rang.

"Fast trip," Josh commented. "Sounds like Superman's paying a call." He got up to stand beside Ginny at the door. When she opened it, she knew immediately who her visitor was.

"Good evening," she said to the figure in the hall. "Won't you come in, Mr. DiBenedetto?"

Twenty-five

Josh looked at their visitor for a moment, then stood aside and, with the formality of an aristocrat's butler, bowed Anthony DiBenedetto into Ginny's living room. Gray stood by his chair, his napkin still clutched in his hand.

Anita's father and Ginny seemed completely at ease. "You recognized me, Mrs. McDougall?"

"Yes. You look a little like Anita. Please sit down, Mr. DiBenedetto. May I offer you coffee?" She looked at him measuringly. He was a big man, tall and barrel-chested. His large head was crowned with a thick crest of iron gray hair. His eyes were brown and watchful. He wore an immaculate camel's hair overcoat and carried a pair of pigskin gloves in one beautifully manicured hand.

He stared at Ginny just as coolly. Whatever he saw seemed to satisfy him, for he took off his coat and folded it carefully. His gray suit was custom-made, and every crease was razor-sharp. Ginny took the overcoat. Before hanging it up, she performed the necessary introductions. "Josh and Gray, this is Anita's father, Anthony DiBenedetto. Mr. DiBenedetto, Grayson Harcourt and Joshua Havilland."

DiBenedetto didn't hold out his hand. He looked both men over as if they were cattle he was thinking of buying and said, in a gruff, cold voice, "Grayson Harcourt, Yale and Harvard. You're the young man Anita Louise thinks she's in love with." He turned to Josh, but Josh wasn't about to let anyone put him in his place and leave him feeling like a butterfly on a pin.

"Joshua Havilland, Mr. DiBenedetto. Princeton, Class of '58, Harvard Law, Class of '61." Josh grinned and, without waiting to be snubbed, took DiBenedetto's hand and shook it. He took the man's coat from Ginny's arms and headed toward the hall closet.

The doorbell rang. Josh looked at Ginny. "Seems you have two visitors this evening. Shall I get it?"

"Please," Ginny said faintly, hoping it wasn't Lisa or Denis. It wasn't.

"Mr. Havilland," came Anita's soft voice, "I was wondering if you'd be here."

"Anita," Josh said, "it's good to see you again. I should tell you, though, that Gray and your father are both here. In case you want to run away."

Anita's voice shook a little, but she made no

move to leave. "No, thank you. I'd like to come in, if I may."

"Of course," said Ginny as she hurried over to take Anita's arm so that she entered the room flanked by two friends. Anthony DiBenedetto hadn't said a word that wasn't civil, but that didn't mean his daughter was wrong to fear him.

"Papa." Anita's voice was a thread and her knees seemed to buckle for a moment. Then she stood up straight as a soldier and stepped away from Josh and Ginny. "Why are you here?" she said, in a stronger voice.

"I found out Harcourt was here, and I figured you were headed here when your cab started downtown." Anthony DiBenedetto's face looked carved from granite, hard and bleak as stone, but there was an expression in his eyes that made Ginny wonder if he was as immovable as he seemed.

"You've had us followed." Anita's expression was despairing. "I was afraid you would."

"I have to know if you're all right." DiBenedetto reached a hand toward his daughter for a moment, then, seeing the icy, set expression on her face, he let it fall to his side. "I've explained to you why that is necessary, *cara mia.* You know the risks to my family because of my business."

"Then give up the business! Retire, and let us

all live in peace!" Anita's voice was passionate, pleading. "Don't make me live this way, Papa."

Gray heard the plea in her voice and came to stand beside her. He curled his arm around her protectively, and faced her father without fear. "Let her go," he said. "That's all we ask. Let her go."

"You have told him, Anita?" DiBenedetto's voice was harsh. "That was very foolish."

"She has told me nothing, except that even though she loves me, she won't marry me because she is afraid of your anger." Gray held Anita tighter. "But I'm not afraid. Let her go. Let her be happy."

Rage as fierce and frightening as a wildfire blazed out of DiBenedetto's eyes. "You tell me how to care for my daughter? You? Get away from her."

"We're engaged. I'm never going to leave her. I don't give a damn what you do."

DiBenedetto laughed, a chilling, unamused sound. "Very good, Anita. You haven't told him. I see our family still means something to you."

Anita bowed her head. She took a deep breath, as if trying to get her second wind. "Papa, of course you and the family mean something to me. I love you. I always will. But I won't let you control my life any longer. I have to do what I believe in my heart is right, even if you don't understand." Anita looked up at him and raised her chin.

"I only want to keep you safe," her father answered. "To be sure the world doesn't hurt you, Anita Louise."

Ginny could see the love in his eyes. He was sincerely afraid of what would happen to his daughter because of him. Ginny stared at the legendary leader of organized crime and saw a man trying to keep his daughter safe and unharmed by his enemies. He didn't want her to pay for his life.

"You can't do that, Papa," Anita responded. "No one can be safe forever."

"I'll keep her safe, Mr. DiBenedetto," Gray said, his arm still around Anita. "You and I want the same things for Anita."

DiBenedetto looked at the man his daughter loved. "I don't want you anywhere near her. You will dishonor her."

Anita and Gray looked at each other, asking and answering a silent question. *Shall we tell him?* Gray's eyes asked. *No!* Anita's look answered. Ginny read it easily, but DiBenedetto had looked only at his daughter.

"I want you to come home with me, Anita Louise," he said, his deep voice rough with emotion. "This little experiment has gone far enough. You have made friends with unsuitable people.

People who don't understand your life, and certainly not mine. Come back with me now."

Anita shook her head. "We've talked about this before, Papa. I'm not coming home. I like my friends and I like my job."

"And Grayson Harcourt ?"

"I—I love him, Papa."

Gray's face lit with happiness and he put his arms around her and held her as carefully as if she were a precious jewel.

"Are you going to marry him? Is it going to go that far?" Anthony DiBenedetto's eyes filled with pain and he closed them. "Please, don't do that, *cara*. You know what that will mean."

"It will mean happiness, Anita, for everyone," Gray said. "Your father will be welcome, my parents will welcome you. And I love you, Anita, with all my heart. Marry me, darling, please." Gray ignored everyone else. For him, only Anita mattered.

But Anthony DiBenedetto was focused on his daughter, too. His eyes never left her. "We can't talk about this in front of outsiders. Come home with me now. Please, dear one. Please."

Anita shook her head. "I can't, Papa. You know you'd never let me leave. And I can't go back to that life. I'd suffocate. I was suffocating, don't you understand?"

"I only want to protect you. You are always in

danger, and I cannot protect you if you insist on living here in the city." He took a step toward her, and Anita took one back. Gray moved to stand slightly in front of her. "It would be a good life, *cara*. There are still enough of us to have a good life."

The three principals were totally wrapped up in their emotions. Ginny and Josh looked on and saw what the three didn't. Ginny moved quietly to the kitchen. Maybe coffee and some cookies would enable everyone to sit down and stop behaving like a scene out of grand opera. *Rigoletto,* perhaps, she thought, remembering her course in Italian opera. The last act where the father's unsavory life catches up with him, and his innocent daughter. But Anita's hero was better than Duke Whatshisname. Ginny had checked on Gray Harcourt with the secretaries and paralegals at Hanson and Hermann. They had all rated him *A* on all counts. Ginny had faith in the judgments of nurses and secretaries. Doctors and lawyers couldn't hide much from them.

What was going on in the living room? She quickly made coffee in her silver pot, got out the sugar and cream, and put it all on a tray with her good cups and saucers and a plate of the bakery's best. Ginny found her hands shaking a little as she headed back to the fray.

Anita stood between the two strong-willed

men in her life and Ginny could understand why she felt like a bone between two dogs. Ginny put the loaded tray down on the coffee table and went to stand beside Anita. She put her arm around her waist and felt the fine trembling in Anita's body, as if she were a tuning fork responding to a note.

"Come and sit down, and let's have some coffee." She led Anita to the wing chair and handed her a cup of coffee. "Here, drink this. It's decaffeinated, so it won't keep you up."

"No, thanks, Ginny. It doesn't seem to agree with me." Anita looked up and Ginny understood. No coffee of any kind. Anita didn't want to take any risks with the baby. Ginny smiled and gave her hand a squeeze.

When she looked up, Ginny saw Gray's eyes study Anita intently. Anita sat with her hands folded in her lap. Gray automatically took the cup of coffee Ginny handed him, and Ginny saw him smile.

He's sure now that she isn't going to have an abortion, Ginny thought, *because she's not drinking coffee. She's thinking of the baby.* Would Anita's father suspect something? Ginny was afraid he might. He couldn't be sure, of course, but the man had extraordinary radar where his daughter was concerned. He had known she was coming to Ginny's this evening.

Ginny handed out coffee and passed the plate of cookies. When she finished and all five of them were seated, Josh stirred his coffee and spoke in his deep, quiet voice. "It seems you all have a problem. Anita and Gray are in love and Anita's father doesn't approve."

"What the hell do you know about this?" Anthony DiBenedetto said, his voice quiet and deadly. "What do you know about me?"

"The situation would be clear to anyone who listened to the three of you this evening," Josh answered, "but as it happens, Anita and Ginny work for the same law firm and are friends."

"I know." Again, his listeners were aware of all that this man had managed to find out about his daughter and her friends.

"Have you had me investigated?" Ginny asked calmly.

"I learn things in many ways, Mrs. McDougall."

"Ms. McDougall."

"Yes, you have been a widow for many years. You are still devoted to your late husband's memory. A woman of honor. Not many women are these days." His voice was approving. "I am pleased Anita Louise has a friend such as you."

Facts Anthony DiBenedetto might have, but he hadn't learned how to interpret them except through the distorting lens of his own experience.

"Papa, please. Leave me alone." Anita's voice trembled. "Leave my friends alone, or I won't have any."

"How many times must I tell you, Anita Louise? You cannot rely on friends, but only on your family. I wish you would learn that." Her father shook his head and looked over at Josh. "Children are so difficult. They refuse to grant that their parents know anything at all about the world. Have you not found that to be true with your son, Mr. Havilland?"

"I've learned that children will make their own mistakes whether we want them to or not." Josh took a sip of his coffee, unsurprised that Anthony DiBenedetto knew he had a son. "I think your daughter is trying to tell you that."

"You don't understand. My daughter is in a special situation."

Josh took a chance. "Because of your line of work, Mr. DiBenedetto? You still believe in the sins of the fathers being visited upon the children? I think you're wrong."

Anthony DiBenedetto's face was suffused with color and his eyes turned hard and cold. "What do you mean?"

Josh shrugged. "Just what you think I mean. You're not the only one to have sources of information available."

DiBenedetto stood up, his gray silk and wool

suit falling into precise place on his bulky body. "Come, Anita Louise. It is time for us to go home."

"Just a damn minute!" Gray surged to his feet and stood with his legs planted pugnaciously and his fists clenched. "Anita doesn't have to go anywhere she doesn't want to go. What the hell right do you have to order her around as if she were underage or mentally handicapped? It's her life, damn it, and it's my life, too! Go away and leave us alone if you won't wish us happiness."

"Don't take that tone with me, you little snot-nosed Connecticut snob. Do you have any idea who you're talking to? Do you know what I could do to you?" If anyone had had any doubt that this was a supremely dangerous man, that doubt vanished at the ugly look on DiBenedetto's face. He took a step toward Gray, when Anita gave an anguished cry and jumped up. She ran like a deer toward the door and snatched up her coat from the pile on a nearby chair.

"Stop it, both of you! I can't stand this!" she cried as she ran out the door and pushed it closed behind her.

For a moment everyone stood frozen, as if in a game of statues. Then the spell was broken. Gray and DiBenedetto started toward each other once again, intent on their struggle. Ginny grabbed her keys and ran out the door with Josh at her heels.

She punched the elevator button savagely, then stared at Josh as he went over to the metal door that led to the stairs. No one took the stairs in Peter Cooper buildings if they lived above the third or fourth floor. Ginny was on the tenth.

"What are you—"

"Hush." Josh opened the fire door and took a half step inside. "I hear footsteps. I think Anita took the stairs. I'll go after her. You wait for the elevator. See you." He took off down the metal stairs.

Ginny returned to punching the elevator call button. When it arrived, she counted the seconds until she arrived at the lobby, praying it wouldn't stop along the way. Once there, she looked around and saw no one, but the two outer doors were just closing. Running now, she sped outside and looked around, trying to see which way Anita had gone. Ginny took the shortest route to First Avenue, where she found Josh looking around frantically.

"I can't see her," he said.

Ginny looked away from First Avenue, toward FDR Drive and the East River. Anita didn't know her way around this part of town. If she paused, maybe they could overtake her.

"There she is," Ginny cried, pointing toward a

running figure, headed east, toward the river. "We've got to stop her!"

Josh was already running, and Ginny took off after him. Dimly, she heard a car start and head in their direction. "Hurry, Josh!" she gasped, as Anita came toward the end of the street.

Anita didn't stop, or look to see what was coming after her. She started across the last crossing. Josh and Ginny were too far behind to catch her. Ginny slowed slightly, but the car she had heard swept by her. It was a black Lincoln, and the driver was bent over the wheel.

It only took a split second. Anita was in the middle of the last crossing. The black car looked as if the driver was trying to block her way. Suddenly there was a sickening squeal of brakes and a thud. Josh didn't pause. Ginny could see him as he reached a dark, crumpled mass in the street.

Ginny stopped beside the car. "What have you done?" she yelled at them. Yelling wouldn't help Anita. She took a deep breath and looked at the two men in the car. Dark overcoats. One man had his hand in his pocket. Dark car that started up when the driver first caught sight of Anita. Without thinking these things consciously, she told the driver, "I'm Ginny McDougall. Call my number and tell Tony D his daughter's been hurt."

"How did you know this was his car? How do you know Tony D?"

"Just do it, for God's sake! Then call 911." She hurried over to where Josh crouched in the street. "How is she?"

"She's alive. I felt a pulse and she's breathing. I don't know where she was hit. Do those guys have a car phone?"

"Yes. They're calling Tony D right now, then 911."

"Why the hell did you have them call her father? He's just going to want to take her back to Long Island."

"Because it's his car that hit her." Ginny had been running gentle fingers over Anita's body as they talked. "I don't think she's broken anything. Ah, no, I'm wrong. It's her leg." Anita's leg was twisted at an angle. It looked as if she had broken at least one of the bones in her calf. When Ginny touched it, Anita moaned.

Ginny began to look around for something to put over Anita. The two men in the black Lincoln were standing by the curb, looking more terrified than anyone Ginny had ever seen. She didn't waste time. "Give me your overcoat," she said to one of them, holding out her hand. He didn't move. "Give it to me. *Now!*" she barked. Both of them shrugged out of their coats and handed them to her immediately.

As she laid them gently over the small, still figure of Anita, she heard running footsteps. "What have you done to my daughter?" Anthony DiBenedetto had lost his suave demeanor. His voice was loud and harsh. The two men who stood by the car visibly shrank. But he wasn't looking at them. His wrath was aimed at Ginny and Josh. He shoved Ginny out of his way and bent over his daughter. "Anita Louise, speak to me. Who did this to you?" He looked at Josh, his eyes wild. "Did you see who did this? Did you?" Before Josh could answer, he continued, "Where are Benny and Gino?" He looked around and saw the men from the car. "Who did this? Was it Wong? He's threatened to move uptown." He bit off his words as if suddenly aware of who was listening.

"Boss, it was—" one of the men swallowed hard. "It was an accident, Boss. Really, it was."

"What do you mean, an accident? My daughter's hit by a hit-and-run driver and you think it's an accident. Fools!" DiBenedetto turned back to his daughter. "Anita, *cara,* I'm here. Papa's here."

There was no response. "Put her in the car. We'll take her out to the compound. She'll be safer there."

"No." Josh's sharp voice silenced DiBenedetto. "She can't be driven out there. She has a broken leg and there may be other injuries. There's an ambulance on the way, and besides—"

"What have you done to her?" a new voice interrupted Josh. Gray arrived, coatless and out of breath. "I called 9ll from the apartment. How badly is she hurt? What about—" He broke off.

Josh knew he had been about to ask about the baby. "She's broken her leg, but we can't tell about any other injuries."

"Put her in the car," DiBenedetto said again. "Someone is trying to get at me through Anita Louise. I have to keep her safe. She has to go home now."

"Absolutely not." Josh's voice was as commanding as DiBenedetto's. The welcome whoop-whoop of an ambulance drew nearer. "Anyway, the EMT's are here."

Without waiting for permission, the ambulance crew went into something very like a close-order drill. They asked few questions and braced Anita's leg before loading her onto a gurney and into the ambulance. A police car pulled up behind, asked everyone to follow the ambulance to Bellevue, where they would meet in the emergency waiting room.

"Bellevue!" Anthony DiBenedetto couldn't believe it. "Why the hell does she have to go there? That's where every street person and crazy in the city's taken. Why can't she go to Cornell Medical Center or Beth Israel?"

"Closest city hospital's Bellevue," one of the police officers explained. "Let's go."

In fifteen minutes, Anita was being examined by one of the emergency room's resident physicians while the other four huddled together in the waiting room. One of the policemen was there, notebook in hand. He had taken their names and addresses and relationships to the injured party and was now questioning Josh, as the one nearest Anita when the accident occurred.

"She was running down the street, toward the East River, when she was hit." Ever the lawyer, Josh was answering only the questions he was asked.

It was in response to the policeman's query that Josh dropped the bombshell. "The car these two gentlemen were in hit her."

"What!" Anthony DiBenedetto whirled around, his fist raised at the two men who huddled together on one of the plastic benches. *"You!* You two hit my Anita, my *cara?"* His voice dropped to a harsh whisper. "You will answer to me. Later."

"But, Boss," said the shorter man in a pleading whisper, "it was an accident, like Benny told you." DiBenedetto ignored him.

"I don't want to hear it. Tell me only—who was driving?"

"I was," the taller man said.

"Benito." The name was a threat, a promise. "We will talk. Later we will talk."

Silence fell for a moment. The policeman had heard the conversation and Ginny thought she saw comprehension in his eyes. There probably weren't many cops who hadn't heard of Anthony DiBenedetto. He could keep his name and picture out of the papers, but he couldn't prevent law enforcement from knowing who he was and having a pretty shrewd idea of what he did.

"Thank you, Mr. Havilland." The policeman turned to Benito. "Now, Mr. Josephs. Would you tell me how the accident occurred. To the best of your recollection."

Ginny moved over to sit next to Gray, who sat with his hands between his knees and his head bent. "How are you?" she asked quietly. "Maybe I could find some coffee. Would you like some?"

"No, thanks, Ginny. Don't bother. God, I hate the waiting. When will they tell us how she is? How the baby is?" He shook his head. "She's got to be all right. She has to." There was a tremor in his voice and Ginny noticed that, when he raised his hand to run his fingers through his hair, they shook.

"She will be, Gray. I'm sure of it."

They waited for what seemed like hours, while the policeman took their statements and went to make telephone calls. Silence held them all. Josh sat beside Ginny and their hands reached for each other and held on tight. He raised their clasped hands and kissed the back of hers. Ginny looked at him and felt strengthened.

At last, the policeman returned and at the same time a weary-looking doctor in hospital greens came into the room. "Mr. Harcourt?" he asked.

"Yes." Gray was on his feet, hope blazing in his eyes.

"Your fiancée wants to see you. Ms. DiBenedetto will be fine. We've set and casted her leg and treated her other injuries, which were superficial bruises and cuts. I'd let her go with you now, but we want to keep her overnight."

"No, goddammit!" Anthony DiBenedetto gave a roar that would have made most men quail. Most men, but not any of those present except Benito and Gino. "I want my daughter at home. We're leaving. *Now!* Get the car, Gino."

Gino leaped up, ready to go anywhere Tony D told him to, but the policeman said, "I'm sorry, Mr. DiBenedetto, but the car has been impounded. It caused an accident and until a final report has been filed, it will stay in impound." He spoke quietly, but there was no doubt he meant what he said.

"That's not normal procedure, is it?" Josh asked.

"It's discretionary." There was no doubt Tony D's car would stay impounded.

"We want to keep her overnight not because of her injuries," the doctor explained, "but to be sure the baby's all right."

That's torn it, Ginny thought wearily. *World War III will now commence.*

Twenty-six

It wasn't World War III, but it was close.

Tony D turned on Gray and loomed over him. "You miserable son of a bitch." He grated the words out between clenched teeth. "I'll kill you!" He meant it, Ginny thought. His hands were curved and he brought them toward Gray's throat. And he was quite capable of doing it, too. Right there in the emergency room waiting area, amid the milling, noisy crowd.

"Mr. DiBenedetto," the policeman said quietly, "sit down." The words seemed to reach DiBenedetto and he backed off.

"You've dishonored my daughter. By rights, you should die."

"I love your daughter. I would marry her tonight if she'd have me." Gray stood up and faced his adversary. "She won't do it because of you. She's afraid of you. You terrify your own daughter, DiBenedetto. The person you claim to love so much."

Gray's quiet voice struck like ice pellets. Anita's

father stood motionless and looked at the man she loved. "You don't know what you're talking about." He dismissed Gray with a contemptuous wave.

"Mr. Harcourt?" A nurse came toward them. Gray stepped forward. "Ms. DiBenedetto wants to see you. You can have a few minutes with her."

"No. I'm her father. I should be the one to see her. I'm prepared to hire an ambulance and take her home tonight."

The nurse ignored DiBenedetto as if he weren't there. "This way, Mr. Harcourt."

When Gray left, DiBenedetto turned around like a bear tied to a stake, trying to find the source of his misery and pain. His eyes lit on Benny and Gino.

"What did you do to Anita Louise? How could this have happened?"

"Boss, we were trying to stop her. We saw her running toward the river and we tried to block her way. We were crawling along, going five, ten miles an hour." Benny was almost in tears.

"You should've stopped her. You should've done it right, goddammit!" Tony D had found a victim, one who wouldn't fight back. "You hurt my daughter, my Anita Louise." His face was a mask of fury and pain. "She could be dying! And it was you. You!" He pointed at Benny.

"Take it easy, Mr. DiBenedetto," said the policeman.

"I'll kill him." His voice was cold, final.

"No, you won't, Mr. DiBenedetto," said the policeman, as calm as if they were discussing the Giants' chances rather than a death threat by a man reputed to be able to carry them out at will.

DiBenedetto turned away, thwarted. "Benny will pay," he muttered.

"Tony," Josh said, laying a hand on his arm, "think about what's important. It was an accident. Benny's telling the truth. He was trying to help. I saw it and I'm sure. Benny was trying to stop Anita from running into the road and being hit."

"All right, all right." DiBenedetto waved his hand, dismissing the topic. But everyone there knew Benny's troubles were far from over.

"Let's talk about Anita and the baby. They're what's important now. And Anita's going to be all right." Josh took DiBenedetto by the arm and led him over to a bench. "You have to know that Gray was right. Anita didn't tell you about the baby because she was afraid of what you'd do."

"Do? What do you mean? I would never hurt my daughter. She knows that. I want to take her home with me, keep her safe, see that she marries a fine young man. One we know." He shook his head. "What are you talking about? Why should she fear me?"

"Because she doesn't want to live with you and she doesn't want to marry a man of your choosing. She would have married Gray if she weren't afraid you would harm him." Josh's voice was controlled and reasonable. He would defuse the excess emotion here if anyone could, Ginny thought.

DiBenedetto looked as if he might be listening to the voice of reason, when Gray returned to the room. He was smiling a little and he went over to Ginny immediately. "Anita wants to see you, Ginny. The nurse said it's all right."

Ginny rose and prepared to go to Anita, when several young men with microphones and note-pads hurried into the waiting room. "Tony D! Tony D!" they called as they pushed their way through the crowd. "What happened to your daughter?"

"Get these bums out of here," said the object of their search. He gestured to Benny and Gino, but the policeman jerked his head and they sat back down. Tony frowned. Someone's orders superseded his own and he clearly didn't like it. Josh went over to the officer and asked if they couldn't make the press wait outside. The officer agreed and began shepherding the reporters toward the door.

"Thanks, Havilland." It wasn't very gracious, but Josh didn't care. All he wanted was to get this mess straightened out so he and Ginny could get on with their lives.

Meanwhile, Ginny followed the nurse down the dingy hall toward the small room that held Anita.

"Hi, sweetheart, how are you?" Anita looked small and forlorn as she lay on her back with her hands folded outside the blanket.

"Take care of Gray, Ginny, please." Anita's voice was a whisper. Ginny had to lean toward her mouth to hear her.

"Of course I will. Until you can do it yourself. And you take care of yourself. The doctor said the baby seems to be fine."

"I know. I guess Papa heard him say it." Anita turned her head on the pillow and Ginny could see tears on her cheek. "What's he going to do to Gray?" She sounded terrified, as Gray had said she was. Ginny had never realized the depth of Anita's fear until now.

"He's not going to do anything. The police are there for one thing and Josh and I won't let him for another. Gray's going to be fine. You just take care of you and your baby. That's what you've got to do."

"Is he angry at Benny and Gino?" Anita asked. "It was an accident. Tell Papa—"

"Hush, now. Papa knows it was an accident. Don't you worry about what Papa's going to do. I have a feeling Papa isn't going to do anything you object to." Ginny smiled a little. "You really scared him, Anita."

"Good." A fleeting smile crossed Anita's face. "Make sure he stays scared." Her eyes drifted closed. Ginny gave her hand a squeeze and tip-toed out of the room.

When she got back to the waiting room, she told DiBenedetto that his daughter was going to be fine, but was sleeping now.

"We might as well leave. I don't think she's going to wake up again tonight."

"I'll stay, just in case," Gray said, sitting back down.

"Then I'll stay, too," said DiBenedetto.

"Neither of you will stay," said Ginny. "You can all come to my place and we'll talk. I want to have everything completely worked out by the time Anita leaves the hospital tomorrow."

"Is there a way out that won't take us by the press?" Josh asked.

"From what I understand, there are a thousand ways in and out of Bellevue," said Ginny. "I'll ask the nurse." She returned in a few minutes and led the rest of them on a trek down dim corridors and tunnels that ran under streets. When they emerged into the night, they were only a few blocks from

Ginny's building and the press were nowhere in sight.

DiBenedetto ordered Benny and Gino to rent a car and return for him in one hour. Gray and Tony D had to talk and her place was better than the emergency room waiting area. She and Josh would make sure they didn't try to kill each other.

Back in the apartment, Ginny sighed. She wasn't really up to hospitality. "Let's get down to business," said Josh, as if he could read her mind. "Ginny, perhaps you should reassure Mr. DiBenedetto about Anita."

"She seemed tired but all right. They had given her a painkiller because of her leg and she was very sleepy, but she knew where she was and she said she felt good except for the bumps and bruises."

"Bumps and bruises." DiBenedetto's voice was anguished. "Oh, my God."

"She's fine and the baby seemed to be fine, too." That was getting down to business with a vengeance. "Now, I'd like to tell you why I know about the baby. Anita came to me because she didn't know anyone else she could turn to. I guess you've kept her pretty well isolated, Mr. DiBenedetto, until she insisted on living in town. Well, I think you and Gray scared her so much, you both seemed so unreasonable, that she needed someone else to confide in and I was the nearest one. So, now I'm going to say what I think. Anita should come home with me until she's feeling better. I can look after her, Josh will help, and my daughter will drop by, too. You two should let her alone until you can come to some accommodation with each other."

DiBenedetto looked at her incredulously. "I don't accommodate. My daughter is my business, and no one else's."

"She's her own business, too, Mr. DiBenedetto," Ginny said quietly. "And she wants to lead her own life. She told me she felt like a bone between two dogs."

Gray looked stricken, as if he could understand how Anita must feel. But her father simply shook his head, unwilling to hear what he couldn't accept.

"She needs to come home," he said. "You people know a little bit about me, so you can at least start to understand how I feel. I can't let anything happen to her."

"Then do what she asked you to do earlier this evening," Josh said. "Retire."

"That won't solve my problems. You're a lawyer, you should know that."

"I think you must have a few bargaining chips you've kept hidden for just this moment. You might start thinking how best to use them." Josh looked at him intently, trying to see if his words were understood.

Ginny looked over at Gray. He sat back in his chair, out of the light. The only one who hadn't known about Tony DiBenedetto's business before this evening, he sat in the background, studying all of the others, unwilling to speak. By now, he must have a pretty shrewd idea of DiBenedetto's business, Ginny thought.

Tony DiBenedetto looked at Josh with growing respect. "You may have something." He grew thoughtful. "I'll think about it. But you—" he gestured toward Gray, "you're not going to be part of Anita's future. You're history, Harcourt."

Gray looked every bit as stubborn as Tony D. He got up and began to pace. "Damn it, Anita's not just your daughter. She's the woman I love and she's carrying my child. Our child. I won't let you take them away from me. I care about them every bit as much as you do. And I'm not going anywhere. If Anita won't marry me, if you succeed in burying her out at that compound of yours, I'll sue for custody of my child."

"Talk!" DiBenedetto said, waving his hand in dismissal at Gray. "You think you know everything, and you know nothing! My daughter could never take my grandchild away from me. Even if she tried. But you—you *will* get out of her life. If you don't know who I am, Ms. McDougall will tell you that I mean what I say, and I can make it true. I can and I will make you disappear if I have to."

"Listen to me, Mr. DiBenedetto." Gray walked over and stood in front of Tony D's chair. "I know who you are. And I know what you can do. To me and to Anita. But I love your daughter and I want to marry her with all my heart. I can give her a good life, the kind of life you can't give her. Safety. Anonymity. Even respectability, if she cares about that. I'm a good lawyer and even if I have to move to the ends of the earth, I can make a living. I'll go anywhere and do anything to protect my wife and my child. You say you can make me disappear." Gray leaned forward, stabbing at DiBenedetto's chest with his forefinger. "I say that you'll have to do that, because as long as there's breath in my body, I'll love Anita and I'll protect her and our baby. You'll have to kill me to stop me, old man."

There was a strange look in DiBenedetto's eyes. Ginny thought perhaps it was the dawn of respect. The best thing for Gray to do was leave now and let his passion and determination take root in DiBenedetto's mind. She was getting used to the fact that Josh could read her thoughts. Her mouth was open to suggest that Gray leave when Josh spoke her thoughts.

"Why don't you go home now, Gray?" said

Josh. He wanted to talk to DiBenedetto. Getting him to see reason was the first step to untying this knot. Anita wouldn't feel safe enough to let Gray into her life permanently until her father stopped trying to get her back into his custody.

"Okay. I'll talk to you tomorrow, Ginny. Thanks for the chicken, Josh." His face was pale and his expression grim, but Ginny knew Gray felt better than he had. He knew Anita was safe, that she loved him and would have their baby. He had finally told Anita's father exactly how he felt and what he would do.

Ginny handed Gray the battered leather jacket he had worn. "Good-night. And don't worry. Anita's fine and everything will work out." Never had she said anything more inane. But never had she had an evening quite like this one.

Josh and Tony D were seated on the couch, eyeing each other. "I know how you feel about protecting your daughter, but you have to realize that there isn't a whole lot you can do. She's grown up and she's going to be a mother. You can't keep her locked up anymore. You might be able to keep her from marrying Gray Harcourt, but you can't make her marry a man you choose for her. You don't even want to if you think about it."

DiBenedetto looked at him. Finally, he said, "You're right. It's all going to be on the news. Even without pictures, everyone will know. Maybe . . . maybe you're right, Havilland." He sat looking out the window, his face expressionless. Josh thought that it was the look he might have worn before sentencing someone to death. Josh could understand Benny's terror.

DiBenedetto looked around and stood up. "I mustn't keep you, Ms. McDougall. I thank you for having Anita here. I don't think anyone will look for her." He turned to Josh. "I'll think about retirement. And I'll let you know about Harcourt." He took his camel hair coat from Ginny and left.

As she closed the door on her departing guest, she felt Josh put warm, possessive hands on her shoulders.

"At last," he breathed into her hair. "I thought they'd never leave. What a night!"

Ginny gave a tired laugh and turned in his arms so she could lay her head on his shoulder. "That was a scene for our memoirs. What did you mean about retirement for Tony D? Would his rivals really let him retire?"

"If they had to." Josh cupped her face in his hands and kissed her gently. "How about some brandy? I could use some."

Ginny nodded and went over to the chest that served as her liquor cabinet and poured them each a healthy dose. Then she went over and sat next to Josh on the couch. They kicked off their shoes and put their feet up on the coffee table.

"Umm, tastes nice," she said as she let the brandy rest on her tongue for a moment before swallowing.

Josh put his arm around her and pulled her closer, so he could kiss her again. "You taste nicer by far."

Ginny pulled away, but not too far. "Do you think Tony D has something incriminating on his enemies?"

"If he's as smart as I think he is, he does."

"But what good would that do? Then they'd try to kill him all the harder."

"Not if he takes it to the Justice Department and makes a deal. If he's got enough good stuff, he can get protection and end up owning a drug-store in a suburb of Council Bluffs, Iowa, under the name of Harry Jones, or something."

"The witness protection program." Ginny nodded. "Yes, that makes sense. But they'd have to give him a New York kind of name. Harry Jones just doesn't have that ring. We need a melting pot kind of name. Sven Abondondo, or Luis O'Connell."

"No, no, the melting pot idea is out of date. It's a gorgeous mosaic now, haven't you heard? Sticking with your ethnic group is okay." Josh grinned at her. "Though Otto O'Connor has a ring to it."

They leaned back and shut their eyes. They had done all they could, now they could sit and hold hands and sip brandy as peace and silence wrapped around them. Looking into each other's eyes, they raised their brandy snifters and saluted themselves.

They sipped.

They kissed.

They sighed.

The phone rang.

Ginny and Josh missed the eleven o'clock news in all the excitement. But across town, Denis had seen it and had immediately called Lisa and filled her in on their parents' latest escapade. They agreed to meet to call their errant elders and find out exactly why they were hanging out with gangsters and hit-and-run drivers.

Denis insisted on coming to Lisa's apartment. "It's not safe for you to be out at this time of night. Look what happened to your mother's friend. I'll be there in fifteen minutes."

Lisa opened her door, wearing something soft and furry-looking in a wonderful shade of buttery yellow, Denis had an almost irresistible impulse to kiss her and keep on kissing her until they both melted onto the floor. Oh, God, what was the matter with him? He must be going crazy. Overwork, that's what it was. Too much time at the office.

"Hello, Lisa," he said in briskest, most businesslike voice. "Shall we get right down to it?"

Lisa stared at him. She couldn't figure Denis out. First he looks at her as if she were covered in chocolate sauce and he hadn't eaten in a week and then he pumps her hand and glares at her as if she were his adversary in some devilish legal maneuver.

She preferred the chocolate lover. "Denis," she said, smiling widely. "Come on in. Would you like some coffee? Tell me about Mother and Josh. What's happened now?"

"Coffee, yes, thank you." He sat down and stared at the bright colors in her living room as if daring them to make him feel better.

Lisa handed him a cup and passed him a box of Godiva chocolates. Denis stared at her. How did she know of his fantasy of licking chocolate sauce off her body? He shook his head. He was going crazy. And it was all his father and Ginny's fault.

"Let me tell you, the whole city knows about your mother's latest caper," he said, biting into a chocolate and staring at her. Yes, it was the chocolate lover. Lisa smiled. "You wouldn't smile if you knew what they'd been up to. Apparently, that young girl in our office that Ginny's been mothering is the daughter of Anthony 'Tony D' DiBenedetto."

"Who's he? Some organized crime guy?"

"Exactly. Only he's not just some organized crime guy. He's more like the head honcho, king of crime, godfather of godfathers according to Channel 2. His daughter was almost run over this evening and your mother went with her, and her unsavory father, to the emergency room at Bellevue."

"I wish you'd stop calling her 'Your Mother' as if there were initial caps on the words." Lisa smiled as she sucked on her candy. "And anyhow, wasn't Your Father there, too?"

Denis tried to look away from her. "Yes, he was. I don't know what his connection with it all is. Just Ginny, I guess. I don't know all the trouble she's gotten him into since he's been here. Poor old Dad."

"Oh, right. Poor old Dad, the Indigo Man." Lisa rolled her eyes in disbelief. "If we want to get them before your father leaves, we'd better call them now. What do you want to say?"

Denis bristled. "To stay out of trouble, what do you think? This is getting entirely out of hand. Who knows what some rival gangster is going to do to them."

"Just because they were seen with Tony D?"

"It could happen. Dad has developed a genius for trouble since he's been here. Did I tell you about Hervé, the super in my building, and his cousin, the wounded Haitian refugee Dad talked me into trying to help?" His sense of grievance was clear.

"It sounds a lot more socially useful than most of the rich scumbags you represent," Lisa commented. "I'll dial, but you talk to them. I'm not sure what to say."

Denis took the receiver. He was annoyed to hear his father's voice. "Who is this?" Josh asked.

"Your son. And Ginny's daughter."

"Good of you to call, son. But we're both all right. Nothing happened." Denis could hear Josh talk to Ginny, telling her that "the children" had called to see if they were all right.

"I'm glad nothing happened to either of you, but you know you were all over the late local news. I wanted to let you know, so you can avoid the press for the next few days."

"Why should we? I don't think anyone's particularly interested in us. It's Tony D and Anita and Gray they'll be interested in." Josh sounded a little amused. "Are you afraid Ginny and I will reflect badly on you and the firm?"

Denis *was* afraid of it, but he wasn't going to admit it. "Not at all. Sanderson and Smith can withstand a little unfortunate publicity, and so can I." Denis wondered if he sounded pompous. "I'm just worried about you and Ginny becoming targets of some other gang's vendetta against Tony D."

"Well, that's nice of you, son, but I don't think that's going to be a problem. I'm pretty sure they'll have other things to worry about in a day or two."

"Well, thank God for that." Denis put his hand over the receiver and asked Lisa if she wanted to talk to Ginny. She nodded and Denis ended his part of the conversation by saying, "What time can I expect you home, Dad? I'm at Lisa's but I'll be leaving soon. Do you have your key?"

"Yes, Denis. Don't worry about me. I'll probably just stay here with Ginny. That way, I won't be a target, in case some trigger-happy member of organized crime comes after me. And I'll be here to protect Ginny in case she's the target. 'Night, son."

Denis sputtered as he handed the phone to Lisa. As her hand grazed his, Denis felt a sizzle of heat ricochet down his arm. Damn, this was becoming a serious inconvenience. He hadn't seen Candy or Janine for a week. Somehow, he just hadn't been interested. Now he wondered whether the reason was that only Lisa sent that sizzle through him when they touched.

Nonsense, he told himself firmly. It was a purely chemical reaction. Caused by the late hour, or the fuzzy yellow robe. Or something. He couldn't, absolutely could not be falling for Lisa McDougall. Why, he didn't even like the girl!

He came back to the present only when he heard Lisa say, "Okay, Momma, but I think you should stay out of the office tomorrow. You'll have reporters all over the place."

"What? What do you mean, she should stay out of the office?" Denis glared at her, and snatched the phone back. "Don't you dare stay out of the office. No one knows where you work. You'll be safer with receptionists and elevators to buffer you. I'll expect to see you as usual. Good-night." He banged down the phone. "What are you trying to do? Ruin my life? I haven't had a peaceful moment since I saw you again." He jumped up and stood over her, shaking a finger in her face. "You encourage your mother to stay out of work. You constantly tell me what a boring, conventional, chauvinistic—"

He reached out and pulled Lisa to her feet. Holding her shoulders in his hands he stared down into her green eyes.

"Well, you are conventional and chauvinistic," Lisa whispered, sliding her arms around his waist. "As well as stuffy, judgmental, and—"

His lips descended on hers. What the hell was he doing? The answer was overwhelming. He was drowning, his heart swooping and diving like a crazy roller coaster, his blood drumming in his ears. He sank into Lisa's softness and fragrance and drank from her lips as if his life depended on it. Maybe it did. Oh, God.

He managed to break away and stood panting, still looking into those mesmerizing eyes. Darkened now with passion, they were the color of jungle leaves in the twilight. How had he thought of that? He had to save himself by remembering her flaws.

He started to enumerate them. "And *you're* feckless and reckless and—"

"I'm not really, you know." Lisa looked up at him and somehow he knew he saw truth in her gaze. "I just do it because it makes you so mad."

"Damn you, Lisa!" He held her shoulders and lifted her to meet his lips for a long, breathless moment. "Damn you, what have you done to me?"

Without waiting for an answer, he jerked open the door and all but ran down the stairs and into the night.

Twenty-seven

"They sounded awfully cross," Ginny said with a yawn. She took another sip of her brandy. "They always seem cross when they're together. It can't just be us. Why do they spend so much time together if they annoy each other so much?" She knew she didn't sound terribly concerned. At this point, she thought, she wouldn't get too concerned about anything less than a pitched gun battle in her living room.

She was there, with Josh's arm around her, his breath ruffling her hair. She smiled and snuggled a little closer.

"They're falling in love," Josh answered.

"You're crazy."

"True, but irrelevant." He kissed the pulse in her temple, sending it into overdrive. "All we have to do is get in a little more trouble and they'll be inextricably intertwingled."

"They'll be inextricably what?" Ginny turned her head to look at him. She kissed his nose, she couldn't resist. It was pure Fifth Century.

"Intertwingled. My evidence professor used to say that and I thought it was very expressive."

"It is. Intertwingled." Ginny savored the word. "Very descriptive. Are we intertwingled?" She leaned back a little.

"Inextricably plus. The original Gordian knot, that's us." Josh smiled and then kissed her, long and softly. When the kiss ended, some time later, he murmured, "It's one o'clock. I think we're safe for at least a few hours. May I stay?"

There was doubt in his eyes. Ginny melted. "Of course." She couldn't resist adding, "Spending the night together is probably just the little more trouble that will send our children into each other's arms. And why do you think that's a good idea? I'm not sure I do. They'll be as unstable as nitroglycerin."

"I don't know if it's a good idea, sweetheart. It doesn't matter. It's going to happen. The way iron filings will go to a magnet. It's a matter of fact, not opinion." He planted soft kisses on her face in between his words.

"I'll think about that in the morning," Ginny stood and held out her hand to him. "Come to bed, Josh darling."

Nestled under the covers, Josh moved slowly at first, until Ginny urged him on. She couldn't wait. She wanted him, needed him. Kissing his neck she moved against him and smiled when she heard him groan.

"You like making me like this, don't you?" he whispered, and she could feel his smile. "Helpless and hungry."

"Umhmmm." She couldn't remember a time when her body wasn't perfectly attuned to his, yet it had been only days. She wouldn't ask how long it would last.

Ginny felt herself shatter only seconds before Josh's body told her that he, too, had reached that zenith. Enfolding him in her arms, she reveled in the aftermath as much as in the act itself. It felt so good to have his body rest heavily against hers. To feel his fingers caress her hair and stroke her cheek.

"I love you, Ginny," he whispered. She couldn't answer. "No protests?" he teased. "No arguments about how it's too soon and I can't possibly know how I feel?"

Ginny shook her head. Her throat felt choked with tears. How had she ever gotten this lucky? "No protests. No arguments."

"You finally believe me?" Josh rolled to the side, leaving one leg thrown across hers, and, resting his head on his hand, looked down at her. "Yes, I think you do. Well, hallelujah. Next thing you know you'll believe that you really love me and that I'm not going to get struck by lightning and turn into Brian some dark and stormy night."

"I've told you," Ginny whispered, barely able to get the words past the lump in her throat, "I love you." Her voice was so tentative that Josh had to chuckle.

"That's the most wobbly, lily-livered declaration of undying passion I've ever heard."

"The passion isn't wobbly and it certainly isn't lily-livered," Ginny said. "The problem is that I don't know if it's undying. How can you tell, Josh?"

He looked down at her, his hazel eyes warm with love and a touch of laughter. "I guess you just know. I'm not sure how."

"But I thought I knew with Brian." Ginny's brow wrinkled.

"Do you feel with me the way you felt with Brian?" If she said yes, he wasn't sure what he'd do. Probably take a running butt at the wall in sheer frustration.

"No, not at all." Ginny smiled. That question was easy to answer. The wonderful way she felt with Josh, in bed and out, was entirely different. "This is so much more, it's like comparing Twinkies with chocolate soufflé."

"I trust I'm the soufflé." Josh bent over and kissed her.

"Absolutely. With ice cream and chocolate sauce."

"Good Lord, when did you ever eat anything that decadent?"

"Years ago, someone took me to a restaurant and that was their special dessert. I've never forgotten it."

"A real landmark moment."

"I can't remember where the restaurant was, but I've always wanted to have that dessert again."

Josh took her in his arms. As long as he was that long-remembered treat, he was happy. And he could live with the memory of Brian now. "I'll show you how good chocolate soufflé can be," he promised her as he pulled her over to lie on top of him. "Starting now."

The next morning, when Josh returned to Denis's, he decided he would have to find a place to live. He had hoped that Ginny would want to marry as much and as quickly as he did, but that was too much to hope for.

Meantime, he hated leaving Ginny's and coming back to his son's chic bachelor pad. He wanted to live with chintz and hanging plants and warmth. He wanted to live with Ginny. But at least he could find his own apartment.

Denis had already left. Thank God! At least today he wasn't going to be subjected to another moralistic lecture from his playboy son. Denis had left coffee on the hot tray and Josh poured himself a cup. He tried to get comfortable on one of Denis's leather chairs, but his knees felt as if they were on a level with his chin, so he struggled to his feet and went upstairs.

His meeting with Mike Scanlon and Mack was set for eleven. While he showered and shaved, he tried to keep his thoughts on Mack's problems, but memories of last night with Ginny kept intruding. Making love with her was unlike anything else in his experience. He couldn't help but think of what his life might have been like if he hadn't found her. He would never have known what he had missed, but there would have been a hole in his life. He had sensed a missing piece before he met her, but never knew the source of that vague discontent, that feeling of incompleteness. Now he knew the shape and size and feel of that piece of himself. It was Ginny, all of Ginny and only Ginny. He'd just have to wait until she felt the same way.

At eleven, he was walking up Fifth Avenue to the steps of the Metropolitan Museum. He could see that Mack was there but there was no sign of Mike Scanlon. Josh was curious about what he wanted. Mikey struck him as the complete follower, one who never had an idea of his own. Probably, this morning's meeting was Tyrone's idea. It would be interesting to see what he wanted.

As he reached the familiar striped umbrella, a long black car slid to the curb.

"Hi, Mack," Josh said. "Did Mikey tell you what he wanted?"

"Morning, Hoosier. No, he just said he'd be here."

The passenger door of the big car opened and Mikey stepped out. "And I'm here. Mr. Tyrone wants to see both of you. Close up the stand, Mack. Someone'll be along in a few minutes to take care of it."

"A few minutes!" Mack exclaimed. "Do you have any idea what can happen in a few minutes to an unattended hot dog stand? What're you, crazy?"

"Someone will be here. Mr. Tyrone wants to see the two of youse." Mikey stood, his huge arms bulging as he folded them across his chest. Josh figured Mikey must spend half the day at the gym to have a physique like that.

With a sigh, Mack folded up his racks, put his grill away in the special compartment, and furled his umbrella. "I hope Eddie knows what he's doing," Mack grumbled.

"Mr. Tyrone to you, Mack."

"Right, right. I still hope he knows what he's doing."

"In the car."

Josh and Mack got in. He hadn't had time to study the car from the outside, but the spacious interior and high head room made Josh sure it was an older model. "Where are we going?" he asked Mikey.

"Never mind. Just shut up and enjoy the view."

Josh didn't know where they were going until they crossed to Brooklyn and he noticed signs for the Verrazano Bridge. He had read Ginny's guidebook and now knew the Verrazano went to Staten Island. Did Eddie Tyrone live there?

The bridge was majestic, an enormous span of steel cables and concrete suspended over the narrow crossing where the river met the ocean. He could see the Statue of Liberty and felt a lump in his throat. Then they were in Staten Island.

"This is part of New York City?" he asked, astonished. It was a suburb. Houses with lawns, villages with main streets two blocks long. "It can't be. No wonder they want to secede from the city."

Mack smiled. "Foreigners always say that."

"Foreigners?"

"Yeah. You guys from outside the city. Appleknockers. Hicks. Foreigners."

"Ah, Mack, I love that sophisticated New York City attitude. It just charms us foreigners. That sense that the world consists of only two parts:

New York City and anywhere else. And that no one with any sense lives anywhere else."

"Yeah," Mack said, totally unmoved by Josh's irony. "That's about right. I'm surprised you understand it so good."

"Shut up. We're here." Mikey pressed a button and the back door opened. Josh looked up to see a tidy split-level house, painted white with green shutters, set in a lawn that even in March showed the result of careful tending.

Eddie Tyrone, Josh thought with an inward smile, the middle-class mobster.

The door was opened by a woman with an elaborate arrangement of improbably blond hair. She wore a ruffled pink-flowered dress and an orange-flowered apron with even more ruffles. High-heeled red pumps completed the outfit. The picture of a Las Vegas showgirl in a fifties sitcom, she seemed to fit right into Eddie Tyrone's improbable life. "Eddie's in the den," she said, with a pouty smile and a flutter of improbably long black eyelashes. "You can go right in."

The den was paneled in knotty pine and had red plaid curtains and slipcovers. There was a Notre Dame pennant on one wall and a painting of a big-eyed urchin on another. But the surprising thing about the room was that it was built to Eddie Tyrone's tiny size. The chairs were small and the desk, behind which Eddie sat, looked almost child-sized. Eddie waved them to seats and Josh immediately felt like the Amazing Colossal Man. He overflowed the seat and his knees were even higher than on Denis's Barcelona chairs.

"Here they are, Boss," Mikey said.

"Hello, Eddie," Mack said in an unnaturally subdued voice.

Josh returned Eddie's nod but said nothing.

"You two"— Eddie nodded toward Mack and Mikey—"go downstairs to the rec room. I got a hot dog stand down there. Mack, I want you to teach Mikey here everything you know." Eddie's gravelly whisper stopped and he swallowed hard. Josh noticed that the knot on his carefully tied necktie rode up and down. "Then Mikey can practice. Maybe you could write it down, step-by-step like."

"But, Eddie, you can't tell who's gonna want what. It's improvisation and you can't teach—" Eddie's ice blue eyes grew even colder than usual, and Mack's voice dwindled to silence. "Right, Eddie," he said after a long pause.

Eddie nodded and the two men went out. Eddie nodded again. "I want to talk to you," he whispered to Josh. "Sit on the couch. It's better for tall fellas." For a moment, Josh was afraid the chair would come with him when he rose. Fortunately, it stayed on the floor and he gratefully went over to the couch. It was still low to the ground, but it allowed him to stretch his legs sideways. He looked at Eddie and saw a faint smile on his thin lips. This was Eddie's way of keeping his visitors off-balance. He fitted the room and they didn't.

"What is it you want to talk about?" Josh asked.

"About all this trouble you've been causing me." Eddie sat as if waiting for a reply. Josh knew the value of silence and said nothing. "I got to provide for Mikey."

"Why?"

The single word lay between them for a minute before Eddie said, "I'm getting old. Eighty-six next birthday." His whisper grew more harsh and he cleared his throat. "Mikey's my sister's last one. The others are all settled, taken care of. They got good jobs, nice homes. But Mikey, he's not like the others. He's a throwback, you understand?"

Josh wasn't sure he did. "A throwback? You mean he wants to be a . . ." What did one call a gangster when talking to a gangster?

"Like me. Yeah." Eddie's thin lips quirked upward for a moment. "An entrepreneur."

Now he knew. *Entrepreneur.* "And you don't think that's the right career path for Mikey?"

"No, not Mikey. The world's changed, but

Mikey, he still wants to be Jimmy Cagney or George Raft."

"Is that why you want Mack to give up his stand? So Mikey will have a safe job?"

"Yeah. It's a job Mikey can do. I want to retire. Mrs. Tyrone—you met her on the way in—Mrs. Tyrone wants to live in Florida." Eddie's eyes had a faraway look. "Hialeah, near the racetrack."

Josh took a gamble. "Have you been married long?"

Eddie shook his head. He held up two fingers. "Two years?" Josh guessed. Eddie shook his head. "Two months?" Eddie nodded. "So you want to get Mikey set up before you leave?" Again, a nod. "But if you're not going to be here, wouldn't it be better to have Mikey work with Mack. So he'd have somebody to answer to, if you see what I mean."

Eddie's head bobbed up and down several times. Josh decided that must mean great approval. "You," Eddie said.

"Me?" Eddie nodded. "Me what, Mr. Tyrone? What do you want me to do?" The minute the question was out of his mouth, Josh regretted it. Whatever Eddie had in mind, Josh was sure he wouldn't want to do it. Even if it was legal.

"Somebody for them to answer to." Josh stared at him. Eddie picked up a piece of paper from the desk. It was covered with spidery handwrit-

ing. "These are my people and what they do."
He shoved it across the desk. It faced Josh and
he could see there were only four names. Mack,
Mikey, Eileen, and Melody.

"Who are Eileen and Melody, Mr. Tyrone?"
Again, the minute he heard the words, he knew
he was getting in deeper and deeper.

"Eileen's Mikey's mother. He forgets to go see
her in the nursing home. I gotta buy the cards
so he can sign them. Somebody's got to remind
him to look after his mother." Eddie picked up
a glass of water that was standing in the middle
of a coaster and took a sip. "Mikey's a good boy
but not too smart."

He couldn't help it. He had to know. "And
Melody?" he asked.

"Mrs. Tyrone's sister. An exotic dancer. But
she's getting a little . . . mature for the art. She
needs a job, maybe waitress. Something in a ca-
sino, maybe. And she needs a nice guy to marry.
I promised Desirée I'd look. But I'm old. Old."
Eddie leaned back in his miniature executive
desk chair and closed his eyes.

"That's it?" Josh asked. "Cards and visits for
Eileen and a job for Melody?" This was the empire of Eddie Tyrone? A family that needed a
daddy?

"That's all that's left, Mr. Havilland." Eddie
opened his eyes. They were as sharp as ever.

"Somebody's got to take care of the ones that are left. I thought of you. A lawyer. A gentleman who wouldn't take advantage of Mikey or Melody. I'd pay you, of course. I've got plenty. I wasn't like some of the others. I saved my money."

Josh didn't know whether to laugh or cry. "Mr. Tyrone, I live in Florida. I'm going to be here awhile longer, and I'd be happy to see if I can find a job for Melody. As for Mikey, don't you think Mack and he could work it out themselves? Then when Mack quits the business, he could help Mikey with the bookkeeping. Wouldn't that work?"

"You're not staying in New York?" Eddie Tyrone looked very tired all of a sudden, the deep furrows in his face turned down and his mouth drooped.

"It's possible. I don't know yet, Mr. Tyrone. I couldn't promise."

"But you would look after Melody as long as you're here?"

Was there a gleam in Eddie's eye? "My fiancée and I would be glad to," Josh said.

"Fiancée," Eddie said sadly.

"Yes. I'm going to be married soon." It was only a slight exaggeration, Josh assured himself. None at all if he had his way.

"I'll take it." Eddie held out his hand. Josh

stood and shook hands. "Would you tell Mikey it's time to go back to the city now? He and Mack can come back any time. I'll set up an appointment. Desirée and I won't be leaving for a few weeks. They can practice till then."

"I'll tell them."

"I'll be in touch, Mr. Havilland. I'd like to have you and your fiancée for dinner. So you can meet Melody."

"I'm sure we'd enjoy that."

On his way back to Manhattan, Josh wondered if Ginny would mind being his fiancée, if only to protect him from Eddie's matchmaking. He had a feeling Eddie could be very persuasive, even at eighty-six and with no other muscle than Mikey Scanlon.

Anita and Ginny arrived at Ginny's apartment later than they had planned because of the end-less paperwork it took to get Anita discharged from the hospital. By the time Ginny tucked her into the bed in Lisa's old room, now rechristened the guest room, Anita was white and wobbly.

"I'll get you your pill and then you can just lie back and rest." Ginny smiled reassuringly at Anita and squeezed her hand. She had just put the kettle on to boil for coffee and poured a glass of orange juice for Anita when the buzzer sounded.

It was a florist delivery boy, bringing two dozen pink rosebuds "from Papa with love." No sooner had Ginny found the pills and started toward the guest room when another bouquet arrived, this one deep red American Beauty roses "from Gray to the mother of my child and my only love." After that, Papa sent chocolates and Gray sent champagne "to celebrate our engagement and your life."

Anita slept through most of the afternoon. Even the frequent ring of the doorbell didn't awaken her. At four, Papa arrived with an enormous tray of five different cheeses and six different kinds of crackers. Ginny refused to let him see Anita until she woke up naturally.

"She needs all the sleep she can get, Mr. Di-Benedetto. Sit down, won't you? Would you like some sherry? Or perhaps wine?"

"Sherry would be fine, Ms. McDougall." He was dressed as elegantly as he had been the night before, but his face was no longer ruddy with health and frequent massages. Instead, he looked as white as Anita. Ginny was almost tempted to tell him to lie down on the couch and cover him with an afghan.

She poured him a glass of sherry, glad her crystal glasses were Waterford. He took a sip.

"Very nice." There was a note of surprise in his voice. "Dry sack?"

"Amontillado." Ginny gave what she hoped was a pleasant smile. She found Anthony Di-Benedetto a little intimidating. "Anita will be happy to see you. But the doctor did say that she shouldn't be upset until she's feeling better. He said there's nothing to worry about, but accidents like hers cause more wear and tear psychologically than we're aware of."

"I won't upset her."

"I hope that means you aren't going to demand that she return to Long Island with you?" Seeing the coldness come back into his eyes, she added, untruthfully, "I don't mean to tell you how to talk to your own child, Mr. DiBenedetto. But sometimes outsiders can see things more clearly than we ourselves can."

"Just what do you mean?"

"I know that Anita's been bitterly unhappy these past weeks because of the estrangement between the two of you. If you could see your way clear to consider her choice of husband, she would be very happy." Ginny crossed her fingers that she'd live through this encounter.

"I appreciate your interest in Anita, Ms. McDougall, but I think I know best what my daughter needs."

"I'm sure you know better than *I* could, but

don't you think Anita knows what she needs better than *you* could?" Ginny's voice was soft and as unthreatening as she could make it.

Tony D sat in silence studying the woman who sat across from him. What he saw must have reassured him, for a thin sliver of a smile crossed his lips. "I understand what you're saying." He took another sip of his sherry. "Perhaps you're right."

Ginny sagged with relief. She had not been pulverized, atomized, or otherwise destroyed. Anthony DiBenedetto didn't need gunmen. The force of his anger alone would have done the trick.

"I'm glad you'll consider it. Anita has become a dear friend, and I worry about her."

"Yes, I can see you do." This time it was a real smile. "May I say that anyone who can call you friend is fortunate."

Ginny inclined her head at the compliment, feeling like a duchess indicating thanks. "Anita loves you very much. She also fears for you." She didn't dare to say more openly that his daughter thought Tony D's life was in danger every day. He refused to heed his daughter, he would certainly resent a stranger telling him such a truth.

"I know. I've thought about everything she said, as well as your friend Mr. Havilland's ideas. I'm beginning to think—"

The soft sound of Anita's voice could be heard calling Ginny. DiBenedetto got to his feet and was halfway down the short hallway to the guest room with surprising speed for such a bulky man.

He opened the door and Ginny heard him say, "Hello, *cara.*" Ginny stayed in the living room, trying to decide what she thought of Anthony DiBenedetto. Loving father, formidable adversary. What else? Organized crime kingpin? Apparently. At least, he hadn't laughed at Josh's idea of seeking out the witness protection program.

The buzzer sounded again. Ginny went to the front door and waited until she heard the elevator doors closing. She was becoming a friend of the delivery boys in the neighborhood who had been beating a path to her door. She glanced through the peephole and then opened the door with a reluctant sigh.

"Hello, Gray, come in." Ginny was not ready for another scene between Anita's father and her fiancé. Last night had been bearable only because Josh stayed on after their guests had left and loved her so completely that there had been no room for worries about problems she couldn't solve. But that wouldn't be possible now that Anita was staying with her.

"I hope it's all right," Gray said a little doubtfully. "I saw Frick and Frack outside with a rental limousine, so I figured Anita's father was here. I'll wait to see her until he leaves, if that's all right with you. I don't want to upset her, but I went to her apartment and brought her some clothes. I'm glad you thought to call me. I'd never have remembered." He gave Ginny an apologetic grin. "I can't leave without seeing her. No scenes, I promise you."

"I'm not sure you can guarantee that," Ginny said, "but I thank you for the thought."

"Gray?" Anita's voice, lifted with hope, came from the guest room. "Is that you, Gray?"

Gray looked inquiringly at Ginny, who nodded. "Go ahead, I'm sure seeing you will be good for her. As long as you don't wear her out with worry."

"I'll be good as gold, I promise." He headed down the short hallway at a pace just short of a run. "Hi, darling! You're looking much better. Hello, sir, how are you?"

Ginny, listening to his voice from the living room thought that there was something to be said for drilling manners into children as Gray's parents had clearly done. It gave you something to fall back on when faced with a disapproving crime lord and father of your true love.

She went into the guest room and found it crowded with not only two men and Anita but the enormous tray of crackers and cheese. "If you gentlemen would excuse us for a few minutes, now that Anita is awake, the doctor wants her to get up and move around on her crutches for a while. We'll be out to join you shortly." Ginny crossed her fingers that she wouldn't be faced with blood and mayhem when she rejoined Gray and Tony D.

Anita and Ginny managed a shower with the aid of a waterproof sleeve for the cast. Getting dressed was more of a challenge. "I feel like a hippopotamus," Anita said as she struggled into a printed turtleneck and denim jumper. "I don't know why my arms don't work right. It's my leg that's broken."

"Well, you look fine." Ginny deftly helped her guest into a soft moccasin. "It's a good thing Gray brought over some clothes for you, isn't it?"

"Do you hear anything?" Anita asked, apprehension clear in her worried eyes and wrinkled brow. "Are they fighting?"

"I don't think so. But my fingers are crossed."

"So are mine!"

"No wonder we're having such a hard time getting you dressed." Ginny laughed. "Come on. Just a little lipstick and you'll be ready."

As Anita made her way slowly into the living room, Ginny saw the looks on the faces of the two men who waited for her. Love and concern showed equally on both and made Grayson Harcourt and Anthony DiBenedetto resemble each other more than many fathers and sons. If only their love far Anita could bring them together instead of tearing her apart!

"Papa, Gray, see how much better I am now that I am awake and dressed." Anita swung herself toward the club chair with the ottoman that sat at right angles to the couch. Both men leaped to assist her but she shook her head. "I have to learn to manage by myself. The doctor said that the exercise is good for me." She maneuvered herself into position and sank into the chair. Gray lifted her leg onto the ottoman and Anita smiled at him.

"I'd like to take you and Ms. McDougall out for dinner, *cara,*" said her father.

"I'd like Gray to come, too, Papa." Anita's tone was level, but it was like tempered steel. She meant to have her way, Ginny thought. She's her father's daughter.

DiBenedetto looked at the two young people, Gray sitting on the arm of Anita's chair, his arm protectively around her shoulders. He sighed. "What do you think, Ms. McDougall? Do you think this soft boy from Darien is going to be able to stand up to his parents when they find out he wants to marry Tony D's daughter?" He looked inquiringly at Ginny, as if he really wanted an answer.

"He stood up to you, didn't he?" Ginny said dryly. "I don't think a mere corporate chief from Fairfield County, Connecticut, would have a chance against him."

Anita smiled. "She's right, Papa. Gray's not afraid of you."

"I'm not sure that speaks well for his intelligence," Tony D said with a chilly look at Gray. "I don't want my daughter hurt because of me. I don't want her ostracized or talked about behind her back. That's why I wanted her to marry someone I knew. Because then I could guarantee it wouldn't happen."

"No one can guarantee that, Mr. DiBenedetto," Gray said. "You can't know what Anita will make of her life, or who will come into it. But you know her. Do you really think Anita would crumble because some jackass insulted you?"

"I'd be much more likely to scratch their eyes out," Anita said. She was, Ginny knew, perfectly serious.

"That's my girl," Gray murmured, smiling proudly into her eyes. "Takes nothing from nobody."

"Better remember that," she replied.

DiBenedetto looked at them both for a long moment. Then he sighed. "I will consider this young man's suit, Anita Louise. So I suppose he had better come along with us to dinner." He rose, like Poseidon from the sea, majestic and powerful. "Ms. McDougall?"

"I would love to come, but I have a previous engagement," Ginny said with the old-fashioned courtesy the invitation demanded.

"Ah," said DiBenedetto, "the fortunate Mr. Havilland. I envy him."

Ginny smiled in acknowledgment of the compliment.

"We shall return Anita by ten o'clock," he added. "Good-night, Ms. McDougall."

"Have a delightful evening," Ginny said as she closed the door after them.

Twenty-eight

Ginny sat on the couch and leaned back into the cushions. She had high hopes that Tony D would give in gracefully to what was inevitable. What a wonderful, fairy-tale ending! She sighed and considered and then decided against pouring herself more sherry.

Josh should be here any time. Ginny stretched and smiled and wiggled her toes. That was a happy ending, too. Well, maybe not a happy ending, but certainly a happy first act curtain.

When the buzzer rang, she was across the room pushing the answering button in two bounds. There was a silly grin on her face and her heart was beating double time when she heard the elevator doors open. She had her door open before he had time to walk down the hall.

"Josh, dar—" The words dried in her mouth. She tried and failed to summon a welcoming smile. "Lisa. Denis," she said with foreboding. "Come on in and tell me what we've done this time."

Their faces were troubled, disapproving. Ginny sighed. She wondered whether she had ever been as tiresome about Lisa as Lisa was being about her. Anytime now, Ginny thought, she'd get a list of "dating do's and don't's" from her daughter.

Lisa and Denis sat side by side on the couch. Ginny couldn't help but recall how they had reacted to each other the first time they had seen each other in recent years. Hard to believe it was just last week. Apparently, concern about their foolish parents had forged a bond. She was still unconvinced that it was anything more than that, no matter what Josh thought.

"Would you like something to drink?" Ginny sat down in the wing chair. If they wanted anything, Lisa could get it. If she was going to have the disadvantages of dealing with grown children, she might as well get some of the perks as well.

They shook their heads. "Well, then, here we are," Ginny said, trying to get them started. Nothing. They continued to stare at her with that more-in-sorrow-than-in-anger expression on their faces. "Okay, let's have it."

"We thought we'd wait until Dad arrived," said Denis, in the mournful tones of a network anchor announcing another failed peace conference.

Ginny tapped her fingers on the arm of the chair. "No," she said after a minute, "I'm not

going to have you sit around here looking like
someone's just died. You'd better tell me what's
up." She sat back awaiting the worst.

"We just wish you'd told us, Momma," Lisa
said with a choke in her voice. "I'd want to know
no matter how I felt."

"You'd want to know what?"

"You know."

"No, dear, I don't."

"That you're getting married."

Ginny took a deep breath and counted to ten.
Then she attempted to explain, calmly and ra-
tionally, in the same tone she had used to explain
to Lisa why she couldn't cross First Avenue by
herself when she was two. "I have no plans to
get married. When I do, I promise you will know.
Okay? Now for the last time, Josh and I are not
going to elope."

Denis shook his head, as if he couldn't believe
what he was hearing. "It's no use, Ginny. The
travel agency called."

Ginny sat expectantly, waiting for the rest of
the sentence. Nothing. Denis just looked at her.
"What did the travel agency say, Denis?" she
asked at last, with what she thought was com-
mendable patience.

"They called with information about your
trip."

Another pause. Was she going to have to extract every bit of information from him like teeth? "Where exactly am I going?"

"Mexico."

"That's nice. I've never been to Mexico. Am I going any place special or touring the whole country?"

"It's not funny, Momma. Josh asked about suites at beachfront resorts. *Honeymoon* suites, Momma."

"That's ridiculous. To the best of my knowledge, I'm not getting married and I'm not going to Mexico." She felt a faint pang as she said the words. "The agency must have been mistaken."

"No, they weren't," Lisa shook her head. "Denis questioned them very carefully. Joshua Havilland asked that they call with the information. Denis thought maybe you were planning to sneak away for a romantic weekend, but I knew you'd never do anything like that. Not after all the lectures I got from you when I was in high school. Besides, I told Denis that people your age don't do impulsive things like that. So, since I knew you'd only go if you were married, that meant—" Lisa stared at her mother with tear-drenched eyes.

Ginny stared back at her daughter. Had it ever occurred to these two that maybe Josh was planning on surprising her with a weekend trip to the Caribbean? That she would like nothing better?

And that their ham-handed meddling had now ruined any surprise? For the first time, Ginny didn't see Lisa and Denis's attitude as comic.

"Look, I don't know what, if anything, Josh planned, but you two have now ruined it." Was there a guilty flash in either pair of eyes? She didn't think so. "As I remember it, Denis, you got very annoyed with Josh when he invited one of your dates over for dinner without checking with you. Yet here you are, acting like some sort of moral policeman." She glared at the two sitting opposite her. They stared back with what looked like a total lack of comprehension.

"We only want what's best for you," Denis said. There was a hurt look in his eyes. "I didn't mean to act like a moral policeman. We're just worried about you."

"Why don't you two get a life?" Ginny said acidly. "Or better yet, two lives. One each," she explained.

"We have lives, Ginny. But you're behaving so strangely that we worry."

"Denis, your father is not a lonely hearts killer. Lisa, your mother is not an idiot." Ginny ran her hand through her hair, wishing Josh were there. Surely he could find a way to explain to their overprotective children that he and Ginny were functioning adults. "Why don't you go plan some trip for yourselves, instead of worrying about what we may or may not do."

Lisa and Denis looked at each other, their eyes bright. Then, simultaneously, they looked away and cleared their throats.

Maybe Josh wasn't crazy after all. Ginny would bet that for just a moment they had each thought of going away together. She smothered a smile.

"Look, why don't you two go out for dinner and a movie? Calm down and try not to worry about your parents. Both of whom can take care of themselves, and in case you've forgotten, took care of you for a number of years."

Lisa caught the sharp tone of her mother's voice. "Okay, okay. You don't have to hit me over the head. I'll never bother about you again." She stood up, raised her chin, and looked like a soap opera diva about to launch into her big scene "I can see you just don't want me around, now that you've found a man."

Ginny was tempted to throw up her hands and let Lisa play the misunderstood child. But she still cherished the hope that Lisa and Josh would become friends. Why she cared when Josh most likely was going back to Florida in a few weeks, was something Ginny didn't care to examine.

"Lisa, darling, you know you're being absurd. I will tell you everything when there's something to tell. But right now there isn't. You know about

Anita and her father. She's staying with me for a few days until she gets used to the cast and crutches. If there is ever anything about Josh and me that you should know, believe me, I will tell you."

"All right, Momma. I believe you. But Denis and I can't help worrying about the two of you, running all over New York, making friends with organized crime figures and Haitian refugees."

"The Haitian is Denis's client." Ginny smiled.

"Only because Dad dragooned me into the mess," Denis said. He still didn't sound happy about it, either, Ginny thought. "It's taking up a lot of time. I must have spent a half hour on the phone today talking to some guy at the INS."

"I wouldn't worry about it, Denis. You know the firm likes lawyers to take on *pro bono* work. I'm even thinking about a project with Josh—" She could have bitten her tongue. Just as she was about to usher Lisa and Denis out the door, she has to bring up another topic, sure to raise Denis's blood pressure.

"What!" Denis's exclamation sounded like a pistol shot. "You're not serious. You just got back from months of traipsing around the city with my father, and now you think that I'll give you a leave of absence so you can do some crazy

public interest work? What is it this time? Legal aid for indigent mob bosses?"

"There are no indigent mob bosses, Denis, you should know that. There are only rich mob bosses and dead mob bosses. Would you feel better if your father and I were going to get paid to work with organized crime figures?"

"Damn straight I would." Denis stood, folded his arms across his chest and frowned.

"Denis!" Lisa exclaimed. "You can't be that much of a barbarian. Even you must have some ethics."

"Stop standing there looking like a cigar store Indian," Ginny said to him impatiently. "This is just a pilot project to help litigants represent themselves in court."

"Oh, my God!" Denis put one hand to his face and shook his head. "I can't believe I'm hearing this. I thought at least Dad was enough of a lawyer to believe that no one should act as their own attorney!"

"That being the first law of lawyering, I suppose." Lisa rose and stood toe-to-toe with Denis. "That lawyers are a necessity of life, like food and air!" Fire flashed from her eyes and Ginny noted that there was a becoming flush on her cheeks. The sparks flying between them were practically visible. Well, thought Ginny, so that's why they fought so often. It turned them on.

"That is not the first law of lawyering, but it isn't fair to encourage people who don't know anything about the law or the court system to try to represent themselves."

"Well, all I can say is—"

"Lisa. Denis. Why don't you go and fight this out somewhere else? I've had a hard day and if there's anything I don't need, its a passionate discussion about the role of lawyers in society."

"There's no passion involved. Absolutely none." Lisa stared at Denis for a moment, then turned on her mother with the same flashing eyes. "It's extremely logical and rational."

"Then go be logical and rational somewhere else." Neither of the combatants paid any attention to her. She decided to go for the jugular. "Lisa, I'm not as young as I used to be, and I'm very tired. I'd like to just sit down and put my feet up and listen to a little Brahms. Could you let me do that, do you think?" Ginny's voice was wistful and quiet. Her shoulders sagged and her eyes were pleading.

Lisa was instantly contrite. "Oh, Momma, of course we'll go. I didn't mean to be so inconsiderate. But you haven't had any dinner. Why don't I just go fix you something—a nice bowl of soup or oatmeal or something? Denis can stay here and talk to you. Nicely. About something you'd enjoy. The fate of the arctic seal, maybe?"

Ginny and Denis looked at each other, horrified. "No, no," said Denis, "I can see that Ginny's tired. And we haven't had dinner either, Lisa. I for one don't feel like soup and oatmeal. We'd better go."

Without waiting for an answer, he swept Lisa out the door and off to a restaurant.

Ginny heaved a sigh of relief. With any luck at all, she should have at least an hour and a half before Anita came back. Ginny hoped that this time there wouldn't be any big emotional scenes. After hearing Tony D and Gray the night before, Ginny thought she should be braced for the worst.

Meanwhile, where was Josh? He had said that he'd be over this evening. They had planned dinner together. He, of course, was going to cook. He had an appointment with Mikey Scanlon, she remembered, but that was supposed to be this morning. Were Mikey and Eddie Tyrone perhaps more fearsome than they appeared?

Now she was really getting worried. They could have shot Josh and left him in some landfill in New Jersey. Josh might be right that Eddie didn't have a gang any more, but it only took one person to fire a gun and Mikey looked big enough to haul a dead body to some out-of-the-way spot. Ginny got up and started to pace the room.

If something happened to Josh, she'd never

forgive herself. Denis was right. New York was no place for a man starting over at fifty-eight.

Now, Virginia, nothing has happened. You're being absurd. He'll be here any minute. What time was it, anyway? She glanced at her watch. Seven-fifteen! *Oh, God, he's dead.*

The doorbell rang. Ginny ran to her front door and looked through the peephole.

Josh! She threw open the door and hurled herself into his arms. In surprise, Josh lurched forward a few steps, propelling them both into Ginny's living room.

"Kiss me again," he murmured, suiting the action to the words. "If this is the way you greet the prodigal, I'll have to get stuck in Brooklyn more often."

"Brooklyn?" Ginny was getting her second wind. "What were you doing in Brooklyn? Alone."

"You mean without you and Theodore?" Josh kept his arms around her.

"Never mind that. What were you doing in Brooklyn?"

"Going to see Sylvia." He backed Ginny towards the couch.

She stopped in her tracks. "Our Sylvia? At the Mordecai Jackson Home?"

He backed up two more steps. "The very same."

She stopped again, and moved to free herself from his embrace. "About her will?"

He bent to kiss her in the sensitive spot behind her ear. "Yes."

She was breathing quickly, but she had enough presence of mind to protest. "Josh, you haven't been admitted to—"

He cupped her face in his hands and kissed her mouth. It was a long, gentle kiss that robbed her of the rest of her breath. "I know, sweetheart, I know," he murmured when he drew back at last. "But I wasn't giving her legal advice."

She had just enough sense left to know that she was about to do her best to kiss him senseless. "Then what were you doing?" she whispered.

He felt her butterfly kisses on the corners of his mouth and rational thought became all but impossible. "Questions," he managed to mutter between kisses. "Oh, yes. Keep doing that, sweetheart."

"I will," she promised. "Questions about her will?"

"Mmmhmm." His tongue traced the outline of her lips and they opened to him.

"Oh, Joshua, do that again," breathed Ginny as soon as she could talk. "Questions to ask her son-in-law, the lawyer?"

"Riiight." He trailed his mouth to her collarbone and nuzzled the base of her throat. "You taste wonderful."

She pulled his shirt out of his pants and caressed his back. "You feel wonderful." She felt her knees sag. She was surprised she was still upright. "I guess that's not . . . practicing . . . law."

"Damn right . . . it's not. Oh, sweetheart, I like that." His hands reached under her sweater. "You feel good, too. Like warm satin." He traced intricate patterns on her back with his fingertips. "She's going to tell him he won't be executor if he misbehaves."

She almost whimpered with need. "An *in terrorem* clause?" she whispered. She tilted her head back, pulled his head down and kissed him.

His breath was uneven when she finally released him. "Sort of." It was all he could say for a moment. "Come make love."

She slid an arm around his waist. "I thought you'd never think of it. I didn't want to rush you."

"You never rush me and I'm always thinking of it."

"Good. Let's go."

The telephone startled them both awake. It was Anita. "Papa's got my old nurse to come and stay with me at my apartment, Ginny. It's the perfect solution. So, I'll send for my stuff tomorrow, if that's all right."

"That's fine, Anita. I'm glad things are going well."

"So far they are. But we haven't talked about the wedding."

"If you need moral support, just let me know." Ginny thought it was a good thing that Anita didn't know that her mentor and friend was lying naked in bed, next to an equally naked man, who was nuzzling the back of her neck.

"Thanks, Ginny. You and Mr. Havilland have already done more than you know. Good-night."

Ginny hung up the phone. "Josh, stop it now. It's very hard to carry on an intelligent conversation when you're in bed with me."

"I certainly hope so." He propped himself on his elbow and grinned at her. "It's almost impossible for me any time you're in the same room. You make a sober discussion of someone's last will and testament sound like phone sex."

"Guess what." Ginny smiled seraphically up at him.

"What?"

"I'm hungry."

"And you expect me to cook?"

"Of course. Unless you'd like soup or oatmeal."

"My God. You need me so you won't get some deficiency disease. Oatmeal for dinner! I don't want to hear where you got that idea." He pulled her into his arms and kissed her.

Dinner was very late.

Lisa and Denis had spent the evening not talking about taking a vacation together. They had ordered paella at a Spanish restaurant in the East Twenties, and stared at each other across the dimly lit table.

"Your mother—I mean, Ginny, is very adamant about leading her own life." His fork seemed to swoop down on a steamed clam. "I've never seen her like that before."

Lisa looked at him. He looked good even when he was chewing. Not many men did. "It's your father. He's changed her."

Denis looked at her. She was very pretty in the subdued light and shadow of the candlelight. Her hair was the color of new pennies and her eyes were emeralds. "Maybe change isn't so bad."

"Do you think so?" she said.

"It can be . . . liberating." He thought maybe his father wasn't so wrong after all. Maybe commitment wasn't such a terrible idea.

"Momma thinks I've been in a rut." Maybe Momma had a point. Denis Havilland was certainly a change, and in this case, Lisa thought change was stimulating to say the least.

"How's the paella?" Denis said more or less at random. "Mine is delicious." He bit into a shrimp and ate it with every appearance of pleasure.

Lisa tingled with awareness. Looking down at her plate, she murmured. "Mine is wonderful." She raised her eyes and their gazes entwined.

They weren't talking about paella.

"Let's go," Denis said abruptly. He felt strongly that the moment had to be seized or he might lose his chance. *Chance at what, you idiot?* he asked himself in vain.

"All right." Tension had Lisa's nerves jumping. When Denis took her hand to help her up, she felt his touch all the way up her arm. *What do you think you're doing?* she asked herself, as if she didn't know.

The waiter rushed up to their table. "Is anything wrong? Why are you leaving? Didn't you like your dinner?" He seemed about to cry. Denis stared at him. This couldn't be a New York waiter.

"Dinner was fine," he said, peeling a bill off his money clip and handing it to the man without looking at it.

"It was wonderful," Lisa said, with a smile that illuminated the room.

The waiter looked at the bill. A hundred should just about cover two plates of paella. Those two looked like they were headed to a fire, he thought, as they ran to catch a cab.

Twenty-nine

They stood close together on the sidewalk out-side the restaurant.

"Where are we going?" Lisa asked. It was a cosmic question.

Denis understood. "A long way, if you want to."

Lisa took his hand. "I'm a little scared."

Denis frowned. "Why? I wouldn't hurt you."

Lisa understood. "I know. Not on purpose any-way. But sometimes things just don't work out for one person, while the other still feels . . ." She trailed off.

"I don't think that will happen." For some rea-son, Denis was sure that everything would work out. In the back of his head, he heard that small, frantic voice of sanity screaming, *"You're out of your mind! Lisa McDougall is a fruitcake who wears orange dresses! She's not tall and willowy! She disagrees with everything you and Rush Lim-baugh stand for! She'll be a disaster at firm par-ties! Stop this right now!"* Denis told the little voice to shut the hell up.

"Are you sure?" Lisa was doubtful. "You think this could be . . ." She was afraid to say it.

"Yes," he said. "I do. The real thing."

She believed him. "Oh, my God."

He took her in his arms. "We won't rush. I'll come over now and we'll just talk."

"Just talk?" Disappointment colored her voice.

"Well, maybe we could fool around a little, too." He held her a little tighter. "May I?"

"Yes." *You are mad, Lisa, mad! This man is nothing you want. He's not just a lawyer, for God's sake, he's a Wall Street lawyer! So, okay, he's good-looking and makes you feel like no one ever has before. That's hormones! That's lust! That's not a deep, true, abiding affection based on shared values and mutual esteem. What are you thinking of?* Lisa smiled. She was thinking of stimulating arguments and even more stimulating kisses. She was thinking of Love with a capital L. "Shall we take a cab?"

In the cab's dark interior, with the lights of Manhattan whizzing by, Denis pulled Lisa into his arms and kissed her, a long, moist kiss that lasted from Twenty-eighth all the way to Ninety-fourth Street. It was exploratory and so exciting that they were both shaking when the cab pulled over to the curb outside Lisa's building.

It took Lisa the minute she spent extracting herself from Denis and the cab to recognize her home. Denis paid the cabby as randomly as he had paid the waiter.

"Thanks, friend!" said the cabby as he pulled away, a fifty tucked carefully in his wallet.

When they finally stood inside her colorful little apartment, Denis put his arms around her loosely and looked down into her eyes. They were dark with an emotion he hoped was passion. "I don't know what to say," he admitted at last. "I've never felt like this."

"What does that mean?" Lisa said, her expression wary.

"It means this is not going to be another affair."

Anger brightened her eyes to emerald again. "What do you mean, *'another affair'*? Are you implying that I—"

He smiled. She was such a firecracker! "No, I meant for me. You're unique. I've never known anyone who makes me feel the way you do."

Her expression was wary again. "What way?"

"Excited, happy. As if something wonderful were about to happen." He'd never talked this way either. It was exhilarating but frightening to be so honest.

"Do you know what's going to happen?"

"Yes. I know what, Lisa, and you know it, too. But I'm not sure when."

She shook her head. "I understood you better

when we were fighting. Now I don't know where I am. You've got me thoroughly confused."

"I know. I feel exactly the same way. Scary, isn't it?" His voice was low and tender, with a thread of laughter in it.

Lisa had never heard him sound like that before. "What are we going to do?"

"I think we should maybe take off our coats and sit down."

"And then what?" Lisa wanted to know the ground rules. Then maybe she could figure out the point of the game.

"A kiss, maybe?"

She thought it over. "For the first one, I think we should keep our coats on. Or at least, we should be standing up." Denis laughed. She heard genuine amusement. "What's so funny?" It was the first time she had had to ask.

"I don't know. Us, I guess, negotiating a contract for a kiss." He hesitated a moment and then bent to touch his lips to hers. Gentle, tentative, searching, it made Lisa's heart pound so hard the blood beat in her ears like a drum. A soft and simple kiss, it shook her like an earthquake, and she could feel the seismic shifts in her body and soul.

"Lisa, Lisa, what's happening to us?" Denis's arms tightened around her, bringing her as close as two wool coats and assorted indoor clothing would allow.

"I don't know." She stood perfectly still while he unbuttoned her orange pea jacket. As she reached up to return the favor and unbutton his gray cashmere chesterfield, she was embarrassed to find that her fingers shook. "Look at me." Her voice was half laugh, half gasp. "I can't even undo buttons."

He waited while she fumbled with his coat, enjoying the sight of her bent head and the excitement he felt when she at last slipped the last button through its hole. He shrugged the coat off, and pulled her into his arms again.

He wanted to devour her and at the same time prolong the moment forever. He wanted to possess her totally and yet leave intact the independent spirit that was the heart of her. He wanted to take everything and give everything, to cherish her like a flower and dive into her core without restraint.

Denis shook his head, trying to clear it. Useless. He didn't know what he wanted, but it seemed to be the very thing that terrified him.

Love.

Oh, God. Love?

He began to kiss her face, savoring every curve, the taste of her satin skin flavored lightly with makeup. The sight of her smiling mouth as he bent to kiss its corners.

"Lisa, Lisa." It was all he could say. Denis Havilland, the silver-tongued lawyer and man-about-models, could think of nothing more to say. Just, "Lisa."

"What are you doing to me?" She was breathless, as if she'd run miles.

"I don't know. The same thing you're doing to me, I hope. Driving you wild. Confusing the hell out of you."

"Yes." It was true. She didn't know how she felt. She had gotten used to the idea that she hated Denis Havilland. It was pretty clear now that hatred wasn't the emotion he inspired. But was it love? Or just the perverse appeal of a good-looking man she didn't like? Could she seriously be considering an affair with the Stud Muffin of Wall Street?

She pulled out of his arms, a move that caused her whole body to shake. Whatever she thought of him, her body—ignorant slut!—wanted him.

"What's wrong?" Denis's voice didn't sound like him. It was soft and concerned. Could he do that at will? she wondered.

"I don't want to go to bed with you." That was certainly straight shooting. But honesty required that she amend that bald statement. "I mean, I don't want to want to."

There was a pause while Denis pondered. Finally, he smiled. "We're not going to do that tonight."

Perversely, she was angry. "Why not? Am I not pretty enough? Too short? Too ordinary? Too—"

He hauled her into his arms and kissed her. It silenced her, robbing her of breath and thought. "Does that feel like you're lacking anything I want?" he demanded angrily when she finally pulled away.

"Then why? I know you don't treat your gorgeous girlfriends this way. Why me?" Should she be insulted? Was this a subtle put-down? Was he going to yell "fooled you" any second now?

"This is different, Lisa. This feels like it might be . . . permanent." What was he saying? A permanent relationship with Lisa McDougall? Oh, God.

Yes.

"You mean it." She stared at him as if seeing him for the first time.

"Yes. What about you? Do I feel like a permanent part of your life?"

Lisa didn't say anything for what seemed like several millennia to Denis. At last, "I'm afraid so," she said.

He took her hands in his. "I don't know what to do with a permanent relationship."

"I don't either."

"I think," Denis said, "that we can take things

easy. We can have romantic dinners and send each other silly cards and call on the phone six or seven times a day. At least," he added, "that's what I think it's like."

"Have you ever done that before?"

"My first girlfriend in high school, maybe. At least it felt sort of the same." He grinned. "Fizzy and obsessive. And I remember the phone calls."

She grinned back. "Yeah. I remember, too. Let's have some romance, Havilland. Roses, champagne. All that stuff."

"Romantic dresses," he said, smoothing his hands over her arms. "Floaty. Soft."

Lisa sensed criticism. "You hate my clothes. How can I have a serious, permanent relationship with a man who hates the way I look?"

"I love the way you look," Denis protested. "It's your clothes I'm not crazy about."

Lisa frowned. "Well, romantic to me isn't three piece suits with a key chain across the vest."

"Where else would I put my Phi Beta Kappa key?" Denis asked reasonably.

"In a drawer." She considered him through narrowed eyes. "Don't you ever relax? Wear sloppy sweatpants and a Yale sweatshirt?"

"Nope. I went to Harvard. No Yale sweatshirts." He couldn't help smiling. "Tell you what though. If you'll wear something soft and floaty, with flowers on it maybe, then I promise to order sweats from the Yale Coop first thing in the morning. Deal?"

"Only if we wear them at the same time."

"Deal." Denis watched her face. She was smiling but she looked tired. For the first time he could remember, he wanted what was best for a woman. His woman. "You should go to bed. You look exhausted." He ran his index finger down her cheek and around the delicate line of her jaw. "I'll leave and let you get some sleep."

"Denis?" Her voice was tentative.

"Yes, love."

"Maybe we should think about taking a trip. Like Momma and your father." She paused and Denis thought that she blushed. "What do you think?"

"A honeymoon?" How did he feel about that? Scared, excited. Pushed?

"No!" Lisa stepped back, horrified. "I didn't mean *that!*"

She didn't want to marry him? He was wounded. Other women had wanted to marry him, and when he couldn't persuade them that marriage to him was a very bad idea, he had fled. "Is it that revolting a thought?"

He sounded hurt. That wasn't what she meant. "No, no. It's not that. It's just that it's so soon. I meant just a trip for a weekend. So that we . . . for the first time . . . I mean—"

He helped her out. "That's a wonderful idea. You start thinking of where you want to go." Taking her face in his hands, he spoke softly, almost in a whisper. "There's no hurry."

"Yes," Lisa sighed. "Isn't that wonderful?"

He kissed her. "Yes, it's wonderful. And so are you. Good-night, love."

"Good-night," she echoed, "love."

The next evening, Josh and Ginny made their weekly trip to the Mordecai Jackson Home. Sylvia Bright was ensconced in a huge wing chair. Her feet dangled above the floor, but she was flanked by her son-in-law, Simon, the lawyer they had met several weeks before, and a middle-aged woman who looked very much like Sylvia.

"Ginny, Mr. Havill, come and meet my Cecilia. She and Simon have just gotten back from Sanibel Island. Look at what they brought me!" Sylvia was all smiles as she pointed to a glass lamp. The base was filled with shells that she proudly told Ginny and Josh had been collected and arranged by Cecilia herself.

"They're lovely, Sylvia," Ginny said, admiring the gift. Sylvia had complained to Ginny more than once that her daughter forgot to bring her anything from her frequent trips with her husband. "It's Simon," Sylvia would say. "He tells her not to, I'm sure. My Cecilia would never forget me."

"Simon picked out the lamp, Mother."

"Nothing's too good for Mother Bright," Simon chimed in with a smile Ginny thought made him look like a hungry pig.

Josh raised his eyebrows and said, "Hello, again, Mr. Miller."

Simon Miller turned toward him with an expression that was more a grimace than a smile. "Havilland. I got your letter and—"

"Did I tell you, Joshua, when you were here that Simon has answered all my questions about my will?" Sylvia beamed at the four younger people.

"I don't think you did, Sylvia, but I'm glad to hear it."

"Yes. We're not having any more difficulties in communication." Again, Simon Miller bared his teeth. "I can assure you of that."

"Good." Josh's eyes were hard and bright. "I was sure you would be able to solve all Sylvia's problems."

"Yes, it's just wonderful," Sylvia said again. "Simon's been so helpful. Just as you said he would be, Joshua."

Ginny looked from one man to the other. She had a few questions to put to Josh. Just what letter had he written to Simon Miller that had made him so amenable?

When they arrived back at Ginny's apartment, she asked him. Josh smiled and said only that he'd get them each a small brandy and then explain it. Ginny went to get their messages from the answering machine.

"We got a dinner invitation from Eddie Tyrone and his wife, Desirée," she said, accepting the snifter from Josh. "They want us to come and meet Melody and Mikey and his wife and Mack and his wife. I'm to call and let them know if we're available this weekend."

Josh shook his head, smiling. "Nope. This weekend we're busy."

"Doing what? I have to tell you, I'm dying to meet all these people. I've only seen them, you know, in the bar. I've never really met them. And I haven't even seen any wives. So what's so important that we can't go?"

"I'll let you know when I'm sure."

"Wait a minute!" Ginny was beginning to lose her temper. It wasn't just this high-handedness in making decisions for them. She didn't mind surprises. It was his smug smile. He had planned something she wasn't to know about. It was something very amusing and he wasn't sharing the joke. "Don't I get a say in this?"

Josh pulled her onto his lap and kissed her.

"Nope. It's going to be my surprise. As soon as I get everything arranged, I'll tell you. But I don't want to get all excited about something if I can't get tickets—" He broke off and frowned, as if he had said more than he meant to.

Ginny sat quiet for a minute. Then she said, "Mexico! We're going to Mexico. Aren't we? Do I have to get a passport, or a visa or shots or—"

"Sshh. I didn't say we were going anywhere. Where did you get that idea?" Ginny peered at Josh's face. He definitely looked guilty.

"Lisa and Denis told me you were making plans to go to Mexico. Cancún, I think they said." Ginny put her hands on either side of his face. "Tell the truth, Josh, is that what you're up to?"

"I can't tell you yet, Ginny. You'll just have to be patient." She grumbled, and took a sip of her drink. "Besides, I thought you wanted to know about Sylvia and Simon."

"Yes. What did you do to make him into such a pussycat?"

"I did exactly what he did to me. I threatened to take him to the Bar Association. They frown on lawyers who don't write the wills their clients want. I wrote him a letter that he got the day he got back from vacation. He called Sylvia and she told me that he wrote the will so even she could understand it. The End."

Ginny chuckled. "I should have guessed you'd think of something that elegant. Now, what about your trip to Mexico?" It had just suddenly occurred to Ginny that a trip for Josh didn't even necessarily mean a trip for Ginny. That made her even crosser.

"I don't know if there is a trip to Mexico. But, believe me, wherever I go, you go. But it's not the weekend yet. We still have that luncheon meeting with court project people tomorrow."

"I'm a little worried about that."

"Why? You took on everyone in the hall when they didn't give paralegals the respect you thought they deserve. Lunch with Sheila Margolies and company can't be worse than that."

"I just hope that they're ready to listen. I have some ideas about who can do what in something like this."

"Good. That's what I'm counting on." He smiled and kissed her. "I think you're going to be the best thing that ever happened to the court system of New York. Maybe of all the court systems in the country."

"Oh, please!" Ginny laughed. "Don't get carried away."

"No, I'm serious. Think of the possibilities. Paralegals in every courthouse in the country, ready to help anyone who wants to represent himself."

"Chill out, Joshua. One step at a time." Ginny shook her head. "You're quite a dreamer. I'll settle for helping a few people in one court."

"Think big, Virginia. Don't settle. Go for broke." He hugged her. "What a team we'll make."

"In the court project?"

"In every way." He grinned. "I love you. And I'm more excited about everything I'm doing now than I can ever remember being. And happier."

"I'm glad." Ginny reached up to kiss him. "I love you, too. Now if you'd just tell me what you're going to do in Mexico, I'd be content."

"Don't jump to conclusions. Nobody but Denis and Lisa said anything about Mexico. Wait. Meanwhile, come to bed and love me."

Denis had never before considered asking anyone for help with a client. But now, as he contemplated going to Hervé's aunt's house to meet with the entire Dumalier family, his heart quailed. He had spent several hours with Hervé and François, trying to persuade them to let him take François's case to the Immigration and Naturalization Service. He had been met with torrents of French, oceans of hot, black coffee that had turned his stomach to roiling acid, and waves of emotion that he simply didn't know how to deal with.

His hand hovered near the telephone. What if she wouldn't come? What if she thought he was trying to put something over on her? With Lisa, he never knew. But somehow he thought if he could get the Dumaliers to Lisa's apartment, they might feel more at home. And with Lisa to smile, and offer chocolates, maybe he could make some progress.

"Hello." Her voice. He found he loved the sound of it.

"Lisa?" Did he sound sappy? "It's me." *Well, of course it's you, stupid. Who else would you say it was? "It's him"?*

"Denis?" Her voice was soft and sexy.

"Yes. It's me. I want to ask a favor of you. You can turn me down. I know it's an imposition, but it would be a big help."

"What are you talking about, Denis?" She didn't sound mad. Just amused. He found he didn't mind it that she thought he was amusing. He didn't need to impress her every minute. How peculiar.

"I need your help with Hervé."

"Is he the Haitian super in your building with the illegal cousin?"

"You remembered!" He was inordinately pleased that she recalled anything at all about his work.

"Sure. He sounds like the one client I'd like."

"Well, I'm supposed to meet with his aunt and a couple of other cousins today and I'd really like them to meet you. And to have the meeting at your apartment. I think they'd feel more at ease there than at my office or even my apartment. And with you." Lisa didn't say anything. Had he insulted her? Did it sound as if he thought her apartment was a mess and she was a simple child of nature, or something? "It's the way you are. The way you live. It's the colors, Lisa. I think they'd like them. And the cushions and the posters. And you. If you could be there, too. You're—it's—warm and colorful. And happy."

Denis had never said anything like this before. He'd never thought anything like this before. He'd had vague feelings that Ginny's apartment, with its plants and cheery chintz, was somehow more welcoming and relaxing than the elegant austerity of his. Lisa's place had struck a chord in him from the first moment he'd seen it. But he'd never been able to put it into words.

"Why, Denis, thank you." Lisa sounded amazed. "Sure, that would be fine. I have a luncheon meeting, but I can leave a key with the super and you and Hervé and the others can go ahead before I get back."

"You'd really do that?"

"Sure. You're not going to wreck the place, are you?"

"No, of course not. But I'd really like you to be there."

"Why?"

"I think you'd put them at their ease. Your clothes—"

"I beg your pardon. What about my clothes?"

"They're so bright. I think they'd make the Dumaliers feel at home. And you're so friendly and warm and—" Was he really saying these things? What was wrong with him? Was he bewitched?

He'd spent hours fantasizing about Lisa on a beach in Cancún or Acapulco, but that shouldn't send his brain on vacation and his tongue into overdrive. "Look, forget it. I don't know what I was thinking of. I'm sorry, Lisa."

"Denis, what is the matter with you? I said it would be fine. Use the apartment. I'll try to wear something truly outrageous today so your friends will feel at home."

"How about that outfit you wore to Ginny's the first time we had dinner together. You remember, the purple tank top and the pink sweater. With the army boots."

"You remembered." Lisa's voice was soft.

"Who could forget? Wear that. Please."

"I can't. I have that lunch today. But I'll find a way to look Caribbean for them. And I'll be there as soon as I can."

"Thank you, Lisa. I—I don't know what to say."

"That's a first. I'll see you this afternoon. 'Bye, Den."

By three o'clock, Denis and the five Dumaliers had disagreed totally about everything possible and Denis was ready to throw in the towel and agree that François should remain an undocumented alien, at least until democracy returned to Haiti.

Then Lisa walked in the door and Denis's senses reeled.

It was a Lisa he had never seen before. A Lisa with a briefcase, polished pumps, and a suit. A tweed suit. Purple tweed, to be sure, but nevertheless a suit. Denis simply stared at her, goggling like a kid at a sideshow.

"L-Lisa, how are you?" He tried to pull himself together. "Let me introduce you to the Dumaliers."

He took her hand and led her around the circle. Her smile was so bright and welcoming. How had he ever thought she was difficult and sarcastic? She sat down beside Tante Amalie, the matriarch of the clan. Before Denis could sit down again, Amalie held one of Lisa's hands in hers and they were conversing in some sort of fractured Creole and pidgin English.

Denis turned to Hervé. "What's going on?" he asked in an undertone.

"My aunt is asking your young lady about

you. Does she trust you? Are you a good lawyer?
Should we believe that you can get François a
fair hearing? Will you stand by us if the hearing
goes against us? That kind of thing."

Denis was afraid to ask what Lisa was saying.
Hervé continued, "She believes in you, your
young lady. She says you are the most capable
lawyer she knows. She says you are fair and
upright and will always do what you say you
will." Hervé looked at Denis and smiled. "You
are a very lucky man, *m'sieu*. I have never seen
this young lady come to your home, but she is
better than the others, I think."

Denis smiled at Hervé. "Yes," he said simply,
"she is."

The meeting became general after that. Denis
explained how François could claim political asy-
lum status, and what facts would sway the INS.
François would meet with Denis and then they
would go together to the hearing. The family
nodded agreement. They would do it. It was a
chance, for if François was denied refugee status,
he would be deported back to Port-au-Prince.

"You are trusting me with his life," Denis said
to the family in slow, careful English. "I will not
betray that trust."

Tante Amalie nodded and gave Denis a slight
smile. It felt like a benediction. *"Bien,"* she said.

"It is good. Marry *Mlle*. Lisa, *m'sieu*. It is good advice I give you. Do not let her escape you."

"No, *Madame*," Denis said with a bow, "I will not let her escape."

He held on tight to Lisa's hand as the family left. "Thank you." He took her into his arms. "I don't know what you did, but I'd tried everything I knew how to get François and the rest to trust to the process, but you won them over in five minutes." He kissed her. "Aunt Amalie told me not to let you get away from me." Lisa wound her arms around his neck. "And I'm not going to. You're mine, Lisa." He kissed her again, and she strained closer to him. "And I'm yours. Now, you'd better explain that briefcase and suit."

Thirty

Lisa smiled and touched Denis's cheek. "It's a long story."

"I have lots of time. Wait!" He went out to her kitchen and brought back a bottle of Dom Pérignon, two champagne flutes, and a dozen cream-colored roses. "Here. You wanted roses and champagne, so . . ."

Lisa took the foaming glass he handed her and sat down on her red, yellow, and green flowered couch. She cradled the roses on her lap, kicked off her shoes, and curled her feet up under her. "Come and sit next to me." She patted the soft cushion.

Denis sat and put his arm around her. "All right. Now I want to hear about this metamorphosis. What happened to the yellow minis and the combat boots? You look like an associate at Sanderson and Smith." He grinned. "Was all that funky chic just to annoy me?"

"No. Don't be so conceited. It's the way I like to dress—and the way I'm going to dress for any stuffy firm parties you take me to, so be warned. But I had a meeting with some people today who were looking for seed money for a project so I wore my power suit."

He looked at her. Her face was full of mischief as she said, "You'll never guess who I had lunch with . . ."

Josh had spent the morning making notes on the presentation to the Barringer Foundation. He frowned. That name seemed familiar, but he couldn't place it. Sheila Margolies had listed the others at the luncheon in rapid-fire order and his notes were incomplete. He was going to meet Ginny and the other participants at the Union League Club, where they were to have a private room so that they could meet over lunch without any interruptions. He arrived early and waited for Ginny in the club's elegant lobby and indulged in his favorite New York occupation, people-watching. How could he go back to Shellfish Cay and miss the parade of humanity he could find every day in this city?

From behind his *Wall Street Journal,* he was looking at the early arrivals for lunch—mostly middle-aged men who he decided were lawyers or brokers, maybe advertising executives. Then he saw a smashing-looking young woman come through the door. She reminded him a little of Ginny. And then he looked again at the trim, businesslike figure.

"Lisa!" he called, and started out of his leather chair and across the room to her. "What are you doing—Barringer!" he exclaimed. "You're the Barringer Foundation!"

She grinned at him. "Yes. Today I'm the Barringer Foundation. If you and Momma would be a little more talkative about what you're up to, I could have told you that Sheila Margolies contacted me several weeks ago about her court project."

"Didn't you know about our adventure at the Columbia symposium?" Josh asked.

"No, you never said anything about it." Lisa smiled a little ruefully. "I guess Denis and I were giving you both such a hard time that you didn't tell us anything you didn't have to." She held out her hand. "Sorry about that."

"Have you turned over a new leaf?" Josh was a little skeptical of Lisa's sudden turnabout. "Business suits and a welcome for your would-be stepdad?"

Lisa shook her head. "I can't go that far. Suits only when necessary. And as for you and Momma, well, I still have to be convinced this isn't some sort of mid-life crisis for you both."

"You still can't understand how anyone older

than you can feel what you do, can you? I don't know what we can do to make you see it. Maybe if we stay together for the next ten years or so you'll think it might last."

Lisa just smiled. "I want the best for my mother. And I don't want someone who'll run out on her like my father did."

"You know about your father?"

"Momma told you?"

"Yes," said Josh, "but I know she didn't tell you. How did you find out about it? Some so-called 'friend' of Ginny's?"

"As a matter of fact, yes."

"Damn. You won't let her know, will you, Lisa? She thinks she's given you a wonderful father to carry in your mind. It makes her happy to believe that."

"No, of course I won't." Lisa looked around. "Here comes Momma now." She smiled with proprietary pride. "Doesn't she look terrific?"

Josh turned. Ginny was wearing a caramel-colored coat. Her shiny cinnamon hair was ruffled by the wind and her green eyes sparkled. She smiled at the doorman and looked around the lobby. When she saw Lisa and Josh standing together, her smile broadened and she hurried forward.

"Not just terrific," he said, "beautiful. Beautiful, inside and out."

The calm conviction in his voice made Lisa

turn and survey him for a moment before she went forward to hug her mother.

"Surprise," she said. "I'm the foundation representative."

"Lisa! Why didn't you tell me?"

"I was just explaining to Josh that you didn't tell me this was one of your projects. All I knew was that Sheila had met a lawyer and a paralegal she thought would be great running the project."

Josh gave Ginny an "I-told-you-so" grin. "And now you know how right Sheila was," he said to Lisa.

Lisa frowned and looked at them. "As a matter of fact, she described you as a lawyer with no hang-ups about lawyers and their image and she said that the paralegal was so bright she scared the men at the conference."

"And you didn't guess it was your mother?" Josh said in mock surprise. "How could you miss a clue like that?"

"Now that I think about it, I don't know. You two would be the ideal cochairs of the project. If you want it, I think it's yours." Ginny beamed at her capable, beautiful daughter. Lisa sounded brisk and businesslike. Sometimes Ginny had trouble remembering that Lisa had a responsible job that she performed very well. Maybe it was true that mothers never saw their children as really and truly grown-up.

"Now all we have to do," Josh added, "is persuade Sheila and the other members of the group that you're right and once they meet your mother, it should be a snap."

"No problem." Lisa agreed, sounding very confident. "If Barringer is providing major funding, we'll have a big say in staffing. And there aren't any two people better qualified. So, let's lay it on them. If you're sure you want it." She looked at her mother. Josh raised his eyebrows in an unspoken question.

Ginny took a deep breath and jumped in. "Yes," she said. "I want to do it very much."

"Consider it done," said Lisa.

That evening, as the setting sun made Ginny's windows blaze with light, Josh and Ginny sat side by side on the couch, sharing a congratulatory glass of champagne.

"We got the job!" said Josh triumphantly.

"I hope we know what we're doing," said Ginny. "This is all so new. We'll have to make it up as we go along."

"That's the fun of it." Josh leaned over, carefully took the champagne glass out of her hand, and kissed her. "The coordinating committee sounded as if they'd help all they can."

"It's scary."

"It's exciting."

Ginny laughed. "Is this the classic case of you see the glass half-full and I see it half-empty?"

"No, it's a classic case of a lady who needs to be helped out of her rut." Josh stroked her cheek and smiled.

"What rut? I haven't done the same thing twice since I met you, Joshua Havilland."

He leaned over and kissed her. "Oh, yes, you have." The gleam in his eye told her exactly what he meant.

Ginny could feel her cheeks grow hot. "I wish you'd stop doing that. I hadn't blushed since high school until I met you."

"I consider that a great compliment." Josh took her hand in his and stroked it gently. Ginny could feel her fingertips begin to tingle. The man had the most amazing effect on her.

Josh's expression grew serious and he looked at her silently. Ginny felt her heart begin to pound. "Are you about to tell me about that mysterious trip to Mexico?"

"I don't think we're going to Mexico," Josh said absently.

"Oh." So much for that. Ginny was disappointed. She knew she shouldn't have believed anything Lisa and Denis said. Though she was beginning to believe that Josh was right about them. "I think Lisa's interested in Denis."

"Denis is in love with Lisa." Josh sounded positive. "And she's fallen for him, too."

"No, it hasn't gone that far yet." Ginny was very sure of herself. A mother knew these things. "Believe me, Lisa's just now beginning to think of it."

"Nope. They're in love."

"Maybe Denis is. But he's not her type at all." Ginny shook her head. "I think you're wrong."

Josh folded his arms across his chest and frowned. "You're absolutely mistaken. Trust me, I'm right about this. They're both hooked. It's happened already and it's serious."

"I think I know both of them better than you do," said Ginny, beginning to resent his cocksure attitude.

"No, you don't. I'm right."

"Oh, yeah?"

"Yeah! What's more, if you're so sure you're right, how'd you like to back up your opinion with a little bet." Josh's eyes gleamed. Clearly, a betting man, Ginny thought.

"Absolutely." She picked up the forgotten glass of champagne and downed the rest of it. "Name the stakes."

"I'll bet you that I can get Denis and Lisa to run away for the weekend. Tonight."

"Run away where?"

"Cancún."

"Where *we* were going to go?" Ginny was beginning to feel her anger rise, like a thermometer in the hot sun. The hot Mexican sun of Cancún, maybe.

"Umm, sort of. Anyway, if I can get them to run away for a weekend together, I win. If I can't, *we'll* go to Cancún."

Ginny stared at him. The man was up to something. She wasn't sure what. But she would certainly enjoy spending the weekend at a Caribbean resort with Mr. Know-It-All. After she demonstrated that he didn't know squat about young love.

Some innate sense of caution made her ask, "And if they go? You win, and what do I have to do?"

"Spend the weekend with me."

"Doing what?"

"Whatever suggests itself." Josh wouldn't look at her but Ginny could see the confident smile.

"Why do I get the feeling that I have just been suckered in a big way?" Ginny asked. The grin on Josh's face told her that things had worked out exactly the way he planned. "Have you been watching three-card monte dealers in Times Square? Is that where you learned to be such a con artist?"

"Nope. I learned that at Harvard. Lawyering 101." He tugged at her arm and pulled her onto his lap. "You are my heart's delight. I love you to pieces, Ms. Virginia McDougall, ma'am."

She held on to his shoulders and raised her face for his kiss. She could live on his kisses, Ginny thought as her lips opened under his. Kisses and champagne.

At last she pulled away from him slightly and leaned back to look at his face. His expression was serious, and his eyes had a hot, hungry look, the lids half-closed. She smiled. "Mr. Havilland, I love you." She took his face between her hands and kissed him, so softly it was more tease than satisfaction.

Josh's arms tightened around her ribs. "Enough to marry me?" he said, his voice a rasp.

"Well, I don't know about—" she began with a smile.

"Don't tease, Ginny. I'm serious."

She could see he was. She tried to maintain the happy, carefree mood but she couldn't. Fear simply ate at her confidence like acid. *Marriage.* It wasn't something she let herself think about. "What's the hurry?" she said. "I need more time to—"

He shook his head. "No, you don't, Ginny. I think you'll always be afraid. You'll never be ready to marry me."

She thought for a moment. It never occurred to her to lie. "Maybe you're right. Would that be so bad, Josh? If we just stayed the way we are. You could get your own place, and I could stay here and we could see each other whenever we wanted."

"I wouldn't be seeing you as much as I want. I want to wake up with you every morning. I couldn't live with less, Ginny. At least not forever." He stroked her back, his hands smoothing their way from her neck to her hips. It was hypnotic, arousing. Ginny swayed toward him. She pulled back with a frown.

"Are you threatening me?" she asked. "Telling me that if I won't marry you, you'll leave me?"

"God, no! I don't have anything to threaten you with. You heard me this afternoon. I'm committed to the court project. I'm going to be in New York for the foreseeable future. Do you think I can be in the same city and stay away from you?" The lines in his face seemed to grow deeper and his mouth curved downward in an expression of pain. "I'll take you on any terms you lay down, but I want to marry you."

"But why? What's the big attraction? Especially when you know it scares me." Ginny put her hands gently on his face, as if to wipe away the lines of fatigue and disappointment.

Josh leaned back, his head against the flowered couch cushion. "I love you. I want to live with you. But not just when it's convenient or fun. I

want to be with you always, good times and bad."
He tried to smile. "And I can't help being disappointed that you don't feel the same way about
me."

Ginny felt her stomach clench, as two warring
ideas fought it out inside her. "I love you that
way, too, Josh." Her voice was low and hesitant.
"I've never loved anyone the way I love you. It
seems so permanent and never-changing that I
know I'll want to spend my life with you."

"But . . ." Josh prompted her when she fell
silent. "I can tell there's a but. What is it?"

Ginny thought for a minute, trying to put her
finger on the source of her fear. When she found
it, she didn't want to tell Josh. But incurable honesty led her to say, in a voice so soft it was almost inaudible, "But eventually you might leave.
It would kill me if I ever lost you."

Josh looked at her and smiled a little half
smile. "I could tell you that I'd never leave you,
but I don't know if you can bring yourself to
believe that, no matter how I wrapped it up in
promises and poetry. But I'll tell you one thing
that you do know deep down inside, Ginny." He
sat up and looked into her eyes, willing her to
hear the truth in his words. "You're no coward.
You don't hide from life because it hurt you in
the past and might hurt you in the future. If you
lost me, if I died or something happened to me,

it wouldn't kill you. No matter how much you love me, you'd go on. Just the way you always have."

Ginny shook her head. "Only a lawyer would try to talk me into marriage by telling me I'll be okay if he leaves."

"I'll never leave voluntarily, Ginny. But I can't promise nothing bad will ever happen to either one of us again. You and I both know that's a promise no one can make."

Ginny felt those words reverberate within her. Josh wasn't telling her that life would be perfect, only that their love was worth taking a chance on, no matter what had happened in the past. She felt the truth of what he said. "But I feel like a coward right now."

He laughed. "Marry me anyway, Ginny."

She was tempted. Oh, how he tempted her! But some instinct for the safe and familiar led her to say, "I thought we had a bet. You'd better be thinking of how you're going to get our children to take off to Mexico."

Josh gave her a self-satisfied grin. "I've already taken care of that."

"You've what? How?"

"I have my methods." If anything, his grin grew even bigger and more fatuous. "Does David Copperfield tell the audience how he does it? Did Merlin spill the beans to King Arthur? I am

bound by the magician's code never to reveal my
secrets."

Ginny glared at him, but she couldn't help but
laugh. She leaned over and began to tickle his
ribs. "Well, code or no code, you'd better start
talking or get ready to die!"

Laughter made speech impossible for a minute, but Josh threw up his hands in surrender.
"All right, all right, I give up. I'll tell you everything." He took a minute to sit up and stop
laughing. Holding her hands away from him to
make sure he was safe, he said, "It really wasn't
that hard. This morning I . . ."

Earlier in the day, Denis found two airline tickets tucked carelessly in his briefcase. Opening
the travel agent's folder, he saw they were two
first class seats to Cancún. For a flight tonight
at seven. Dad and Ginny's tickets. How had they
gotten in his briefcase?

He called home and caught his father about to
leave to meet Ginny and some other people for
lunch. Something about that court project they'd
talked about. Helping people to represent themselves. Denis frowned. He didn't approve.

"Dad, I have your airline tickets. They're for
this evening. Maybe you'd better stop down here
and pick them up after lunch."

"Tell you what, son. I'm going to be pretty busy all afternoon. Why don't you come on out to Kennedy and say bon voyage to us. So we'll know you don't begrudge us our little fling." Josh had his fingers crossed. Would Denis take the bait?

There was an excruciating wait before Denis said, "Oh, all right. But you know, Dad, I don't really . . . I mean, at your age, if you want to go to concerts or plays together I understand, but the Caribbean for a weekend is different."

"What's wrong with the Caribbean?" Josh tried to sound anxious, but he was beginning to smile. It was working.

"Nothing. It's not that. But it seems sort of a young and . . . carefree kind of thing to do."

"I'm hoping to talk Ginny into marrying me. You know, rum drinks on the beach, moonlight swims. Get her in the mood. I think it has a good chance of working. You should try being carefree while you're young, Denis. But you'd never take a woman to Cancún for the weekend, would you?" Josh tapped his fingers impatiently as he waited for an answer.

"I don't know," Denis said, thinking about Lisa and the conversation they had had the night before. He thought about going with her to some place with moonlight and palm trees. Someplace like the resorts in the posters on her wall. For their first time together. For their honeymoon? The thought made his stomach quiver. He had never before considered doing anything this exciting, this spontaneous. Not ever. But maybe, with Lisa, he could learn to take a chance. Maybe he could work up the courage to ask her—his mind veered from the thought. He said hesitantly, "I never have. But—"

That was the word Josh was waiting for. "Well, think about it. When you come to see us off, you could make your own reservations."

"Is Lisa coming to the airport?"

"I don't know. Why don't you call her?"

Silence made Josh screw up his eyes, thinking, *Do it! Go ahead and say you'll do it! You're dying to and you know it. Say it, Denis!*

"I'll call her. See you at Kennedy at"—Denis looked at his watch—"six-thirty. Bye, Dad."

"Bye, son." Josh hung up the phone. "So far, so good," Josh said to himself, restraining a desire to rub his hands in satisfaction. He set off for the Union League Club whistling "Let's Get Away From It All."

Ginny leaned closer to Josh and reached around the floor for the champagne bottle. "And you think that when we don't show up they'll go to Cancún in our place?" Ginny shook her head. "I think you're crazy. All right, they don't hate each other, I'm willing to admit you were right about that. But I can't believe that either one of them would—" She shook her head. Lisa? Denis? Lisa and Denis? "Besides, I'm not sure I approve of my daughter going off with some man she's not even engaged to—"

Josh burst out laughing. "Well, now I see where your daughter gets it."

"Gets what?"

"The idea you each have that the other one should behave perfectly, but you don't have to. She doesn't think you and I should be seeing each other. And you think it's okay for you and me to make love, but not for your daughter and—" He saw the look on her face and thought, *Oh, damn, Havilland, now you've done it.*

"You're right." Ginny was seeing things she had ignored before. "I don't know why I thought it was a good idea for Lisa to get involved with Denis. I know how he is. And look at me! What kind of parent am I being? Sleeping with you every chance I get." Her hands began to twist in her lap and she looked at Josh with reproach.

He looked at her with a tender smile in his eyes. "I guess there's only one answer to that dilemma, sweetheart. You'll just have to set a good example and make an honest man of me.

Then we can worry about Lisa taking Denis for better or worse."

Ginny shook her head. "Lisa and Denis, *Married?*"

"Why is it whenever you say *married* it's in exactly the tone of voice you'd use to say *earthquake* or *plague?*" Josh took her hands in his. "Come on, show the younger generation the way."

Ginny opened her mouth and Josh waited.

The telephone rang.

"It's seven-fifteen," Josh said, glancing at his watch. "I'll bet that's Denis calling. Either from the airport or from the plane. It should have taken off about fifteen minutes ago."

At six-thirty on a Friday evening, Kennedy Airport was seething with humanity, everyone with a place he simply had to get to, everyone ignoring the rest of humanity. Denis arrived fifteen minutes early and had been scanning the crowd ever since. At last, he spotted her!

"Lisa, over here!" Denis waved but the crowd cut her off from his view. Then he saw Lisa's copper-colored head move in his direction. Eventually, she found her way to the gate where he waited.

"Denis! What are we doing here?" Was he going to kiss her?

"Saying bon voyage to our parents." He debated whether or not to kiss her. She licked her lips. He grabbed her arms and hauled her to him. "I've missed you," he murmured before his mouth found hers.

She emerged breathless from his embrace. "But we don't approve of their running off like this."

"We don't? But we talked about doing the same thing."

Lisa's brow furrowed and her mouth turned down. "I know we did. But this just shows how wrong—"

Oh, damn, Havilland, you've blown it! Denis thought.

"Would Mr. Denis Havilland and Ms. Lisa McDougall please come to the ticket counter?" The disembodied voice that sounded like long distance from Mars actually came from one of the airline employees manning the counter ten feet away.

Exchanging puzzled looks, Lisa and Denis approached the man behind the counter, who greeted them with a beaming smile.

"I have a surprise for you!" he said, happily, and reaching behind the counter he pulled out a small flight bag with a note pinned to it. "Here, this is for you! Someone left it at our midtown office and one of the pilots brought it out here."

Denis took the bag. "That's Dad's handwriting," he told Lisa. He looked at the bag as if it held a ticking bomb. "I wonder what he's up to. Some kind of silly treasure hunt, I suppose."

"Well, open it, for heaven's sake! Don't just stand there staring at it." Lisa shook his arm. "Come on."

Denis opened the envelope and took out the letter. He began to read it aloud. *"Dear Denis and Lisa, I'm sending you both on a treasure hunt.* What did I tell you? It's some kind of dumb game. He used to always have them at my birthday parties. I hated them. One time—"

"Read the letter!" Lisa was practically dancing in her impatience to hear what Josh had written.

". . . a treasure hunt. The treasure is in Cancún. To start the hunt, use the tickets Denis has in his briefcase. Once you're airborne, the attendant will open the champagne that I ordered for you. When you get to Cancún, there are hotel reservations in the flight bag. I've also included a bathing suit for each of you and a bottle of suntan lotion. That should take care of your needs, except for stuff like food and drink and you can charge all that on Denis's uranium credit card. The treasure? Well, everyone has to find it for themselves. Good luck and bon voyage." Denis turned the paper over. "That's all there is."

"What are we going to do?" Lisa looked at

him. Denis couldn't read her expression, but he thought it was eager and apprehensive both.

To his surprise, he found he had no doubts at all. "We're going to get on that plane." He grabbed her hand and went back to the counter. "We're checking in."

The man at the counter smiled. "I'm glad. Everyone should have a weekend in the Caribbean sometime."

Lisa looked at Denis and smiled. "For someone who looks like a lawyer, you're awfully daring and spontaneous."

"You haven't seen spontaneous yet, my dear. Just wait till we get to that hotel. And as for daring—" Denis grinned at her and pulled her into his arms. Their kiss might have gone on much longer if the public address system hadn't squawked, "All passengers should now be aboard the airplane. Mr. Havilland, Ms. McDougall, the crew is waiting."

Still holding hands, Lisa and Denis ran down the runway.

Ginny and Josh smiled at each other. They had just hung up from talking to their children on the flight to Mexico.

"I guess you win," Ginny said. She was still a tiny bit worried about her little girl going off with a man whose womanizing she knew about all too well.

"He loves her, Ginny," Josh said, his arms going around her to hold her against him. "It's nothing like those other relationships. I can tell."

"I guess you're right. They fought too much to be indifferent to each other." Ginny snuggled against Josh's chest, her ear over his heart. "Anyway, I've lost the bet. And like a good loser, I stand ready to pay up. Tell me the worst. What am I going to be doing this weekend? Scrubbing the windows on the World Trade Center? Running a marathon?"

"Well," said Josh, giving the word five syllables, "I was thinking—"

The phone rang.

"Don't you dare answer it," Josh said, suddenly making up his mind. "I'll tell you what we're doing. We're going to Maryland."

"We're going where? To Maryland? Josh, it isn't summer. We can't go to the shore."

"Then we'll go to Baltimore and see the aquarium and eat crab cakes." He was determined. He got to his feet and turned off the answering machine before it could begin recording the message. "We're going for two reasons."

Ginny stood up and faced him, her jaw set at a pugnacious angle. "And they are?"

"First, no one will know where we've gone,

so you won't get a thousand calls from people who want one or both of us to do something. Second, we can get married without a waiting period in Maryland."

Ginny's jaw dropped. "I haven't said I'd marry you. I haven't told Lisa or Denis or anyone. I don't have a dress—"

"I want to marry you now. I don't want to wait. Too many things can happen to people in love, and we're old enough to know what they are. We can't be sure we'll have world enough and time to love each other the way we want. I'm not willing to waste a second." He took her hands in his, his blue eyes dark with emotion. "I love you, Ginny. If you love me the way I think you do, marry me. Marry me now."

Ginny looked deep in his eyes and read such love and conviction there that her own eyes filled. She searched her heart and found that there was no more doubt, no more fear. She loved Josh. Together, they had found the love and sharing that everyone longs to find.

"Yes," she said. "You're right. I love you very much, and I want to live with you forever. Let's go to Maryland and get married this weekend."

"Thank God," Josh breathed. "I was afraid you wouldn't—"

The phone rang.

"Now!" he said, grabbing her hand and pulling

her toward the bedroom. "Throw something into an overnight bag and let's get out of here before somebody decides to come over and ring the—"

The downstairs buzzer sounded.

"Stop packing. We'll buy what we need when we get there. Come on, we'll sneak down the stairs."

When they reached the lobby, they heard voices. Josh put his finger to his mouth.

"They must have gone out." It sounded like Gray's voice.

"Oh, I'm so sorry. I wanted Ginny to be the first to know that Papa's agreed to be at our wedding." Anita sounded disappointed.

"Well, it isn't until you get your cast off next month. We have plenty of time to tell everyone," Gray said. "Come on, let's go get some dinner. It's late."

Ginny could hear the outer door close behind them.

"Dinner," she said. "We haven't had dinner."

"Think crab cakes. Think Maryland," Josh said. "Think love."

"Always," Ginny said as they went out the door and headed toward Maryland and forever.

Coming next month
from To Love Again romances:

Lovers and Friends by Claire Bocardo
and
Garden of Love by Eileen Hehl

IT'S NEVER TOO LATE FOR LOVE AND ROMANCE

JUST IN TIME (4188, $4.50/$5.50)
by Peggy Roberts

Constantly taking care of everyone around her has earned Remy Dupre the affectionate nickname "Ma." Then, with Remy's husband gone and oil discovered on her Louisiana farm, her sons and their wives decide it's time to take care of her. But Remy knows how to take care of herself. She starts by checking into a beauty spa, buying some classy new clothes and shoes, discovering an antique vase, and moving on to a fine plantation. Next, not one, but two men attempt to sweep her off her well-shod feet. The right man offers her the opportunity to love again.

LOVE AT LAST (4158, $4.50/$5.50)
by Garda Parker

Fifty, slim, and attractive, Gail Bricker still hadn't found the love of her life. Friends convince her to take an Adventure Tour during the summer vacation she enjoys as an English teacher. At a Cheyenne Indian school in need of teachers, Gail finds her calling. In rancher Slater Kincaid, she finds her match. Gail discovers that it's never too late to fall in love . . . for the very first time.

LOVE LESSONS (3959, $4.50/$5.50)
by Marian Oaks

After almost forty years of marriage, Carolyn Ames certainly hadn't been looking for a divorce. But the ink is barely dry, and here she is already living an exhilarating life as a single woman. First, she lands an exciting and challenging job. Now Jason, the handsome architect, offers her a fairy-tale romance. Carolyn doesn't care that her ultra-conservative neighbors gossip about her and Jason, but she is afraid to give up her independent life-style. She struggles with the balance while she learns to love again.

A KISS TO REMEMBER (4129, $4.50/$5.50)
by Helen Playfair

For the past ten years Lucia Morgan hasn't had time for love or romance. Since her husband's death, she has been raising her two sons, working at a dead-end office job, and designing boutique clothes to make ends meet. Then one night, Mitch Colton comes looking for his daughter, out late with one of her sons. The look in Mitch's eye brings back a host of long-forgotten feelings. When the kids come home and spoil the enchantment, Lucia wonders if she will get the chance to love again.

COME HOME TO LOVE (3930, $4.50/$5.50)
by Jane Bierce

Julia Delaine says good-bye to her skirt-chasing husband Phillip and hello to a whole new life. Julia capably rises to the challenges of her reawakened sexuality, the young man who comes courting, and her new position as the head of her local television station. Her new independence teaches Julia that maybe her time-tested values were right all along and maybe Phillip does belong in her life, with her new terms.

WATCH AS THESE WOMEN LEARN
TO LOVE AGAIN

HELLO LOVE (4094, $4.50/$5.50)
by Joan Shapiro
Family tragedy leaves Barbara Sinclair alone with her success. The fight to gain custody of her young granddaughter brings a confrontation with the determined rancher Sam Douglass. Also widowed, Sam has been caring for Emily alone, guided by his own ideas of childrearing. Barbara challenges his ideas. And that's not all she challenges . . . Long-buried desires surface, then gentle affection. Sam and Barbara cannot ignore the chance to love again.

THE BEST MEDICINE (4220, $4.50/$5.50)
by Janet Lane Walters
Her late husband's expenses push Maggie Carr back to nursing, the career she left almost thirty years ago. The night shift is difficult, but it's harder still to ignore the way handsome Dr. Jason Knight soothes his patients. When she lends a hand to help his daughter, Jason and Maggie grow closer than simply doctor and nurse. Obstacles to romance seem insurmountable, but Maggie knows that love is always the best medicine.

AND BE MY LOVE (4291, $4.50/$5.50)
by Joyce C. Ware
Selflessly catering first to husband, then children, grandchildren, and her aging, though imperious mother, leaves Beth Volmar little time for her own adventures or passions. Then, the handsome archaeologist Karim Donovan arrives and campaigns to widen the boundaries of her narrow life. Beth finds new freedom when Karim insists that she accompany him to Turkey on an archaeological dig . . . and a journey towards loving again.

OVER THE RAINBOW (4032, $4.50/$5.50)
by Marjorie Eatock
Fifty-something, divorced for years, courted by more than one attractive man, and thoroughly enjoying her job with a large insurance company, Marian's sudden restlessness confuses her. She welcomes the chance to travel on business to a small Mississippi town. Full of good humor and words of love, Don Worth makes her feel needed, and not just to assess property damage. Marian takes the risk.

A KISS AT SUNRISE (4260, $4.50/$5.50)
by Charlotte Sherman
Beginning widowhood and retirement, Ruth Nichols has her first taste of freedom. Against the advice of her mother and daughter, Ruth heads for an adventure in the motor home that has sat unused since her husband's death. Long days and lonely campgrounds start to dampen the excitement of traveling alone. That is, until a dapper widower named Jack parks next door and invites her for dinner. On the road, Ruth and Jack find the chance to love again.

YOU WON'T WANT TO READ
JUST ONE — KATHERINE STONE

ROOMMATES (3355-9, $4.95)
No one could have prepared Carrie for the monumental changes she would face when she met her new circle of friends at Stanford University. Once their lives intertwined and became woven into the tapestry of the times, they would never be the same.

TWINS (3492-X, $4.95)
Brook and Melanie Chandler were so different, it was hard to believe they were sisters. One was a dark, serious, ambitious New York attorney; the other, a golden, glamourous, sophisticated supermodel. But they were more than sisters — they were twins and more alike than even they knew
. . .

THE CARLTON CLUB (3614-0, $4.95)
It was the place to see and be seen, the only place to be. And for those who frequented the playground of the very rich, it was a way of life. Mark, Kathleen, Leslie and Janet — they worked together, played together, and loved together, all behind exclusive gates of the *Carlton Club*.

Available wherever paperbacks are sold, or order direct from the Publisher. Send cover price plus 50¢ per copy for mailing and handling to Penguin USA, P.O. Box 999, c/o Dept. 17109, Bergenfield, NJ 07621. Residents of New York and Tennessee must include sales tax. DO NOT SEND CASH.

CATCH A RISING STAR!

ROBIN ST. THOMAS

FORTUNE'S SISTERS   (2616, $3.95)

It was Pia's destiny to be a Hollywood star. She had complete self-confidence, breathtaking beauty, and the help of her domineering mother. But her younger sister Jeanne began to steal the spotlight meant for Pia, diverting attention away from the ruthlessly ambitious star. When her mother Mathilde started to return the advances of dashing director Wes Guest, Pia's jealousy surfaced. Her passion for Guest and desire to be the brightest star in Hollywood pitted Pia against her own family — sister against sister, mother against daughter. Pia was determined to be the only survivor in the arenas of love and fame. But neither Mathilde nor Jeanne would surrender without a fight. . . .

LOVER'S MASQUERADE   (2886, $4.50)

New Orleans. A city of secrets, shrouded in mystery and magic. A city where dreams become obsessions and memories once again become reality. A city where even one trip, like a stop on Claudia Gage's book promotion tour, can lead to a perilous fall. For New Orleans is also the home of Armand Dantine, who knows the secrets that Claudia would conceal and the past she cannot remember. And he will stop at nothing to make her love him, and will not let her go again . . .

SENSATION   (3228, $4.95)

They'd dreamed of stardom, and their dreams came true. Now they had fame and the power that comes with it. In Hollywood, in New York, and around the world, the names of Aurora Styles, Rachel Allenby, and Pia Decameron commanded immediate attention — and lust and envy as well. They were stars, idols on pedestals. And there was always someone waiting in the wings to bring them crashing down . . .